THIS SPECIAL SIGNED EDITION
IS LIMITED TO 1000 NUMBERED COPIES.

THIS IS COPY 963.

KELLY ROBSON

ALIAS SPACE

AND OTHER STORIES

ALIAS SPACE

AND OTHER STORIES

KELLY ROBSON

SUBTERRANEAN PRESS
2021

Edited by Yanni Kuznia.

See page 459 for individual story credits.

First Edition

ISBN
978-1-64524-025-9

Subterranean Press
PO Box 190106
Burton, MI 48519

subterraneanpress.com

Manufactured in the United States of America

For Nanny

TABLE OF CONTENTS

INTRODUCTION

AS I SIT DOWN TO WRITE, IT'S May 25, 2020. The midday sunlight filters through the lime-green leaves of the birches outside the window of our condo. A quick glance at the Days Until counter on my phone shows that my wife Alyx and I have been in COVID-19 lockdown for 73 days.

We've been fine here in downtown Toronto. Alyx and I have been calling this the Prosciutto Quarantine, because we've been pouring our budget into supporting the local small businesses we love—Sanagan's Meat Locker, Blackbird Bakery, Global Cheese, Forno Cultura, Death in Venice, and Hot Black Coffee. I've been working at home since mid-March, and until my day job cuts my hours (which could happen very soon), we have the luxury of income to spread around.

It's fair to say we lack for nothing. Nothing, except we are unable to visit family and friends, and we have no way to know, with any reasonable confidence, what tomorrow will bring. These are not small things, and in this way we are no different from anyone else in the entire world at this moment in history.

What will the world look like in a year, when this book comes out? I have a powerful urge to be twee and ask you, but it's a completely frivolous question. So I'm just going to rise from this vertiginous moment and take a leap of faith.

You and I both know, now, how 2020 became 2021, and I trust and hope that all our friends and loved ones, our neighbors, colleagues, acquaintances stretching out in braided networks to encompass everyone in the whole world—that all of us are okay.

The stories in this collection were all written between 2013 and 2020, with "Waters of Versailles" the oldest and "Alias Space" the newest. Social interconnectedness—the importance of those braided networks for survival—is a broad theme that runs through my work, and it's something Peter Watts and I argue about nearly every time we see each other.

If you're familiar with Peter's excellent Science Fiction, you know it's bleak. He's absolutely convinced that humanity is lemming at top speed and the cliff is very close indeed. When he talks about this approaching doomsday, he's the happiest guy in the world, and though I don't have much success in these arguments—he's louder than me, thinks faster, and has a PhD—Peter can't make me think like him. No way. I can't. Because if I thought humanity was doomed, I simply couldn't live.

Jeffe Kennedy, with whom I'm chatting in Google Hangouts as I draft this, sums it up this way: "Writing a book is an act of hope for the future we can't yet imagine."

Yes, exactly. I write this introduction in May 2020 for some time in 2021, trusting those days will come. It's an act of hope. So I would argue with Peter (who isn't here and thus can't dizzy me with one of his whiplash arguments) that even *he* believes enough in the future to write books. To toss his time and passion into the void and trust it will come out the other side.

But I will never change his mind, any more than he will change mine. Because we're not arguing about facts, we're arguing about ways of understanding the world.

What do I believe? What's my counter argument to Peter's doomsday scenario? This book is soaked in it. I think strangers can care for other strangers. I think the act of nurturing changes a person for the better. I think that love, trust, hope, and all the higher values are real and possible. I think humans are strongest when we find ways to work together, even though lasting cooperation is hellishly difficult to achieve.

And I fervently believe that humanity will survive to the stars.

I think we have to. Whatever drives us won't be satisfied until humans occupy every habitat we see, however marginal, however dangerous, and without regard for whoever or whatever was living there before us. We are the species that colonizes. We are the species that causes problems—for ourselves, for other species, for ecosystems, for the planet. Humans can make trouble out of two sticks and a bit of tinder, and we like nothing better than to tell stories about how we took a bold risk and survived.

Here are some of those stories. Some are dark indeed. Having hope is hard when you know how people work—how we create and destroy at the same time, love and hate with equal fervor, cling to fantasies and reject facts. With a clear understanding of human nature, it's much easier to predict a bad outcome than imagine a route to something more equitable. Falling apart is easy. All destruction requires is for people to stop trying. Building something, fixing something? That's hard.

But we do build, we can fix—and at a heck of a pace when motivated. And often, all we need is the right story to get us moving in the right direction.

I have loved short stories my whole life. The first short fiction I remember reading were Saki's and Oscar Wilde's in an anthology that ended up in my hands at the age of seven. At that age, most books came to me by chance, and getting enough of them was always an issue because reading was everything to me, in a way nobody understood.

I have always been a book-based lifeform, but as a child I had no books. My family would scoff at that, but what they don't understand is that if you read two books a day, you need hundreds per year, not six or eight. For me, access to books was a survival issue.

I could go on. Small town—no bookstores. Town library in the high school, full of scary older kids. When my parents divorced, my mother moved to Edmonton and worked at a mall which had a library, but that's a saga about the *Black Stallion* series and ended with me never going in there again, despite the kind librarian who waived a year of late fees.

I could get (more) dramatic about this, but really, all I'm trying to say is that my devotion to fiction is practically primordial.

When I discovered the Science Fiction and Fantasy section of the mall bookstore, my life got much, much better. Then a life-changing event happened.

December 1983. My family stopped for gas in Blue River, one of the tiny towns spaced an hour apart on the Yellowhead Highway amid the mountains of central-eastern British Columbia. Inside the gas station shack, on the shelf above the cashier's head, was a copy of *Asimov's Science Fiction* with Connie Willis' "Blued Moon" on the cover. Never was there a magazine cover better suited to catch a teenage girl's eye. A cat, a moon, an intriguing title. And the story! Playful, intellectual, romantic. It changed me.

Connie's story made neurons fire that had never seen a spark. And from that moment, I was a different person. A teenager steeped in cutting-edge short SF of the 1980s, who haunted the drugstore waiting for the next issue of Asimov's, Analog, F&SF, and Omni. My thought processes, my politics, my beliefs shaped by the work of Connie, James Tiptree, Jr., Octavia Butler, James Patrick Kelly, John Kessel, and later Maureen McHugh, Michael Bishop, and Walter Jon Williams. At university, I just wanted to be Connie Willis when I grew up. I married an SF writer. Eventually, I evolved into one myself.

What took so long? I guess it's that I knew what a good story was, and I could recognize it when my own work didn't make the grade. It took a lot of practice to get to this point.

Now here we are. These stories are me, for better and for worse. I hope they bring you joy.

TWO-YEAR MAN

GETTING THE BABY THROUGH SECURITY WAS EASY. Mikkel had been smuggling food out of the lab for years. He'd long since learned how to trick the guards.

Mikkel had never been smart, but the guards were four-year men and that meant they were lazy. If he put something good at the top of his lunch pail at the end of his shift, the guards would grab it and never dig deeper. Mikkel let them have the half-eaten boxes of sooty chocolate truffles and stale pastries, but always took something home for Anna.

Most days it was only wrinkled apples and hard oranges, soured milk, damp sugar packets and old teabags. But sometimes he would find something good. Once he'd found a working media player at the bottom of the garbage bin in the eight-year man's office. He had been so sure the guards would find it and accuse him of stealing that he'd almost tossed it in the incinerator. But he'd distracted the guards with some water-stained skin magazines from the six-year men's shower room and brought that media player home to Anna.

She traded it for a pair of space heaters and ten kilos of good flour. They had dumplings for months.

The baby was the best thing he'd ever found. And she was such a good girl—quiet and still. Mikkel had taken a few minutes to hold her in the warmth beside the incinerator, cuddling her close and listening to the gobble and clack of her strange yellow beak. He swaddled her tightly in clean rags, taking care to wrap her pudgy hands separately so she couldn't rake her talons across that sweet pink baby belly. Then he put her in the bottom of his plastic lunch pail, layered a clean pair of janitor's coveralls over her, and topped the pail with a box of day-old pastries he'd found in the six-year men's lounge.

"Apple strudel," grunted Hermann, the four-year man in charge of the early morning guard shift. "Those pasty scientists don't know good eats. Imagine leaving strudel to sit."

"Cafe Sluka has the best strudel in Vienna, so everyone says," Mikkel said as he passed through the security gate.

"Like you'd know, moron. Wouldn't let you through the door."

Mikkel ducked his head and kept his eyes on the floor. "I heated them in the microwave for you."

He rushed out into the gray winter light as the guards munched warm strudel.

Mikkel checked the baby as soon as he rounded the corner, and then kept checking her every few minutes on the way home. He was careful to make sure nobody saw. But the streetcars were nearly empty in the early morning, and nobody would find it strange to see a two-year man poking his nose in his lunch pail.

The baby was quiet and good. Anna would be so pleased. The thought kept him warm all the way home.

Anna was not pleased.

When he showed her the baby she sat right down on the floor. She didn't say anything—just opened and closed her mouth for a minute. Mikkel crouched at her side and waited.

"Did anyone see you take it?" she asked, squeezing his hand hard, like she always did when she wanted him to pay attention.

"No, sweetheart."

"Good. Now listen hard. We can't keep it. Do you understand?"

"She needs a mother," Mikkel said.

"You're going to take her back to the lab. Then forget this ever happened."

Anna's voice carried an edge Mikkel had never heard before. He turned away and gently lifted the baby out of the pail. She was quivering with hunger. He knew how that felt.

"She needs food," he said. "Is there any milk left, sweetheart?"

"It's no use, Mikkel. She's going to die anyway."

"We can help her."

"The beak is a bad taint. If she were healthy they would have kept her. Sent her to a crèche."

"She's strong." Mikkel loosened the rags. The baby snuffled and her sharp blue tongue protruded from the pale beak. "See? Fat and healthy."

"She can't breathe."

"She needs us." Why didn't Anna see that? It was so simple.

"You can take her back tonight."

"I can't. My lunch pail goes through the X-ray machine. The guards would see."

If Anna could hold the baby, she would understand. Mikkel pressed the baby to Anna's chest. She scrambled backward so fast she banged her head on the door. Then she stood and straightened her maid's uniform with shaking hands.

"I have to go. I can't be late again." She pulled on her coat and lunged out the door, then turned and reached out. For a moment he thought she was reaching for the baby and he began to smile. But she just squeezed his hand again, hard.

"You have to take care of this, Mikkel," she said. "It's not right. She's not ours. We aren't keeping her."

Mikkel nodded. "See you tonight."

The only thing in the fridge was a bowl of cold stew. They hadn't had milk for days. But Mikkel's breakfast sat on the kitchen table covered with a folded towel. The scrambled egg was still steaming.

Mikkel put a bit of egg in the palm of his hand and blew on it. The baby's eyes widened and she squirmed. She reached for his hand. Talons raked his wrist and her beak yawned wide. A blue frill edged with red and yellow quivered at the back of her throat.

"Does that smell good? I don't think a little will hurt."

He fed her the egg bit by bit. She gobbled it down, greedy as a baby bird. Then he watched her fall asleep while he sipped his cold coffee.

Mikkel wet a paper napkin and cleaned the fine film of mucus from the tiny nostrils on either side of her beak. They were too small, but she could breathe just fine through her mouth. She couldn't cry, though, she just snuffled and panted. And the beak was heavy. It dragged her head to the side.

She was dirty, smeared with blood from the incineration bin. Her fine black hair was pasted down with a hard scum that smelled like glue. She needed a bath, and warm clothes, and diapers. Also something to cover her hands. He would have to trim the points off her talons.

He held her until she woke. Then he brought both space heaters from the bedroom and turned them on high while he bathed her in the kitchen sink. It was awkward and messy and took nearly two hours. She snuffled hard the whole time, but once he'd dried her and wrapped her in towels she quieted. He propped her up on the kitchen table. She watched him mop the kitchen floor, her bright brown eyes following his every move.

When the kitchen was clean he fetched a half-empty bottle of French soap he'd scavenged from the lab, wrapped the baby up tightly against the cold, and sat on the back stairs waiting for Hyam to come trotting out of his apartment for a smoke.

"What's this?" Hyam said. "I didn't know Anna was expecting."

"She wasn't." Mikkel tugged the towel aside.

"Huh," said Hyam. "That's no natural taint. Can it breathe?"

"She's hungry." Mikkel gave him the bottle of soap.

"Hungry, huh?" Hyam sniffed the bottle. "What do you need?"

"Eggs and milk. Clothes and diapers. Mittens, if you can spare some."

"I never seen a taint like that. She's not a natural creature." Hyam took a long drag on his cigarette and blew it over his shoulder, away from the baby. "You work in that lab, right?"

"Yes."

Hyam examined the glowing coal at the end of his cigarette.

"What did Anna say when you brought trouble home?"

Mikkel shrugged.

"Did the neighbors hear anything through the walls?"

"No."

"Keep it that way." Hyam spoke slowly. "Keep this quiet, Mikkel, you hear me? Keep it close. If anyone asks, you tell them Anna birthed that baby."

Mikkel nodded.

Hyam pointed with his cigarette, emphasizing every word. "If the wrong person finds out, the whole neighborhood will talk. Then you'll see real trouble. Four-year men tromping through the building, breaking things, replaying the good old days in the colonies. They like nothing better. Don't you bring that down on your neighbors."

Mikkel nodded.

"My wife will like the soap." Hyam ground out his cigarette and ran up the stairs.

"There now," Mikkel said. The baby gazed up at him and clacked her beak. "Who says two-year men are good for nothing?"

Four-year men said it all the time. They were everywhere, flashing their regimental badges and slapping the backs of their old soldier friends. They banded together in loud bragging packs that crowded humble folks off busses and streetcars, out of shops and cafés, forcing everyone to give way or get pushed aside.

Six-year men probably said it too, but Mikkel had never talked to one. He saw them working late at the lab sometimes, but they lived in another world—a world filled with sports cars and private clubs. And who knew what eight-year men said? Mikkel cleaned an eight-year man's office every night, but he'd only ever seen them in movies.

Nobody made movies about two-year men. They said four-year men had honor, six-year men had responsibility, and eight-year men had glory. Two-year men had nothing but shame. But it wasn't true. Hyam said so. Two-year men had families—parents, grandparents, uncles and aunts, brothers and sisters, children and wives who depended on them. They had jobs, humble jobs but important all the same. Without two-year men, who would grub away the garbage, crawl the sewers, lay the carpets, clean the chimneys, fix the roofs? Without two-year men there would be nobody to bring in the harvest—no sweet strawberries or rich wines. And most important, Hyam said, without two-year men there would be no one parents could point at and say to their sons, "Don't be like him."

Hyam was smart. He could have been a four-year man easy, even a six-year man. But he was a Jew and that meant a two-year man, almost always. Gypsies too, and Hutterites, and pacifists. Men who couldn't walk or talk. Even blind men. All drafted and sent to fight and die in the colonies for two years, and then sent home to live in shame while the four-year men fought on. Fought to survive and come home with honor.

Hyam returned swinging a plastic bag in one hand and a carton of eggs in the other. A bottle of milk was tucked under his arm.

"This is mostly diapers," he said, brandishing the bag. "You'll never have too many. We spend more on laundry than we do on food."

"I can wash them by hand."

"No you can't, take my word for it." Hyam laughed and ran up the stairs. "Welcome to fatherhood, Mikkel. You're a family man now."

Mikkel laid the baby on the bed. He diapered and dressed the baby, and then trimmed her talons with Anna's nail scissors. He fitted a sock over each of the baby's hands and pinned them to her sleeves. Then he wedged Anna's pillow between the bed and the wall, tucked the baby in his arms, and fell into sleep.

He woke to the clacking of the baby's beak. She yawned, showing her colorful throat frill. He cupped his hand over her skull and breathed in the milky scent of her skin.

"Let's get you fed before Mama comes home," he said.

He warmed milk in the soup pot. A baby needed a bottle when it didn't have a breast, he knew, but his baby—his clever little girl—held her beak wide and let him tip the milk into her, teaspoon by teaspoon. She swallowed greedily and then demanded more. She ate so fast he could probably just pour the milk in a steady stream down her throat. But milk was too expensive to risk spitting up all over the kitchen floor.

"Mikkel," said Anna.

She was standing in the doorway in her scarf and coat. Mikkel gathered the baby in his arms and greeted Anna with a kiss like he always did. Her cheek was cold and red.

"How was your day?" he asked. The baby looked from him to Anna and clacked her beak.

Anna wouldn't look at the baby. "I was late. I got on the wrong bus at the interchange and had to backtrack. Mrs. Spiven says one more time and that's it for me."

"You can get another job. A better one. Closer to home."

"Maybe. Probably not."

Anna rinsed the soup pot, scooped cold stew into it and set it on the stove. She was still in her coat and hat. The baby reached out and hooked Anna's red mitten out of her pocket with the trimmed talon poking through the thin gray knit sock. The mitten dangled from the baby's hand. Anna ignored it.

"Sweetheart, take off your coat," Mikkel said.

"I'm cold," she said. She struck a match and lit the burner.

Mikkel gently pulled on her elbow. She resisted for a moment and then turned. Her face was flushed.

"Sweetheart, look," he said. Anna dropped her gaze to the floor. The baby clacked her beak and yawned. "I thought we could name her after your mother."

Anna turned away and stirred the stew. "That's crazy. I told you we're not keeping her."

"She has your eyes."

The spoon clattered to the floor. Anna swayed. Her elbow hit the pot handle and it tipped. Mikkel steadied it and shut off the flame.

Anna yanked back her chair and fell into it. She thrust her head in her hands for a moment and then sat back. Her eyes were cold and narrow, her voice tight. "Why would you say that? Don't say that."

Why couldn't Anna see? She was smart. So much smarter than him. And he could see it so easily.

Mikkel searched for the right words. "Your eggs. Where did they go?"

"It doesn't matter. I needed money so I sold my ovaries. That's the end of it."

Mikkel ran his fingers over his wife's chapped hand, felt the calluses on her palm. He would tell her the awful things, and then she would understand.

"I know where your eggs went. I see them in the tanks every night. And in the labs. In the incinerator. I mop their blood off the floor."

Anna's jaw clenched. He could tell she was biting the inside of her cheek. "Mikkel. Lots of women sell their ovaries. Thousands of women. They could be anyone's eggs."

Mikkel shook his head. "This is your baby. I know it."

"You don't know anything. What proof do you have? None." She laughed once, a barking sound. "And it doesn't matter anyway because we're not keeping her. People will find out and take her away. Arrest you and me both, probably. At the very least, we'd lose our jobs. Do you want us to live in the street?"

"We can tell people you birthed her."

"With that beak?"

Mikkel shrugged. "It happens."

Anna's flushed face turned a brighter shade of red. She was trying not to cry. He ached to squeeze her to his chest. She would just pull away, though. Anna would never let him hold her when she cried.

They ate in silence. Mikkel watched the baby sleep on the table between them. Her soft cheek was chubby as any child's, but it broadened and dimpled as it met the beak, the skin thinning and hardening like a fingernail. The baby snuffled and snot bubbled from one of her tiny nostrils. Mikkel wiped it away with the tip of his finger.

Mikkel checked the clock as Anna gathered the dishes and filled the sink. Only a few minutes before he had to leave for the lab. He snuggled the baby close. Her eyelids fluttered. The delicate eyelash fringes were glued together with mucus.

"You have to go," said Anna. She put his lunch pail on the table.

"In a minute," he said. Mikkel dipped his napkin in his water glass and wiped the baby's eyes.

Anna leaned on the edge of the sink. "Do you know why I married you, Mikkel?"

He sat back, startled. Anna didn't usually talk like this. He had wondered, often. Anna could have done better. Married a smart man, a four-year man, even.

"Will you tell me, sweetheart?"

"I married you because you said it didn't matter. I explained I could never have babies and you still wanted me—"

"Of course I want you."

"I told you why I was barren. Why I sold my ovaries. Do you remember?"

"Your mother was sick. You needed the money."

"Yes. But I also said it was easy because I never wanted babies. I never wanted to be a mother." She leaned forward and gripped his shoulders. "I still don't. Take her back to the lab."

Mikkel stood. He kissed the baby's forehead. Then he put the baby in Anna's arms.

"Her name is Maria," he said. "After your mother."

Mikkel was tired walking up the street toward the bus stop. But that was fatherhood. He would get used to it. Anna would get used to being a mother too. He was sure. All women did.

The thought of his wife and child kept him warm all the way to the Josefstadt streetcar station. Then a four-year man shoved an elbow in his ribs and spat on his coat. Mikkel watched the spittle freeze and turn white. He stood shivering at the edge of the curb, taking care to stay out of everyone's way.

Mikkel relied on Anna's kindness, sure she would always do the right thing, the generous thing. She was good to him, good to everyone. For ten years she had taken care of him, cooking, cleaning, making their two rooms into a home. In return he did his best to fill those two rooms with love. It was all he could do.

As he stood in the wind at the edge of the station, doubts began to creep in with the cold. Why would Anna say she didn't want to be a mother? It couldn't be true. They lived surrounded by families—happy, noisy, families—three and four, even five generations all living together. Healthy children, happy mothers, proud fathers. Aunts, uncles, cousins, grandparents. Family everywhere, but he and Anna only had each other.

Anna must regret being barren. Some part of her, buried deep, must long for children. But she said she didn't, and if it was true, then something in her must be broken.

He had seen broken men during his two years in the colonies, men with whole bodies and broken minds, who said crazy things and hurt themselves, hurt others. Anna could never be like them.

But his doubts grew with every step further from home. By the time he could see the lights of the lab glowing through the falling snow, the doubts were clawing at him. He imagined coming home in the morning to find Anna alone, ready to leave for work, pretending Maria had never been there.

He turned back home, but then one of the four-year men shouted at him through the glass doors.

"You're late, you stupid ass."

Mikkel watched his lunch pail slide though the x-ray. The guards ran it back and forth through the machine, just to waste time. Mikkel had to run to the time clock. He stamped his card just as it clicked over to eight.

Normally Mikkel loved the rhythm of work, the scrubbing, mopping, wiping. Even cleaning toilets brought its own reward. He knew the drip of every tap, every scratch on the porcelain and crack in the tiles. He took an inventory of them night by night as he cleaned, taking his time, double-checking every corner for dust, scanning every window and mirror for streaks, even getting down on his knees to swab behind the toilets, scrubbing away any hint of mildew from the grout, finding all the little nooks and crannies.

Tonight he rushed through his work, but each room felt like it took twice as long as usual. He kept checking the time, sure he was falling behind. Thinking about Anna dragged on the clock hands. Worrying made him forgetful, too. He left the four-year men's bathroom with no memory of cleaning it. He had to go back and check just to be sure.

In the tank room he began to feel better. He loved the noise of the tanks—the bubbling pumps and thumping motors. Here he always took his time, no matter what. It was his favorite place in the whole building. He wasn't supposed to touch the tanks, but he always took a few extra minutes to polish the steel and glass and check the hose seals. He even tightened the bolts that fixed each heavy tank to the floor and ceiling.

The tinted glass was just transparent enough to show the babies floating inside. Mikkel watched them grow night by night. He kept a special rag just for polishing the tanks, a soft chamois that a six-year man had discarded years ago. It was specially made for precious things—the logo of a sports car company had long since worn off. He always polished the glass with long slow caressing strokes, sure the babies could feel his touch.

Two of the tanks were empty. Mikkel polished them too, in their turn, making them perfect for the next baby. Maria's tank was in the last row on the far side of the room, two from the end. It was refilled but the baby was still too small to see, just a thin filament dangling from the fleshy organ at the top of the tank.

"Your sister says hello," Mikkel whispered. "Her mama and papa are proud of her. Maria is going to grow up smart and strong."

The filament twisted and drifted in the fluid. Mikkel watched it for a few minutes, wondering what Anna and Maria were doing at that moment. He imagined them curled up in bed, skin to skin, the baby's beak tucked under Anna's chin. He squeezed his eyes tight and held the image in his mind, as if he could make it real just by wanting it so badly. And for a few minutes it did feel real, an illusion supported by the comforting tank room sounds.

But he couldn't stay there. As he lugged his bins and pails upstairs to the offices, worry began gnawing at him again.

Women abandoned babies all the time. The mothers and grandmothers in the tenement always had a story to tell about some poor baby left out in the cold by a heartless and unnatural mother. Once, when they were first married, Anna told the woman next door that people did desperate things when they had run out of options. That neighbor still wouldn't speak to her, years later.

What if Anna bundled Maria up and put her on the steps of some six-year man's house? Or left her at the train station?

He could see Maria now, tucked into their big kitchen pail and covered with a towel. He could see Anna, her face covered by her red scarf, drop the pail on the edge of the Ostbahnhof express platform and walk away.

No. His Anna would never do that. Never. He wouldn't think about it anymore. He would pay attention to his work.

On the wide oak table in the eight-year man's office he found four peach pastries, their brandy jam dried to a crust.

The bakery box was crushed in the garbage bin. When he was done cleaning the office he re-folded it as best he could and put the pastries back inside. Four was good luck. One for each of the guards. Then he made his way down to the basement.

The incinerator was an iron maw in a brick wall. For years, Mikkel had walked down those concrete steps in the hot red light of its stare to find the sanitary disposal bin bloody but empty, its contents dumped by one of the four-year men who assisted in the labs. Back then, all Mikkel had to do was toss his garbage bags in the incinerator, let them burn down, then switch off the gas, bleach the bin, hose the floor, and mop everything dry.

But now there was a new eight-year man in charge, and Mikkel had to start the incinerator and empty the disposal bin himself.

The light from the overhead bulb was barely bright enough to show the trail of blood snaking from the bin to the drain. Mikkel felt his way to the control panel and began the tricky process of firing up the incinerator. The gas dial was stiff and the pilot light button was loose. He pressed it over and over again, trying to find the right angle on the firing pin. When the incinerator finally blasted to life Mikkel had sweated through his coveralls.

The room lit up with the glow from the incinerator window and he could finally see into the bin. The top layer of bags dripped fluid tinged red and yellow. Most were double-and even triple-bagged, tied with tight knots. But they were torn and leaked. Sharp edges inside the disposal chute hooked and tore on the way down.

Maria had been single-bagged. Her beak had pierced the plastic, ripped it wide enough for her to breathe. And she had landed at the far edge of the bin, mostly upright. If she had been face down or if another bag had fallen on top of her she could have suffocated.

Mikkel wrenched open the incinerator door and began emptying the bin, carefully picking up each wet bag and throwing it far into the furnace. Some bags were tiny, just a few glass dishes and a smear of wax. One bag was filled with glass plates that spilled through a tear and shattered at his feet. The biggest bags held clear fluid that burst across the back wall of the incinerator with a hot blast that smelled like meat. He set the bloodiest bags aside, put them down safe on the pitted concrete floor, away from the glass.

As the bin emptied, a pit began to form in Mikkel's stomach. He turned away and kicked through the glass, pacing along the far wall where it was a little cooler.

The tank room had two empty tanks. He'd polished them just a few hours ago, but he hadn't paid much attention. He'd been thinking about Anna and Maria.

He knew those babies, the ones who had been in the empty tanks. One was a little boy with a thick, stocky body covered in fine hair. The other was a tiny girl with four arms that ended in stubby knobs. Where were they now? Had they been sent away to the crèche or put down the chute? If they'd gone down the chute they would be in the bin, waiting for him to throw them into the fire with the blood and tank fluid. With all of the failed experiments.

Mikkel picked up a bloody bag and hefted it by the seal, feeling the contents with his other hand. The fluid sloshed heavily and clung to the sides of the bag like syrup. There were a few solid pieces inside the bag, but nothing big enough to be a baby, not even a tiny one. He threw it into the incinerator and picked up the other bag.

Maria would probably be gone when he got home; he understood that now. The thought made a hollow in his chest, a Maria-shaped hole where he'd cuddled her to his heart. But if Maria was gone, if Anna had taken her to the train station and abandoned her, that only meant Anna needed time. He would give her time. He would be patient, like she always was with him, and gentle too. What was broken in her would heal and she would love their children. She would be a wonderful mother. Maybe not today, but soon.

He would find more babies. Night after night he'd search for them. Maria had survived, so others would survive, too, and he would find them. Find every baby and bring them all home until Anna healed. He would fill their home with love. It was all he could do.

NOTES ABOUT "TWO-YEAR MAN"

Just as I can remember the exact moment I came across Connie Willis' "Blued Moon," I can also recall the exact moment of genesis for most of my stories. "Two-Year Man" came to me when editors Christie Yant and Seanan McGuire announced the *Lightspeed* special issue *Women Destroy Science Fiction*.

I was unpublished at the time, but of course I wanted to be a part of that anthology—everyone did—and even more so for me because I have such fond memories of editor Shawna McCarthy's all-women *Space of Her Own* anthology, a one-off digest which came out at the end of 1983, just when teenage-me was discovering contemporary short Science Fiction.

"Two-Year Man" combines elements from worldbuilding I'd been cogitating for months, about a Europe where the World Wars never happened, along with ideas that had stuck with me for two decades after reading Maureen McHugh's terrific story "Nekropolis." I wanted to write a story about a person who becomes emotionally attached to a tank-gestating person.

To this, I added a decades-long grudge against one of my least-favorite teachers from back in high school. He considered the people who clean up our messes—janitors, chambermaids, house-keepers—to be less worthy and less valuable than anyone else, which to this day makes me livid. The people who clean up our messes cannot be thanked or appreciated enough, and are just as capable of heroism as anyone.

A STUDY IN OILS

HALFWAY UP THE WINDING CLIFF-SIDE GUIDEWAY, ZHANG Lei turned his bike around. He was exhausted from three days of travel and nauseated, too, but that wasn't the problem. He could always power through physical discomfort. But the trees, the rocks, the open sky above, and the mountains closing in—it was all too strange. He kept expecting something to drop on his head.

He pinged Marta, the social worker in Beijing Hive who'd orchestrated his escape from Luna seventy-two hours earlier.

Forget Paizuo, he whispered as his bike coasted the guideway's downslope. *This is too weird.*

Turn that bike back around or I'll hit your disable button, Marta whispered back.

You wouldn't.

He turned the bike's acceleration to maximum.

I would. You can spend the next two weeks lying at the bottom of a gully while the tribunal decides what to do with you. Turn around.

No, I'm going back to the Danzhai roadhouse.

When she scowled, her whole face crumpled into a mass of wrinkles. She didn't even look like a person anymore.

I'd do anything to keep you alive, kid, and I don't even like you. She jabbed at him with an age-spotted finger, as if she could reach across the continent and poke him in the chest. *Turn back around or I'll do it.*

He believed her. Nobody had hit his disable button since he'd left Luna, but Marta was an old ex-Lunite and that meant she was both tough and mean. Zhang Lei slowed his bike, rotated back to the guideway's uphill track, and gave the acceleration dial a vicious twist.

You don't like me? he asked.

Maybe a little. Marta flipped through the graphs of his biom. She had full access to that too, and could check everything from his hormone levels to his sleep cycle. *You're getting dehydrated. Drink some water. And slow your bike. You're going to make yourself puke.*

I feel fine, he lied.

Marta rolled her eyes. *Relax. You'll love Paizuo. Nobody wants to kill you there.*

She slapped the connection down, and the image of her elderly face was replaced by steep, verdant mountainside. Danzhai County was thick with an impossible greenness, in layers of bushes, trees, grasses, and herbs he had no name for.

Everything was unfamiliar here. He knew he was deep in southwestern China, but that was about all. He knew he was surrounded by mountains, with Danzhai's transit hub behind him. It was a two-pad skip station, the smallest he'd ever seen, next to a narrow lake surrounded by hills, everything green but the sky—which actually was blue, like everyone always said about Earth—and the buildings. Those were large, brown, and open to the air as if atmospheric weather was nothing.

An atmosphere people could breathe. That was Earth's one unique claim. Unlike Luna, or Venus, or Mars, or any of the built environments in the solar system, here in Danzhai and a few other places on Earth, humans lived every day exposed to weather. It was traditional, or something.

Weather was overrated, Zhang Lei decided. The afternoon was so humid, he'd sweated through his shirt. And the air wasn't clean. Bits of fluff floated in it, and it smelled weird, too. Birds zipped through the air like hovertoys launched from tree limbs—were they even birds? He'd seen so few on Luna.

At least he was alone. A year ago, he would have hated not having anyone to goof around with or show off for. No coach, no team, no fans. Now he was grateful. Marta was watching out for him, always on the other end of a ping if anything went wrong. It was a relief not having to stay ultra-alert.

He pinged Marta.

How long do I have to stay in Paizuo?

Her face appeared again. She was shoveling noodles into her mouth with a pair of chopsticks. The sight of the food made his stomach heave.

At least two weeks. More if I can wrangle an extension. Ideally, I'd like you to stay until the tribunal decides your case.

Okay.

Two weeks. Fine. He'd keep doing what she said, within reason. Drinking water, yes. Slowing the bike down, no. He wasn't going to toil up the mountain like some slack-ass oldster.

Wasn't long before he regretted that decision. The nausea wouldn't be denied any longer. He shifted on the bike's saddle and hung his head over the edge of the guideway. His mouth prickled with saliva until his guts heaved, forcing what was left of his luxurious, hand-cooked Danzhai lunch—black fungus, eggplant, cucumbers, and garlic with pepper, pepper, and more pepper—up, out, and over into the green gulch below. The nausea eased.

When he got to the Paizuo landing stage, the guideway came to a dead end. He couldn't believe it. Just a ground-level platform with a bike rack on one side and a battery of cargo floats on the other. Zhang Lei had never even seen a landing stage with only one connection, not even in the bowels of Luna's smallest hab. Everywhere was interconnected. Not Paizuo, apparently.

He hooked his bike on the rack, shouldered his duffle bag, and wiped his mouth on his sleeve, flicking away a few stray pepper seeds. His lips burned.

I said you'd puke, Marta whispered. No visual this time, only a disembodied voice. *Bet you feel like shit.*

Yeah, but you look like shit.

It was the traditional Lunar reply. Marta laughed.

Don't pull that lip here, okay? You're a guest. Be polite.

He shifted his bag from one shoulder to the other. Nobody seemed to be watching, aside from Marta. Behind the trees, a few brown houses climbed the side of the mountain. Where was the village? A few people were visible through the trees, but otherwise, Paizuo was a wilderness—a noisy wilderness. Wind in the leaves, birds chirping, and buzzing—something coming up behind him.

Zhang Lei spun, fists raised. A cargo conveyor zipped up the guideway. It slid its payload onto a float and slotted itself into place on the underside of the landing stage. The float slowly meandered up a leafy path.

A hospitality fake showed him the way to the guest house, where he stumbled to his room, fell on top of the bed, and slept fourteen hours straight. If someone had wanted to kill him then, they easily could have. He wouldn't have cared.

The other three artists in the guest house were pampered oldsters from high-status habs. They made a big show of acting casual, but Zhang Lei caught each of them exchanging meaningful looks. They were probably pinging his ID to ogle his disable button, marveling at the label under it that said KILLER—FAIR GAME, and discussing him in whispers.

During lunch, Zhang Lei ignored them. Instead of joining their conversation, he watched a hygiene bot polish the floor.

"The wood bothered me at first," said Prajapati, gesturing with a beringed hand at the guest house's wooden walls, floor, and ceiling. She looked soft, her dark skin plush with fat and burnished with moisturizers. Her metadata identified her as sculptor from Bangladesh Hell. "But organic materials are actually quite hygienic, if treated properly."

"I don't like the dirt," said Paul, an ancient watercolorist from Mars. "It's everywhere outside."

"It's not dirt, it's soil," said the sculptor. She picked a morsel of flesh out of the bubbling pot of fish soup in the middle of the table.

"People from the outplanet diaspora forget that soil is life," said Han Song, a 2D photographer from Beijing Hive.

"Yes, we've all been told that a thousand times," replied the watercolorist with a smile. "Earth thinks very well of itself. But I have to say, I like Paizuo. The Miao traditional lifestyle is extremely appealing."

A woman shuffled into the dining room bearing plates of egg dumplings and sweet millet cake. The oldsters smiled and thanked her profusely. The woman wore a wide silver torque around her neck, hung with tiny bells and charms. They tinkled as she arranged the dishes. She was slender, but the profile of her abdomen showed a huge tumor under her colorful tunic.

"What a waste of billable hours," the watercolorist said once the chef was gone. "Couldn't they task a bot with the kitchen-to-table supply chain? I know tradition is important to the Miao, but the human ability to carry plates is hardly going to die out."

The chef had tagged the food with detailed nutritional notes, and it said millet was good for digestive upset. After vomiting his Danzhai lunch yesterday, he couldn't face more peppers. But the millet cake was good—honey-sweet and crunchy. The egg dumplings were delicious, too. He could eat the whole plate.

Marta pinged him.

I thought you'd never wake up. Listen, don't worry about the other guests, okay? We've had them investigated. They're all nice, quiet, trustworthy people. They agreed not ask too many questions.

He shoved another dumpling in his mouth. Zhang Lei knew he ought to be grateful but he wasn't. The three oldsters were getting something out of the deal, too. They would be able to tell stories about him for the rest of their lives. *I once shared accommodations with a murderer. Well, not a murderer, I suppose, not exactly, my dear, but a killer. No, I never asked him what happened but you should have seen the disable button on his ID. It said KILLER right under it. I couldn't help but stare.*

Zhang Lei finished the dumplings and claimed the rest of the millet cake. He left the table still chewing, and slammed the front door behind him.

What did you tell them about me? he asked Marta.

Not much. I said you weren't responsible for what happened and we're working to have the disable button removed.

I was responsible, though.

Zhang Lei, we've discussed this. Do you want to ping a peer counselor? Talk therapy is effective.

No. I hate talking.

The guest house was part of a trio of houses, fronted by a cabbage patch. Large birds—domestic poultry he guessed—pecked at the gravel walkway that led to the guest house's kitchen door. Nearby, a huge horned mammal was tethered in the shade, along with a large caged bird that stalked back and forth and shrieked.

Zhang Lei trudged toward a peak-roofed pavilion. The midday sun stood high over the valley, veiled by humid haze. Not at all hot, but in the unfamiliar atmosphere, sweat beaded on his scarred forearms.

The pavilion overlooked the terraced fields descending the valley and the hazy fleet of mountains on the horizon. No blue sky today. He might as well be in a near-Sun-orbit greenhouse hab, deep in the eye of its dome, every sprout, bud, and bloom indexed and graphed. The locals probably used the same agricultural tech here. Each of the green-and-yellow plants in the terraces below was probably monitored by an agronomist up the mountain, watching microsensors buried in the soil and deploying mineral nutrition with pinpoint accuracy.

Zhang Lei pinged one of the plants. Nothing came back, not even an access denial. He tried pinging one of the farmers working far below, then a nearby tree. Still nothing. Frantic, he flung pings across the valley.

All of the Paizuo guest houses answered immediately. A map highlighted various routes up and down the valley. The guideway landing stage sent him the past two days of traffic history and offered average travel times to various down-slope destinations. A lazy stream of ID information flowed from the guest artists, thirty in total.

Several hazard warnings floated over their targets: *Watch for snakes. Beware of dog. Dangerous cliff.* But no pings from the locals, or any of the crops, equipment, or businesses. Not even from the wooden hand-truck upended over a pile of dirt at the side of the path. But no way this village ran everything data-free.

His pings summoned the hospitality fake. It hovered at his elbow, head inclined with a gently inquiring look.

"Why can't I get a pingback from anything here?" he demanded.

It gave Zhang Lei a generic smile. "Paizuo data streams are restricted to members of the Miao indigenous community."

"So I can't find out anything?" His face grew hot with anger. Stuck here for weeks or more, totally ignorant, unable to learn anything or find out how the village worked.

The fake nodded. "I'll be pleased to answer your questions if I'm able."

Zhang Lei wasn't in the mood for crèche-level games. He slapped it down, hard. The fake misted away, immediately replaced by Marta in full length. She had her fists on her hips and didn't look pleased.

Feeling a little aggressive, Zhang Lei? You didn't say two words to your fellow guests, and now you're getting testy with a fake.

I'm sorry, okay? Embarrassing. He should have controlled himself. *I hate this place.*

No, you don't. You're out of your element. Nothing here is any threat to you. She grinned. Not unless you have a phobia of domestic animals.

Hah, he grumbled.

Go for a walk. Do a little sketching. Get familiar with the village. There's lots to see, and it's all gorgeous. There's a reason why artists love Paizuo.

Okay. He booted up his viewcatcher. Marta gave him an approving nod and dissolved.

True, Paizuo was beautiful. From the pavilion, mountains thick with trees stretched sharp and steep over the valley, where green and yellow terraced fields stepped up and down the lower slopes, punctuated by small groups of wooden houses under tall trees. He framed the composition in his viewcatcher. It was perfect, pre-chewed—the whole reason the pavilion had been built there in the first place. The fang-like form of the tallest mountain clutched in the spiral fist of the golden mean. Nice.

Even though the view was pre-packaged, framing it in his viewcatcher was satisfying. And what a relief to be able to do it openly. Back on Luna, he had to be careful not to get caught using the viewcatcher, or he'd get smacked by one of his teammates or screamed at by his coach. Zhang Lei was allowed to draw cartoons and caricatures, but everything else was a distraction from training and a waste of time and focus.

Total commitment to the game, that's what all coaches demanded.

"What do you love better, hockey or scribbling on little bits of paper?" Coach had demanded, and then smacked him on the back of the head when he hesitated.

"Hockey," he answered.

"Right. Don't forget it."

So he drew cartoons of his teammates, their rival teams, and stars from the premier leagues they all wanted to get drafted into. He got good. Fast. Accurate. In thirty seconds, he could toss off a sketch that got the whole team hooting. Coach liked it, said it was good for morale. But quick, sketchy work didn't satisfy. Neither did the digital-canvas painting he snuck past Coach on occasion, but both were better than nothing.

He padded down a trail to the first terrace, flipping his viewcatcher through its modes—thirds to notan to golden mean to phi grid—as he strode along the edge. The earthen berm bounding the terrace was less than a meter wide, and seemed to be made entirely of dirt. The next terrace was ten meters below on his left.

He blacked out edges of the view, widened the margins until nothing was visible outside his constantly expanding and contracting search for a composition. He swept back and forth across the landscape. Then he slipped and fell. The viewcatcher framed a close-up of green plants in brown water.

Zhang Lei lurched sideways, regaining his footing, the right leg of his pants wet to the knee and slimy with mud. He dismissed the viewcatcher and stared incredulously around him.

The matrix of the terraces was liquid, not soil. Water and mud. He'd seen it glinting between the greenery, but he hadn't realized it was water. And now he was covered in it.

A fleeting thought—*I'm going to die here*—easily dismissed. All he had to do was watch where he put his feet as he explored.

Paizuo wasn't what Zhang Lei expected. The village wasn't all one piece like ancient towns in crèche storybooks. It was spread thin, covering the whole valley, the houses clustered in groups under the trees and separated by fields and paddies. The Miao didn't build on flat or even sloping land—those areas seemed dedicated to crops. Instead, they chose the precipitous and rocky landscape for their multi-level wooden homes. Each house stood on stilts over the canted landscape, the weight of the structures leaning back on the mountainside. Livestock sheltered in the shade beneath, some tethered or penned, some roaming free.

Actual live animals, like the ones behind the guest house, and a lot of them. With humans living literally on top of them.

A deep voice knocked Zhang Lei out of his thoughts. Unfamiliar syllables. When he turned to look, the translation word balloon hung over the man's head:

"Hello, can I help you?"

No ID accessible, but the balloon was tagged with his name: Jen Dang. Not tall, but broad-shouldered and athletic, with skin deeply burnished by the sun and a wide, strong face. Old, but not an oldster.

Zhang Lei switched on his translation app.

"I arrived yesterday," Zhang Lei said. "Trying to get used to everything."

Jen Dang scanned the balloon overhead.

"Are the insects troubling you?"

"Insects?" Zhang Lei frowned and scanned the ground. "I haven't seen any yet."

"Right there." Jen Dang pointed at one of the fluttering creatures he had no name for.

"Oh, I thought insects lived on the ground. I'm from—" He almost said Luna but caught himself in time. "I've never been on Earth before. It's different."

"Most of our guests use seers to help them identify plants and animals. Paizuo is a biodiversity preserve, with thousands of different species."

"I'll do that, thanks."

Jen Dang fell silent. Zhang Lei could feel himself warming to the stranger. Lots of charisma and natural authority. He'd do well on Luna.

"The food is really good here," he said.

A shadow of a smile crossed Jen Dang's face.

"Jen Dla is my daughter. She's an experienced chef."

"I'm sorry," Zhang Lei said, and other man squinted at him. "I couldn't help but notice she's sick." He gestured vaguely in the region of his stomach.

Jen Dang shook his head. "You're a guest. There are lots of things guests can't understand. Would you like to see another?"

Two large baskets lay under a tree. Jen Dang plucked them from the ground and led Zhang Lei down a tree-lined path, the slope so extreme the route soon turned into uneven stairs, cut into the dirt and haphazardly incised with slabs of rock. Mammals grazed on either side, standing nearly on their hind legs while cropping the ground cover.

They descended five terrace levels before Zhang Lei's thighs started getting hot. Stairs were a good workout, mostly cardio but some leg strength, and uneven steps were good balance training, too. For a moment he lost himself in the rhythm of their rapid descent. It was enjoyable. He could run the stairs in morning and evening before doing his squats and lunges—but then he remembered. He wasn't an athlete anymore. And with the disable button on his ID labeling him a killer, nobody in Danzhai, Miao or guest, needed to wonder what he was training for, or if he was chasing someone.

He slowed, letting the distance widen between himself and the farmer. If someone got worried and hit the button, he'd roll right down the mountain.

Jen Dang shucked his shoes and rolled up his trouser legs as he waited for Zhang Lei at one of the lower terraces.

"Many guests are squeamish of the rice paddies, but it's only water and mud," he said when Zhang Lei joined him. "And worms. Bugs of course. A few snakes. And fish." He hefted the large basket. It was bottomless—an open, woven cylinder.

“Not a problem.” Zhang Lei pulled off his shoes, but didn’t roll up his pant legs. One was still damp. The other might as well get wet, too.

Jen Dang handed him the smaller basket and waded into the sodden paddy, bottomless basket clutched in both hands.

“Step between the rice plants, never on them. Try not to stir up too much mud, or you can’t see the fish.”

Jen Dang demonstrated, moving slowly and looking at the water through the basket. Zhang Lei followed. The mud was cool. It squelched through his toes.

“Use the basket to shade the water’s surface,” the farmer said. “Look for movement. A flash of scales or the flick of a tail.”

As Zhang Lei followed the farmer through the paddy, he took care to keep his feet away from the knee-high rice plants. Each one was topped by knobby spikes—the grain portion of the crop, he assumed. Some of the grain was coated with a milky substance, and some was turning yellow.

Jen Dang plunged the bottomless basket in the water and said, “Come look.”

A fish was trapped inside. Jen Dang reached into the water and flipped it into Zhang Lei’s basket. It struggled, thrashing.

“That’s one, we need six. You catch the rest.”

Zhang Lei made several tries before he trapped a fish large enough to meet Jan Dang’s standards. Catching the rest took a full hour. The sky cleared and turned Earth-blue. The older man betrayed no trace of impatience, even though it was a ridiculous expenditure of effort to procure basic foodstuffs when a nutritional extruder could feed hundreds of people an hour, with personalized flavor and texture profiles and optimal nutrition.

When they finished, Zhang Lei’s eyes ached from squinting against the flare of sun on water. He wiped his fish-slick hands on his pants and followed the farmer up the stairs.

"Why do you do this?" he asked.

Jen Dang stopped and eyed the word balloon over Zhang Lei's head.

"Stubbornness. That's what my wife says. She's an orthopedic surgeon, takes care of all the Miao in Danzhai county. She won't farm. Says her hands are meant for higher things. She loves to cook, though. She taught all our daughters."

"But why do manual labor when you could use bots?"

"We use some, but we're not dependent on them. If we don't do the work, who will?"

"Nobody."

"Then nobody will know how to do it. All traditional skills and knowledge will be lost, along with our language, stories, songs—everything that makes us Miao. We do it to survive."

"You could write it down."

Jen Dang laughed. He lifted the fish basket to his shoulder and ran up the stairs two at a time. His word balloon blossomed behind him.

"Some things can only be mastered with constant practice."

That was true. Nobody could learn to play hockey by watching a doc. Or learn to draw or paint without actually doing it.

An insect landed on a nearby plant. Its wide, delicate wings had eye-like patterns in shades of gold and copper. Zhang Lei framed it in his viewcatcher, then panned up to include the mountains in the composition. Gold wings and green slopes, copper eyes and blue sky. Perfect.

Another insect hung in the sky, hovering motionless, shaped like a half circle and very faint. Zhang Lei stared for a whole minute before realizing what he was looking at.

The moon. Luna itself. The home of everything he knew, and everyone who wanted to hurt him. Watching.

Over the next week, the moon turned its back on him, retreating through its last quarter to a thinning sickle. In the morning, when he ventured onto the guest house's porch for a stretch, there it was, lurking behind the boughs of a fir tree, half-hidden behind mountain peaks, or veiled in humid haze to the east. Sometimes it hid on the other side of the globe. Then the next time he looked, it was right overhead, staring at him.

Night was the worst. The lights of the habs glared from the dark lunar surface aside the waning crescent—the curved sickle of Purovsk, the oval of Olenyok, the diamond pinpoint of Bratsk, the five-pointed star of Harbin.

A few years back, an investment group had tried to float a proposal to build a new hab on Mare Insularum, its lights outlining a back-turned fist with an extended middle finger. Zhang Lei and his teammates had worn the proposed hab pattern on their gym shirts for a few months, the finger mocked up extra large on a dark moon, telling Earth and all its inhabitants what Lunites thought of them.

He could stay inside at night, but he couldn't hide from the moon during the day. It watched him with a sideways smile. *We see you—we're coming to get you.*

He tried not to think about it, and concentrated on finding compositions with his viewcatcher. He made sketches and studies, and looked up plants and animals with his seer, and tried to learn their names. When he ran into artists from the other guest houses, they were friendly enough, but all much older than him.

At night, he worked on studies and small canvases in his room, door closed and windows dark. They were disasters: muddy greens, lifeless brushwork, flat compositions. He tried all the tricks he'd learned in the crèche—glazing, underpainting, overpainting, scraping with a palette knife, dry brush, but nothing worked.

Why don't you try some familiar subjects? Marta suggested. *Limber up first, then branch out into new things.*

If you say so.

He was so frustrated he'd try anything. He lugged his easel and kit up to the guest house's communal studio and set up in his own corner of the work space.

"I was beginning to think we'd never see you up here," said Paul. "Welcome."

"The light's especially good in the afternoon," said Prajapati.

Han Song paused his hands over his work surface for a moment and nodded.

Nothing motivated Zhang Lei like competition. He would destroy the watercolorist with his superior command of light and shadow, teach the sculptor about form, show the photographer how to compose a scene.

His old viewcatcher compositions and stealthily-made reference sketches were gone forever, so he worked from memory. He attacked the canvas with his entire arsenal, blocking out a low-angle view of Mons Hadley and the shining towers of Sklad, with the hab's vast hockey arena in the foreground under a gleaming crystal dome. The view might be three hundred and eighty thousand kilometers away, but it lay at his fingertips, and he created it anew every time he closed his eyes.

The paint leapt to Zhang Lei's brush, clung to the canvas, spread thin and lean and true exactly where it should, the way it should, creating the effects he intended. After a week of flailing with sappy greens and sloppy, organic shapes, he finally had a canvas under control. He worked late, muttering good night to the other artists without raising his eyes from his work. When dawn stretched its fingers through the studio's high windows, the painting was done—complete with a livid crimson stain spreading under the arena's crystal dome.

He didn't remember deciding to paint blood on the ice, or putting crimson on his palette. But the color belonged there. It was the truth. It showed what he did.

Zhang Lei lowered himself to the floor, leaned his back against the wall with his elbows on his knees, and rested his head in his hands. He pinged Marta. She blinked blearily at him for a few seconds, her eyes swollen with sleep. He pointed at the canvas.

Have any of the other artists seen this? she whispered.

I don't know. I don't think so.

It's important they don't. Okay? Do you understand why?

Because people are looking for me.

Not only that. She scrubbed her eyes with the heels of her hands. *The Lunite ambassador is trying to block your immigration application. If the media gets interested we'll have to move you, fast. And yes, people are searching. Three teams of Lunite brawlers have been skipping all over the planet, asking questions. They found someone in Sudbury Hell who remembers you getting on a skip bound for Chongqing Hive. That's too close for comfort.*

I can destroy the canvas, he said, voice flat and scraped clean of emotion. It was the first real painting he'd done since he left the crèche. But he couldn't look at it. When he did, his flesh crawled.

No. Don't do that. Hide it.

He nodded. *It's a decent painting.*

Yeah. Not bad. You worked out the kinks.

He knocked his head against the wall behind him. Wood was harder than it looked. He swung his head harder.

Stop that.

There's no point, Marta. Those brawlers are going to find me.

No, they won't. And chances are good the tribunal will rule in your favor. We have to be patient.

Even if I get to live in Beijing, people will still find out what I did.

They'll assume you had no choice. Everyone knows Luna is the most dangerous place in the solar system.

I did have a choice—

Marta interrupted. *It was a mistake. An accident. It could happen to any hockey player.*

I aimed for Dorgon's neck.

You did what you were taught, and so did Dorgon. Playing hockey isn't the only way to die on Luna. If you live in a place where getting killed is accepted as a possible outcome, then you also accept that you might become a killer.

But we don't understand what it means.

No. Marta looked sad. *No, we don't.*

The day after he'd killed Dorgon, Zhang Lei's team hauled him to a surgeon. Twenty minutes was all it took to install the noose around his carotid artery, then two minutes to connect the disable button and process the change to his ID. His teammates were as gentle as they could be. When it was all done, the team's enforcer clasped Zhang Lei's shoulder in a meaty hand.

"We test it now," Korchenko said, and Zhang Lei had gone down like a slab of meat.

When he woke, his friends looked concerned, sympathetic, even a little regretful.

That attitude didn't last long. After the surgery, the team traveled to a game in Surgut. Zhang Lei's disable button was line-of-sight. Anyone who could see it could trigger it. He passed out five times along the way, and spent most of the game slumped on the bench, head lolling, his biom working hard to keep him from brain damage. His teammates had to carry him home.

For a few weeks, they treated him like a mascot, hauling him from residence to practice rink to arena and back again. They soon tired of it and began leaving him behind. The first time he went out alone he came back on a cargo float, with a shattered jaw and bootprint-shaped bruises on his gut. That was okay. He figured he deserved it.

Then one night after an embarrassing loss, the team began hitting the button for fun. First Korchenko, as a joke. Then the others. Didn't take long for Zhang Lei to become their new punching bag. So he ran. Hid out in Sklad's lower levels, pulling temporary privacy veils over his ID every fifteen minutes to keep the team from tracking him. When they were busy at the arena warming up for a game, he bolted for Harbin.

He passed out once on the way to the nearest intra-hab connector, but the brawler who hit his disable button was old and drunk. Zhang Lei collected a few kicks to the ribs and one to the balls before the drunk staggered off. Nobody else took the opportunity to get their licks in, but nobody helped him, either.

Boarding the connector, he got lucky. A crèche manager was transferring four squalling newborns, and the crib's noise-dampening tech was broken. The pod emptied out—just him and the crèche manager. She ignored him all the way to Harbin. He kept his distance, but when they got to their destination, he followed her into the bowels of the hab.

She was busy with the babies and didn't notice at first. But when he joined her in an elevator, she got scared.

"What do you want?" she demanded, her voice high with tension.

He tried to explain, but she was terrified. That big red label on his button—KILLER—FAIR GAME—didn't fill people with confidence in his character. She hit the button hard, several times. He spent an hour on the floor of the elevator, riding from level to level, and came to with internal bleeding, a cracked ocular orbit, three broken ribs, and a vicious bite mark on his left buttock.

He limped down to the lowest level, where they put the crèches, and found his old crèche manager. She was gray, stooped, and much more frail than he remembered.

"Zhang Lei." She put a gentle palm on his head—the only place that didn't hurt. "I was your first cuddler. I decanted you myself. I won't let anyone hurt you."

If he cried then, he never admitted it.

Zhang Lei watched Jen Dla carry a pot of soup into the dining room. She moved awkwardly, shifting her balance around that bulbous gut. He couldn't understand it. Why hadn't she had an operation to remove the tumor? Her mother was even a surgeon.

Terminal, he guessed, and then realized he'd been staring.

Jen Dla nestled the pot on the stove in the middle of the table, and lit the flame. He caught the chef's eye as she adjusted the temperature of the burner.

"Your father must be an important man here in Paizuo," he said.

Jen Dla laughed.

"He certainly thinks so." She laid her hand on the embroidered blouse draped over her bulging abdomen. "Fathers get more self-important with every new grandchild."

She tapped her finger on her stomach. Zhang Lei sat back in his chair, abruptly. She wasn't sick, but pregnant—actually bearing a child.

"Are all Miao children body-birthed?" he asked.

She looked a little offended. "Miao who choose to live in Paizuo generally like to follow tradition."

Abrupt questions leapt behind his teeth—*does it hurt, are you frightened*—but her expression was forbidding.

"Congratulations," he said. She smiled and returned to her kitchen.

After talking to Marta, he'd taken the painting down to his room and hidden it under the bed, then collapsed into dream-clouded sleep. The arena at Sklad, deserted, the vast spread of ice all his own. The blades of his skates cut the surface as he built speed, gathered himself, and launched into a quad, spinning through the air so fast the flesh of his face pulled away and snapped back into place on landing. He jumped, spun, jumped again.

Dreams of power and joy, ruined on waking. He'd pulled the painting from under his bed and hid it behind the sofa in the guest house lounge.

Jen Dla's soup began to bubble. Tomatoes bobbed in the sour rice broth. Zhang Lei watched the fish turn opaque as it cooked, then pinged one word at the three artists upstairs—*lunch*. They clattered down.

"Looked like you were having a productive session yesterday," Prajapati said. "Good to see."

"Don't stop the flow," Han Song added.

Paul grinned. "Nothing artists love more than giving unwanted advice."

"It's called encouragement," said Prajapati. "And it's especially important for young artists."

"Young competitors, you mean."

"I don't see it that way." She turned to Zhang Lei. "Do you?"

All three artists watched him expectantly. Zhang Lei stared at his hands resting on the wooden tabletop. He'd forgotten to roll down his sleeves. His forearms were exposed, the scarred skin dotted with pigment. He put his hands in his lap.

"I think the fish is ready," he said.

After lunch, while exploring for new compositions, he found Jen Dang behind the guest house. The water buffalo—one of the first creatures he'd looked up on his seer—was tethered to a post by a loop of rope through its nose. It was huge, lavishly muscled, and heavy, with ridged, back-curving horns, but it stood placidly as Jen Dang examined its hooves.

"Stay back," Jen Dang said. "Water buffalo aren't as friendly as they look. He's not a pet."

"Yeah, I know," said Zhang Lei. When he'd sketched the water buffalo, a stern warning had popped into his eye: *Do not approach. Will trample, gouge, and kick.*

He lifted his viewcatcher and captured a composition: Jen Dang stooping with his back turned to the water buffalo, drawing its massive hindquarter between his own legs and trapping the hoof between his knees.

"All he has to do is back up, and you'll get squashed," said Zhang Lei.

"He knows me." Jen Dang dropped the hoof and patted the animal's rump. "And he knows the best part of his day is about to begin."

The farmer untied the rope from the post and led the animal up the narrow trail behind the houses. Zhang Lei followed. A bird stalked from between the trees, its red, gold, and blue body trailing long, spotted brown tail feathers. His seer tagged it: *Golden Pheasant*, followed by a symbol that meant *major symbolic and cultural importance to the indigenous people at this geographical location*. Which was no different from most of the plants and animals the seer had identified.

"So, I've been using a seer," he said, as if his rice paddy conversation with Jen Dang had happened that morning instead of days before. "It doesn't explain anything. Why is every butterfly important to Miao but not the flies? Why one species of bee but not the other?"

"The butterfly is our mother," Jen Dang said.

"No, it's not. That's ridiculous."

"I might ask you who your mother is, if I were young and rude, and didn't know better."

"I don't have a mother. I was detanked."

"That means you're the product of genetic advection, from a tightly edited stream of genetic material subscribed to by your crèche. How is that less strange than having a butterfly mother?"

"Is the butterfly thing a metaphor?"

Jen Dang glanced over his shoulder, his gaze cold. "If you like."

The water buffalo lipped the tail of Jen Dang's shirt. He tapped its nose with the palm of his hand to warn it off. The trail widened as it began to climb a high ridge. The water buffalo was heavy but strong. It heaved itself up the slope, like a boulder rolling uphill. Jen Dang ran alongside to keep pace, so Zhang Lei ran after. The exertion felt good, scrambling uphill against the full one-point-zero, with two workout partners. So what if one of them was an animal? Zhang Lei would take what he could get.

When the trail widened, he took the chance to sprint ahead. He made it to the top of the ridge a full ten seconds before the water buffalo. Jen Dang looked him up and down.

"Not bad. Most guests are slow."

Zhang Lei grinned. "I train in the dubs."

"Dubs?"

"Double Earth-normal gravity. You know. For strength."

"I never would have guessed."

"I know," Zhang Lei said eagerly. "I look bottom-heavy, right? Narrow above a wide butt and thick legs. That's what makes me a good skater."

Shut up, Marta hissed in his ear. But he couldn't stop. Finally a real conversation.

"I train for optimal upper body flexibility, like all center forward play—"

One twinge in his throat, that was all it took to send Zhang Lei plummeting to the ground. He twisted and rolled when he hit the dirt—away from the edge of the hill, and then the world faded to mist.

Zhang Lei clawed his way to consciousness.

You're fine, you're fine, nobody's touched you.

Okay, he mumbled.

You've only been down five minutes, Marta added. *Tell him you have a seizure disorder and your neurologist is fine-tuning your treatment protocol. Say it.*

Zhang Lei struggled to focus. His eyelids fluttered as he tried to form the words.

“I get seizures.” He licked his lips. “Doc’s working on it.”

Jen Dang said something. Zhang Lei forced his eyes to stay open. He was collapsed on his side, cheek pressed to the dirt. Three ants crawled not ten centimeters from his eye. He flopped onto his back to read the farmer’s word balloon.

“Your medical advisory said it wasn’t an emergency, and I shouldn’t touch you.” Behind Jen Dang, the water buffalo cast a lazy brown eye over him and shook its head.

Tell him you’ll be fine, Marta demanded. *Ask him not to mention it to anyone.*

“I’m fine.” Zhang Lei pushed himself onto his elbows, then to his knees. “Don’t talk about this, okay?”

The farmer looked dubious. He gathered the water buffalo’s lead rope.

“I’ll walk you back to the studio.”

“No.” Zhang Lei jumped to his feet. “There’s nothing wrong with me. It won’t happen again.”

Better not, Marta grumbled.

Zhang Lei led the way up the trail. Jen Dang followed. The water buffalo wasn’t dawdling anymore, it was moving fast, nearly trotting. The track converged on a single-lane paved road, which snaked up the valley in a series of switchbacks. They were higher now, the guest houses far below, and everywhere, rice terraces brimmed with ripening grain yellow as the sun. He could paint those terraces with slabs of cadmium yellow. Maybe he would.

“Which way?”

Zhang Lei needn’t have asked. The water buffalo turned onto the road and trundled uphill. Before long, the slope gentled. Houses lined the road, with gardens and rice paddies behind. The road ended at a circular courtyard patterned with dark and light stones and half-bounded by a stream. At the far end, a footbridge arched over the water, leading to more houses beyond.

The animal's tail switched back and forth. It trotted toward the water, splayed hooves clopping on the courtyard's patterned surface. A hygiene sweeper darted out of its path. At the stream's edge, where the courtyard's stone patterns gave way to large, dark slabs, the water buffalo paused, lowered its head, and stepped into the water.

A man called out from one of the houses across the bridge. Jen Dang shouted a reply. No word balloon appeared.

Jen Dang offered the lead rope to Zhang Lei.

"He'll stay in the water. I'll only be a few minutes."

Zhang Lei leaned on the bridge railings, flipping the rope to keep it from tangling in the animal's horns as it luxuriated in the water below. The stream wasn't deep, only a meter or so, but the beast lay on its side and rolled, keeping its white beard, eyes, and horns above water.

When Jen Dang returned, the water buffalo was scratching its long, drooping ear on a half-submerged rock. Zhang Lei kept the rope.

"It's fun," he said. "Best part of my day, too."

The farmer sauntered across the courtyard and joined a pair of friends working in the shade of a mulberry tree.

Zhang Lei composed a series of canvases. The water buffalo with its eyelids lowered in pleasure, lips parted to reveal a gleaming row of bottom teeth. Three women in bright blue blouses weaving in an open workshop, their silver torques flashing. A man in deep indigo embroidered with pink and silver diamonds, sorting through a table piled with feathers. Jen Dang leaning on a low stone wall, deep in conversation with two friends using gleaming axes to chop lengths of bamboo. A white-haired woman in an apron stirring a barrel of viscous liquid with a wooden paddle. A battery of pink-cheeked, scrubbed children racing across the courtyard as a golden pheasant stalked in the opposite direction. A row of cabbages beside the road. Herbs clinging to a slate outcropping. A dragonfly skipping over the water. The tallest peak puncturing the western horizon like a fang on the underjaw of a huge beast.

Aesthetically pleasing, peaceful, picturesque. But all communities had tensions and contradictions. Only a Miao could identify the deeper meaning in these scenes. Only a great artist could paint the picturesque and make it important. He wasn't Miao and he was no great artist. Could he capture the water buffalo's expression of ecstasy as it pawed the water? Not likely. But he could paint the mountain. Nothing more banal than another mountain view. But he loved that unnamed peak. He'd loved Mons Hadley, too.

Jen Dang waved. A word balloon blossomed over his head: *Let's go.*

He jiggled the rope. The water buffalo ignored him. He flapped it, then gave the gentlest of tugs. The buffalo snorted and heaved itself out of the water. It stood there dripping for a moment, then its skin shivered. It lowered its head, shaking its great bulk and coating Zhang Lei in a local rainstorm.

Zhang Lei wiped his face on his sleeve. The men were still laughing when he joined them. Nothing more fun than watching a rookie fall on his ass.

Jen Dang was still chatting. Zhang Lei waited nearby, in the shade of a house. Along the wall was a metal cage much like the one behind the guest house. A rooster stalked back and forth, its face, comb and wattle bright red, its bare breast and scraggly back caked with clean, healing sores. It stared at

Zhang Lei with a malevolent orange eye, lifted one fiercely-taloned yellow leg, and flipped its water dish.

"Stupid bird," Zhang Lei muttered.

Around the corner was another cage, another rooster in similar condition, its comb sliced in dangling pieces. When it screamed—raucous, belligerent—the other bird answered. Zhang Lei knew an exchange of challenges when he heard it.

"Are these fighting cocks?" he asked when Jen Dang joined him.

"You don't have them on Luna?" he answered.

Shit, whispered Marta. *Tell him you're from the Sol Belt. You've never been to Luna.*

Why don't you hit my disable button again? Load me on a cargo float and stick me in a hole somewhere? Or better yet—a cage. Evict one of the birds and get me my own dish of water.

I might have to do that. Listen kid, it's never been more important for you to be discreet.

Why? Are they coming for me?

Silence.

They are, aren't they? Answer me.

A Lunite team tracked you to the Danzhai roadhouse, but don't worry. We've got people on the ground, planting rumors to lure them to Guiyang. Even if they don't take the bait, Danzhai County has lots towns and villages. You're still safe.

"I'm from the Sol Belt," he told Jen Dang. "I've never been to Luna."

The farmer didn't look convinced.

Zhang Lei's hand stole up to his throat. Under his jaw, where his pulse pounded, the hard mass of the noose waited to choke off his life.

When Zhang Lei got back to the studio, the other three artists were upstairs. He shoved the sofa aside. The painting leaned against the wall, facing out, a layer of breathable sealant protecting the drying oil paint. He was sure he'd turned it to face the wall, but apparently not. It didn't really matter. He wanted it gone.

He sprayed the canvas with another layer of sealant, trying not to look at the thick wet bloody gleam on the arena's ice. He wrapped it in two layers of black polymer sheeting, and requested a cargo wrap to meet him at the guideway landing stage.

When he got there, the area was packed with Miao arriving on sliders and bikes, whole families crowded onto on multi-seat units, laughing and talking. He edged his way to the cargo drop, slid the cargo wrap around it, addressed it to Marta, and shoved the painting inside the conveyor. Done. He'd never have to think about it again.

The Miao were on holiday. Women wore their blue blouses with short skirts trailing with long, flapping ribbons, or ankle-length red and blue dresses. All the women's clothing was dense with colorful embroidery and tinkling with silver, and all wore their silver torques. The younger women pierced their top-knots with flowers. Mothers and grandmothers layered their torques with necklaces, and wore tall silver headdresses crowned with slender, curving horns. Silver everywhere—charms in the shape of flowers, bells, fish, and butterflies dangled from their jewelry, sleeves, sashes, and hems.

They were, in a word, gorgeous. Happy-laughing, leading children, carrying babies, holding hands with their friends, and among them, men of all ages in embroidered black, blue, and indigo. The men were also happy, also laughing, also embracing their friends, helping their children and elders. But the young women—ah. They caught his eye.

Zhang Lei retreated to the side of a corn patch, capturing compositions while watching the steady flow of arrivals. Some pinged for mobility assistance, and rode float chairs up the road, but most walked. Some eschewed the road, and ran uphill toward the guest house, making for the steep shortcut up the ridge. Zhang Lei followed.

Paul, Prajapati, and Han Song watched from the studio porch. Zhang Lei joined them.

"Jen Dla told me we can go watch the festival after supper," Prajapati said. "It's called Setting Free Your Daughter, or something like that."

"Setting them free from what?" asked Han Song.

Six young women ran toward them, through Jen Dla's cabbage patch.

"Family control, I would imagine," Paul answered.

The girls didn't even glance up. At home, he never had to work to get a girl's attention—nobody on the team did. Unless coach called a ban for training reasons, sex was on offer everywhere he looked. Here, he might as well be invisible. But then, he hadn't exactly been making himself available. If the girls were being set free, and he was in the right place at the right time, maybe one of them would land in his lap. All he had to do was get them to notice him.

"I'm going to the festival," Zhang Lei said.

"I'll go too," said Han Song. "I haven't done enough exploring."

"We'll all go," said Prajapati. Paul nodded.

After Jen Dla served them an early supper, Zhang Lei led the oldsters up the winding road to the village center. They admired the views from every switchback as if they hadn't already had a week to explore, and examined every clump of flowers as if Paizuo wasn't one big flower garden. Guests from the other studios joined them, which made the whole group even slower.

Zhang Lei was tempted to leave them all behind, run to the village center and see if the girls had been set free yet. He jogged up a few switchbacks, and then thought the better of it. Even the most adventurous girl would flee from a lone man bearing a disable button labeled KILLER. If he wanted someone to take a chance on trusting him, he'd better stick with the group.

Zhang Lei sat on a boulder at the side of the road and waited for the oldsters to catch up. They weren't bad people. All three were kind and clever in their own ways. And patient. He'd been unfriendly but they hadn't taken offence.

"We should really walk faster," Prajapati told the other two when they caught up. "We don't want Zhang Lei to miss his chance with the girls."

Zhang Lei grinned. "I could ping you a cargo float."

She laughed and took his arm.

The roadside floating lights winked on, turning their route into a tunnel of light snaking up the mountainside. When they got to the village center, night had fallen. The courtyard was lit with flaming torches and in the middle of the crowd, a bonfire blazed, sending up a column of sparks to search the sky. Faces flickered with shadows. Silver glinted and gleamed. Laughter pealed. A singer wailed.

"I don't know when I last smelled something burning," said Han Song.

"Is that what the stench is?" asked Paul.

"Wood smoke is the most beautiful scent," said Prajapati. "Primal."

Most of the guests stayed on the courtyard's edge. They joined a group under the mulberry tree, a gender-free triad of performance artists from Cusco Hab. Zhang Lei had seen them around the village. They always looked like they were in a meeting—heads down, conferring, arguing, making notes.

"Have the daughters been set free yet?" Han Song quipped. "Asking for a friend."

The triad laughed.

"Apparently it's only one daughter, and no, the ceremony hasn't begun yet," said Aiko, the tallest of the three.

"Just one girl?" Zhang Lei said. "Then what's the point?"

"Shakespeare! One performer, one night only. The complete works." Aiko was obviously joking but their face was perfectly sober.

Prajapati grinned. "Don't tease the boy."

Another pair of artists joined them, a cellist from Zurich and an opera singer from Hokkaido. They seemed to know more about the festival than anyone else.

"We won't catch much of the performance unless the girl throws the switch on her translation balloon," the cellist said in a low voice. "The one last year didn't."

"Someone told me they translate in Kala, for the tourists visiting from Danzhai Wanda Village," said Aiko.

"Paizuo is more traditional than Kala. Which is why we come here." The cellist shaded her eyes against the torches' flare and scanned the crowd.

"It's better they don't translate," the opera singer said. "What the girl says won't make sense if you don't know the context. It's more meaningful to watch the reactions of the Miao."

With so many people in the square, Zhang Lei could only catch glimpses of the action. He put his viewcatcher on full extension, sent it a meter overhead and switched its mode to low lux. Much better. The musicians were at the far end of the courtyard, near the bridge, playing drums and tall, upright bamboo flutes. The singer stood with them, wearing her silver headdress like a crown. Jen Dang and his family didn't seem to be around. But he spotted the girl—the one who was being set free. She was alone. No friends, no fussing parents, no little siblings hanging on her arms.

She wore hoops of silver chain around her torque, a blue blouse and short black skirt embroidered with butterflies, and a woven sash around her waist. A deep-red flower pierced her top-knot. Her hands rested at her sides. She didn't pick at her nails or play with her jewelry like Lunite girls. She looked prepared, like a goalie in a crease, waiting for the game to begin.

He zoomed in on her face. His age or a little younger. Pretty, like all the Miao girls. Tough, too. What would a girl like her think of him?

Not much, he suspected.

The music stopped, the crowd hushed. The girl's lips thinned in concentration. She stepped toward the bonfire and the circle of elders welcomed her into their arms. No drums this time, no bamboo flutes, no practiced wail from a powerful throat. The elders sang softly, their song a hum in the night, drowning under the buzz of the cicadas and crickets.

Near the artists at the back of the crowd stood a mother with a baby clutched to her chest. She wore little silver, and looked upset.

"Poor thing," said Prajapati.

The woman scowled at her and made a hushing motion.

Zhang Lei waited for something to happen, some reason why the Miao were paying such close attention. The girl wasn't doing anything, just standing in the circle of softly singing elders, eyes closed, face tight with concentration. Maybe nothing would happen—that was the point? Perhaps it was a test of her patience. It certainly was a test of his.

As he was considering sneaking away, the girl began singing along. Her voice was high, with an eerie overtone that pierced the sky. She sang higher and higher, drowning out the elders' voices. The Miao were rapt, breathless. When she spoke—loud as if amplified—the crowd exhaled a collective sigh of wonder.

"No translation balloon," Aiko breathed. "Damn."

Zhang Lei expected the crying mother to turn and scold them again, but she was pushing through the crowd, sobbing and holding her baby out like an offering.

"Must be her dead husband," said the cellist, quietly. "You see? They set the girl's soul free to visit the spirits, and now she's bringing messages back."

"Messages?" said Zhang Lei. "What kind of messages?"

"Every kind. Instructions. Admonitions. Warnings. Blessings. What kind of messages would you send from beyond if you could?"

"I don't know, maybe something the girl could easily guess?" said Han Song.

"Hush," said Prajapati. "This is serious."

It was serious. Zhang Lei didn't even have to look up to know the new moon was watching him, the lights of its habs inscribed like a curse on the sunless black disc punched through the middle of the Milky Way.

On Luna, hockey was a blood sport. Lunar hockey was played at one-sixth gravity on a curved surface, with a Stefoff field to keep the puck low and snap players back to the ice. One of the major defensive moves was to disable the other team's players. Clubbing with weighted carbon fiber hockey sticks resulted in a penalty, though all referees were selectively blind. Slashing with skate blades, however, was a power move. An over-dominant team could cut their way through their opponents' starting lineup, into the benched players and fourth-rates, and by the end of the fourth quarter stage an assault on a undefended goalie.

Deaths were rare. Heads, legs, torsos, and groins were armored. Arms and throats were not. Medical bots hovered over the ice, ready to swoop in for first response, but rookies from the crèches quickly picked up scars, even playing in the recreational leagues. Anyone who remained unscarred was either a goalie or a coward.

Zhang Lei's crèche manager had tried to do right by him, direct his talents so he'd have choices when he left the crèche. She nurtured his talent for drawing and painting as much as possible. But she was practical, too. Luna had far more professional hockey teams than artist collectives. All her children were on skates as soon as they could walk.

With powerful legs and a low center of gravity, Zhang Lei could take a hit and keep his speed. He could jump, spin, and kick. He could slice an opposing defenseman's brachial artery, drag his stick through the spurting blood, and spray the goalie as he slid the puck into the net. The fans loved him for it. His teammates too.

It made him a target, though. He spent more time on the bench than anyone else on the team, healing wounds on his forearms. No matter. The down time gave him the opportunity to perfect the rarest of plays—jump and spin high enough to slice a blade through an opponent's throat. He practiced it, talked about it, drew cartoons of it. He gave up goals attempting it, which got him a faceful of spittle whenever Coach chewed him out.

Then finally he did it.

Dorgon wasn't even Zhang Lei's favorite proposed target. He was just a young, heavy-duty defenseman with a loud mouth who wasn't scared of Zhang Lei's flying blades.

He should have been.

Dorgon bled out in ten seconds. The med bot wrapped him in a life support bubble and attempted a transfusion right there on the ice, but stumbled over the thick scars on the defenseman's arms. When it searched for alternate access, Dorgon's coach was too busy screaming at Zhang Lei to flip the master toggle on his player's armor.

Whose fault was it, then, that Dorgon died?

"Your fault, Zhang Lei," the Miao girl said. "You opened a mouth in my throat and my whole life came pouring out."

She pointed to him, standing under the mulberry tree with the other guests. Heads turned. He should have ran but he was frozen, breathless as if in a vacuum. He might have collapsed without the tree trunk behind him.

Marta? he whispered. *Help.*

No answer. Prajapati grabbed his arm.

"Ignore her, it's a trick," she said. And then louder: "That's not funny."

The crowd parted to allow the girl a clear sight of him.

"There's nowhere you can go that I won't follow. I'm inside your mattress when you sleep. Behind the door of your room, inside the closet. When you painted the Sklad arena, who do you think put the blood on the canvas? It was me."

She raised her fists and swung them toward him, as if shooting a puck with a phantom hockey stick.

"You're fair game."

The girl's head snapped back. She coughed once, and began speaking her native language again. The crowd turned away.

Marta? Answer me.

Prajapati tugged on his sleeve. "It's late. Walk me home. We'll take the shortcut."

She took his arm again, pretending to need it for balance on the rocky path, but in truth she was holding him up. Han Song and Paul trailed behind, talking in low voices.

Marta? Marta!

She answered before they got to top of the ridge.

Sorry, kid. I was in a closed-session meeting. Total privacy veil.

Are they coming for me?

What? No. Is there a problem in Paizuo?

Zhang Lei groaned. Prajapati looked at him sharply. Worry lines creased her plump face.

They know who I am. What I did.

Who knows?

Everyone. And all their relatives. From all over. Dorgon told them.

That's impossible.

He grabbed his viewcatcher, pinched off the last ten minutes of data, and fired it to her.

Watch this.

The path descending the ridge was treacherous, lit by nothing but stars. If he'd been alone, Zhang Lei would have ran down the ridge. If he fell and broke his neck, he deserved it. But the oldsters needed his help.

He took Prajapati's hand—warm, dry, strong—and used the fill flash on his viewcatcher to light each step while Han Song shone the brighter light from his camera down the trail. The two oldster men helped steady each other, Paul's hand on the photographer's shoulder. When Han Song slipped, Paul caught him by the elbow.

Yeah, okay, Marta whispered. *Someone figured out who you are and told the girl. I'll talk to the security team. Don't do anything stupid, okay? We're on this.*

When they got to the studio, Paul fetched a bottle of whiskey from his room. He poured four glasses and handed the largest one to Zhang Lei.

"I found the news feed from Luna a couple days ago," Paul said. "But I didn't tell anyone."

"I found the painting," said Prajapati. "I wasn't looking for it, but the sofa was in the wrong place. I showed it to Paul and Han Song. It's effective work, Zhang Lei. Palpable anguish."

"If you want to keep something private," said Han Song, "don't put it in the common areas."

"None of us told anyone," Prajapati added.

"So, how did the story get to the Miao girl?" Paul asked. The other two oldsters shook their heads.

"Jen Dla?" Han Song ventured.

"I'll ask her in the morning." Prajapati patted Zhang Lei's knee. "Try to get some sleep."

The whiskey burned Zhang Lei's throat and filled his sinuses with the scent of bonfire. *What kind of messages would you send from beyond if you could?* Vengeance. Dorgon had watched and waited for his opportunity. The news would travel fast. Brawler teams were searching the county for him.

Zhang Lei poured the rest of the whiskey down his throat.

"When they come for me, keep hitting my disable button," he said.

The three oldsters exchanged confused looks. A whirring sweeper bot bumped Zhang Lei's foot. He nudged it away with his toe and headed for the stairs.

Don't be so dramatic, Marta whispered.

"When who comes for you?" Prajapati asked.

"Let them do whatever they want to me," he said. "Don't put yourself in danger. But if you can, keep knocking me out. Please."

Marta sighed. *Honestly.*

You, too. Keep hitting the button. Whatever they do to me, I don't want to know about it.

He climbed the stairs two at a time. If his life was about to be crushed under the boots of a Lunite brawler gang, there was only one thing he wanted to do.

The scarred face of the new moon glared through the high windows of the communal studio. Zhang Lei chose the largest of his prepared canvases and flipped through his viewcatcher compositions. The water buffalo lying in the stream. Jen Dang catching a fish. Ripening rice terraces under golden mist. Jen Dla carrying a pot of sour fish soup, a lock of hair stuck to the sweat of her brow.

The fighting cocks in their cages, separated by the corner of a house, their torn flesh healing only to be sliced open another day.

He flipped the canvas to rest on the long side and projected the composition on its surface. How to make the three-dimensionality of the scene clear in two dimensions—that was the main problem. Each cock each knew the other was just out of sight. If they could get free, they would fight to the death.

It's in their nature, he whispered.

What nature? Marta asked. *Oh, I see. Are you going to paint all night?*

I'll paint for the rest of my life.

Okay, ping me if there's a problem.

First, he drafted with a light pencil, adjusting the composition. The corner of the house dividing the canvas into thirds, with one caged brawler directly in front of the viewer and the other around the corner. It was a difficult compositional problem—he had to rub out the draft several times and start again. Then he began a base layer in grays, very lean and thin. What the old masters called *en grisaille*. Solve the painting problems in monochrome before even thinking about color. The texture of the wooden walls of the house, the figures of the birds filling the canvas with belligerence. It took all night.

A few hours before dawn, Han Song brought him a cup of tea.

"That's good," he said, squinting at the canvas. "I've got some pictures of those birds, too." He settled at his workstation and sipped his own tea as he ruffled through his files. "You can use them for reference if you want."

A package hit Zhang Lei's message queue—the only communication he'd received since leaving Luna that didn't relate to his immigration status. The photos were good. Details of the cocks' livid faces and dinosaurian legs, the pinfeathers sprouting from their bald backs, the iridescent sheen of their ruffs.

He added crimson and madder to his palette and used Han Song's photo of the cock's flayed wattle to get that detail exactly right, then moved on to the next problem. He thinned the paint with solvent to make a glaze. No time to wait for fat oils to oxidize, for thick paint layers to cure. In places, the paint was so thin the texture of the canvas showed through. That was fine. He would never be a master painter, but this would be the best painting he could make.

His friend's photos helped. Gradually, color and detail began to bring the painting to life.

"Thank you," Zhang Lei said, hours later. Han Song didn't hear him. Prajapati smiled from across the studio, her hands caked with clay to the elbow.

"Don't skip lunch," she said. "Even painters need to eat."

"And sleep," Paul added.

Sleep. He had no time for it. And Dorgon was in his mattress, behind his door, in his closet. He would join Dorgon soon enough, and next year, when Paizuo's rice crop had turned yellow, they could scream public challenges at each other through a Miao girl.

Until then, there was only the work. Work like he'd never known before. As an athlete, he practiced until instinct overtook his mind. On the ice, he didn't think, he just performed. In the studio, he used his whole body—crouching, stretching, sweeping his arms—continuing the action of his brush far off the canvas like a fighter following a punch past his opponent's jaw. And then small, precise movements—careful, considered, even loving. But his intellect never disengaged. He made choices, second-guessed himself, took leaps of faith.

It was the most exhausting, engrossing work he'd ever done.

The eye of the cock flared on the canvas, trapped in the pointlessness of its drive to fight and fight and die. Zhang Lei hovered his brush over that eye. One more glaze of color, and another, and another, over and over until nobody looking at the painting could misunderstand the meaning of that vicious and brainless stare.

Paul put his arm around Zhang Lei's shoulders.

"Come on down to lunch. The painting is done. If you keep poking, you'll ruin it."

"Ruin yourself, too," said Han Song.

"He's young, he can take it," said Prajapati.

They fed him rice and egg, bitter green tea, and millet cake. No fish soup. No Jen Dla.

"She's giving birth," Prajapati explained. "Went into labor last night. Brave woman."

"We should break out Paul's whiskey again," said Han Song. "Drink a toast to her."

Paul laughed. "Maybe. We have something else to celebrate, too."

They all looked at Zhang Lei. His mouth was crammed with millet cake.

"I don't know. What?" he said though the cake.

"Your button is gone, dear," Prajapati said gently.

He swallowed, pinged his ID. Zhang Lei, Beijing resident. No caveats, no equivocations. And no button.

Marta, he whispered. *Is it done?*

The notice has been sitting in your queue for half an hour. I pinged you when it came through. Looked like you were too busy painting birds to notice.

Are the brawlers gone? he whispered.

They're on their way home. They can't touch you now and they know it. I don't recommend going to Luna anytime soon, but if you did and there was a problem, at least you could fight back.

Zhang Lei excused himself from the table and stumbled out of the guest house. He skirted the cabbage patch and followed the trail to the pavilion, with its perfectly composed view. Up and down the valley, farmers walked the terraces, examining the ripening rice.

How? You said it would be weeks, at least. Maybe never.

I took your painting directly to the tribunal.

That made no sense. His painting was upstairs in the studio, on his easel.

They were impressed, Marta added. *So was I.*

I don't understand.

The wet blood. Smart move. Visceral. The tribunal got the message.

Blood?

On the ice. They brought in a forensic expert to examine and sequence it. That gave me a scare because I had assumed the blood was yours. Didn't even occur to me it might be somebody else's. If it had been, things wouldn't have turned out so well.

My blood?

I guess the tribunal wanted to be convinced you regretted killing Dorgon.

Zhang Lei leaned on the pavilion railing. A fresh breeze ruffled his hair.

I do regret it.

They know that now. I'll keep the painting for you until you get a place of your own. So keep in touch, okay?

I will, he whispered.

On the terrace below, Jen Dang walked along the rice paddy with four of his grandchildren. The farmer waved. Zhang Lei waved back.

NOTES ABOUT "A STUDY IN OILS"

Artists often have trouble explaining why we make art. Why do we do this thing that takes so much learning and practice, and requires huge effort and dedication, when at the same time we must work another job to keep the rain off? The answer is complex and multi-layered. It can be difficult to put into words.

Maybe the best answer is a variation on the old mountaineer's quip, "because it's there." *Because if I don't do it, it won't exist.*

But there are some practical answers, too, and one of them is that having a successful artistic practice opens opportunities that would otherwise be closed. "A Study in Oils" is a good example of this.

In 2018, my wife Alyx and I were both invited by the Chinese online magazine *Future Affairs Administration* to attend the Danzhai SF Camp, which was an all-expenses paid trip to Guizhou province, to tour anti-poverty initiatives and write stories inspired by the trip. We leapt at the chance (when you get offers like this, do not refuse them!) and had an experience that I can only describe by flinging my arms around wildly and making screeching noises.

We also got to hang out with Chinese SF writers like Han Song, Jiang Bo, Lucia Liu, and others, who are wonderful people and terrific, thoughtful artists.

Just like in Canada, the most impoverished people in China are indigenous communities in remote areas. The village that appears in "A Study in Oils" really exists. Paizou is a Miao village whose residents are enacting a plan to beat poverty by promoting themselves as an international destination for art retreats. In "A Study in Oils," I imagined a future where these kinds of initiatives have provided the Miao of Danzhai with the economic power that allows them to thrive on their traditional lands, practice their ceremonies and traditions, and speak their language hundreds of years in the future. Because the future is for indigenous people, too.

I gratefully thank the Future Affairs Administration and Danzhai SF Camp for their generous support.

INTERVENTION

When I was fifty-seven, I did the unthinkable. I became a crèche manager.

On Luna, crèche work kills your social capital, but I didn't care. Not at first. My long-time love had been crushed to death in a bot malfunction in Luna's main mulching plant. I was just trying to find a reason to keep breathing.

I found a crusty centenarian who'd outlived most of her cohort and asked for her advice. She said there was no better medicine for grief than children, so I found a crèche tucked away behind a water printing plant and signed on as a cuddler. That's where I caught the baby bug.

When my friends found out, the norming started right away.

"You're getting a little tubby there, Jules," Ivan would say, unzipping my jacket and reaching inside to pat my stomach. "Got a little parasite incubating?"

I expected this kind of attitude from Ivan. Ringleader, team captain, alpha of alphas. From him, I could laugh it off. But then my closest friends started in.

Beryl's pretty face soured in disgust every time she saw me. "I can smell the freeloader on you," she'd say, pretending to see body fluids on my perfectly clean clothing. "Have the decency to shower and change after your shift."

Even that wasn't so bad. But then Robin began avoiding me and ignoring my pings. We'd been each other's first lovers, best friends since forever, and suddenly I didn't exist. That's how extreme the prejudice is on Luna.

Finally, on my birthday, they threw me a surprise party. Everyone wore diapers and crawled around in a violent mockery of childhood. When I complained, they accused me of being broody.

I wish I could say I ignored their razzing, but my friends were my whole world. I dropped crèche work. My secret plan was to leave Luna, find a hab where working with kids wasn't social death, but I kept putting it off. Then I blinked, and ten years had passed.

Enough delay. I jumped trans to Eros station, engaged a recruiter, and was settling into my new life on Ricochet within a month.

I never answered my friends' pings. As far as Ivan, Beryl, Robin, and the rest knew, I fell off the face of the moon. And that's the way I wanted it.

Ricochet is one of the asteroid-based habs that travel the inner system using gravity assist to boost speed in tiny increments. As a wandering hab, we have no fixed astronomical events or planetary seasonality to mark the passage of time, so boosts are a big deal for us—the equivalent of New Year's on Earth or the Sol Belt flare cycle.

On our most recent encounter with Mars, my third and final crèche—the Jewel Box—were twelve years old. We hadn't had a boost since the kids were six, so my team and I worked hard to make it special, throwing parties, making presents, planning excursions. We even suited up and took the kids to the outside of our hab, exploring Asteroid Iris's vast, pockmarked surface roofed by nothing less than the universe itself, in all its spangled glory. We played around out there until Mars climbed over the horizon and showed the Jewel Box its great face for the first time, so huge and close it seemed we could reach up into its milky skim of atmosphere.

When the boost itself finally happened, we were all exhausted. All the kids and cuddlers lounged in the rumpus room, clipped into our safety harnesses, nestled on mats and cushions or tucked into the wall netting. Yawning, droopy-eyed, even dozing. But when the hab began to shift underneath us, we all sprang alert.

Trésor scooted to my side and ducked his head under my elbow.

"You doing okay, buddy?" I asked him in a low voice.

He nodded. I kissed the top of his head and checked his harness.

I wasn't the only adult with a little primate soaking up my body heat. Diamant used Blanche like a climbing frame, standing on her thighs, gripping her hands, and leaning back into the increasing force of the boost. Opale had coaxed her favorite cuddler Mykelti up into the ceiling netting. They both dangled by their knees, the better to feel the acceleration. Little Rubis was holding tight to Engku's and Megat's hands, while on the other side of the room, Safir and Émeraude clowned around, competing for Long Meng's attention.

I was supposed to be on damage control, but I passed the safety workflow over to Bruce. When we hit maximum acceleration, Tré was clinging to me with all his strength.

The kids' bioms were stacked in the corner of my eye. All their hormone graphs showed stress indicators. Tré's levels were higher than the rest, but that wasn't strange. When your hab is somersaulting behind a planet, bleeding off its orbital energy, your whole world turns into a carnival ride. Some people like it better than others.

I tightened my arms around Tré's ribs, holding tight as the room turned sideways.

"Everything's fine," I murmured in his ear. "Ricochet was designed for this kind of maneuver."

Our safety harnesses held us tight to the wall netting. Below, Safir and Émeraude climbed up the floor, laughing and hooting. Long Meng tossed pillows at them.

Tré gripped my thumb, yanking as if it were a joystick with the power to tame the room's spin. Then he shot me a live feed showing Ricochet's chief astronautics officer, a dark-skinned, silver-haired woman with protective bubbles fastened over her eyes.

"Who's that?" I asked, pretending I didn't know.

"Vijayalakshmi," Tré answered. "If anything goes wrong, she'll fix it."

"Have you met her?" I knew very well he had, but asking questions is an excellent calming technique.

"Yeah, lots of times." He flashed a pointer at the astronaut's mirrored eye coverings. "Is she sick?"

"Might be cataracts. That's a normal age-related condition. What's worrying you?"

"Nothing," he said.

"Why don't you ask Long Meng about it?"

Long Meng was the Jewel Box's physician. Ricochet-raised, with a facial deformity that thrust her mandible severely forward. As an adult, once bone ossification had completed, she had rejected the cosmetic surgery that could have normalized her jaw.

"Not all interventions are worthwhile," she'd told me once. "I wouldn't feel like myself with a new face."

As a pediatric specialist, Long Meng was responsible for the health and development of twenty crèches, but we were her favorite. She'd decided to celebrate the boost with us. At that moment, she was dangling from the floor with Safir and Émeraude, tickling their tummies and howling with laughter.

I tried to mitigate Tré's distress with good, old-fashioned cuddle and chat. I showed him feeds from the biodiversity preserve, where the netted megafauna floated in mid-air, riding out the boost in safety, legs dangling. One big cat groomed itself as it floated, licking one huge paw and wiping down its whiskers with an air of unconcern.

Once the boost was complete and we were back to our normal gravity regime, Tré's indicators quickly normalized. The kids ran up to the garden to check out the damage. I followed slowly, leaning on my cane. One of the bots had malfunctioned and lost stability, destroying several rows of terraced seating in the open air auditorium just next to our patch. The kids all thought that was pretty funny. Tré seemed perfectly fine, but I couldn't shake the feeling that I'd failed him somehow.

The Jewel Box didn't visit Mars. Martian habs are popular, their excursion contracts highly priced. The kids put in a few bids but didn't have the credits to win.

"Next boost," I told them. "Venus in four years. Then Earth."

I didn't mention Luna. I'd done my best to forget it even existed. Easy to do. Ricochet has almost no social or trade ties with Earth's moon. Our main economic sector is human reproduction and development—artificial wombs, zygote husbandry, natal decanting, every bit of art and science that turns a mass of undifferentiated cells into a healthy young adult. Luna's crèche system collapsed completely not long after I left. Serves them right.

I'm a centenarian, facing my last decade or two. I may look serene and wise, but I've never gotten over being the butt of my old friends' jokes.

Maybe I've always been immature. It would explain a lot.

Four years passed with the usual small dramas. The Jewel Box grew in body and mind, stretching into young adults of sixteen. All six—Diamant, Émeraude, Trésor, Opale, Safir, and Rubis—hit their benchmarks erratically and inconsistently, which made me proud. Kids are supposed to be odd little individuals. We're not raising robots, after all.

As Ricochet approached, the Venusian habs began peppering us with proposals. Recreation opportunities, educational seminars, sightseeing trips, arts festivals, sporting tournaments—all on reasonable trade terms. Venus wanted us to visit, fall in love, stay. They'd been losing population to Mars for years. The brain drain was getting critical.

The Jewel Box decided to bid on a three-day excursion. Sightseeing with a focus on natural geology, including active volcanism. For the first time in their lives, they'd experience real, unaugmented planetary gravity instead of Ricochet's one-point-zero cobbled together by centripetal force and a Steffof field.

While the kids were lounging around the rumpus room, arguing over how many credits to sink into the bid, Long Meng pinged me.

You and I should send a proposal to the Venusian crèches, she whispered. *A master class or something. Something so tasty they can't resist.*

Why? Are you trying to pad your billable hours?

She gave me a toothy grin. *I want a vacation. Wouldn't it be fun to get Venus to fund it?*

Long Meng and I had collaborated before, when our numbers had come up for board positions on the crèche governance authority. Nine miserable months co-authoring policy memos, revising the crèche management best practices guide, and presenting at skills development seminars. All on top of our regular responsibilities. Against the odds, our friendship survived the bureaucracy.

We spent a few hours cooking up a seminar to tempt the on-planet crèche specialists and fired it off to a bunch of Venusian booking agents. We called it 'Attachment and Self-regulation in Theory and Practice: Approaches to Promoting Emotional Independence in the Crèche-raised Child.' Sound dry? Not a bit. The Venusians gobbled it up.

I shot the finalized syllabus to our chosen booking agent, then escorted the Jewel Box to their open-air climbing lab. I turned them over to their instructor and settled onto my usual bench under a tall oak. Diamant took the lead position up the cliff, as usual. By the time they'd completed the first pitch, all three seminars were filled.

The agent is asking for more sessions, I whispered to Long Meng. *What do you think?*

"No way." Long Meng's voice rang out, startling me. As I pinged her location, her lanky form appeared in the distant aspen grove.

"This is a vacation," she shouted. "If I wanted to pack my billable hours, I'd volunteer for another board position."

I shuddered. *Agreed.*

She jogged over and climbed onto the bench beside me, sitting on the backrest with her feet on the seat. "Plus, you haven't been off this rock in twenty years," she added, plucking a leaf from the overhead bough.

"I said okay, Long Meng."

We watched the kids as they moved with confidence and ease over the gleaming, pyrite-inflected cliff face. Big, bulky Diamant didn't look like a climber but was obsessed with the sport. The other five had gradually been infected by their crèche-mate's passion.

Long Meng and I waved to the kids as they settled in for a rest mid-route. Then she turned to me. "What do you want to see on-planet? Have you made a wish list yet?"

"I've been to Venus. It's not that special."

She laughed, a great, good-natured, wide-mouthed guffaw. "Nothing can compare to Luna, can it, Jules?"

"Don't say that word."

"Luna? Okay. What's better than Venus? Earth?"

"Earth doesn't smell right."

"The Sol belt?"

"Never been there."

"What then?"

"This is nice." I waved at the groves of trees surrounding the cliff. Overhead, the plasma core that formed the backbone of our hab was just shifting its visible spectrum into twilight. Mellow light filtered through the leaves. Teenage laughter echoed off the cliff, and in the distance, the steady droning wail of a fussy newborn.

I pulled up the surrounding camera feeds and located the newborn. A tired-looking cuddler carried the baby in an over-shoulder sling, patting its bottom rhythmically as they strolled down a sunflower-lined path. I pinged the baby's biom. Three weeks old. Chronic gas and reflux unresponsive to every intervention strategy. Nothing to do but wait for the child to grow out of it.

The kids summited, waved to us, then began rappelling back down. Long Meng and I met them at the base.

"Em, how's your finger?" Long Meng asked.

"Good." Émeraude bounced off the last ledge and slipped to the ground, wave of pink hair flapping. "Better than good."

"Let's see, then."

Émeraude unclipped and offered the doctor their hand. They were a kid with only two modes: all-out or flatline. A few months back, they'd injured themselves cranking on a crimp, completely bowstringing the flexor tendon.

Long Meng launched into an explanation of annular pulley repair strategies and recovery times. I tried to listen but I was tired. My hips ached, my back ached, my limbs rotated on joints gritty with age. In truth, I didn't want to go to Venus. The kids had won their bid, and with them off-hab, staying home would have been a good rest. But Long Meng's friendship was important, and making her happy was worth a little effort.

Long Meng and I accompanied the Jewel Box down Venus's umbilical, through the high sulphuric acid clouds to the elevator's base deep in the planet's mantle. When we entered the busy central transit hub, with its domed ceiling and slick, speedy slideways, the kids began making faces.

"This place stinks," said Diamante.

"Yeah, smells like piss," said Rubis.

Tré looked worried. "Do they have diseases here or something?"

Opale slapped her hand over her mouth. "I'm going to be sick. Is it the smell or the gravity?"

A quick glance at Opale's biom showed she was perfectly fine. All six kids were. Time for a classic crèche manager-style social intervention.

If you can't be polite around the locals, I whispered, knocking my cane on the ground for emphasis. *I'll shoot you right back up the elevator.*

If you send us home, do we get our credits back? Émeraude asked, yawning.

No. You'd be penalized for non-completion of contract.

I posted a leaderboard for good behavior. Then I told them Venusians were especially gossipy, and if word got out they'd bad-mouthed the planet, they'd get nothing but dirty looks for the whole trip.

A bald lie. Venus is no more gossipy than most habs. But it nurses a significant anti-crèche prejudice. Not as extreme as Luna, but still. Ricochet kids were used to being loved by everyone. On Venus, they would get attitude just for existing. I wanted to offer a convenient explanation for the chilly reception from the locals.

The group of us rode the slideway to Vanavara portway, where Engku, Megat, and Bruce were waiting. Under the towering archway, I hugged and kissed the kids, told them to have lots of fun, and waved at their retreating backs. Then Long Meng and I were on our own.

She took my arm and steered us into Vanavara's passeggiata, a social stroll that wound through the hab like a pedestrian river. We drifted with the flow, joining the people-watching crowd, seeing and being seen.

The hab had spectacular sculpture gardens and fountains, and Venus's point-nine-odd gravity was a relief on my knees and hips, but the kids weren't wrong about the stench. Vanavara smelled like oily vinaigrette over half-rotted lettuce leaves, with an animal undercurrent reminiscent of hormonal teenagers on a cleanliness strike. As we walked, the stench surged and faded, then resurfaced again.

We ducked into a kiosk where a lone chef roasted kebabs over an open flame. We sat at the counter, drinking sparkling wine and watching her prepare meal packages for bot delivery.

"What's wrong with the air scrubbers here?" Long Meng asked the chef.

"Unstable population," she answered. "We don't have enough civil engineers to handle the optimization workload. If you know any nuts-and-bolts types, tell them to come to Vanavara. The bank will kiss them all over."

She served us grilled protein on disks of crispy starch topped with charred vegetable and heaped with garlicky sauce, followed by finger-sized blossoms with tender, fleshy petals over a crisp honeycomb core. When we rejoined the throng, we shot the chef a pair of big, bright public valentines on slow decay, visible to everyone passing by. The chef ran after us with two tulip-shaped bulbs of amaro.

"Enjoy your stay," she said, handing us the bulbs. "We're developing a terrific fresh food culture here. You'll love it."

In response to the population downswing, Venus's habs had started accepting all kinds of marginal business proposals. Artists. Innovators. Experimenters. Lose a ventilation engineer; gain a chef. Lose a surgeon; gain a puppeteer. With the chefs and puppeteers come all the people who want to live in a hab with chefs and puppeteers, and are willing to put up with a little stench to get it. Eventually the hab's fortunes turn around. Population starts flowing back, attracted by the burgeoning quality of life. Engineers and surgeons return, and the chefs and puppeteers move on to the next proposal-friendly hab. Basic human dynamics.

Long Meng sucked the last drop of amaro from her bulb and then tossed it to a disposal bot.

"First night of vacation." She gave me a wicked grin. "Want to get drunk?"

When I rolled out of my sleep stack in the morning, I was puffy and stiff. My hair stood in untamable clumps. The pouches under my eyes shone an alarming purple, and my wrinkle inventory had doubled. My tongue tasted like garlic sauce. But as long as nobody else could smell it, I wasn't too concerned. As for the rest, I'd earned every age marker.

When Long Meng finally cracked her stack, she was pressed and perky, wrapped in a crisp fuchsia robe. A filmy teal scarf drifted under her thrusting jawline.

"Let's teach these Venusians how to raise kids," she said.

In response to demand, the booking agency had upgraded us to a larger auditorium. The moment we hit the stage, I forgot all my aches and pains. Doctor Footlights, they call it. Performing in front of two thousand strangers produces a lot of adrenaline.

We were a good pair. Long Meng dynamic and engaging, lunging around the stage like a born performer. Me, I was her foil. A grave, wise oldster with fifty years of crèche work under my belt.

Much of our seminar was inspirational. Crèche work is relentless no matter where you practice it, and on Venus it brings negative social status. A little cheerleading goes a long way. We slotted our specialty content in throughout the program, introducing the concepts in the introductory material, building audience confidence by reinforcing what they already knew, then hit them between the eyes with the latest developments in Ricochet's proprietary cognitive theory and emotional development modelling. We blew their minds, then backed away from the hard stuff and returned to cheerleading.

"What's the worst part of crèche work, Jules?" Long Meng asked as our program concluded, her scarf waving in the citrus-scented breeze from the ventilation.

"There are no bad parts," I said drily. "Each and every day is unmitigated joy."

The audience laughed harder than the joke deserved. I waited for the noise to die down, and mined the silence for a few lingering moments before continuing.

"Our children venture out of the crèche as young adults, ready to form new emotional ties wherever they go. The future is in their hands, an unending medium for them to shape with their ambition and passion. Our crèche work lifts them up and holds them high, all their lives. That's the best part."

I held my cane to my heart with both hands.

"The worst part is," I said, "if we do our jobs right, those kids leave the crèche and never think about us again."

We left them with a tear in every eye. The audience ran back to their crèches knowing they were doing the most important work in the universe, and open to the possibility of doing it even better.

After our second seminar, on a recommendation from the kebab chef, we blew our credits in a restaurant high up in Vanavara's atrium. Live food raised, prepared, and served by hand; nothing extruded or bulbed. And no bots, except for the occasional hygiene sweeper.

Long Meng cut into a lobster carapace with a pair of hand shears. "Have you ever noticed how intently people listen to you?"

"Most of the time the kids just pretend to listen."

"Not kids. Adults."

She served me a morsel of claw meat, perfectly molded by the creature's shell. I dredged it in green sauce and popped it in my mouth. Sweet peppers buzzed my sinuses.

"You're a great leader, Jules."

"At my age, I should be. I've had lots of practice telling people what to do."

"Exactly," she said through a mouthful of lobster. "So what are you going to do when the Jewel Box leaves the crèche?"

I lifted my flute of pale green wine and leaned back, gazing through the window at my elbow into the depths of the atrium. I'd been expecting this question for a few years but didn't expect it from Long Meng. How could someone so young understand the sorrows of the old?

"If you don't want to talk about it, I'll shut up," she added quickly. "But I have some ideas. Do you want to hear them?"

On the atrium floor far below, groups of pedestrians were just smudges, no individuals distinguishable at all. I turned back to the table but kept my eyes on my food.

"Okay, go ahead."

"A hab consortium is soliciting proposals to rebuild their failed crèche system," she said, voice eager. "I want to recruit a team. You'd be project advisor. Top position, big picture stuff. I'll be project lead and do all the grunt work."

"Let me guess," I said. "It's Luna."

Long Meng nodded. I kept a close eye on my blood pressure indicators. Deep breaths and a sip of water kept the numbers out of the red zone.

"I suppose you'd want me to liaise with Luna's civic apparatus, too." I kept my voice flat.

"That would be ideal." She slapped the table with both palms and grinned. "With a native Lunite at the helm, we'd win for sure."

Long Meng was so busy bubbling with ideas and ambition as she told me her plans, she didn't notice my fierce scowl. She probably didn't even taste her luxurious meal. As for me, I enjoyed every bite, right down to the last crumb of my flaky cardamom-chocolate dessert. Then I pushed back my chair and grabbed my cane.

"There's only one problem, Long Meng," I said. "Luna doesn't deserve crèches."

"Deserve doesn't really—"

I cut her off. "Luna doesn't deserve a population."

She looked confused. "But it has a population, so—"

"Luna deserves to die," I snapped. I stumped away, leaving her at the table, her jaw hanging in shock.

Halfway through our third and final seminar, in the middle of introducing Ricochet's proprietary never-fail methods for raising kids, I got an emergency ping from Bruce.

Tré's abandoned the tour. He's run off.

I faked a coughing fit and lunged toward the water bulbs at the back of the stage. Turned my back on two thousand pairs of eyes, and tried to collect myself as I scanned Tré's biom. His stress indicators were highly elevated. The other five members of the Jewel Box were anxious, too.

Do you have eyes on him?

Of course. Bruce shot me a bookmark.

Three separate cameras showed Tré was alone, playing his favorite pattern-matching game while coasting along a nearly deserted slideway. Metadata indicated his location on an express connector between Coacalco and Eaton habs.

He looked stunned, as if surprised by his own daring. Small, under the high arches of the slideway tunnel. And thin—his bony shoulder blades tented the light cloth of his tunic.

Coacalco has a bot shadowing him. Do we want them to intercept?

I zoomed in on Tré's face, as if I could read his thoughts as easily as his physiology. He'd never been particularly assertive or self-willed, never one to challenge his crèche mates or lead them in new directions. But kids will surprise you.

Tell them to stay back. Ping a personal security firm to monitor him. Go on with your tour. And try not to worry.

Are you sure?

I wasn't sure, not at all. My stress indicators were circling the planet. Every primal urge screamed for the bot to wrap itself around the boy and haul him back to Bruce. But I wasn't going to slap down a sixteen-year-old kid for acting on his own initiative, especially since this was practically the first time he'd shown any.

Looks like Tré has something to do, I whispered. *Let's let him follow through.*

I returned to my chair. Tried to focus on the curriculum but couldn't concentrate. Long Meng could only do so much to fill the gap. The audience became restless, shifting in their seats, murmuring to each other. Many stopped paying attention. Right up in the front row, three golden-haired, rainbow-smocked Venusians were blanked out, completely immersed in their feeds.

Long Meng was getting frantic, trying to distract two thousand people from the gaping hole on the stage that was her friend Jules. I picked up my cane, stood, and calmly tipped my chair. It hit the stage floor with a crash. Long Meng jumped. Every head swiveled.

"I apologize for the dramatics," I said, "but earlier, you all noticed me blanking out. I want to explain."

I limped to the front of the stage, unsteady despite my cane. I wear a stability belt, but try not to rely on it too much. Old age has exacerbated my natural tendency for a weak core, and using the belt too much just makes me frailer. But my legs wouldn't stop shaking. I dialed up the balance support.

"What just happened illustrates an important point about crèche work." I attached my cane's cling-point to the stage floor and leaned on it with both hands as I scanned the audience. "Our mistakes can ruin lives. No other profession carries such a vast potential for screwing up."

"That's not true." Long Meng's eyes glinted in the stage lights, clearly relieved I'd stepped back up to the job. "Engineering disciplines carry quite the disaster potential. Surgery certainly does. Psychology and pharmacology. Applied astrophysics. I could go on." She grinned. "Really, Jules. Nearly every profession is dangerous."

I grimaced and dismissed her point.

"Doctors' decisions are supported by ethics panels and case reviews. Engineers run simulation models and have their work vetted by peers before taking any real-world risks. But in a crèche, we make a hundred decisions a day that affect human development. Sometimes a hundred an hour."

"Okay, but are every last one of those decisions so important?"

I gestured to one of the rainbow-clad front-row Venusians. "What do you think? Are your decisions important?"

A camera bug zipped down to capture her answer for the seminar's shared feed. The Venusian licked her lips nervously and shifted to the edge of her seat.

"Some decisions are," she said in a high, tentative voice. "You can never know which."

"That's right. You never know." I thanked her and rejoined Long Meng in the middle of the stage. "Crèche workers take on huge responsibility. We assume all the risk, with zero certainty. No other profession accepts those terms. So why do we do this job?"

"Someone has to?" said Long Meng. Laughter percolated across the auditorium.

"Why us, though?" I said. "What's wrong with us?"

More laughs. I rapped my cane on the floor.

"My current crèche is a sixteen-year sixsome. Well integrated, good morale. Distressingly sporty. They keep me running." The audience chuckled. "They're on a geography tour somewhere on the other side of Venus. A few minutes ago, one of my kids ran off. Right now, he's coasting down one of your intra-hab slideways and blocking our pings."

Silence. I'd captured every eye; all their attention was mine.

I fired the public slideway feed onto the stage. Tré's figure loomed four meters high. His foot was kicked back against the slideway's bumper in an attitude of nonchalance, but it was just a pose. His gaze was wide and unblinking, the whites of his eyes fully visible.

"Did he run away because of something one of us said? Or did? Or neglected to do? Did it happen today, yesterday, or ten days ago? Maybe it has nothing to do with us at all, but some private urge from the kid's own heart. He might be suffering acutely right now, or maybe he's enjoying the excitement. The adrenaline and cortisol footprints look the same."

I clenched my gnarled, age-spotted hand to my chest, pulling at the fabric of my shirt.

"But I'm suffering. My heart feels like it could rip right out of my chest because this child has put himself in danger." I patted the wrinkled fabric back into place. "Mild danger. Venus is no Luna."

Nervous laughter from the crowd. Long Meng hovered at my side.

"Crèche work is like no other human endeavor," I said. "Nothing else offers such potential for failure, sorrow, and loss. But no work is as important. You all know that, or you wouldn't be here."

Long Meng squeezed my shoulder. I patted her hand. "Raising children is only for true believers."

Not long after our seminar ended, Tré boarded Venus's circum-planetary chuteway and chose a pod headed for Vanavara. The pod's public feed showed five other passengers: a middle-aged threesome who weren't interested in anything but each other, a halo-haired young adult escorting a floating tank of live eels, and a broad-shouldered brawler with deeply scarred forearms.

Tré waited for the other passengers to sit, then settled himself into a corner seat. I pinged him. No answer.

"We should have had him intercepted," I said.

Long Meng and I sat in the back of the auditorium. A choir group had taken over the stage. Bots were attempting to set up risers, but the singers were milling around, blocking their progress.

"He'll be okay." Long Meng squeezed my knee. "Less than five hours to Vanavara. None of the passengers are going to do anything to him."

"You don't know that."

"Nobody would risk it. Venus has strict penalties for physical violence."

"Is that the worst thing you can think of?" I flashed a pointer at the brawler. "One conversation with that one in a bad mood could do lifelong damage to anyone, much less a kid."

We watched the feed in silence. At first the others kept to themselves, but then the brawler stood, pulled down a privacy veil, and sauntered over to sit beside Tré.

"Oh no," I moaned.

I zoomed in on Tré's face. With the veil in place, I couldn't see or hear the brawler. All I could do was watch the kid's eyes flicker from the window to the brawler and back, monitor his stress indicators, and try to read his body language. Never in my life have I been less equipped to make a professional judgement about a kid's state of mind. My mind boiled with paranoia.

After about ten minutes—an eternity—the brawler returned to their seat.

"It's fine," said Long Meng. "He'll be with us soon."

Long Meng and I met Tré at the chuteway dock. It was late. He looked tired, rumpled, and more than a little sulky.

"Venus is stupid," he said.

"That's ridiculous, a planet can't be stupid," Long Meng snapped. She was tired, and hadn't planned on spending the last night of her vacation waiting in a transit hub.

Let me handle this, I whispered.

"Are you okay? Did anything happen in the pod?" I tried to sound calm as I led him to the slideway.

He shrugged. "Not really. This oldster was telling me how great his hab is. Sounded like a hole."

I nearly collapsed with relief.

"Okay, good," I said. "We were worried about you. Why did you leave the group?"

"I didn't realize it would take so long to get anywhere," Tré said.

"That's not an answer. Why did you run off?"

"I don't know." The kid pretended to yawn—one of the Jewel Box's clearest tells for lying. "Venus is boring. We should've saved our credits."

"What does that mean?"

"Everybody else was happy looking at rocks. Not me. I wanted to get some value out of this trip."

"So you jumped a slideway?"

"Uh huh." Tré pulled a protein snack out of his pocket and stuffed it in his mouth. "I was just bored. And I'm sorry. Okay?"

"Okay." I fired up the leaderboard and zeroed out Tré's score. "You're on a short leash until we get home."

We got the kid a sleep stack near ours, then Long Meng and I had a drink in the grubby travelers' lounge downstairs.

"How are you going to find out why he left?" asked Long Meng. "Pull his feeds? Form a damage mitigation team? Plan an intervention?"

I picked at fabric on the arm of my chair. The plush nap repaired itself as I dragged a ragged thumbnail along the arm rest.

"If I did, Tré would learn he can't make a simple mistake without someone jumping down his throat. He might shrug off the psychological effects, or it could inflict long-term damage."

"Right. Like you said in the seminar. You can't know."

We finished our drinks and Long Meng helped me to my feet. I hung my cane from my forearm and tucked both hands into the crease of her elbow. We slowly climbed upstairs. I could have pinged a physical assistance bot, but my hands were cold, and my friend's arm was warm.

"Best to let this go," I said. "Tré's already a cautious kid. I won't punish him for taking a risk."

"I might, if only for making me worry. I guess I'll never be a crèche manager." She grinned.

"And yet you want to go to Luna and build a new crèche system."

Long Meng's smile vanished. "I shouldn't have sprung that on you, Jules."

In the morning, the two young people rose bright and cheery. I was aching and bleary but put on a serene face. We had just enough time to catch a concert before heading up the umbilical to our shuttle home. We made our way to the atrium, where Tré boggled at the soaring views, packed slideways, clustered performance and game surfaces, fountains, and gardens. The air sparkled with nectar and spices, and underneath, a thick, oily human funk.

We boarded a riser headed to Vanavara's orchestral pits. A kind Venusian offered me a seat with a smile. I thanked him, adding, "That would never happen on Luna."

I drew Long Meng close as we spiraled toward the atrium floor.

Just forget about the proposal, I whispered. *The moon is a lost cause.*

A little more than a year later, Ricochet was on approach for Earth. The Jewel Box were nearly ready to leave the crèche. Bruce and the rest of my team were planning to start a new one, and they warmly assured me I'd always be welcome to visit. I tried not to weep about it. Instead, I began spending several hours a day helping provide round-the-clock cuddles to a newborn with hydrocephalus.

As far as I knew, Long Meng had given up the Luna idea. Then she cornered me in the dim-lit nursery and burst my bubble.

She quietly slid a stool over to my rocker, cast a professional eye over the cerebrospinal fluid-exchange membrane clipped to the baby's ear, and whispered, *We made the short list.*

That's great, I replied, my cheek pressed to the infant's warm, velvety scalp.

I had no idea what she was referring to, and at that moment I didn't care. The scent of a baby's head is practically narcotic, and no victory can compare with having coaxed a sick child into restful sleep.

It means we have to go to Luna for a presentation and interview.

Realization dawned slowly. *Luna? I'm not going to Luna.*

Not you, Jules. Me and my team. I thought you should hear before the whole hab starts talking.

I concentrated on keeping my rocking rhythm steady before answering. *I thought you'd given that up.*

She put a gentle hand on my knee. *I know. You told me not to pursue it and I considered your advice. But it's important, Jules. Luna will re-start its crèche program one way or another. We can make sure they do it right.*

I fixed my gaze pointedly on her prognathous jaw. *You don't know what it's like there. They'll roast you alive just for looking different.*

Maybe. But I have to try.

She patted my knee and left. I stayed in the rocker long past hand-over time, resting my cheek against that precious head.

Seventy years ago I'd done the same, in a crèche crowded into a repurposed suite of offices behind one of Luna's water printing plants. I'd walked through the door broken and grieving, certain the world had been drained of hope and joy. Then someone put a baby in my arms. Just a few hours old, squirming with life, arms reaching for the future.

Was there any difference between the freshly detanked newborn on Luna and the sick baby I held in that rocker? No. The embryos gestating in Ricochet's superbly optimized banks of artificial wombs were no different from the ones Luna would grow in whatever gestation tech they inevitably cobbled together.

But as I continued to think about it, I realized there was a difference, and it was important. The ones on Luna deserved better than they would get. And I could do something about it.

First, I had my hair sheared into an ear-exposing brush precise to the millimeter. The tech wielding the clippers tried to talk me out of it.

"Do you realize this will have to be trimmed every twenty days?"

"I used to wear my hair like this when I was young," I reassured him. He rolled his eyes and cut my hair like I asked.

I changed my comfortable smock for a lunar gray trouser-suit with enough padding to camouflage my age-slumped shoulders. My cling-pointed cane went into the mulch, exchanged for a glossy black model. Its silver point rapped the floor, announcing my progress toward Long Meng's studio.

The noise turned heads all down the corridor. Long Meng popped out of her doorway, but she didn't recognize me until I pushed past her and settled onto her sofa with a sigh.

"Are you still looking for a project advisor?" I asked.

She grinned. "Luna won't know what hit it."

Back in the rumpus room, Tré was the only kid to comment on my haircut.

"You look like a villain from one of those old Follywood dramas Bruce likes."

"Hollywood," I corrected. "Yes, that's the point."

"What's the point in looking like a gangland mobber?"

"Mobster." I ran my palm over the brush. "Is that what I look like?"

"Kinda. Is it because of us?"

I frowned, not understanding. He pulled his ponytail over his shoulder and eyed it speculatively.

"Are you trying to look tough so we won't worry about you after we leave?"

That's the thing about kids. The conversations suddenly swerve and hit you in the back of the head.

"Whoa," I said. "I'm totally fine."

"I know, I know. You've been running crèches forever. But we're the last because you're so old. Right? It's got to be hard."

"A little," I admitted. "But you've got other things to think about. Big, exciting decisions to make."

"I don't think I'm leaving the crèche. I'm delayed."

I tried to keep from smiling. Tré was nothing of the sort. He'd grown into a gangly young man with long arms, bony wrists, and a haze of silky black beard on his square jaw. I could recite the dates of his developmental benchmarks from memory, and there was nothing delayed about them.

"That's fine," I said. "You don't have to leave until you're ready."

"A year. Maybe two. At least."

"Okay, Tré. Your decision."

I wasn't worried. It's natural to feel ambivalent about taking the first step into adulthood. If Tré found it easier to tell himself he wasn't leaving, so be it. As soon as his crèche-mates started moving on, Tré would follow.

Our proximity to Earth gave Long Meng's proposal a huge advantage. We could travel to Luna, give our presentation live, and be back home for the boost.

Long Meng and I spent a hundred billable hours refining our presentation materials. For the first time in our friendship, our communication styles clashed.

"I don't like the authoritarian gleam in your eye, Jules," she told me after a particularly heated argument. "It's almost as though you're enjoying bossing me around."

She wasn't wrong. Ricochet's social conventions require you to hold in conversational aggression. Letting go was fun. But I had an ulterior motive.

"This is the way people talk on Luna. If you don't like it, you should shitcan the proposal."

She didn't take the dare. But she reported behavioral changes to my geriatric specialist. I didn't mind. It was sweet, her being so worried about me. I decided to give her full access to my biom, so she could check if she thought I was having a stroke or something. I'm in okay health for my extreme age, but she was a paediatrician, not a gerontologist. What she saw scared her. She got solicitous. Gallant, even, bringing me bulbs of tea and snacks to keep my glucose levels steady.

Luna's ports won't accommodate foreign vehicles, and their landers use a chemical propellant so toxic Ricochet won't let them anywhere near our landing bays, so we had to shuttle to Luna in stages. As we glided over the moon's surface, its web of tunnels and domes sparkled in the full glare of the sun. The pattern of the habs hadn't changed. I could still name them—Surgut, Sklad, Nadym, Purovsk, Olenyok…

Long Meng latched onto my arm as the hatch creaked open. I wrenched away and straightened my jacket.

You can't do that here, I whispered. *Self-sufficiency is everything on Luna, remember?*

I marched ahead of Long Meng as if I were leading an army. In the light lunar gravity, I didn't need my cane, so I used its heavy silver head to whack the walls. Hitting something felt good. I worked up a head of steam so hot I could have sterilized those corridors. If I had to come home—home, what a word for a place like Luna!—I'd do it on my own terms.

The client team had arranged to meet us in a dinky little media suite overlooking the hockey arena in Sklad. A game had just finished, and we had to force our way against the departing crowd. My cane came in handy. I brandished it like a weapon, signaling my intent to break the jaw of anyone who got too close.

In the media suite, ten hab reps clustered around the project principal. Overhead circled a battery of old, out-of-date cameras that buzzed and fluttered annoyingly. At the front of the room, two chairs waited for Long Meng and me. Behind us arced a glistening expanse of crystal window framing the rink, where grooming bots were busy scraping blood off the ice. Over the arena loomed the famous profile of Mons Hadley, huge, cold, stark, its bleak face the same mid-tone gray as my suit.

Don't smile, I reminded Long Meng as she stood to begin the presentation.

The audience didn't deserve the verve and panache Long Meng put into presenting our project phases, alternative scenarios, and volume ramping. Meanwhile, I scanned the reps' faces, counting flickers in their attention and recording them on a leaderboard. We had forty minutes in total, but less than twenty to make an impression before the reps' decisions locked in.

Twelve minutes in, Long Meng was introducing the strategies for professional development, governance, and ethics oversight. Half the reps were still staring at her face as if they'd never seen a congenital hyperformation before. The other half were bored but still making an effort to pay attention. But not for much longer.

"Based on the average trajectories of other start-up crèche programs," Long Meng said, gesturing at the swirling graphics that hung in the air, "Luna should run at full capacity within six social generations, or thirty standard years."

I'm cutting in, I whispered. I whacked the head of my cane on the floor and stood, stability belt on maximum and belligerence oozing from my every pore.

"You won't get anywhere near that far," I growled. "You'll never get past the starting gate."

"That's a provocative statement," said the principal. She was in her sixties, short and tough, with ropey veins webbing her bony forearms. "Would you care to elaborate?"

I paced in front of their table, like a barrister in one of Bruce's old courtroom dramas. I made eye contact with each of the reps in turn, then leaned over the table to address the project principal directly.

"Crèche programs are part of a hab's social fabric. They don't exist in isolation. But Luna doesn't want kids around. You barely tolerate young adults. You want to stop the brain drain but you won't give up anything for crèches—not hab space, not billable hours, and especially not your prejudices. If you want a healthy crèche system, Luna will have to make some changes."

I gave the principal an evil grin, adding, "I don't think you can."

"I do," Long Meng interjected. "I think you can change."

"You don't know Luna like I do," I told her.

I fired our financial proposal at the reps. "Ricochet will design your new system. You'll find the trade terms extremely reasonable. When the design is complete, we'll provide on-the-ground teams to execute the project phases. Those terms are slightly less reasonable. Finally, we'll give you a project executive headed by Long Meng." I smiled. "Her billable rate isn't reasonable at all, but she's worth every credit."

"And you?" asked the principal.

"That's the best part." I slapped the cane in my palm. "I'm the gatekeeper. To go anywhere, you have to get past me."

The principal sat back abruptly, jaw clenched, chin raised. My belligerence had finally made an impact. The reps were on the edges of their seats. I had them both repelled and fascinated. They weren't sure whether to start screaming or elect me to Luna's board of governors.

"How long have I got to live, Long Meng? Fifteen years? Twenty?"

"Something like that," she said.

"Let's say fifteen. I'm old. I'm highly experienced. You can't afford me. But if you award Ricochet this contract, I'll move back to Luna. I'll control the gating progress, judging the success of every single milestone. If I decide Luna hasn't measured up, the work will have to be repeated."

I paced to the window. Mons Hadley didn't seem gray any more. It was actually a deep, delicate lilac. Framed by the endless black sky, its form was impossibly complex, every fold of its geography picked out by the sun.

I kept my back to the reps.

"If you're wondering why I'd come back after all the years," I said, "let me be very clear. I will die before I let Luna fool around with some half-assed crèche experiment, mess up a bunch of kids, and ruin everything." I turned and pointed my cane. "If you're going to do this, at least do it right."

Back home on Ricochet, the Jewel Box was off-hab on a two-day Earth tour. They came home with stories of surging wildlife spectacles that made herds and flocks of Ricochet's biodiversity preserve look like a petting zoo. When the boost came, we all gathered in the rumpus room for the very last time.

Bruce, Blanche, Engku, Megat, and Mykelti clustered on the floor mats, anchoring themselves comfortably for the boost. They'd be fine. Soon they'd have armfuls of newborns to ease the pain of transition. The Jewel Box were all hanging from the ceiling netting, ready for their last ride of childhood. They'd be fine, too. Diamante had decided on Mars, and it looked like the other five would follow.

Me, I'd be fine, too. I'd have to be.

How to explain the pain and pride when your crèche is balanced on the knife's edge of adulthood, ready to leave you behind forever? Not possible. Just know this: when you see an oldster looking serene and wise, remember, it's just a sham. Under the skin, it's all sorrow.

I was relieved when the boost started. Everyone was too distracted to notice I'd begun tearing up. When the hab turned upside down I let myself shed a few tears for the passing moment. Nothing too self-indulgent. Just a little whuffle, then I wiped it all away and joined the celebration, laughing and applauding the kids' antics as they bounced around the room.

We got it, Long Meng whispered in the middle of the boost. *Luna just shot me the contract. We won.*

She told me all the details. I pretended to pay attention, but really, I was only interested in watching the kids. Drinking in their antics, their playfulness, their joyful self-importance. Young adults have a shine about them. They glow with untapped potential.

When the boost was over, we all unclipped our anchors. I couldn't quite extricate myself from my deeply padded chair and my cane was out of reach.

Tré leapt to help me up. When I was on my feet, he pulled me into a hug.

"Are you going back to Luna?" he said in my ear.

I held him at arm's length. "That's right. Someone has to take care of Long Meng."

"Who'll take care of you?"

I laughed. "I don't need taking care of."

He gripped both my hands in his. "That's not true. Everyone does."

"I'll be fine." I squeezed his fingers and tried to pull away, but he wouldn't let go. I changed the subject. "Mars seems like a great choice for you all."

"I'm not going to Mars. I'm going to Luna."

I stepped back. My knees buckled, but the stability belt kept me from going down.

"No, Tré. You can't."

"There's nothing you can do about it. I'm going."

"Absolutely not. You have no business on Luna. It's a terrible place."

He crossed his arms over his broadening chest and swung his head like a fighter looking for an opening. He squinted at the old toys and sports equipment secured into rumpus room cabinets, the peeling murals the kids had painted over the years, the battered bots and well-used, colorful furniture—all the ephemera and detritus of childhood that had been our world for nearly eighteen years.

"Then I'm not leaving the crèche. You'll have to stay here with me, in some kind of weird stalemate. Long Meng will be alone."

I scowled. It was nothing less than blackmail. I wasn't used to being forced into a corner, and certainly not by my own kid.

"We're going to Luna together." A grin flickered across Tré's face. "Might as well give in."

I patted his arm, then took his elbow. Tré picked up my cane and put it in my hand.

"I've done a terrible job raising you," I said.

NOTES ABOUT "INTERVENTION"

Editor Jonathan Strahan invited me to write a story for his original SF anthology *Infinity's End*. I love getting these opportunities, because the story seeds that come out of them are often a surprise. Just getting that email gets the neurons sparking.

Though because of schedule considerations I can't always submit a story when I get an invitation, story ideas always come out of them. Walter Jon Williams once told me that when he receives an anthology invitation, he imagines what other writers will submit and then tries to write something completely opposite. So I try to do that, too.

Despite the fact that I don't have kids and have never wanted them, I write about parenthood a lot. I can't seem to get away from it. Part of the reason is that I'm blessed/cursed with vivid and detailed childhood memories. I've never forgotten what it's like to be a kid—how terrifying it is, how boring, how lonely. I don't feel compelled to explore childhood from a child's perspective, but I can't seem to stop examining it from an adult point of view.

"Intervention" deals with the professionalization of childrearing. It's not an unfamiliar subject for SF, but usually the take is horrific. But why?

Imagine a situation where children are raised only by people who want to do it, are emotionally and psychologically suitable, and who receive training and support. Imagine what a joy the job of child-rearing would be if caregivers didn't have to juggle a hundred other responsibilities while constantly being told they're missing out on life.

Fine, says you, *but where's the conflict?* Oh, dear. Don't you know humans can find conflict absolutely anywhere?

LA VITESSE

March 2, 1983, 30 kilometers southwest of Hinton, Alberta

"ROSIE," BEA SAID UNDER HER BREATH, BUT the old school bus's wheels were rumbling over gravel, and her daughter didn't hear. Rosie was slumped in the shotgun seat, eyes closed. She hadn't moved since Bea had herded her onto La Vitesse at six-fifteen that morning. She wasn't asleep though. A mother could always tell.

Bea raised her voice to a stage whisper. "Rosie, we got a problem."

Still no reaction.

"Rosie. Rosie. Rosie."

Bea snatched one of her gloves off the bus's dashboard and tossed it. Not at her kid—never at her kid; it bounced off the window and landed in Rosie's lap.

"Mom. I'm sleeping." Big scary scowl. Bea hadn't seen her kid smile since she'd turned fourteen.

"There's a dragon right behind us," she said silently, mouthing the words. None of the other kids had noticed, and Bea wanted to keep it that way.

Rosie rolled her eyes. "I don't read lips."

"A dragon," she whispered. "Following us."

"No way." Rosie bolted upright. She twisted in her seat and looked back through the central aisle, past the kids in their snowsuits and toques. "I can't see it."

The rear window was brown with dirty, frozen slush. Thank god. If the kids saw the dragon, they'd be screaming.

"Come here and look."

Rosie crawled out of her seat and leaned over her mother, hanging tight to the grab bar behind Bea's head. Her too-tight black parka carried a whiff of cigarettes.

Bea flipped open her window and adjusted the side-view mirror for Rosie. Behind the bus, a long, matte-black wing beat the air in a furious rhythm. The pale winter sun glinted on the silver scales that marked the wing's fore-edge.

"Wow," Rosie said, her voice so low it was almost a growl.

Bea stepped on the gas. La Vitesse surged ahead, revealing the dragon's broad chest, rippling with flexed muscles. It lifted its taloned forelegs as if reaching for the bus, and showed them the barest glimpse of a lissome neck and triangular, snake-like head before it caught up to the bus and disappeared into the mirror's blind spot.

Rosie pushed her ragged bangs out of her eyes and leaned closer to the mirror.

"No fire. Why isn't it trying to roast us?"

"I don't know. Maybe it's breathing too hard," Bea said. "But honey, you got to help me. Herd the kids into the front seats. Pack them in tight."

Rosie wasn't listening, though. She stared at the mirror, transfixed, watching the dragon's wing flexing from hooked tip to thick shoulder.

"Rose, please." Bea slapped the wheel with both hands. "Get the kids up front."

"Yeah, okay." Rosie straightened, then leaned over her mother again for one last look.

Even Bea had to admit her kid looked scary, especially lately, with her death metal T-shirts and her angry slouch.

Not yet sixteen, but so big and tall she looked twenty. Add all that to the black eyeliner Rosie melted with a match and applied smoldering, and the spiky haircut she'd given herself in grade ten and kept short with Bea's only pair of good scissors, and yeah, Bea could understand why other mothers gave her hell for letting her kid look so rough.

Bea couldn't do anything about it. Rosie had always been more trouble than Bea could handle. But as long as she came home on the bus with Bea every day, nothing else mattered.

But Bea didn't like the way her daughter looked at the dragon. She wasn't scared, not even a bit. Maybe she was even glad to see it.

Bea drove the longest and most remote bus route in the school district. Starting at her trailer south of Cadomin, she headed north and picked up kids along the Forestry Trunk Road all the way past Luscar and the Cardinal River coal mine, then turned east on the Yellowhead Highway, and hauled the kids through town to drop them off at all three schools.

The round trip took five hours—two and a half each way. La Vitesse was a fast bus with a big V8 engine but Bea drove slow. She had to. The Forestry Trunk Road was gravel, heavily corrugated with washboard created by runoff from the surrounding mountains. The soft shoulders on either side of the gravel road could easily pull a vehicle into the ditch or off a cliff, and moose lurked around every corner—often right in the middle of the road. Bea had seen what hitting a big bull moose could do to a bus, and she didn't want anything to do with it.

So Bea drove slow. She was kind, too. School bus drivers were allowed to leave kids behind if they weren't outside on time, waiting by the road, but Bea never did. Bears were common fall and spring, and cougars hunted year-round. A kid waiting for the bus made a nice warm snack.

And lately, Bea worried about dragons, too.

Rosie herded the kids into the front rows, three and four to a seat. Too rough; Rosie was always too rough with other kids, but it didn't matter now.

"We're playing a game," Bea sang out in her best sunny voice and smiled into the rear-view mirror. "Let's see how fast La Vitesse can stop. I'll honk my horn ten times. You all count with me. On the tenth honk, I'll hit the brakes. Everyone hang on tight. Brace yourselves, okay?"

In the rear-view, hoods and toques framed twenty pairs of big, scared eyes. They knew something was wrong. Kids always did.

"It'll be fun," she said, smiling wider. "Ready?"

The kids counted along as she honked. She hoped the horn might drive the dragon off, but she'd already tried that and it hadn't worked.

On the tenth honk, they were on a good flat straight-away. Decent gravel, no pot holes or washboard. Shallow ditches on either side, lined with slender young spruce. If La Vitesse skidded off the road they'd be okay. The bus would stick though, Bea had faith.

When she slammed on the brakes, one kid screamed. Several whimpered. The dragon hit the back of the bus with a hollow *thunk*. La Vitesse skidded but stayed square in the middle of the road. Bea shifted to first gear and slammed the gas. La Vitesse's engine roared, then screamed. Bea let the revs build and shifted to second, her foot flat on the floor.

In the side-view, the dragon lay crumpled on the gravel, wings canted like a broken tent.

Bea held her breath, flicking her gaze from road to mirror to road. Dead, she hoped. Let it be dead.

The dragon lifted its head and yawned. A tongue of blue flame licked from between its fangs. It clawed the gravel with the hinges of its wings and staggered to its feet. In the early morning light, its eyes sparked a keen and murderous ice-white.

Bea had seen the first dragon in 1981, two years back, when she was bringing home a bus full of soccer players after a tournament in Jasper.

She'd been cruising east along the Athabasca River, heading toward the Jasper park gates. The sunset light turned the mountains mellow orange, and the trees threw long, spear-shaped shadows across the highway. La Vitesse's speedometer was two fingers below the speed limit. The wheels hummed on the gently curving highway. Bea was thinking about making barbeque ribs for Sunday supper when she spotted the dragon perched on the massive cliff-edge of Roche Miette.

On the mountain high above the highway, the dragon's red scales gleamed bloody in the sun. It stretched its wings and beat them once, then pointed its narrow head at the highway below. It dropped off the cliff, kited low, and disappeared behind the trees.

When La Vitesse rounded the curve, the red dragon hunched spread-winged atop the dynamite-blasted rock face where mountain met highway, a bighorn sheep clamped in its jaws.

"Look," Bea squeaked. But the kids were making too much noise to hear. She floored the gas and watched the dragon recede in the rear-view mirror. If she busted the speed limit all the way home, nobody noticed.

Twenty kids, and Rosie made twenty-one. The youngest not yet six, and Rosie the oldest at nearly sixteen. More than half of them were crying.

"Brake check all done!" Bea's voice was high with tension. She hunched in her seat and twisted from side to side, scanning the sky through the side-view mirrors. "The brakes are fine! La Vitesse is a good bus."

She patted the dashboard like it was a horse.

"Mom. They heard it hit us," Rosie growled. "Fucking tell them."

"A moose ran up the ditch," Bea said. "Gave us a little knock on the bum but we're fine."

The kids wailed louder. Tony Lalonde yanked his toque down over his eyes and howled.

"The moose is fine, too," Bea insisted. "Everything's okay."

But it wasn't okay. The dragon wasn't hurt. It flew a dozen car lengths behind, wings beating hard, mouth gaping. On every downstroke, that blue flame licked the road. Was it hot enough to melt her tires? Probably. She couldn't afford to find out.

Behind her, Rosie stood in the aisle, surfing the bumps. When the dragon tore the emergency exit off its hinges and lunged up the aisle, Rosie would be its first victim. It would rip her daughter's head off and slaughter the kids one by one while Bea sat behind the wheel. She had to think of something.

"Rosie, honey," she said in the sweetest voice she could muster. "Come and drive the bus."

When Bea reported the red dragon to the Hinton RCMP, the Mountie at the front desk had just smiled.

"Imagination goes wild in the mountains," he said. "I had a coal miner in here the other day saying a giant black cat was lurking around his dragline."

"Yeah, okay, but have you been to Jasper lately?" Bea asked. "You know the bighorn sheep along the highway? The ones that graze under Roche Miette? They're gone. All of them."

The Mountie smirked. "Last summer a bunch of campers said they saw a Bigfoot at Jarvis Lake."

Bea gave up. He was from Toronto. What did he know? Nothing.

Bea and her family weren't coal miners and they sure weren't campers. The mountains weren't terra incognita to her. She'd been born in the bush, like her parents, and their parents and so on back all the generations. Her ancestors lived in Jasper before it was a park, until they were kicked out and resettled in Cadomin. Those Rocky Mountain ranges were her true home, so when Bea said she saw a dragon, she saw it. No matter what some Mountie said.

"You want me to drive La Vitesse?" Rosie said. "Are you fucking kidding?"

From the back of the bus came a high-pitched rasping sound, like metal on metal, and if Bea had been unsure, she wasn't any longer.

"I'm not kidding. Take the wheel, please."

They exchanged positions awkwardly. Bea's ample hips didn't leave much room, but Rosie slid in behind her. What mattered most—after staying on the road—was keeping pressure on the gas pedal. Bea hung from the grab rail and stretched to keep her toe on the pedal, like a swimmer testing the water.

"Let go, let go, I got it." Rosie dug her shoulder into her mother's hip, hard.

"Okay, honey. Keep it above fifty, even on the curves. Floor it on the straightaways. And if you see anyone coming, lean on the horn and don't let up." Bea grabbed the fire extinguisher from the stepwell. When she stood, Joan Cardinal glared at her from under her glossy black bangs.

"I'm going to tell on you," Joan said, fully thirteen and fierce.

"That's okay, honey. You do that." Bea cradled the fire extinguisher like a baby.

"Let's play another game. Here are the rules. Everybody stay in your seat. Don't get up. Hold tight to your seat buddies, stay quiet, and do everything I say. If you do, we'll stop at Dairy Queen on the last day before Easter break. My treat."

Every kid's mouth dropped open. Ice cream was the bus driver's secret weapon.

"Sundaes or cones?" asked Sylvana Lachance, ten years old and already a master of negotiation.

"That depends on how good you are." Bea gave them a big motherly smile. "Now take off your snowsuits."

Rosie only had her learner's license but she'd been driving since she was ten. Out in the bush, all kids drove early. She learned on Bea's rusty Chevy Blazer, a four-speed with a sticky clutch, and had been driving it with confidence for years. Maybe the Blazer was nothing like La Vitesse, but Bea had no choice. She couldn't do anything about the dragon while stuck in the driver's seat.

Bea knelt in the aisle and stuffed her own parka inside Michelle Arsenault's tiny pink snowsuit, then padded the legs and arms with all the toques and scarves within reach.

"Who's got meat in their lunch today? Anyone?" The kids shrunk in their seats. "If you've got it, I want it."

Blair Tocher threw her his lunch bag. Bea ripped it open and tore through the plastic wrap with her fingernails. Peanut butter, that was fine. All animals liked that, right? She smeared the insides of the sandwich all over the snowsuit.

"Nobody's got baloney for lunch? Sausage? Spam?" She tried to sound normal, but her voice was high and shrill.

"Give her your lunches," came a growl from the driver's seat, where Rosie hunched over the wheel. "Do it or I'll take us into the ditch."

Bags rained on Bea's head. Pork sausage on thick homemade bread with mustard and a lick of golden syrup—that would be Manon Laroche's grandkids. Baloney and cheese on brown—could be anyone's. Cookies, apples, celery with Cheez Whiz, those all went inside. The meat she smeared on the outside, grinding the greasy dregs into the snowsuit's knit cuffs and fuzzy hood.

"Okay," Bea said. She hefted the snowsuit in one arm and grabbed the fire extinguisher with her other hand. Then La Vitesse hit a pothole and the whole world spun around her.

"Try steering around them, Rose," Bea called from the floor.

"We got a logging truck coming." Rosie's voice was strangely deep.

"The horn. Hit the horn, honey!" Bea scrambled up the aisle on all fours. "He's got a radio, he'll call for help."

She waved her arms as Rosie blasted the horn. High in the truck's cab, a man in a trucker hat and stubble. Sunglasses though it wasn't even full light yet. One hand on the wheel with fingers raised in a lazy wave while the other hand brought a white styrofoam coffee cup to his lips for a sip. The truck flashed by.

"Did it work?" Rosie asked.

Bea ran to the first empty row and dived for the side window. She pressed her forehead against the cold glass and watched the truck disappear around a curve.

"No," Bea said. "He wasn't looking."

She limped up the aisle.

"I didn't turn on the hazard lights." She reached around her daughter and flicked on the hazards. She hit the warning lights too, the big orange traffic flashers front and back. Then she turned to the kids and took a deep breath.

On her left and right, all twenty kids, their precious little upturned faces. Tear-stained. Some contorted in fear. Most blank with shock. Her fault. She'd failed them all.

"It's a dragon," she said. "A big one."

Hinton didn't have a real library. Technically, the high school library was open to the public during school hours, but the librarian had ideas about the kinds of people who should be allowed to walk through the door. And in grade eleven, Bea had been banned. That might be sixteen years ago but as far as she knew, she was still banned.

Still, Bea needed information and the library was the only place to get it.

After talking to the Mountie, she'd parked her bus at the hockey arena and walked over the playing fields toward the high school. Across the road, the pulp mill's stink-stacks belched rotten-egg vapor that drifted over the high school in a yellow haze.

She slipped into the library, walked softly to the reference shelf on the back wall, and pulled out *Encyclopedia Britannica* Volume D. The entry on dragons was subtitled "mythological creature." She examined the illustrations. Clearly her dragon was the European type. Its snaky head and batlike wings matched the picture.

In European myth, it said, dragons terrorized entire valleys. After eating all the sheep, they'd start eating children.

Sheep. The sheep in the picture were fairy-tale versions, white and fluffy—nothing like bighorn sheep, with their sleek brown fur and curling horns. But the sheep under Roche Miette were gone. Did that mean the children were next?

"Bea Oulette."

Bea slammed the encyclopedia closed. Mrs. English watched her over the edge of her reading glasses.

"You're not allowed in here," she said. "You're banned."

Bea slipped the book back on the shelf and padded toward the door, keeping her eyes low.

"High school was a long time ago," she said softly as she passed the check-out desk.

"Not for me," the librarian snarled. "Don't come back."

Bea stood on a bus seat, reached high, and yanked open the rooftop safety hatch. It popped up easily—Bea kept the hinges well oiled. She steadied herself with one hand on the hatch's open edge and put her foot on the seatback, holding the greasy stuffed and smeared snowsuit between her teeth. With both hands, she shoved the hatch fully open.

Still awkward, but steadier now as she poked her head and shoulders through. Her hair whipped her face.

The dragon kited behind the bus. It scrabbled at the roof with its forelegs, raking its talons along the metal, looking for purchase. It lost its grip and fell behind, twisted in the air, then extended its long neck and beat its wings hard to catch up again.

All along the roof, long shiny marks gashed the paint and road dust. It was only a matter of time before it hooked a talon into La Vitesse.

Bea yanked the stuffed snowsuit through the hatch.

"Here," she yelled. "Do you want dinner?" She held the snowsuit by its waist and danced it, the arms and legs flopping. She pitched it at the dragon, then grabbed the hatch handles and slammed the hatch closed.

"Floor it, Rosie," she yelled.

But La Vitesse was already moving fast, and the highway intersection was on the horizon. No choice, they had to turn.

Bea lunged up the aisle.

"Slow down, honey! You won't make the turn."

"It didn't work." Rosie had her eyes on the side mirror. She wasn't even watching the road.

"Slow down now!"

Bea grabbed Rosie's shoulder and tried to pull her from the seat. The bus swerved. Rosie hunched over the wheel, gripping it with both hands, knuckles white, her whole body tense.

"Get out of the seat." Bea's voice rose, high and shrill. "Rosie, get out now."

A ripping sound of nails on metal. A gash of sunlight appeared in the ceiling over the left rear seat.

"That's a problem," Rosie said in a low, ominous voice.

"Slow down or we'll flip," Bea pleaded.

Rosie nudged the speed down a little. Bea grabbed two armfuls of kids from the seats behind Rosie and pushed them into seats opposite.

"Everyone on the right side." No time to be gentle. She grabbed arms and shoulders—whatever she could get a grip on, and then leaned in, pressing a seat full of the littlest kids under her belly. "Hold tight."

A popping sound. Bea twisted to look. Just above the smeared rear window, three talons punctured the bus's roof. The window itself was dark. The dragon hung from the back of the bus.

"Sundaes," Bea shouted. "If we make this turn, I'll buy you all sundaes."

"Hot fudge," Rosie said, and swung the wheel.

When she was a teenager, Bea took books from the high school library. Not often. Not every book. Just the good ones. But it wasn't stealing, not at first. When she started, she'd bring the books back. That's how she got caught.

First day of grade eleven, she was returning the books she'd taken home for the summer. Her plan was to slip them onto a shelf in the morning, make herself scarce, then sneak back in the afternoon like she'd never been there. But the load was too heavy. The books tore through the paper bag and spilled across the library linoleum, right in front of Mrs. English.

In the vice principal's office, Bea kept her eyes hooded and looked at the floor. Never confront them, that was the survival strategy. It's what her grandpa did when hunters crossed the ridge where he set up his sweat lodge. It's what her mother did when the grocery store manager followed her through the aisles. Eyes down, calm breaths, wait for them to lose interest.

Getting banned only kept her out of the library for a week. Mrs. English wasn't always watching. The student volunteers didn't care, and best of all, nobody else seemed to know what Bea knew. To steal a library book, all you had to do was sandwich it between two other books, say a binder and a math textbook, and hold the stack horizontal as you walked through the exit door. Held flat, the magnetic strip wouldn't set off the detector.

So Bea still had all the books she wanted, even though Hinton had no place to buy them but the drugstore's rack of boring bestsellers. She stocked up. After getting roasted by Mrs. English and the vice principal, she felt absolutely fine about it.

La Vitesse's rear wheels screeched as they skidded sideways over the gravel-coated asphalt at the Forestry Trunk Road intersection. One rear wheel parted from the ground. The chassis shivered like it was Bea's own flesh.

She clung to the seatbacks with her nails and wrapped her sneaker-clad foot around a seat strut. Under her belly, she pressed the littlest kids hard into their seat. As La Vitesse fishtailed, the dragon's claws ripped through the roof—four jagged rents lengthening in a clockwise curve as the dragon swung like a pendulum. A wing slapped the left rear windows, once, twice. A foot scrabbled at the glass, talons clacking in rapid staccato.

Warm wet spread across the thigh of Bea's jeans. One of the little kids was peeing himself. The dragon hung from the bus's side, talon tips hooked into the window seals. Its head whipped back and forth like a flag, bashing La Vitesse's side windows.

Under Bea, Tony Lalonde wailed. But if he could cry, he could breathe, and that was all that mattered to Bea.

The bus fishtailed onto the highway, spun across two wide eastbound lanes, and spat gravel across the median. The dragon's maw opened in a scream, but instead of sound—a lick of blue fire, transparent, like the propane flame from Bea's camp stove. Then it lost its grip and fell. One talon dangled from the window, smearing ashy gore from its root.

Bea plunged up the aisle and scrabbled at her daughter's shoulders.

"Out of my seat, now," she demanded.

"This is almost over." Under the caked eyeliner, Rosie's narrowed gaze was flinty. "Take care of the kids. They hate me."

"Rosie. No."

"That's okay. I hate them, too."

No use. Bea had never been able to stand up to her daughter. But Rosie wasn't wrong. It was almost over. She turned to face the huddled kids.

"We're going to be fine." She gave them her best motherly smile. "Rose will drive us to the RCMP station. Five minutes."

Those little tear-streaked faces just about broke her heart. Theresa Lalonde held tight to her little brother. He sobbed into his big sister's sweater. Bea stooped over them.

"Did I hurt you, Tony? I'm so sorry."

"This is your fault," Theresa said. And she wasn't wrong. Bea had known about the dragons for months, and what had she done? Nothing.

"It's okay. Someone will rescue us," she said, but she knew it wasn't true.

Encyclopedia Britannica Volume D was the first book Bea had stolen in sixteen years. She hadn't lost her touch. All she had to do was wait for Mrs. English's smoke break. The teenage girls behind the check-out desk didn't look up when Bea walked in, or when she took the volume off the reference shelf. Bea walked through the anti-theft gate, the heavy book held flat at stomach-level.

The book fit perfectly over La Vitesse's steering wheel. Bea read through the Dragon entry twice to make sure she hadn't missed anything, but there wasn't much. European dragons were voracious. They slaughtered, consumed, and laid waste to the land until finally stopped by a great hero.

Bea had lived all her life in the bush, but she knew this much about the world: Heroes were more mythical than dragons. They simply didn't exist.

"Slow down, honey," Bea said. "Turn on Switzer."

La Vitesse shuddered. Rosie had the gas pedal flat on the floor. They'd be in the RCMP parking lot in minutes. But first, they had to take a sharp right onto Switzer Drive.

"I said slow down," Bea repeated.

Rosie didn't slow.

"What are you doing?" Bea screeched as they blew through the intersection.

"Do you want it to grab us again?" Rosie said.

Rosie flipped the latch on the driver's side window, stuck her hand out and pointed the mirror at the sky behind them. The dragon was still following, ten lengths behind and high above the highway.

"We've got lots of room," Bea pleaded. She gripped her daughter's shoulder and pointed at the last access point to the service road, coming up fast on their right. "Slow down and turn."

Rosie shrugged off her mother's hand. "Too late now."

Tears sprung to Bea's eyes. "Rosie, baby. You can't do this."

The rest of the highway was a straight shot through Edson and on to Edmonton. Three and a half hours of bush. But Hinton had service roads lining either side of the highway, busy with gas stations and strip malls. Not much traffic this early in the morning, but someone must have spotted the dragon by now. They were probably already running to a pay phone.

Bea raced to the back of the bus. The glass was clearer now, its coat of grime smeared thin by the dragon's swinging body. A little red Datsun chugged along in the right lane. Bea caught a glimpse of the driver's shocked expression, their mouth open in a perfect *O* as La Vitesse roared past.

High above the highway, the dragon folded its wings. It seemed to hover in the air. Then it dropped toward the tiny car like a torpedo.

It hit with all fours like a pouncing cat, talons puncturing the flimsy fiberglass roof. The car swerved through the median and plunged across the oncoming lanes. The dragon rode the car like a rodeo cowboy, legs flexing, wings slapping the air as if it could lift the car right off the road.

"Brake, brake," Bea whispered. "Throw it—Oh no."

Hinton's Husky station was the biggest in town, impossible to miss with the massive Canada flag snapping above. Big diesel pumps for the semis, four banks of regular pumps for the summer tourist traffic. And the Datsun was out of control. It missed the first pump but hit the second. The station went up with a *whump*.

Orange flames. Boiling smoke. And from the conflagration rose the dragon. Its wings fanned the flames with long, lazy beats.

"Go, Rosie!" Bea howled. Maybe they could get around the next curve before it spotted them. "Faster!"

Maybe the dragon would attack another car, blow up another station. Did she want that? No—it was horrible—but neither did she want the dragon on their tail again.

Then La Vitesse's horn blasted. One long, insistent, unending bellow.

"No, Rose!" Bea screamed.

The dragon's wings hitched. It flipped and turned, graceful as a swallow, scales shedding streams of smoke. Its eyes gleamed, two chilly points, square and level.

Bea lived in the bush. She'd seen plenty of cougars, and she knew this: when a predator's eyes focus on you, two orbs in perfect alignment, you are meat, meat, and nothing but meat. Whether you live or die is no longer in your control. Your fate lives between the claws and teeth of another.

"Honey, why?" Bea moaned. But there was no answer, never any answer with Rosie. She did as she pleased.

From the time her daughter was born, Bea's one goal was to keep her at home for as long as possible. With a kid as strong-willed as Rosie, that meant giving in, always. It also meant feeding her well. Tasty food, and lots of it. Though tiny as a baby, Rosie had always been a good eater. She'd grown big and tall—nearly six feet and still growing—with broad shoulders and big hands and feet.

The food was an important strategy. Bea knew from experience that, aside from weekend bush parties, going for pizza or fries with friends was pretty much the only thing a Hinton teenager could do to beat the boredom. Bea had been caught in that trap herself.

At sixteen, instead of getting on the school bus for the long ride home, she'd head to Gus's Pizza. Then, she'd wait outside the IGA grocery and try to catch a ride home with a neighbor. But that didn't always work, so she started hitchhiking. The first two times were fine. But the third time, her social studies teacher picked her up. For a half an hour, he'd lectured her about the dangers of hitchhiking, and then pulled over and slipped his hand into her jeans. That's how she got pregnant.

Bea didn't want that to happen to her girl. So if the poutine at the L&W was good, Bea's was better—the fries crispier, the cheese gooier, the gravy dark brown and chunky with lumps of salty hamburger. And that was just the start. Bea's nut-crusted elk roast was perfection and her open-fire flatbread with homemade jam beat any cake. So when Rosie got to that dangerous age, she never even thought about staying behind after school. Why would she hang out with kids she hated and eat substandard snacks when her mom's food was so good?

Rosie scared her teachers, but Bea didn't care. If her daughter sat in the back of every class and did the bare minimum of work to pass, that was fine with Bea. And if she stomped down the hallways with her elbows out, glaring at the other kids from under her ragged, dyed-black bangs and wore the same two Slayer T-shirts for a year, that was better than fine. Nobody would ever take advantage of her Rosie. Anyone who tried never tried twice.

La Vitesse blasted east, the speedometer topping out, the dragon still chasing them, and nothing ahead but open highway. Soon, they'd start climbing Obed Mountain. The engine couldn't take it at speed. Bea had to do something but she was too scared to think. Scared of what the dragon would do when the bus began toiling up that long, steep slope. And also, for the first time in her life, she was scared of her daughter.

Rosie hunched in Bea's seat, her mouth set in a permanent sneer. The remnants of her blue-black lipstick smeared her chin. Maybe the biggest danger they faced wasn't the dragon. Maybe it was Rosie. Maybe it always had been.

The kids knew Rosie was dangerous. They'd always known. Bea made a habit of looking away when the kids scooted past Rosie's shotgun seat as if it were on fire. She ignored it when Rosie snarled at a tardy kid, and when she snagged a treat out of one of their backpacks, Bea treated it like a joke.

Bea knelt beside the driver's seat and put a gentle hand on her daughter's thick wrist.

"Honey, whatever I've done, I'm so sorry. But take it out on me, not the kids."

Rosie's brow furrowed. The bridge of her nose crinkled like she smelled something rotten.

"Don't talk shit, Mom," she snarled.

Bea moved her hand up to her daughter's bicep and tried again.

"You've been angry for a long time, haven't you? And now you're in control. And you do have control. You're making all the choices. So make the right one, honey. Turn us around."

"Fuck, Mom, what do you think I am?" Rosie said. She took a deep breath and screamed, "Hang on!"

Rosie slammed on the clutch and brakes and spun the wheel. The momentum threw Bea down the stepwell. She hit her head on the door, hard. By the time she'd shaken off the pain and climbed to her feet, La Vitesse sat idling in the middle of Pedley Road, a gravel-top dead-end with nothing along it but a few old houses tucked back deep in the bush.

"Good girl, thank you. I'll drive now." Bea laid a hand on her daughter's thick shoulder. It was solid as stone. Rosie's right hand strangled the steering wheel and her left stuck stiffly out the window, twisting the side-view mirror to scan the sky behind them.

"No," Rosie said quietly. "Stop touching me."

Rosie shifted the bus into first gear, then second. They rolled up the road. Over the soft crunch of wheels on gravel and the engine's low hum, the *whump-whump* of wide wings sounded, louder and louder. Behind Bea, the children sniffled and sobbed. Maybe Bea did too. She knew she should fight—but how? Bea had never hit anyone. Certainly not her child. Not ever. How could she have known it was a mistake?

"I'm sorry," Bea whispered. "I didn't know what I was doing. I was too young."

When Rosie answered, her voice was flat and emotionless. "Stop. I'm trying to think."

"I should have made you play with the other kids. I wanted to keep you home. Keep you safe. I didn't know what it would mean. That you'd be isolated. That it would be bad for you."

Bea leaned her left cheek against Rosie's arm as La Vitesse rolled toward the Pedley railway crossing. The lights flashed red under the white-and-black crossing sign. A train was coming, but Rosie was utterly focused on the side mirror, jaw clenched, eyes narrow.

The train's low horn sounded in the crossing pattern. Two short blasts, one long, one short. Bea put a soft hand on her daughter's fist where it gripped the wheel.

"We have to stop before the tracks, honey."

No answer. Bea climbed to her feet. The fire extinguisher lay in the aisle, beside a tiny sneaker that had slipped off the foot of a terrified child. A child who was in her care. A child she had to keep safe.

She hoisted the heavy extinguisher in her arms. Bea knew herself. Violence wasn't in her nature. She'd never raised a hand to anyone, even when she should have. Even when they were hurting her. Now she had to hurt her daughter. Had to. Lift the extinguisher high and drop it on Rosie's head. That's all.

But she couldn't. She put the extinguisher down and turned away.

The bus's front wheels bounced over the rails. The train raced toward them, a massive stack of silver metal topped by a curved glass windshield. Close now, so close Bea could see its wipers stuck at a low angle across the glass. Its horn screamed as it bore down on them with all its murderous weight and velocity. Rosie still had her hand out the side window, yanking at the mirror with her thick fingers.

Behind La Vitesse, at the bus's grimy rear window, a shadow reached out to wrap its wings around the bus. Then a wall of silver speed obliterated it.

Rosie couldn't get the bus door open. Not even with both hands and all her muscle and weight.

"Mom, how the fuck do you do this?"

"There's a trick to it." Bea slipped her soft hands over her daughter's and flicked the rubber thumb control on La Vitesse's spring-latched handle. She cranked the door open, just as she'd done a thousand times before, but never with such relief.

The train was still rolling past, brakes howling and throwing sparks. When it had cleared the crossing, Bea ushered the kids off the bus.

"You too," she told Rosie, and followed her daughter down to solid ground.

Bea wrapped her sweater around little Michelle Arsenault and lifted her up to settle on her hip. She wiped the child's nose with a crumpled tissue from her jeans pocket, then lifted Tony Lalonde onto her other hip.

At the railroad crossing, the tar-smeared sleepers and silver rails were painted with red-brown gore, thick and smoking. The dragon's head lay beside La Vitesse's right rear wheel. Bleeding pits marked the milky sclera of its eyes, and a blue liquid leaked from its fanged jaws.

Rosie heaved the dragon's head so it lay chin-down on the road.

"Where's the rest of it?" Michelle Lalonde whispered from under Bea's elbow.

"Here, in the ditch," Rosie said. She slipped down the icy incline and hefted a tattered wing, then dragged it up to the road and deposited it beside the dragon's head.

"That's not good meat," said Blair Tocher, eleven years old and an experienced hunter. "Smells like bear gone bad. You can't eat that."

"I think Rosie could," Joan Cardinal said.

Bea shivered, cold without her sweater, and her forearm was wet where she was supporting little Tony Lalonde against her body. His arms gripped Bea's neck and his little snot-smeared face burrowed into her.

"Is someone coming to help us?" he asked in a whisper.

"Soon, I think."

Far up the tracks, the train had finally stopped. The engineer would have already reported the incident. She couldn't hear the sirens yet, but it wouldn't be long.

Rosie dragged the dragon's torso from the far side of the tracks. Its gut had split open, revealing a nest of mottled entrails padded with honeycombed tissue.

"The dragon you saw on Roche Miette was red, Mom." Rosie stripped off her gore-soaked gloves and dropped them on the ground. "That's what you said."

"That's right," said Bea. "And you didn't believe me."

"Then this isn't the only dragon." Rosie shaded her eyes with her hand and scanned the sky.

Bea nodded. "There must be one more at least."

Tony whimpered. Bea hitched him up higher on her hip.

"We're okay. We're safe," she told the kids. "Right, Rose?"

Rosie shrugged and drew a pack of menthols from her pocket. A cigarette dangled from her lips as she fished for her lighter. She glanced at Bea, furtively, as if she needed her mother's permission to light up in front of the kids. Bea almost laughed.

She'd thought there were no heroes, but she was wrong. Dead wrong.

"Go ahead and smoke, honey," Bea said. "You earned it."

NOTES ABOUT "LA VITESSE"

When Jonathan Strahan invited me to contribute a story to the anthology *The Book of Dragons*, I knew I wanted to set the story in my hometown of Hinton, Alberta. But there was a problem. Dragons are a myth foreign to North America. You can't airdrop them into a story set in North America and pretend they belong. Or, you *could*, but it's shitty. Indigenous territories have their own mythical ecosystems, and unless we belong to those communities, we need to keep our sticky fingers off them.

But does that mean I can't write a fantasy story about the place where I grew up? Of course I can, but I have to be thoughtful about it.

I solved the problem by treating dragons as an invasive species, something dangerous that needs to be eradicated. My sister drives a school bus: problem solved. I set the story in 1983, which let me ventriloquize all my feelings about the town where I spent my teenagerhood. It's not the kind of place that ever gets written about, but there are lots of stories to tell there, and I hope to write more.

A couple more things about "La Vitesse" that give me great joy: Fans of the comedian Eddie Izzard may enjoy the joke embedded in the story's title. And all library thievery techniques are absolutely authentic and tested by teenage me.

SO YOU WANT TO BE A HONEYPOT

WHEN SHE WAS A GIRL, VASILISA WANTED to be a sniper. She'd grown up listening to tales of the valiant Stalingrad sharpshooters who had bolstered the city's resistance to the German invasion in the Second World War. She enlisted in the army as soon as she was old enough, and trained hard with her rifle, but when she applied for specialty training, that career track was closed. Instead, she was recruited for a new program.

Vasilisa learned seduction from a lithe Uzbek of slippery gender, who taught classes in three cramped trailers along the shores of the Caspian Sea. The trailers were welded into a row and doorways had been sliced though the metal sides, allowing the instructor to stalk back and forth between the three sex stations like a parade marshal.

If she could learn to be alluring under those conditions, she could seduce anyone, anywhere.

"Desire. You will use it like a weapon," her instructor said.

"Yes, comrade instructor," Vasilisa answered in concert with her classmates.

Vasilisa buried herself in her studies. Explored her five classmates' orifices with eyes, fingers, tongue. Learned what made them keen with pleasure, sob, weep. And she lusted after her instructor. They all did.

"You will embody desire. Use it. Wield it. Exude it from every hole. But you will never feel it."

"No, comrade instructor."

"The hand goes like this," the instructor said, with a sly glance. They held their fist high, closed into a cone, index finger knuckle protruding like a mountain's apex. "The knuckle is key. When you are inside, rotate your hand by bending at the wrist until you find the spot that makes them scream."

The lone man among them stared at his closed fist, puzzled.

"Not you, child. Your hands are too large." The instructor lowered their plush, plummy lips to Axel's knuckle and kissed the air above it. Vasilisa nearly swooned.

The instructor's head snapped up.

"Desire controls others," they said. "It will never control you."

"Never, comrade instructor."

That was the point of all their lessons: rejection of desire. Vasilisa and her classmates satiated their lust for their instructor by banging each other raw. By the end of the six months, all six had learned to master themselves. Desire was nothing. Control was everything. And love? Love didn't exist.

Upon graduation, she changed her name to Claudia and forgot Vasilisa had ever existed.

Her classmates chose similarly seductive names—Valentina, Monique, Silke, Axel, Erika. Vasilisa would never know the names their mothers had given them. The six of them were so intimate she could recognize each of them blindfolded, using just the tip of one finger. She'd made them shiver and shake, and had been shaken in her turn, but she didn't know them, not really. And then they were parted, so she never would.

Claudia, the fresh new girl in Vasilisa's head, sulked on the long, hot train to Sofia. The danger of the border crossing into Turkey couldn't lift her mood, and by the time she boarded the passenger liner in Istanbul's thronging port, she was truly melancholy.

"A beautiful girl like you shouldn't look so sad."

Claudia raised the wide brim of her hat. The man who spoke was Canadian, his military background obvious from his posture. Canadians were inconsequential, but still, she allowed him to amuse her on the three-day trip to Naples, let him try to lift the sadness from her eyes. Then on the last night of their trip, she fucked his wife three times, in the first officer's empty cabin, deploying comrade instructor's knuckle trick to thunderous effect.

When she stepped onto Italian soil at six in the morning, she set her small bag at her feet, lifted her fingers to her mouth and licked them, savoring the woman's scent. It smelled like desire satiated. Like power. Like winning.

Come north, the breeze whispered. *Everything you want is here.*

A week of pasta put an exclamation point on Claudia's décolletage. American men had simple tastes; Claudia's breasts would attract them like bears—well, like bears to honey. She bought new clothes, semi-fashionable, from stalls in the back streets of the Vomero. And scent, mysterious iris and cedar. Then she caught a slow train north.

After the bustle of Naples, Stuttgart was gray, bleak, and joyless. The frigid winds of autumn came early; only a few leaves jittered on the boughs of the city's tortured trees. Every third building lay in rubble, and bland civic buildings punctuated pitted thoroughfares colorless as a Moscow dawn.

Her first instinct was to stalk the city until she found an American with stars on his epaulettes, then drag him into an alley and leave him with his eyes rolling and his trousers around his ankles, but no, that would be a disaster. She restrained herself.

She found an attic apartment, a source for nylon stockings, and a job as a hostess at the Kiss Club. Slow nights, Monday to Wednesday to start.

Her first night at the Kiss Club, she saved a young American captain from falling down stairs. Just a discreet hand on his elbow. He didn't even realize he'd stumbled, but he certainly noticed her touch.

"Who are you?" he asked.

"Just a girl from Obersdorf, come to make my way in the big city." She used her most gentle seductive glance, but he didn't even notice. He was too busy making a grab for her left ass cheek.

Claudia dodged his grip and let him go unmolested. She could have hauled him into an alcove and made him scream, but he had no stars on his shoulders, and her mission was too new to compromise on a whim.

The Kiss Club was Stuttgart's most notorious gathering place, but Claudia soon learned it was staid as a neighborhood coffee house. The club's steamy atmosphere, dark corners, and steady trickle of uninformed foreigners might overwhelm an innocent small-town girl. But Claudia had higher standards. She was a talented soldier with sharp eyes, keen reflexes, and a flexible mind. Those qualities made her an effective seductress, but she wasn't patient.

Three weeks later, when her handler found her, she begged him to give her some work.

"I have skills. Talents. And I'm forgetting them all. Let me do an information drop. Equipment transfer. Anything."

"Hush," he commanded.

Her handler told her to call him grandpa, and he did look the part. A kindly little old man, squat and skinny, with short suspenders that held his baggy trousers up to his armpits.

"All you have to do is work, sleep, and watch for opportunities. Is that so hard?"

"No, Opa," she said softly and dropped her eyes.

"Ah." He pulled a flask from his breast pocket and unscrewed the cap. "Nerves. Liquor helps. Drink."

Claudia let him think she was nervous, and that a sip of schnapps helped. She knew what happened to troublesome operatives. Managing her handler was just as important as managing her marks, and she would not fail at either. But still, she was uneasy. At night, the wind skittered over the attic's roof. The loose terracotta tiles rattled like broken teeth.

North, it said. *You miss them. Come north.*

Claudia rose to the rank of senior Kiss Club hostess just in time for the club's winter lull. Early snowfall muffled Stuttgart. The Americans stayed in their barracks, officers straying from their compounds only on Friday and Saturday nights, and then junior officers, only. Callow young men with little access to secrets, and useless to Claudia. The senior officers rarely left their compounds, and when they did, they brought their wives and children with them.

As the weeks piled up, the highest she got was a pathetically romantic signals officer from Texas, who would kiss but not fuck her.

"I'm waiting for my wedding night," he drawled. "Just like Jesus did."

"That's lovely," Claudia said, gazing up into his thick glasses.

He invited her to worship with him, and when she walked onto the base, Claudia grinned in triumph. Church was held in the concrete basement of the administration building. From there, all the base's secrets would fall into her lap. Three Sundays later, she had the combinations to the general's safe (his daughter's birthdate), and had stolen a list of codes from a young airman's pocket.

Opa pocketed the safe combination, but he wasn't impressed with the codes.

"These aren't encryption keys, they're guitar chords."

Claudia was embarrassed. "My mistake, Opa."

"It doesn't matter. Don't risk yourself. Just marry him, and wait."

Claudia hadn't realized marriage was on the table. She swallowed carefully, mastering herself.

"But he's only a captain."

"He will rise."

"That could take years."

"It will take as long as it takes." He offered her a sip from his flash. She pushed it away, but gently, like a good, obedient girl would.

The next day, she boarded a northbound train to Frankfurt and wandered through the city. She listened to the whisper in the air—*north, north*—and when it quieted, she found herself in a dirty, dangerous club—the kind of place the Kiss Club wanted to be—where shadowed pairs writhed on the dance floor, their movements bearing no relation to the discordant music served up by a quartet of blade-faced jazz musicians.

There, in the club's north corner, she found three of her classmates. Claudia nearly launched herself into their laps.

"Is it what you thought it would be?" Silke asked.

"Not at all," Claudia blurted. "It's so boring."

Axel laughed. "At least you're in a city. Ramstein is this big." He showed her the polished nail of his smallest finger.

"In Grafenwoehr, sheep block traffic daily," Silke said.

"Did you think your life would be enjoyable?" Valentina's voice carried over the din. Axel and Silke snapped to attention, automatically. "We are tools. We wield ourselves like weapons."

"And how many Americans have succumbed to your weapon so far, Valentina?" Claudia asked.

Valentina pursed her lips. "I have one in my sights."

"We were made for sex. Drugs. Parties. American decadence, not church and chastity," Claudia said. "Opa wants me to marry my American. Can you believe it?"

"Obey him. What do you care?" Valentina snapped. "You have no needs or desires. None."

Claudia nodded her head in time with the music, feigning agreement. Valentina would never understand the agony of a restless mind. In bed, Valentina was the softest, most scrumptious morsel, delicious from eyebrows to toes. Upright, she was a rigid pedant.

"Have you seen Monique and Erika?" Claudia squinted into the murky depths of the club, expecting the last two members of their cohort to appear.

Axel looked sad. "Not yet, but they'll find us."

Silke slid her long, delicate hand up Claudia's inner thigh and nuzzled her ear.

"Perhaps if we make enough noise, they'll hear," she breathed.

One trip to Frankfurt every two weeks or so. That's all Claudia allowed herself. It was so little. But still, Opa didn't like it.

"Don't give the American any reason to doubt you're a good Christian."

"No, Opa. I won't."

Claudia didn't mind spending time with the signals officer. He was boring but not stupid; turned out the Jesus comment had been a joke. And she enjoyed the church services, which were heavy on music and light on preaching.

An energetic trio played the hymns—a Black master sergeant singing and playing guitar, with two stocky airmen on drums and double bass. The church band made the hymns energetic, rakish, even wicked—the kind of music you could dance to, fuck to, turn into a religion and lose yourself in.

Could she do what Opa wanted? Marry the American, live on the base, cook his meals, have his babies? Occasionally root out small pieces of information that, if not useless, were likely redundant?

If so, at least she was guaranteed some up-tempo church music every Sunday.

Monique found them soon after New Year's. Five of them together again, every two weeks at Frankfurt club. Only Erika was still missing.

"If all they wanted were good little American wives, they should have chosen people more suited to it," Monique said. "It's like hitching a racehorse to a plow."

"Where would you rather be?" Valentina snapped. "Digging the Bratsk Reservoir? Guarding a Mongolian border crossing?"

"Hush, Valentina," Silke said.

Valentina's mouth snapped shut. Silke had landed a Major General, which gave her automatic status and authority. But Silke hated him.

"It's like milking a cow. Thirty minutes of steady work, and when he falls asleep, I drink half a bottle of whiskey and masturbate on the sofa." Silke's eyes glittered. "I used to be a soldier."

Valentina squared her delicate shoulders and drew in a deep breath, clearly gearing up to deliver some more well-used platitudes. Monique stopped her with an elbow to the ribs.

"Turn on the radio before you start," she suggested gently. "You'll have something to listen to."

Claudia tipped the last drops of her beer onto the table's filthy, pitted surface. She drew wet spirals with her finger.

"My American gives chaste little kisses and moons at me through his glasses. He'll propose soon and then I'll be stuck. I know I shouldn't complain. I'm not soft—I can take almost anything, but it's too dreary."

"You could drink," said Monique.

"If I get married, I might have to."

"Pawn him off on a new girl," Silke suggested. "A little frau to turn his head."

"I've tried. He loves me. Who knows why? I've barely given him a reason."

"Should I visit?" Axel slapped his chest. "Maybe he'd prefer some of this."

Claudia grinned. "I'd like to see that."

"When you are married, you'll be content," Valentina said. "Marriage is what women are for. It's our duty."

Axel sipped his beer contentedly. Of course he did. For him, it was self-evident that a woman wanted to be married. But Monique and Silke stared into the club's shadows, frowning. Even Valentina looked unconvinced.

On Monday morning, she woke to find Opa perched on her one rickety chair.

"I have a problem," he said, and dropped a train ticket on her table. "You wanted a job. Take care of it."

It was a return trip to Hamburg.

"Does the problem have a name?" she asked.

"Erika," he said. "Find her and kill her. If you do well, I may give you other jobs."

Erika. She had the tiniest wrists Claudia had ever seen, easily circleable with her thumb and forefinger with room to spare. Her ankles were delicately boned, and her baby toe fit between Claudia's lips like a nipple. When that toe was sucked, Erika seemed to float off the bed.

"Certainly," Claudia said. "I'll need a weapon." With a rifle, even a rusted relic, it would be the work of a moment. Death at a distance—her childhood dream. Anonymous. Efficient. Final.

"You're a smart girl." He rose from the chair, so old and creaky his joints groaned. "Improvise."

On the train north to Hamburg, Claudia had no questions, no doubts. She didn't need a rifle to kill Erika. Any weapon would do. When the train pulled into Hamburg, she transferred a razor from her purse to her pocket, stepped out onto the platform, calmed her breathing, and listened.

Erika. With her little cleft chin and sensual gap between her front teeth. Breath that tasted of cinnamon and fresh snow, and nipples that turned tomato-red with arousal.

Nothing at first, no wind, just the chug and huff of trains. And then, gently: *West*.

West of central Hamburg lay the red light district of St. Pauli. It only took three hours to find Erika in a noisy club. The dim room had a low stage at the end, no bigger than a bed. Five skinny boys crowded on it, attacking their instruments with more passion than skill, their heads skimming the ceiling.

Erika bounced by the side of the stage, her back to the crowd, completely vulnerable. Claudia drifted through the room, let herself be gently pushed across by the ebb and flow of bodies until she was standing right behind Erika.

It would have been so quick, so easy to slice that razor through her classmate's throat and disappear in the press and confusion. Instead, she put her arms around Erika and squeezed tight. Erika squealed, bounced against her, and covered her face with little kisses.

"I knew you were coming!" Erika shouted in Claudia's ear to make herself heard over the din. "I'm so glad you're here."

"No, you're not. They sent me to kill you."

Erika grinned and turned back to the stage. Claudia pulled her close.

"Did you hear me? They want you dead. You have to run. Find a new life somewhere."

"I can't do that, kitten," Erika yelled back.

Erika bounced in time to the music. It wasn't good music—the church band was better—but the beat was insistent. Soon, Claudia was bouncing, too.

"They'll send someone else," she yelled.

"I know. They sent Silke last week. I don't care. I'm staying here."

When the song ended, Erika jumped and screamed. The band grinned in appreciation and swung into another song.

Hours later, in the dim light of morning, Claudia broke into the Hamburg morgue. She razored the littlest finger from the corpse of a young woman, wrapped the bloodless member in a handkerchief, and ran to catch a southbound train. In the train toilet, she polished and filed the fingernail. Would it satisfy Opa? Likely not, but it was the best she could do.

Silke turned up at Claudia's apartment on Sunday morning, just as she was about to leave for church.

"I heard you killed Erika," she whispered. "Is it true?"

"Yes, of course," Claudia answered loudly.

Silke drooped. Claudia bundled her out the door, downstairs, and onto the streetcar. At the gate, she told the military policeman Silke was her sister. He signed them in with a smile.

"No, I didn't," she said when the first hymn was in full strain. "I told her to cut and dye her hair, gain some weight, try to be inconspicuous."

"You're smarter than me. I came back and told my opa I couldn't do it," Silke said. "I said if he wanted to find another girl to milk the Major General, he should just slit my throat right then."

"Why would they send us to kill her?"

"It could be a message. Do your duty and don't complain or..." Silke drew a manicured finger across her throat. Up in front, the drummer caught the movement and blinked at them, startled. Claudia threw him a sunny smile and patted Silke's hand.

"Will your ruse work, do you think?" Silke asked before they parted at the railway station.

"I don't know. I hope so," she said. "But one thing's for sure, I'm not bored anymore."

The next time Claudia visited Frankfurt, Silke hauled Valentina off to the toilet, giving Claudia time to tell the other two about Erika.

"What if my opa sends me to Hamburg?" Axel asked. "What do I do?"

"Don't kill her, that's what." Claudia rapped her knuckle on Axel's sternum for emphasis. He batted her hand away.

"Stop. You just want to touch me."

"Everyone does, dear." Monique patted the boy's beefy shoulder. "I wonder why she won't leave. She could have a lover, I suppose."

"Maybe you should go ask her." Claudia meant it as a joke, but Monique's eyes brightened with purpose.

"She's obsessed with the music," Monique said the next week, her breath hot in Claudia's ear. "Did you notice?"

Claudia nodded. The Hamburg songs were similar enough to the church band for Claudia to see the appeal, with riffs, backbeats, and harmonies, sly bent pitches, noisy timbres, and sudden clear tones that echoed in Claudia's skull from Sunday to Sunday.

"Is she being sensible?" Claudia asked.

"She did what you said. Cropped her hair and bleached it blonde. But she's noticeable. The short hair makes her eyes this big." Monique circled her thumbs and forefingers and raised them to her eyes like goggles.

"Let's hope nobody looks for her."

That hope lasted only until midnight, when Claudia spotted the corner of a train ticket peeking from between the lips of Valentina's velvet clutch.

"Angel, darling," Claudia purred. "Why are you sitting so far away?" She slid her knee between Valentina's thighs and moved in close, gently forcing her classmate against the padded seat. After a moment of resistance, Valentina melted into her arms. She lowered her lips to the silken skin under Valentina's ear, reached behind, and slid the clutch over to Monique.

Twenty minutes later, when Valentina reached for it, her clutch was right at hand. She clicked it open, retrieved her powder and lipstick, and discreetly repaired her smeared complexion.

At the end of the night, Claudia, Silke, and Monique were far back in the coat-check queue. Axel had escorted Valentina to the front of the line, like the gallant boy he was.

"It's what you thought," Monique said later. "Return to Hamburg."

"Oh no," Silke groaned. "Valentina will never let her get away."

"It's worse than that," Monique whispered. "They've given her a pistol."

Erika had been warned twice; she knew the risks. If she wouldn't save herself, what could any of them do? The four of them agreed to go home, not interfere, let Valentina complete her mission. In the dark of early morning, they kissed and hugged and pretended to go their separate ways, but they all got on the north-bound train anyway. Valentina in first-class, the others squished into the third-class car.

Claudia slid into the seat beside Silke.

"We are ridiculous," she said.

Silke shrugged.

"We have the advantage. We know where she's going. Perhaps we can help."

"Help do what? Save Erika, or kill her?"

"Save them both. If Valentina goes through with this, she'll never forgive herself."

Claudia shook her head grimly.

"It's true," Silke insisted. "I know her true nature."

"That's pure romance." Claudia took Silke's hand between both of hers. "You can never know what's in a person's heart."

"When a person is at their most unguarded, their most passionate, that's who they really are. I've seen that side of Valentina a hundred times. So have you. She's a darling."

Claudia grimaced. "No, she's a rigid survivor with a pistol in her purse."

In Hamburg, they scrounged disguises from the station's lost items kiosk—hats, scarves, a widow's veil for Silke, a knit cap with ear flaps for Axel. Claudia tugged it over his hair and pulled the narrow brim down to his eyebrows. He stuffed his hands into the pockets of his woolen coat and tried to look inconspicuous. It didn't work.

"You're too big to hide," Monique said. "You'll have to stay here."

"I will not," he said, stubborn as a child.

They followed Valentina at a discreet distance. Valentina gripped her clutch so tightly, she'd poked her fingers through the tips of her knit gloves.

"You see, she's nervous," Silke said. They were stopped at a busy street corner, cowering together against the frigid North Sea wind that scoured the intersection. "She won't be able to do it."

"If she doesn't kill Erika, we'll have to," Claudia said.

The other three stared at her in horror. When the traffic cleared, Claudia led them across the street.

"Think about it. The opas don't need us for this. Erika could have been dead weeks ago. They want to see where our training went wrong, and whether it can be put right. It's an experiment. A test. Silke failed it. I failed it. How many more chances will they give us?"

They'd come to a four lane road thick with industrial traffic from the port. Valentina was far ahead, just a speck in the distance. Claudia stepped off the curb, raised her hands to stop the trucks, and then shooed her classmates across the road.

"If we want to live, we have to kill Erika," she said when they had all reached the sidewalk safely.

"No," said Silke.

"No," said Axel.

"Absolutely not," said Monique.

"Then we have to let Valentina kill her." That didn't fly with her classmates either. "Do you have a better suggestion?"

"We could go home and kill our opas," Silke said. "It would be easy."

"I'm not killing anyone," Monique said. "I was made for love, not murder."

Axel nodded. "Me too."

"It wouldn't work, anyway," Claudia said. "There's always more opas."

If Opa had given her a rifle, Claudia would have killed Erika the first time. Death at a distance, like a Stalingrad sniper. Her failure to complete the mission was Opa's fault. If he hadn't played games with her, this all could have been over weeks ago.

A pistol. That's what Claudia needed. She'd leave the others to distract Valentina, sneak into the club and kill Erika. It was the only option. But first, she'd have to find one.

It was possible. Hamburg's red light district was notorious. She could find a pistol tucked into the belt of a pimp or loan shark, or even just a scared country boy come into the big city for a night on the town, bringing his daddy's Luger along for protection.

As they entered St. Pauli, Claudia began assessing the men they passed, guessing which ones might be carrying weapons, and trying to spot any tell-tale lumps under their coats.

When they got to the club, a bass riff leaked from the door, punctuated by the rhythmic thump of a low-pitched drum. Valentina slipped inside and the other three followed close behind. Claudia paused for a moment, looking around, trying to make her best guess at a likely mark. She chose a short, thin man. He wore a thickly padded jacket and looked like the kind who would need a pistol for confidence. She glided past him and pretended to catch her heel. When he reached to catch her, she slid her fingers along his belt. Nothing. He scowled and pushed her away, then checked for his wallet. She gave him an innocent smile.

Her clumsy attempt didn't dishearten her. Inside would be better, where every sense was deadened by the press of bodies jouncing to the beat.

Silke, Axel, and Monique had intercepted Valentina and hauled her off into a corner of the foyer. Inside Valentina's purse, clutched in her arms, was the one weapon Claudia could locate with certainty. She could join them, take the clutch from Valentina. If she moved fast, they might not even have a chance to stop her. But she didn't even know if Erika was in the club. So instead of joining her friends, she made her way to the bar and positioned herself at the end, where she could survey the people jostling for drinks.

When a thick-necked man waved to get the bartender's attention, Claudia caught a glint of metal under his jacket, and the leather strap of a shoulder holster against his white shirt. The bartender passed him a foaming pint. He drained half of it in two gulps, then held the glass high as he moved through the press toward the stage. Claudia followed.

If she could be slick enough, quick enough, he wouldn't know who had taken his pistol. He would make a scene but that was fine—she could use it for cover while she did her job, because there was Erika, at the side of the stage. Her bleached hair caught the light like a target.

One smooth movement, perfectly timed. She slid her hand inside the thick-necked man's jacket just as a young woman swung her ample hips into his thigh. As he reached out to steady himself on the shoulder of a friend, Claudia palmed the pistol. Then she ducked low and moved through the crowd, deer-swift and graceful.

Claudia knelt under a table, checked the ammunition; thumbed the safety. The weapon was heavy, its grip cold on her palm. Seconds now, only seconds. If the thick-necked man was as competent as he looked, he'd soon notice soon the missing weight. She stood, raised the pistol, and framed Erika's bright head in her deadly sights.

The music, the band, the crowd, the thick-necked man—they all disappeared. All that was left was Erika, the pistol, and her four dear friends arguing in the foyer. If she killed Erika, she'd be gone forever—and then she'd lose more. Silke, Monique, Axel, and even Valentina, gone from her life, leaving her with Opa and a future she couldn't face.

She lowered the pistol and flipped the safety lever. She shouldered her way across the floor and dropped the weapon on the thick-necked man's foot.

"Keep it," she told him. And then she grabbed Monique's elbow. She pulled her across the dance floor and out to the foyer, where the others were still huddled in a corner, arguing in whispers.

"Let's go," she told them. "We've delayed long enough."

"Delayed?" Silke repeated.

"Delayed what?" Monique asked.

"Our lives." Claudia grinned. "No opas. No Americans. Just the six of us, and the whole wide world. It's all waiting."

NOTES ABOUT "SO YOU WANT TO BE A HONEYPOT"

In 2014, when Ian Fleming's books entered the public domain in Canada, David Nickle and Madeline Ashby edited an anthology of James Bond stories. I contributed a novelette called "The Gladiator Lie." It's filled with sex and violence, and writing it was just about the most fun I've ever had.

This is not that story, for obvious copyright reasons. I wrote "So You Want to be a Honeypot" in 2019, hoping to produce something at least as much fun as that riotous James Bond story.

What's almost never acknowledged is that spy stories are romances, variations on a well-trodden path paved with specific tropes. The honeypot is a fun trope, but it's also, you know, ridiculous: The beautiful woman who wants to seduce and betray the hero, with whom she fights a battle of wits until she either falls slavishly in love with him, or he has to murder her to survive, or both? Sigh. It's a fantasy with no basis in reality. The possibility of a honeypot situation happening approaches zero. It never happens, ever.

But it's awfully fun to play with.

TWO WATERSHEDS

"THEY TOLD ME YOU'RE A SPECIAL CASE," the tech said. "Do you feel okay?"

"Totally," Kayla said. "I'm a gamer, so this is all familiar."

The Avatar's visual horizon bloomed over Kayla's eye. A cyan line zipped across the bottom third of the black-and-gray grid-textured field. A buttercup-yellow sun misted into existence at the top left and slowly descended to kiss the artificial horizon.

"Calibration complete," the tech said. "Here come your apps."

A digital clock appeared at the bottom left of Kayla's eye and ticked the seconds down from thirty. A map icon appeared beside it, then a remote sensing interface with LIDAR, radar, and satellite feeds, and finally a social media chat window on the far right. Kayla flipped through the interfaces.

At zero, the artificial sky brightened to pale blue. Mountains coalesced on the horizon, and behind them, fingers of peach clouds reached toward heaven. Kayla's own personal heaven. Her Rocky Mountains. She loved them so much. Even grainy old photos made her misty. Several times, when showing her mountains' craggy faces to friends after a few glasses of wine, she'd actually cried. She lived less than an hour's drive away, but access restrictions had kept her away for more than three years. Finally, she was back, in the middle of the valley she loved.

"Three-sixty and live," said the tech. "The Avatar is all yours, Ms. Maskuta. Ping me if you need anything."

"Hello beautiful," she said, her voice breathy. "I've missed you so much."

The illusion of being in the Athabasca valley was flawless as a full-sensory gaming surround, but all-the-more-perfect because it was far, far from perfect. Because that hazy sky overhead was barely saturated enough to be called blue, the mountains that bit into the horizon weren't drawn by a talented ARtist, and the scraggly bushes and tough forbs underfoot hadn't been designed for optimized sensory feedback. No. This was raw landscape. Glaciers had clawed it from early Cambrian stratigraphy, a testimony to the inexorable power of flowing water.

But that was then, and this was now. The once-mighty Athabasca River trickled at her feet, and the wide, dry floodplain was rapidly turning to desert.

Kayla's social media feed pulsed for her attention. Her public feed chattered with lookie-loos and gawkers, many of them riding along with her in full VR surround. The pulse was from her family's direct message feed, and Kayla had promised not to ignore it.

Are you feeling okay? Natalie whispered. *Any pain? Any distress?*

I'm fine. Don't fuss.

I can't help but worry.

Kayla shrugged. Her pack slipped off the Avatar's shoulder. It swung to the ground and swiped through the soapberry bush at her right hip.

We talked about it, Nat. This is a once-in-a-lifetime opportunity.

It's just a research grant, Natalie replied. *You didn't have to take it. There are other grants.*

You always choose the worst time to pick a fight, Kayla said. *Do you really want to do this?*

Kayla re-adjusted her backpack and stepped into the shallow river. The slippery cobbles shifted with every step, but the Avatar was balance stabilized. And if she fell, so what? It's not like she'd get hurt.

No, I don't want to fight, Natalie whispered. *Not today.*

Thanks, hon.

But tell me if you feel any pain. No matter how minor, okay?

I will, I promise. But don't worry. This is the best day of my life.

Actually, Kayla wasn't fine. Her lower back throbbed. But the pain wasn't much worse than the backaches she'd endured every month since she was twelve. Keeping it from Natalie might be a lie, but just a tiny one. Kayla gave herself a pass; she had much bigger things to worry about.

She swiped a finger over the social media interface, and a transparent window bloomed across her eye. She struck a pose in the middle of the river with one of her staff gauges and flicked her status to *Live*.

"Hello," she sang out. "I'm Kayla Maskuta, and I'm a restoration ecologist with the Yellowhead Regional District, based out of Hinton, Alberta. Today, we'll be planting a hundred flow gauges in the upper reaches of the Athabasca River. This is an important moment, in a very important place, and I'm glad you're here with me."

She checked her radar and LIDAR readouts to be sure she had the right placement, then positioned the heavy, screw-shaped end of the gauge on riverbed. She had to wiggle it around to get past the cobbles, but after that, installing it was easy. All she had to do was clip her portable motor drive over the shaft, flick a switch, and hold tight as it screwed the gauge into the substrate.

"The gauges will provide streamflow information in real time, accessible to everyone via live stream, beginning right now." Kayla booted the gauge, eyed the incoming data, and then fired the link into her feed. "This data will be absolutely invaluable to our river restoration efforts."

She waded to the riverbank and began jogging upriver toward the next gauge site. Even though it was still early, her feed hummed, questions flying by so fast she could barely read them. But she didn't need to. She'd been training her smart agent to handle public relations basics, and this was the perfect opportunity to try it out.

"I've put my fake in charge of picking questions. She'll choose the most unique and interesting ones, so get creative."

A cramp fluttered across Kayla's belly. Should she tell Natalie? No, the next moment it was gone. And she didn't have time to worry about it—she had a long-term, high-profile project to fund. Eyeballs meant funding. She'd wear a clown costume and dance up and down the highway if it got her grants.

She chatted with her feed while installing the next ten gauges at half-kilometer intervals, but the questions were boring. *How does the gauge work?—Why is the river so low?—The water is brown, does that mean it's polluted?* She'd never keep her audience interested by fielding slow balls, so she told her fake to try choosing more mediagenic questions.

How did you vote in the referendum?

Kayla told her fake to kill the question. She'd heard that question before, and had muted every possible version. Her fake should have dumped it.

Why don't you use robots to place your equipment?

"If someone wants to build us a custom bot for free, please let me know." Kayla grinned. "I get to use this Avatar four times a year for the next five years. The YRD was really lucky to get the grant. Without it, we couldn't place these gauges. In three months, I'll be back to check on them, and you can come with me."

When Kayla got to the old Wabasso campground, she climbed up to the viewpoint and gave her audience a view of the stark peaks, the washed-out highway, and the tangled piles of snags the last flood had deposited on the flats.

What happened to the highway?

It was the perfect question at the perfect time.

"Mother Nature, that's what. The climate on the eastern slopes of the Rockies used to be unusually stable and predictable, and in these steep valleys, flooding was brief and highly contained. No more. A catastrophic flood washed out the highway. A new climatic regime is taking hold. The river is changing. It's my job to learn how we can live with it."

The gauge site at kilometer ten was just below Athabasca Falls. Once, it had been a class five cataract and one of the most powerful waterfalls in the Canadian Rockies. Now it was...not a trickle, exactly. There was still enough water to drown in, and enough velocity to sweep her off her feet.

Kayla stepped into the weighted boots that a drone had dropped on the riverbank, then walked slowly through the white water, admiring the sheer limestone walls that held the falls in a close embrace. The mighty flow had hewn a rock channel six school busses wide and eight high, creating a gorge that clawed its way through geological time, with a roar you still had to shout to be heard over, even with the dramatically reduced flow.

"Athabasca Falls. Impressive skookumchuck, isn't it?"

Social media pulsed in the affirmative. Her numbers swelled to twenty thousand, the feed streaming to classrooms and lecture halls all over the province.

Kayla rattled off some basic geology for the kids. After placing the gauge, she waded right up to the falls, so close the droplets stung her face. Here, she was part of the ecosystem, like the old photo of a grizzly standing in the rapids, jaws gaping, a startled salmon flying into its maw.

"Take a good look," Kayla said. "From here, things are going to change."

She ditched the weighted boots and ran to her next gauge location at the head of the falls. What had once been a broad stretch of white water was now one deep, narrow channel, excavated two years back by a contractor Kayla had hired.

Oh my god.

What happened here?

Horrid. Just horrid.

Who did this?

The shocked exclamations came as no surprise. It was ugly—so ugly it pained Kayla to look at it. Thick walls of medical-grade acrylic lined the sides of the artificial channel, dividing the water from the speed lichen that furred the dry riverbed. Drone bots hovered overhead, closely monitoring the lichens' spread.

Kayla had pre-recorded a twenty-minute media package that explained the reasoning behind the excavation, carefully laying out the long term plan, and—of course—thanking the funding bodies that had made the expensive project possible. She fired the package at the social media feed, then slipped on a thick layer of lichen. Kayla gasped as the Avatar lurched sideways, then quickly righted itself.

Kayla's DMs pulsed.

Is this still the best day of your life? Natalie whispered.

Kayla grimaced and shuffled slowly to the edge of the falls, where the water took its first plunge. She hefted a gauge over the acrylic berm and slipped it into place.

This channel was necessary. And it's nothing compared to what Edmonton did to this watershed.

You don't have to tell me, Natalie whispered.

Adaptive management is a long-term, iterative process.

I've heard it. Tell them.

The numbers were falling off of her feed. The people who stayed demanded answers. She told her fake to pick a question.

Do you feel guilty, knowing you did this to the river?

"No. The communities along the Athabasca River have healthier water than they would otherwise. This artificial channel is the best strategy we've found to keep the speed lichen toxins at minimum."

I think this is a catastrophe. Don't you?

"The original catastrophe was the flow diversion into the North Saskatchewan. But that's the way the vote went and what's done is done. Our challenge now is to manage the watershed. This is a long-term adaptive management project, with a lot of unknowns. We deal with uncertainty by constantly monitoring and adjusting our approaches."

How long is long-term?

"We won't see results for years. Probably decades."

How did you vote in the referendum?

That question again. Kayla slapped it down, and shot a logic correction at her fake.

Can't you get rid of the lichen?

Complicated question, too complicated. Kayla stammered a reply. She wasn't feeling great. The backache gripped her abdomen, her torso from ribs down vise-clamped and aching.

She put the questions on hold and opened the DM feed.

Okay. I'm having cramps.

Thank god, Natalie whispered. *I was so worried. I was just about to pull the plug on this Avatar thing.*

Don't you dare!

Kayla leaned over the berm and shoved her gauge into the riverbed with all her strength.

Don't you dare pull me out of this, she repeated. *I'm serious, Nat. I'll never forgive you. Ever.*

You don't get it, do you? Natalie said. *This is the best day of my life, too. And you're not here. Your body is, but you're far away.*

I have to do this.

Save it. Soon, this is going to get serious and you'll have to pay attention to what's going on with your body. You won't have a choice.

Kayla slapped down the social media feed—public feed, DMs, and all. To hell with them.

She stomped uphill to her second drone drop site by the highway, and tore the package open. Inside were another thirty gauges and a hundred sample bags. She stuffed them in her pack and headed back down to the river.

Low flow wasn't the only threat in the watershed—maybe not even the worst. New and invasive species were also a problem, and speed lichen the worst of all. When it was first discovered in the Ob River watershed in Siberia, the worldwide scientific community pooh-poohed the evidence. When it colonized the upper reaches of China's Yellow River, they'd tsk-tsked—clearly the Chinese had done something wrong. But when it was found in the Colorado River, climbing the storied walls of the Grand Canyon, marring its sunset-shaded elegance with a furry gray-green blight, only then had it been declared an emergency.

Still, there were so many emergencies.

Kayla filled sample bags at her first ten randomly-chosen sites. The rhythm of sterilize-grab-stuff-seal-store calmed her down, and she addressed her feed again.

"I'm gathering speed lichen samples for one of our research partners at the University of Alberta. So little is known about this organism, but in less than ten years, it's colonized nearly two-point-five percent of the Northern Hemisphere's temperate terrain. That might not sound like a lot, but trust me. It is."

She knelt at a sample site where the lichen covered the rocks like layers of puff pastry. She coated her hands in sterilizer, and then gently pulled up a handful of lichen along with the rock it clung to. She slipped it in a sample bag.

Is this lichen the same species as the first samples gathered in Russia and China?

Kayla bit back her instinct to admit ignorance. She didn't know. Nobody did. But she couldn't say that, not when funding was at stake.

"When we discuss lichen, we're not just talking about one species. It's a complex of microorganisms. In the past, lichen have been characterized by extraordinarily slow metabolisms. These new ones aren't like that. They're fast. Profoundly fast for a plant."

A cramp plunged through Kayla's gut, so strong she had to bend over and groan. She counted the duration—one Mississippi, two Mississippi, all the way to eleven. When the pain subsided, she grabbed her stopwatch app and hit start.

Two part question: Will the lichen move to the North Saskatchewan watershed, and if so, what will happen to Edmonton's water supply?

Kayla gasped, still reeling from the cramp.

"I don't know," she blurted, and then quickly backtracked. "North Saskatchewan watershed managers are extremely vigilant. Yes, speed lichen can jump from watershed to watershed, but don't worry. They'll make sure it doesn't."

Not good enough. The feed bristled with emojis, thousands of pairs of cartoon eyes staring at her in alarm. She mouthed a few platitudes and then fell silent. In some cases, the less said the better. She couldn't speak for the NoSask managers, after all.

Kayla filled eighteen sample bags before another cramp tore into her. This time the pain was so intense she couldn't even count. When she came back to herself, she was on her knees by the shallow upper Athabascan trickle, hemmed in on either side by the lichen's fruitcose fronds.

No more chatting, just sampling. Seventeen bags later, another cramp. Then twenty. They weren't getting closer. Maybe she had time—maybe. But they were agonizing. Her pulse pounded, her hands shook.

Kayla slapped open her DMs.

This is not my fault, she whined.

Okay, Natalie said. *What's not your fault?*

Forget it, Kayla said, and slapped down the feed.

It wasn't her fault the province had voted to divert eighty percent of the upper Athabasca watershed's flow into the North Saskatchewan. The choice had been simple—either you provided enough water for two million people, or you didn't. In comparison, the Athabasca was under-allocated, serving fewer than two hundred thousand people. Of course the diversion was a catastrophe for the Athabasca, but it had been the right choice.

Another cramp stabbed Kayla's gut. She bent double and groaned, and a slick petty impulse floated into focus.

She would stay in the Avatar for as long as she could. She'd finish installing the gauges, then do some extra surveying all through the night until her full twenty-four hours were up. Whatever was happening to her body, it could happen without her. She could do it, easy. Just like a marathon gaming session.

Kayla got her hundred samples. She lugged them to the drop site, and sealed them into the sterile duffle. Later, a drone would pick them up and deliver them to Kayla's research partner, who would use the samples to map the organism's mutualistic relationships.

She hiked up the riverbed, stopping at regular intervals to breathe through the cramps, and planted gauges in the narrowing Athabasca until the river ran dry. Then she retraced her steps to the confluence with the Sunwapta, and followed that flow until it died. She ignored her social media feed. When the cramps hit, she didn't even bother to time them.

Then they started coming on in waves. One every minute, or more, so many she couldn't walk. A help message in multiple languages floated across her eye, repeated by soothing audio in English, French, and Blackfoot.

If you find yourself fatigued, engage the Avatar's auto-guidance controls. Click the icon or say "Yes."

"Yes," she groaned. The target in the middle of her eye misted away. As the Avatar straightened, Kayla felt a disconcerting sense of bodily disjunction. She was helpless, bent double in pain, and at the same time, she walked up the riverbed, brandishing a gauge like a spear.

Kayla slapped open her DMs.

Goddamn it, Nat.

Does it hurt, honey? Natalie's voice dripped with sympathy, which made Kayla angrier.

I want that epidural, she demanded. *Now.*

Sure. We're ready, Natalie said in the gentlest of tones. *Are you going to join us here?*

God, no. That's the last place I want to be.

Okay, you're in charge. But think carefully. Do you really want to miss this?

Having a baby was important to Natalie. She'd told Kayla that on their first date. Six months later, Kayla was so deeply in love she'd agreed to carry it. She hadn't even considered how that one decision would devastate her life.

Fuck you, Nat, Kayla moaned. *Fuck you.*

I'd take the pain in a second if I could.

No, you wouldn't.

I love you, my sweet girl. Here comes the needle.

A cold and blissful numbness descended over Kayla's flesh. From the ribs down, nothing. She was a head, arms, and a bit of torso, and yet her legs guided her up the river, stepping around snags and over boulders, avoiding the patches of fruiting lichen, thick with spores.

The release from pain was so delectable, Kayla laughed.

A hundred meters downstream, a lone barren-ground caribou lifted its head to gaze at her, then stepped its stick-thin legs delicately onto the riverbed and lipped at the lichen.

Kayla pinged the caribou's RFID, which identified it as part of a study group monitored by the University of Tuktoyaktuk. The elegant, splay-antlered cow had migrated more than a thousand kilometers southwest over the past year.

"Have you outcompeted the locals?" Kayla laughed again. "At least somebody's getting some benefit out of this goddamned lichen."

The RFID reported the caribou cow was gravid.

"Why did you get pregnant?" Kayla shouted. "Don't you know the world is ending?"

Kayla pinched off a minute of visuals and complementary time-and-location metadata. She tossed it to her fake and instructed it to send the data to the Caribou research group at Tuk-U.

One more gauge to go. Kayla turned her social media feed to *Live*.

"Okay, more questions. Hit me."

How did you vote in the referendum?

Someone had hacked her fake. That was the only explanation. But it was an important question; one of the most critical of the past decade.

"I don't have to answer that. But I will, as long as you all understand my personal political choices do not reflect the official policy of the Yellowhead Regional District."

The feed ripped with nodding emojis.

Kayla stood in a ribbon of water hardly deep enough to cover her feet. The mountains enveloping her looked taller than when she was a child. Then, they'd been pine-green halfway to the sky. Now they were bare and brown.

"Even though I live in Hinton, I voted to divert the Athabasca headwaters into the North Saskatchewan. I did it because Edmonton is a big city and it was in crisis. I have friends there. Family. But still, it was a really hard choice."

She told her fake to choose one last question.

Why?

"It's no use pretending the world hasn't changed. It changes all the time. Every choice we make, every person we meet, has the potential to transform our lives. When that happens, we adapt. Manage. Cope."

Kayla shoved the last gauge into the trickling river. The motor drive whirred.

"I'm having a baby."

Forty-one weeks into her pregnancy, and she'd never said those words aloud before. When Natalie broke the news to everyone, Kayla pretended it didn't have anything to do with her.

"I'm having a baby," she repeated. "It's the biggest leap of faith a human can take. And I'm doing it because I believe humanity has a future. We are capable of undoing the damage we've caused. Maybe not all of it, but some. We can make better choices in the future, with careful, flexible long-term planning."

She opened her DMs so Natalie could hear her.

"Our child's world might not be as beautiful as our past, but it'll have glories we can't even imagine."

With that, she walked up to the broken highway, set Avatar in *Wait* mode, and left to meet her future.

NOTES ABOUT "TWO WATERSHEDS"

In 2019, Ann VanderMeer kindly invited me to contribute a story to the *Avatars Inc.* anthology, organized by XPRIZE Foundation to provide fictionalized use cases for telepresence technology. I knew right away that I wanted to write another story set in the area I grew up in, the Athabasca River Valley in and around Jasper National Park.

Why do some places get written about over and over again, when others never do? Each year, hundreds of novels are set in London, Paris, New York, San Francisco, but these are not the only places worth telling stories about. The land where I grew up never gets fictionalized, but it holds just as many dramatic possibilities as any other locale. It has just as much history and tragedy, and the residents live full lives just like anyone else.

In "Two Watersheds," I draw on fifteen years of experience working with restoration ecologists, along with this idea: If the people most intimate with a problem can find reasons to hope, there's no excuse for the rest of us to give up.

THE DESPERATE FLESH

THE KAREN KAIN CENTRE FOR CONVALESCENT CARE was generously endowed, rumor said, by a bisexual Rosedale matron who'd nursed a lifelong crush on the prima ballerina. When Margaret took the job as director, she tried to find out the mysterious benefactor's identity. Not to out her, of course, or even to share the juicy gossip among her friends, but to satisfy her burning curiosity. No go, though. The secret was buried under a tangle of trusts and numbered companies, and soon Margaret had too much work on her plate to keep digging.

She'd expected to be busy in her new job, but hadn't expected to face a scandal right away—and certainly not one that included flashing both geriatric and barely-legal flesh in the accessible seats in the opera house's dress circle, in front of thousands of white-haired opera fans.

The posters on Margaret's wall rattled as Betty and Pia shut the office door behind them. The black and white portrait of Karen Kain stared down from the back wall—strength, grace, power, and flexibility encapsulated in one simple gesture, a pair of hands laid on a flawless cheek as if in prayer. If anyone could help Margaret get through this day with dignity, it was her.

Saint Karen, help me now, Margaret thought. She took a deep breath and turned to face her two employees.

"The last time I checked, the opera house wasn't a nudist colony." Margaret tried to sound calm and graceful, keep her movements controlled yet relaxed, just like a dancer's. "Do you want to explain what happened?"

"Serena can move fast when she wants to," said Pia.

"We couldn't do anything," said Betty. "The overture was already playing."

"You didn't want to disturb the performance?" Margaret said. The two women nodded. "So I suppose your clothes just fell off, Betty?"

Betty raked her fingers through her thick pink hair. "I didn't want Serena to be the only one showing skin."

"Really? Because it seems like you came prepared."

Betty pulled down the collar of her cowgirl-patterned scrubs to reveal a scarlet pasty complete with a dangling tassel. Margaret winced as the sequins gleamed in the light of the overhead fluorescents. Wearing a costume piece under scrubs didn't do any harm, but it was so trashy. So tasteless.

"Just a coincidence." Betty tugged the tassel. "I'm trying out a new adhesive."

"So you weren't planning to strip during the opera?"

"It wasn't a tease. It was just nudity. I could show you the difference—"

"No." Margaret lurched to her feet. She steadied herself on her desk, tried to make the movement look natural. "I can't believe I have to say this, Betty. No stripping when you're on my clock. None."

Betty rolled her eyes. "Being naked isn't stripping. There's a difference."

Margaret stole a glance at the gorgeous calm form on the poster behind her, that paragon of strength and femininity, muscles sheathed in flawless flesh, and costumed in perfect harmony with taste and tradition. When she turned back to her employees, she tried to look generous, yet imperious.

"That's enough," she said, "you can go."

Betty slipped out. Pia lingered in the doorway.

"I don't blame you," Margaret said in a hushed voice. "Supervising staff isn't your responsibility."

Pia fingered her crucifix. "This isn't going to stop," she said.

It would have to stop, Margaret thought. Her entire career depended on it.

Karen Kain's mission was to house and care for Toronto's geriatric lesbian population. With only eighteen beds in a compact heritage mansion on the corner of Queen and University, Karen could hardly house them all, but the city also had Ivan Coyote house, a hundred-bed long-term care home on Church and King. Together, Karen and Ivan were the bulwark against scattering women to the far edges of the city to live side-by-side with old men who sprung semis when they heard the word lesbian.

The next incident happened at City Hall, just a few days later. When Margaret got the call, she peeled out the door, ran full out for three blocks, and staggered through Nathan Philips Square with a vicious stitch in her side. Out of shape; out of control. Once, Margaret had been a ballet dancer. Tireless, dedicated, unflappable. Now she was a mess. A mess in charge of a mess.

Margo, Titus, and Trinh sat on folding chairs in a quiet corner of the City Hall lobby, clothes crumpled underfoot, gray wool blankets draped over their bare shoulders. Betty stood beside them—clothed, thank goodness. A few steps away, Pia flirted in Spanish with a tall police officer whose duty belt fit snugly around ample hips. Pia's navy blue scrubs were the exact shade of the officer's uniform.

"I don't think there'll be a problem," Betty whispered to Margaret. "That cop is on our side."

"Mmm," said Titus. "Sure is."

Margo grinned and shrugged the blanket off her shoulders. A ray of sunlight highlighted her plummy areolas. Trinh dropped her blanket too. Margaret snatched the blankets from the floor, fumbled them, folded them into bulky wads. When she finished, she placed them across the two women's laps, covering their spare gray bushes. It wasn't much, but it would have to do. Titus lifted herself creakily from her chair, drew her blanket from beneath her butt, folded it herself, and settled back down with the fabric neatly draped across her bony thighs.

The officer glanced over, adjusted her sunglasses, and turned her attention back to Pia.

The elevator dinged. The General Manager of Long-Term Care pushed through the parting doors and stalked across the lobby, glaring at Margaret as he adjusted the already-perfect knot in his tie.

"The police might be on our side," said Margaret. "But the city isn't."

The city had never been on Karen Kain's side. They wanted the building for a museum, maybe a cultural center, anything but an old-age home for lesbians. Margaret's job was to change the city's mind.

Ivan Coyote house was a charmless brutalist structure from the 1960s; four stories on a quarter block of downtown real estate dwarfed by steel-and-glass multi-use towers. The city had squatted on the land for decades, waiting for developers to get desperate. Now the city had a sweetheart deal clutched in its greedy fist, and Ivan Coyote house faced demolition.

Sure, the development proposal promised space in the new building for long-term care. Three hundred beds, as long as the developer didn't find a loophole and renege on the commitment. But where would Ivan's residents go? Dispersed to the suburbs to be forgotten, that's where. The city would never dedicate a shiny new home to old lesbians. No, when Ivan died, the city would never resurrect her.

Margaret squeezed her butt into the chair opposite the General Manager's desk. It was an unforgivingly narrow seat, but she would have fit it with room to spare, once. Margaret checked the buttons of her cream silk blouse and smoothed her pencil skirt over her thighs. On the outside, she was perfect. A tiny bit fleshy, but plenty of former dancers broadened out. On the inside, well, it was obvious the manager could see right through to the fraud she was. The manager took his time settling himself in his big, black leather master-of-the-universe chair.

"I know what you're trying to do, Margaret," he said, finally. "And I can't believe you'd use your residents as pawns."

Margaret's breath left her in a puff, half-laughing from shock. "I don't have anything to do with this."

"You're trying to attract media attention."

"Attention for what? The residents came to visit the library. City Hall is our local branch."

"One of your staff is a stripper."

"Betty's a dancer—a burlesque artist. Let me see the security vid."

The manager slapped his laptop lid shut.

"The Ivan Coyote redevelopment is going forward. The final vote happens on Friday. Lose the pink haired girl and keep out of the media, or I'll have you shut down."

Margaret squeezed forward, perching on the edge of her too-small chair. "You can't shut Karen Kain down. We own the building—"

"If you try to block us," he interrupted. "The heritage department will review your building's appropriate-use status. Keeping a historic building in private hands is a waste. It's a city treasure."

Arguments whirled through Margaret's mind, but there was no point saying anything before consulting Karen Kain's lawyer. She bit her lip until the manager's power trip ran out of juice. She reassembled her dignity in the elevator and took her women home for lunch.

Karen Kain's lawyer was an alarmingly hairy trans man with a gleaming smile behind an abundant raven-black beard. More hair poked out from between his shirt buttons and from under his cuffs. If David dropped his clothes in the middle of City Hall, Margaret thought, nothing would play peek-a-boo.

Nudity *per se* didn't bother Margaret. She'd spent years in crowded dressing rooms filled with sweaty dancers. Those were perfect bodies, though. Perfect like hers had been, once. Graceful, toned, hairless, elegant.

"Don't worry," David said. "Nothing can touch Karen Kain."

"It's not just the appropriate use review," Margaret said. "The residents have been acting up, and the manager said he could have us investigated for abuse. He could get our license yanked."

David laughed. “I’d like to see him try. We could hit the city with a dozen lawsuits. The billable hours would be massive.”

Margaret stared. He laughed again and patted her hand. “It’s okay. Trust me. Karen’s fine. Too bad about Ivan Coyote, though. I wish I could do something for her.”

“Can’t you?”

“There’s no point. The city always planned to redevelop the lot. That’s why they never properly maintained the building.” He looked thoughtful. “And if you think about it, that’s the only reason Ivan exists in the first place. Lesbians have little economic power and no political pull. They’re easy to uproot.”

Margaret nodded. She’d quit ballet so she wouldn’t have to face growing old in poverty. Many of the other dancers had husbands to bankroll their art. Margaret’s few love affairs had been with other lesbian artists—a muscled sculptor who eked out a living as a community college sessional instructor, a spoken-word poet who cleaned offices on the graveyard shift, a photographer who worked in a day care. No savings, no pension; just one run of bad luck away from homelessness.

Ivan was filled with women just like Margaret’s old lovers, women who’d thumbed their noses at fate for decades in the name of rejecting patriarchy and not buying into the status quo. And now their last bulwark was about to fall. Ivan was just a charmless concrete slab—leaky, drafty, and remarkably energy-inefficient. Nobody would fight for her. But she was filled with women who would disappear if scattered. Who would fight for them?

Not Margaret. She’d made her choices, and she knew better than to fight a losing battle.

"You said no stripping on your clock," Betty said. "I'm on the clock, and I've got all my clothes on."

Betty's scrubs were patterned with 1960s pulp covers: teased bouffants and scarlet pouts above missile-shaped foundation garments. They disturbed Margaret, deeply. Not because of the inane titles (*She Wanted It*; *Babes Behind Bars*; *Trash Talking Tramps*) but because the models looked quite a bit like her mother.

Behind Betty, all the residents were crowded into the common room. Elsie posed in front of the fireplace, delicately shrugging the straps of a pink negligee off her age-spotted shoulder. The wattles of her upper arms quivered; her pursed mouth disappeared in a pucker of wrinkles. When Elsie's clothes finally dropped, pasties festooned with rhinestone pills dripped from the tips of her pendulous breasts.

One of the oldest residents was recording the show on her iPhone—probably live streaming direct to Facebook.

Margaret cradled her head in her hands. She could see the lawsuits on the horizon already.

Betty would have to go. She was a disturbance Margaret couldn't afford to tolerate. But when she called Betty into her office, Pia came too.

"Before you say anything, please let me speak." Pia looked over Margaret's head at Karen Kain, as if gathering courage. "I grew up in the Philippines, and I learned early on that women who love women have to be invisible."

Betty nodded. "Protective coloration."

"If I act just like everyone else," Pia added, "I can't be mistreated for who I am. But I'm not like everyone else. If I pretend to be what I'm not, who am I?"

"Pia," Margaret said. "This isn't appropriate. I need to talk to Betty in private."

"Betty's done nothing wrong. All she's done is be herself." Pia smoothed the front of her chrysanthemum-patterned scrubs. Then she reached out and took Betty's hand. "At some point, we must protect the people who are like us."

"Pia, it's not—"

"I know. It's not my responsibility to supervise the other staff members. But I've been here longer than anyone. If you fire Betty, I'll leave too. And I'll take all the staff with me."

After Pia and Betty left the office, Margaret stared up at the poster of Karen Kain for a solid twenty minutes. *What would Karen Kain do?* Dance, of course. But dancing wouldn't help, not here, not now, not ever.

Words were the only weapon in Margaret's arsenal. She pulled out her favorite fountain pen and several sheets of creamy rag paper and began to write.

Margaret fumed as she sat in the City Council visitor's gallery. The final hearing on the fate of Ivan Coyote house was the concluding item on a long agenda. The vote wouldn't happen until the early hours of Saturday morning. Of course, the city would schedule it at the end of a long session when everyone had gone home. Margaret would have to wait all night to make her speech. But would it even matter? She could speechify all she liked, but it wouldn't do any good if nobody was there to listen.

Margaret was wearing her best suit—the one she'd worn to her final interview with Karen Kain's board of directors. A tailored two-piece in gray wool: staid, responsible, and feminine.

It said: "You can trust me with your multi-million dollar charitable foundation. I'm not going to do anything weird."

Protective coloration. Looking at Margaret now, who would guess what was really in her heart—how desperate she was, and how much she cared?

The General Manager of Long-term Care was sitting a few rows ahead of her, the lights gleaming off a patch of shiny scalp barely concealed under a few strands of carefully combed, thinning hair. Margaret toyed with a tin of mints. The urge to toss them at him was nearly unbearable. She could hit his bald spot, easy, one by one. Embarrass him in public. He deserved it.

Margaret laughed to herself. *What would Karen Kain do?* Definitely not throw candy at a bureaucrat. High school tactics wouldn't get her far in life.

Opposite the visitor's section, the tiny media gallery emptied as the night wore on. At half past midnight, the council was still droning over a routine parks board report, and the last few journalists were packing up their laptops.

Ivan Coyote house was dead.

There was only one thing left to do.

Margaret shook the tin of mints. The loud rattle turned all the heads in the visitor's section. She shook them louder. Loud enough to be heard by the media gallery. The journalists paused for a moment, then went back to packing their laptop bags. She stood and stepped gracefully onto the seat of her chair. The spike heels of her black leather pumps sunk into the padding, but Margaret was a dancer; she could perform on any stage.

The persistent rhythm of the mint tin rattle provided a compelling beat as Margaret flicked open the buttons of her high-necked blouse and slid the long sleeves down her arms.

Her body wasn't perfect anymore, but it didn't matter. All eyes were on her, and there was no denying it: The clothes were coming off.

NOTES ABOUT "THE DESPERATE FLESH"

I wrote "The Desperate Flesh" after the 2016 US election, at the invitation of editor Anna Yeatts for the Kickstarter anthology *Nasty: Fetish Fights Back*. This is the first of a three-story cycle set in Toronto, which all draw on the experiences of my friends in the theater and burlesque communities. Though "The Desperate Flesh" isn't SF, the two stories that grew out of it certainly are. "Alias Space" and "Skin City" follow.

"The Desperate Flesh" also reflects one of my core anxieties: that when I am old and unable to care for myself, I might have no option but to live in a long-term care home where, as an elderly queer woman, I would be at risk, considered an outsider and a target. So I took Campbell House, a favorite building from my Toronto neighborhood, and turned it into an old folks home for lesbians. Problem solved.

ALIAS SPACE

WHEN NELLIE LEFT TORONTO, AGNES KNEW SHE'D have to fight to keep her troupe together. Agnes would never quit—she'd dance with her friends all the way to long-term care—but Cat and Susanna were both restless. That's why, when the three of them hugged Nellie goodbye in the middle of the street, Agnes couldn't let go. When it started to rain, Nellie pulled herself out of their arms and lunged up the steps of her boyfriend's vintage motorhome. The door hissed shut.

"Twenty years," Cat said. Never one to keep quiet about her pain, she'd been wailing all morning.

"Honey, we know," said Susanna with some heat. "You don't have to keep saying."

Twenty years, Agnes thought. Rain trickled down her face, acrid with run-off from her hair spray. *I want twenty more.*

The motorhome lumbered silently down the street, tree boughs grazing its rusty roof. Maybe Nellie waved goodbye, maybe not. Impossible to see through the tinted windows. The last thing they saw were the stickers on the bumper:

FREE LIVE FREE
SEE YA TO-RENT-O
SURVEILLANCE=DEATH.

Rain poured, not individual drops anymore, but sheets of water buffeted by the wind. By the time they got to the subway station, Agnes, Cat, and Susanna were soaked through. They left puddles in the station's hygiene chute. As they bathed in the blue light of the disinfector, Agnes examined her friends. Though Cat had brought the drama all morning, now she looked fine. But Susanna's face was puffy, nose and eyes red, stoic façade cracking.

On the train, Agnes led them to a family seat and draped her arm around Susanna's shoulders.

"You okay?"

"Nell's gonna be miserable," she said. "What'll she even do up north?"

"Whatever she wants, I imagine," Agnes replied. "I'm betting she'll check in with us a lot."

"Only when her privacy freak boyfriend finds a public connection he can encrypt. How often is that going to happen?"

"She'll keep designing costumes," Cat said. "She's not giving that up. She promised."

"The motorhome is full of junk," said Susanna. "She'll have no room to prototype."

Agnes gathered Cat into the snuggle. She laid her head on Agnes' shoulder, boneless and unresisting as a sleepy baby.

Halfway down the subway car, a white woman with flat blonde hair switched seats. Maybe she wanted some space, or more likely a better view. She stared at them over her corporate-blue mask.

The blonde woman fired a pointer arrow at the *FAMILY SEATS* label over Agnes's head and another at the *NO TOUCHING* sign over the doors. The pointers were freeware, no style, zero customization. But now that the woman had made first contact, nobody could fault Agnes for spamming her.

Timing was everything. She waited until the woman relaxed slightly, thirty seconds, forty. Then Agnes shot a promo streamer at her.

ALIAS SPACE
Toronto's Favorite CanuckleNerd Burlesque

Featuring:
Susanna Moonie
Nellie McCling
Catharine Bar-Trail
Agnes MacFlail

The History Nerdlesque shows you never knew you needed...
And now you can't live without

The woman jumped, eyes like ping pong balls above her mask. She slapped Agnes with a block, which was fine. Blocks went both ways. If the woman didn't want to get spammed, she had to give up playing behavior cop.

The promo streamer bounced around the subway car. Nellie had given it a revamp just a few weeks back and it was gorgeous, with neon lettering and fresh vid clips. Spam-Agnes in a marcelled wig and granny glasses blew a kiss. Spam-Cat in widow's weeds ripped off her lace cap and flipped her hair. Spam-Susanna in skimpy skirts let a foam axe fly at a prop tree, unleashing a sparkling swarm of cartoon bees. And Nellie. Nellie with a saucy grin peeled off her lace cuffs and tossed them.

The spam cuffs landed in Agnes's lap and dissolved into a bookmark, which the spam target could save or snooze or ignore as they pleased. Agnes had the powerful urge to clutch the bookmark to her bosom, as if it were Nellie herself, but that would mean letting go of Cat and Susanna. She watched the bookmark sparkle until it dissolved.

A lesson in that, she told herself sternly. Pointless to hang on to something that's gone.

TOWER OF CARS
Park in the places where you used to play

"I'm sorry your friend left, but I don't get why you're upset. I mean, with the way you girls live, shouldn't you be happy she found a man? Traditional values and all that."

Overcommunicate. That was one of the key tenets of Agnes' day job. For her manager, that meant long Monday morning chats. Usually, Agnes didn't mind oversharing. She was pretty comfortable being an open book. But it didn't mean her manager understood the difference between aesthetics and social traditionalism, no matter how often Agnes explained.

"But three still makes a troupe, right?" Her manager leaned into the chat window and beamed.

Maybe, Agnes thought.

Agnes had worked at Tower of Cars almost as long as she'd been dancing. She'd started out supervising parking violation bots, back before Toronto outlawed street parking, and tap-danced her way into new roles as the company responded to changes in city policies and bylaws. Now she managed a deluxe garage stack in the base of the CN Tower, and made sure the car daddies didn't have to wait more than a minute for their beloved vintage vehicles to appear at the doors of their financial district offices.

Tower of Cars was one of the last bastions of Toronto car culture. Even though the city charged a fortune for private car permits, lawyers, traders, and analysts were still coming downtown to preen and display, and wanted to do it in style. Agnes figured her job was one of the safest in the city.

"Do you want to talk about it?" her manager prompted.

Agnes dredged up a smile.

"Change is hard." She patted her hair, adjusting the artful 'do she'd sculpted that morning. "But I'll roll with it."

"That's great, because I need you to tap you in on a sales lunch."

"Can do," Agnes said.

Technically, she didn't do sales, but Tower's suits-and-buttons staff often trotted her out at events and parties, taking advantage of her space age girly-Q aesthetic whenever they felt like the company could use a little pizzazz. *This is our deluxe package stack manager. Who could say no to this kind of value-add?*

"It's a cold call that won't go away," her manager said. "They've been hounding me for days. Enjoy the free lunch but don't give them any reason to hope."

Agnes spent the rest of her morning battling a supply chain problem. Tower's maintenance bots couldn't quite reach some spots on the vintage cars—the sinuous hood of the Corvette Stingray specifically—and the software patch that had fixed the problem two months back had been overwritten in a firmware update. Luckily, Agnes only had one Corvette at the moment. Its car daddy was a litigator who worshipped his service contract like gospel. One under-buffing and he'd be screaming at Tower's ombudsperson, so Agnes solved the situation towing the car to her underground kiosk and polishing it by hand.

The Corvette's nanny bot zeroed in on her butt as she leaned over the hood. The car daddy was watching, so Agnes took her time, gave him a free show in her pink-and-white pedal pushers and cherry sling-backs. A little bump and grind cheered her up. Took her mind off Nellie. And it was a genuine pleasure because the car was gorgeous. Too bad her NDA kept her from trapping vid.

When she was done, she summoned a hygiene bot to bathe the Corvette in blue light. Then she patted the towbot and sent the car back to its stack. When she returned to her desk, she filed a support ticket and requested a new software patch, but that could take weeks. Until then, she'd polish the Corvette daily.

It wasn't the worst problem to have, or the most difficult situation she'd ever solved, not by far. Bots couldn't be expected to do everything on vintage cars, the shapes and details were too unique. A few years back, when the car daddies had developed a yen for baby moon hubcaps and whitewall tires, Agnes had spent hours cleaning up after the bots, fixing the spots they'd missed. Compared to that, a little polishing was nothing.

When she left for lunch, she was a bit rumpled and smelled of lemon WhizWax, but her winged eyeliner was perfect, hair freshly sprayed. With her Tower-branded bomber jacket draped casually around her shoulders and a kissy-face mask, she was a picture. If it weren't for Nellie, she'd have felt as good as she looked. But maybe lunch would distract her. A little frisson, maybe some flirting.

Unfortunately, the pair of salespeople who appeared on the booth's high-res screen were blander than vat steak. Mason and Avery, sitting stiffly side by side, blue suits buttoned to the jaw. The drinks in front of them looked like ice water.

"We're so happy to finally meet you, Agnes," said Avery. "You're our Holy Grail."

"Tower of Cars is a giant in your industry," said Mason.

Agnes settled against the booth's velvet upholstery. A barbot dropped off her drink—Tom Collins with extra cherries.

"Your company performs like a champ."

"We've got a great service model," Agnes said. "Nothing tops the personal touch."

"Exactly," Avery said. "Everyone wants to be you."

Agnes checked the garage stack dashboard. It was performing optimally; no sticky problems to troubleshoot. Maybe she could finish off the afternoon here, have another drink after the salespeople left, and stagger back to wave goodbye as the car daddies summoned their babies home. Hadn't she earned a break?

Mason and Avery's ties were tight as nooses around their throats. They might be stiff, but they looked far too engaged, like they expected something from her. Maybe Agnes should break the news that she had zero signing power? No, not until she'd ordered dessert.

"How do you feel about your current towbot fleet?" Mason asked.

"I love my bots," Agnes wiped a trace of lipstick off the edge of her frosty coupe glass. "Without them, I'd be nowhere."

"They have no style, though," said Avery. "Towbots are just slabs that pull things. They don't do anything else for you."

Agnes plucked a cherry from her glass and toyed with the stem.

"I don't know if they have to do anything else. Parking cars isn't rocket science."

Mason laughed. Had she said something funny?

"Tower of Cars is always at risk of losing clients to the convenience of the self-driving fleet. You have to work to keep Joe Trader and Jack Attorney zeroing out their credit on vintage cars."

"Exclusivity will always be sexy to a certain type of person," she said.

The two salespeople beamed, their smiles headlight-bright, but cold. Lupine. Or maybe that was just Agnes' mood. The world without Nellie gone glacial.

"Sexy. Exactly. What if Tower of Cars could extend your kind of personal touch throughout the stack?"

"Mmm hmm," Agnes agreed. "Sounds great."

She drank her Tom Collins, ate her steak, and pretended to be interested as they peppered her with words like synergy, affordances, integration. By the time her Crêpes Suzette arrived, Agnes still wasn't sure what they were selling. Upgraded bots, obviously, and sure, that would be nice.

"I wouldn't say no to better bots," she said.

Mason and Avrey both smirked. She knew what they were saying to each other: *I bet she doesn't say no to anything.* Now was the time to let them down easy.

"Purchasing will want to see return-on-investment analyses. That has nothing to do with me."

"Don't count yourself out," said Avery. "Adoption starts at the customer-service interface, and that's all you, Agnes. You're the star of the show."

It is a truth universally acknowledged that a burlesque troupe grieving for a lost member must return to the site of their last performance.

Agnes took the girls to the fancy pod-bar next to the Art Gallery of Ontario. Drinks only a tourist from Vancouver or Cape Breton could afford, but she had a little room on her credit, and this was medicine. No memories to claw at them, no wounds to open. They could huddle in a privacy pod, bleed their hurt into a puddle on the floor, then leave and never come back. That was Agnes' plan.

Only problem was, Cat and Susanna were fine. Cheery, even. Excited by a rumor that the US might offer free tourist visas in the summer, chattering about the possibility of scoring a flight on Trash Panda Air.

"A long weekend of sun and sand would be perfect," said Susanna. "I would murder to get out of the city. Maybe I'll hang a shingle on Barterbot. Cute Kills for Frequent Flyer Points."

"Don't say things like that," Agnes murmured, but it was just a reflex. She'd paid for privacy, but she'd been planning for a heart-to-heart, not morbid jokes.

"Sounds nice. Flight lotto is a scam, though," said Cat.

Susanna fired Trash Panda's lottery app across the table. She paged through it, walking her fingers across the tabletop, rhinestone-studded nails flashing.

"Myrtle Beach has great odds," she said.

"That's because they made those dikes out of cotton candy and stucco," Cat said. "The coast is gone in the next category three."

"Atlantic City?"

"If your idea of sun and sand is a plexi-pod on stilts."

"Cape Breton?"

Cat wiped the app off the table. "Did you get an inheritance you didn't tell us about?"

"Go ahead, buy a ticket," said Agnes. "Lotteries are a license to dream."

Susanna knocked back the dregs of her watermelon martini and grinned. She fired up the app again and paged through to Trash Panda's *World At Your Feet* lottery. Cheap, but sky-high odds, and the winner accepted whatever destination they got. Even Orlando, its soggy airport surrounded by levees.

Susanna bought a threesome ticket. Three. After only one day, Nellie was already out of the picture. Agnes put her elbows on the table and lowered her forehead to the heels of her hands, but only for a moment. If she wanted to get sloppy, she'd have to wait and find somewhere to do it solo.

She treated the girls to three drinks each and tried her best to be bubbly. That would have been the end of the night, but under the blue light in the bathroom, she snagged a last-minute entry window for the art gallery.

Well-lubricated, they sauntered next door and gravitated upstairs to the Henry Moores in the sculpture court, where they'd performed *Shelter* the previous week. Agnes knew she should stay away, but she couldn't. Maybe it was a law of nature.

Cat posed beside *Three Piece Reclining Figure No. 1* and threw her head back, mirroring its form. She'd dressed in High Victorian pathos, and with the sculptural lighting, the tubercular hollows under her eyes made her face spooky.

"*Shelter* was a great show," said Cat. "Our greatest."

"It was a lot of work to produce," said Agnes.

"Worth it, though." Susanna pulled Agnes in for a hug. "You're amazing."

Agnes relaxed into her friend's embrace, grateful for the comfort. She'd worked hard on *Shelter*. Two solid years of grant applications, proposals, auditions, rehearsals and meetings—endless meetings with the gallery curators. But the girls were right, the show had worked. Beneath the looming Henry Moores, in the dim and flickering light of a World War Two London air raid shelter, the four members of Alias Space had performed on a floor carpeted in bodies huddled under gray wool blankets. One by one, they'd broken out of their cocoons to commune with the sculptures, transforming from anonymous figures into living, breathing women who demanded—no, *grabbed* the audiences' attention, forcing them to recognize their sexuality, their individuality, their worth.

The show was getting backlash in Toronto's burlesque community, though. Complaints on all the feeds, mostly vague but some loud. Alias Space produced one of the most high profile shows the city has ever seen, but Agnes included only the members of their own troupe. It wasn't right. Shows should be inclusive, not exclusive. It set a bad example. And who cared about European history anyway? Canadian artists should do Canadian art.

"I should have expanded the show, booked more performers," Agnes said into Susanna's neck.

"People love to bitch and complain," said Cat.

"Stop beating yourself up, Ag," Susanna said. She squeezed Agnes hard, then let her go and pulled Cat away for a clinch. As her friends necked in the middle of Moore's *Two Large Forms*, Agnes wandered to the artist's studio display, a selection of twisted bones and broken driftwood under glass.

When the ten-minute bell rang for closing, Agnes was slumped on the bench in front of William Kurelek's "A

Ukrainian Canadian Prairie Tragedy." That painting, its stark flat snowy plain surrounding a cinder-soot smoking heap of what-once-had-been-a-house, that was where she lived now. A blasted landscape, bleak and comfortless. No Nellie. Susanna and Cat ready to run off on their own. And slings and arrows being fired at her from all directions.

"Closing time, Agnes," said Ashley, one of the docents, but he let her sit there until the last minute.

"I loved the show," he said as he escorted her to the elevator. "It was terrific."

She smiled and thanked him.

"Was it? I don't know," she said to herself when the door closed.

The bar bill zeroed out Agnes' credit but it didn't matter. Who cared about money when the world was falling apart?

Kitten Heel Floozy has Emotional Breakdown on Richmond Street

Getting to the weekend took every bit of sunny-side-up determination Agnes could muster. Usually she was a pretty agile troubleshooter, but Mason and Avery had been blizzarding her with spam for four days, destroying her concentration. Because she'd accepted the free lunch, it'd be weeks before she could block them.

Finally, she gave up and pinged them back.

"I'm so sorry," said Avery, and she did look sincerely regretful. "The spam schedule is controlled by the customer relations management algorithm."

"Okay," Agnes said. "Is there anything we can do to stop it?"

"All we have to do is move to the next stage of the sales process," said Mason, smoothly.

"Just agree to let us send you a sample," Avery added. "In a week we'll check in with you and get your feedback. No purchase obligation."

Agnes had no choice, but she was finally free from the hurricane of spam. She walked home feeling proud about surviving the week without alienating her manager, offending a client, or causing a bot pileup. Then she stepped on a subway ventilation grate and ripped off a heel.

The shoes were favorites—faux-fur pumps shaped like pouncing kittens—so even on the best of days she would have been upset. As it was, she planted herself beside a bed of roses in full view of every pedestrian, drone, and stationary camera on the block, and bawled her mask soppy.

The only thing that got her on her feet again was the thought of ending up as a lead article on BlogTO, with video clips from multiple angles, right under *Raccoon Hijacks Cop Drone* and *Toronto Named Vertical Orchard Capital of the World.*

She was forty. Undeniably an adult, with so many small business loans and lines of credit that her bank manager sent her a birthday card every year. But still, she couldn't let people go. Not without feeling as if they'd taken one of her organs with them.

She limped east on Queen Street, one leg four inches longer than the other. If Nellie could leave so easily, what kept Susanne and Cat from following? And why shouldn't they leave, if they wanted? It was inevitable they would, some day. If biological family wasn't a life sentence, chosen family wasn't, either.

Home was an old brick-and-beam retail space on Church Street. Rent through the roof but Agnes made it work. With the wide window frontage, live audiences could watch from the street when Alias Space trapped their shows.

A large package leaned outside the door. A black resin flat-pack, long as Agnes was tall. The glossy black logo on the lid seemed vaguely familiar.

Rain began to pockmark the package with raindrops. A tiny security bot buzzed in close to scan Agnes' eye, then scooted off to guard someone else's delivery. Agnes put her arms around the package and tried to lift it. It was heavy and awkward, just a bit too thick to get her hands around. Finally, she tucked it under her arm and dragged it inside, ripping the resin off the bottom edge. She tipped it onto its long end and pushed it through the studio's threshold. Susanna and Cat looked up from their workbenches.

"What's that?" said Susanna.

"I don't know. Something for work. A sales sample."

Agnes stripped off her sodden mask and let it fall to the floor. Cat pushed her rolling seat away from her sewing machine and looked the package up and down.

"Wow, that looks like the Skinless logo."

"A sex bot." Susanna's voice rose to a screech. "Really, Ag? You want to replace Nell with a bot?"

"It's for Tower of Cars. Listen..." But Agnes couldn't summon the energy for an explanation, much less an argument. She brandished her broken shoe. "I've had a really bad day."

"Yeah, you're a mess. Want some tea?" Cat didn't wait for an answer. She abandoned her workstation, where a waterfall of pink tulle spilled to the floor on its way to becoming a petticoat, and began filling the kettle.

Agnes dragged the package to her room and tipped it up to lean against the frosted room divider. Then she freshened her face and slipped into a pair of fluffy slippers. When she rejoined the girls, the package loomed behind the plexiglass like a tombstone. Cat and Susanna ignored it, and Agnes took their cue and ignored it, too.

If she had to get up in the middle of the night and move the package out of sight, it wasn't because the contents unnerved her. Bots were bots. Tools like any other.

Lucy Bot Montgomery
Margaret Botwood
Botty Sainte-Marie
Hayley Bottenheiser

When Agnes got up on Saturday, all her community feeds were roaring with gossip. The package had sat in front of the studio door long enough to fuel the rumor mill. A lot of the comments were vicious: Agnes MacFlail drained the royalties from *Shelter* to buy a sex bot, and Nellie McCling had objected, so the other three ran her out of town. Some were funny, including a long thread of bot stage names, but Agnes couldn't laugh.

After twenty years in the community, Agnes should have banked enough trust to keep the hyenas from ravaging her reputation. But no matter what she did, how many big shows she'd produced or fundraisers she'd organized, she couldn't make everyone happy. Someone always felt left out or overlooked. Agnes tried to let the criticism slide off her, but each barb stung.

So she fixed herself up, makeup casual but perfect, hair artfully undone, and trapped several versions of the same statement to post on the feeds.

I know it looks bad [disarming laugh] *but it's not a sex bot. It's a sales sample for my day job. Last time I checked, Tower of Cars isn't in the sex trade.* [graceful shrug] *Not quite sure why they sent it to the studio.* [kind smile] *But in any case, don't worry. I've been working hard on the next group show and I want it to be totally inclusive—slots for everyone who wants to perform.*

It wasn't quite a lie. Of course she was working on a new show—she always was. And she wanted to include everyone—oldies, newbies, casual dancers, fringe acts. That was always the plan in the early stages. Cuts would come later, when she had to give in to reality.

But now she'd said it in public, she'd have to make it happen somehow. Maybe a fundraiser marathon? That might work.

On Saturday mornings, Agnes taught a free fan-dance class to fifty students from Houston to Hangzhou, her image trapped by the cameras mounted in the corners of the studio. Each student was there for a different reason: curiosity, novelty, nostalgia. Some wanted to experiment with femme power, some were struggling to come to terms with their bodies, others were dancers stretching their skills. Agnes welcomed them all. Nobody could predict who might catch the burlesque bug, and new dancers kept the art alive.

The class was important to Agnes. So when Nellie pinged—finally, after nearly a week!—and the students were cooling down, Agnes didn't even consider ending class a few minutes early. She couldn't. She had to leave the students with an important message.

Agnes dropped her fans and let her breasts beam out across the world high res-and in real time.

"Let's talk about breasts," she told the students. "If you have them, you probably want to change them. Maybe even get rid of them. If you don't have them, maybe you want them something awful. Almost nobody is happy with what they have. Does this ring bells for anyone?"

A general affirmative across the stream. Emojis nodding, bells ringing, hearts flying.

"I'm glad." She gave her students a motherly smile. "Because they are pretty wonderful, aren't they? These little darlings are human life in a nutshell, or a coconut shell, or a couple of melons." Laughter and joy emojis from her students. "The great thing is, everyone is wearing them right over their hearts. Even if you've had surgery, like me. Even if you were assigned male at birth. Your breasts are right there."

She patted the side of her left breast and let it jiggle for a moment, then swatted her chest on the right, above her mastectomy scar.

"Is this where love happens?" she asked. "Or is it all in our heads? Philosophers can argue about it all they want, but I know one thing for sure. When you were a baby, you knew. Survival comes from the breast. This should be the most uncomplicated relationship in the world, but it's not. It's fraught."

She raised her fans and fixed the main camera with her most intense, most seductive stare. She moved toward them slowly, feinting, flirting.

"How can something," she intoned in rhythm with each footfall, "so basic to survival also be a focus of cultural obsession?" She paused and smiled demurely, fans quivering. "I'm not young. My body's not perfect. I have scars. But when I present myself in a certain way, people howl and drool." She smoothly switched her fans. "Some get upset and retreat behind their prejudices. Why? We all have skin."

One of her students piped up, a primary school teacher from the Philippines. The translation appeared in a word bubble: *They're scared of you.*

"I'm not sure. I'm pretty vulnerable when I'm doing this." She shimmied her fans; the feathers shivered. "These are hardly weapons."

Another word bubble, from a student in France: *Maybe not you, but what you represent.*

"What's that?"

Freedom, said a student in Newfoundland. *You look like you could fly away if you wanted to.*

No, they're frightened because they're confused, said a student in Nigeria. *They don't know what to think.*

"That's right. So when you're dancing, always know why you're doing it. If your purpose is clear in your own mind, the audience will take the hint—for at least as long as you're performing."

Agnes framed herself tight in the blank unblinking eye of the camera and drew the fan across her chest, revealing the worm-pink scar that still itched, after all these years.

"And remember, for as long as you're on stage, you're in control of the world. Nobody can ignore you."

Mayday, mayday, mayday
Toronto on the Street torpedoed by Canadian border closure

When Agnes joined the girls, Susanna was still giving Nellie a hard time.

"I'm not telling you to come home—"

"Oh really?" Nellie interrupted, her tone acid. "Thanks. Because I don't follow orders. I'm not a bot."

Nellie's video froze to a smear of brown and pink on a leaf-green background, with a disembodied finger jabbing at the camera. No matter. Agnes could picture Nellie in her mind. Fist on hip. Jaw thrust. Feet planted wide. Her favorite rainbow boa quivering with anger—no, not the boa. Nell had packed it up with the rest of her things, and left it all in a corner of the studio, the boxes piled like a ziggurat.

"All she's saying," Cat said in a gentle tone, "is you can't disappear for six days and not even ping us. We thought you'd been murdered."

"Oh, come on. Drama-drama-drama—"

Nellie's image stuttered and pixelated as the stream squeezed through a data bottleneck somewhere north of Kapuskasing. With one flick of her finger, Agnes could smooth out the image, let the app approximate her friend's facial expressions, but no. She might miss something, a flick of the eyelid or quirk of the lip that signaled—Agnes didn't know what—distress, confusion, anger, pain, even boredom. Something, anything that might indicate a route to getting Nellie back.

"Look at Agnes!" Susanna flung her hand at Agnes's cheekbone. "She's been a mess."

"I'm fine," Agnes said. "As long as you're happy, honey, that's all that matters."

"Are you happy, though?" asked Cat.

"Oh yeah." The image snapped into high-res as Nellie grinned wide. "You have no idea how peaceful it is to have absolutely nothing to do."

"Except cooking and cleaning?" Susanna asked, her tone vinegary.

"I don't clean and you know it." A scowl clouded Nellie's face but quickly cleared. "I'm not turning into Miss Canada 1955. Don't worry. Bob cooks."

She went on to extol the virtues of food made on an open fire. Fresh-caught rainbow trout slathered in foaming butter. Potatoes and onions wrapped in foil and slow-roasted under coals. Foraged berries washed down with cold air and primordial silence. And as long as that pastoral dream gleam lit her friend's eyes, Agnes knew better than to question her choices.

"We miss you," Agnes said.

"I miss you too," Nellie said.

"A week," said Susanna after they'd all blew their goodbye kisses. "I give her one more week before she's back, desperate with boredom."

"Five days," said Cat.

"No bet," said Agnes. "As long as she's safe and happy, I'm happy. You should be too."

Seeing Nellie lifted Agnes' mood. The past six days of worrying and wallowing seemed frivolous. Wasted time, wasted energy. She should have started working on the marathon show weeks back, began figuring out how to pull funding out of thin air.

The audience was there. Toronto's young population lived and worked in tiny condos. Five million people all looking for something exciting to do after work—get out of their own heads, prove the world was fabulous and scintillating and they were a part of making it that way.

When Agnes had started dancing, small dive bars could pack eighty people elbow-to-hip, and when the crowd cheered in such a small space, the noise was so fierce it popped ears to static. Those tiny bars hadn't been enough to match demand, not for the number of acts that wanted to perform, or for the audiences, either. Rooms sold out, but even so, troupes just scraped by. Big venues were the only way to produce a profitable show, but they cancelled burlesque bookings the moment they got a wink from a richer act. As a young producer, Agnes had been bitten by big rooms so many times she'd given up on them. Then social distancing changed the whole live performance ecosystem.

Now the glory days of crowded venues were a nostalgia trip, but Agnes remembered them clearly enough to know they were glorious only in retrospect. Crowded meant hot and sweaty in Toronto's humid summers, hot and sweaty carrying a parka during winter's deep freeze. It also meant no sight lines—which were so important to burlesque audiences. And in the little dive bars, only an acrobat could get the bartender's attention. For performers, the small rooms meant no amenities. If they were lucky, they'd use a toilet for a communal dressing room, but most of the time, they'd change behind a curtain at the back of the bar.

And maybe the bouncer would catch their stalkers on the way in. Usually not. So there was that, too. Never knowing what obsessed idiot was on the floor, or whether he was really violent or just annoying and scary—Agnes didn't miss that. So when she got into discussions about whether or not the good old days were really that good, Agnes always took the negative.

Sure, she'd love to throw a party for a hundred of her most passionate fans in some dark, sultry venue, where the proprietor was a spectacular trans business-woman who served drinks old-school and full-strength. But it couldn't happen. Those days were gone. Other days had come.

Days that looked like these: With Agnes lounging in bed on Saturday night, trying to ignore the sounds of Cat and

Susanna boning each other raw on the far side of the studio. Agnes' frilly pink comforter spilled over the side of the bed onto the still-sealed bot box, its glossy sheen signaling the exclusivity and expensiveness of the contents. Then a new post on the city's festival discussion boards caught her eye:

URGENT. Do you work with street performers? Next weekend's street performance festival full of holes. Ping me anytime day or night. Srsly.

The message was from Pilip, a producer Agnes knew, vaguely. Every year, the city put together artsy meet-and-greets, and Agnes often ended up in a corner with him, on the opposite side of the room from the theater and literature crowd. He was a juggler who couldn't keep his hands still, she was a burlyQ who specialized in history acts. They had nothing and everything in common.

"I've been working on this trick since I was six." Pilip had tossed a neon-pink ball into the air. He caught it on his nose, let it spin down to his forehead, then across one cheek to the other. With his lips, he bounced the ball high into the air and caught it on his heel. "Do you know how long it took me to learn tricks on a giraffe unicycle?"

"Not long?" she guessed.

"An afternoon. But the unicycle brings the tips. Or, it used to." He bounced the ball from his lips to brow, and back again. "How do you keep street art alive when nobody's on the street? If a ball drops on the concrete and nobody sees it, did it really happen?"

"We're all struggling to keep our audiences." Agnes glanced at the artistic director of the Canadian Opera Company, deep in conversation with the federal Minister of Culture and Canadian Heritage, their champagne glasses leaning toward each other as if magnetized. “Do you think he wants to keep programming *Cosi Fan Tutti* and *Carmen?* What he really wants to do is commission new work, revitalize opera as an art form. Get people excited.”

“I don’t know.” Pilip produced a half dozen balls from his pocket and spun them around his fingers.

“If he doesn’t, he’s not an artist anymore. He’s just an administrator, filling the schedule.”

If either of them could have spat politely at that moment, they would have. But filling the schedule was important work, too.

Hi, Agnes messaged Pilip from the comfort of her bed. *Can I help?*

She only had to wait a few moments for a reply.

I have thirty international acts that can’t get though the border. How many performance slots can you fill by next Thursday AM?

It depends. Can I see your paperwork?

She examined the festival license and the city bylaws it referenced. No morality clauses, no content restrictions, well-armored artist protections. Pilip sent his interactive venue map, with the local acts in green and the missing international acts flashing in red. It looked like a Christmas tree, with the broad expanse of the city’s southern waterfront tapering on either side of Yonge Street to Uptown.

All of them. I can fill all of them.

I love you.

There’s a catch, though. Late afternoon and evenings are best. Definitely no mornings.

Anything you need. I’ll juggle the schedule.

Agnes sat up tall in her bed, crossed her legs and closed her eyes. Four days to recruit, contract, schedule, organize, and support two hundred burlesque performances over three days, in venues across the city.

Impossible. But she'd done impossible things before. She'd convinced the fine art crowd that real live naked people belonged in their gallery just as much as the ones made of oil paint and bronze. If she could do that, she could convince the city that they belonged on the street, too.

You probably don't want to grind on a fire hydrant.

Sunday morning, the replies to Agnes's call started streaming in. Enthusiastic affirmatives, mostly, with a few wary questions. Agnes trapped a live Q&A session in full surround, drawing on all her resources of confident body language and palpable enthusiasm.

Q: Am I going to get arrested?

A: Absolutely not. The festival license contains no content restrictions. [happy grin] *City bylaws are still in play, so wear a thong and pasties as always.*

Q: Am I going to get sued?

A: No way. [relaxed but confident posture; reassuring smile] *You're covered by the festival's artistic license guarantees, which are underwritten by the Toronto Arts Council. Having said that, remember burlesque is about seduction. Go ahead and push the envelope, but be smart about it.*

Q: What about cosplay?

A: If you want to riff on a trademarked character, make your take transformative.

Q: Won't people just walk away from us?

A: Sure, street performers get that all the time. It's your job to make sure they don't want to. [serious, piercing look] *Who is better trained for that than a burlesque dancer?*

Q: What happens if it rains?

A: [grin] *You still get paid.*

Q: What kind of acts do you want?

A: Anything. Everything. [arms spread wide; beatific smile] *This is a fantastic opportunity to bring your art to those who don't know they need it. How do you meet that challenge? I can't say. The answer will be different for everyone. But I know you'll be amazing. You're going to blow us all away.*

Q: Have you opened up your bot yet?

A: [laugh] *No, but I'm taking it to work tomorrow so I better crack it open tonight.*

Q: Post an unboxing.

A: [nervous giggle] *Seriously?*

Q: Yeah we all want to see it.

A: [reluctantly] *Okay…*

Smooth like Barbie

Sunday night, Agnes dragged the package to a spot-lit circle in the middle of the studio. Cat and Susanna perched in the shadows, one controlling the cameras, the other on sound.

"Going live in three, two…" Cat gave her a silent one with her index finger and shot it at her.

"Hi," said Agnes. "You all know me, but in case you don't, I'm Agnes MacFlail, a Toronto burlesque dancer and producer.

A few days ago, the Skinless Corporation sent me a bot, and I'm going to unbox for you."

Cat made a circular gesture with her finger: *Keep it rolling*. Then two fingers: *Two minutes*. She flipped her hand upside down and made a walking gesture.

"People are still joining us, so let's talk." Agnes sat beside the bot box and crossed her legs. She laid a gentle hand on the Skinless logo. "Some of you were pretty upset when you saw this sitting outside my door. That's okay. I understand. We all have strong opinions about sex bots."

The green-light camera hovered in for a closeup. Agnes gave it a fond, motherly smile.

"Most of you saw the urgent call I made for Toronto on the Street next weekend. If you haven't responded yet, you've got another day to think about it. In the meantime, I'm going to focus on making it a great festival. And now, let's see what's inside."

The lid of the package moved slowly, the suction from the tight seal producing just enough resistance to make the procedure feel significant.

"This box is more expensive than my mattress," Agnes joked. "Okay, here's our first look."

Cushioned in dark, form-fitting foam, the bot was pale from head to toe. Its eyes were closed, its body eerily still, like a corpse on a slab. A thin white shift covered it from shoulders to ankles.

"I think we're all getting the Snow White reference, here, right?" Agnes looked up at the camera again. "I have to admit this is a bit disturbing. I work with bots all day long, but they're task specialized. Usually you can tell what a bot does by just looking at it."

She rose to her feet in one fluid motion and stepped back, arms crossed.

"I don't know what this bot is for." Wary, she poked its arm with the tip of one finger, then laid her palm flat on its surface. "Feels kind of skin-ish. Cool, but it warms up fast."

She stood back to let the camera trap a tracking shot of the bot's whole body. Then she then knelt and leaned in to examine its face. Between the bot's lips was a clear plastic tab.

"I guess I'm supposed to pull this."

She made a concentrated effort to be gentle. Having worked with bots for years, Agnes was well acquainted with the human urge to abuse them. She felt it herself. When one of Tower's hygiene bots malfunctioned, when a towbot stalled, her first impulse was to give it a kick. Once, years ago, she'd accidentally booted a spinning polisher so hard it had flown across the garage and smashed into the wall. When she went to retrieve it, the bot was desperately trying to polish a tiny spot of concrete, whirring brokenly.

"Here's what I think." The plastic tab seemed stuck, so Agnes knelt beside the box, and braced herself with a gentle hand on the bot's forehead. "We should treat bots the same way we do anything. Would you punch a hole in the wall because your window broke? Would you kick the subway escalator because the train is late? Would you tell your phone it's a piece of shit because it can't answer your question? They say it's okay to abuse bots because they're just things, but it shows what kind of person you are."

She wiped her fingers on her blouse.

"This thing is really slippery."

She pinched the tab and pulled hard. It gave way with a snap. The bot lunged up, folding itself into a ninety degree angle at the hips. Agnes scurried backward, scrabbling along the floor like a crab, but the bot just sat there, open-eyed, rock-still, and unbreathing.

Agnes did a straddle jump to standing.

"We're all wondering the same thing. Is this a sex bot or isn't it?" She looked into the bot's face. "Can you stand up?"

The bot stood and stepped clear of the box. Its feet were the least humanlike thing about it. Wedge-shaped, toeless, with a thick, grippy antibac sole.

"Whatever it is, it's not for foot festishists. Okay, let's see." When she lifted the bot's garment, it helpfully raised its arms.

"It's definitely not a sex bot." No orifices. Not even the suggestion of them. No navel or nipples. She poked at its mouth with her pinkie. It had lips but the teeth were fused into a single plate. "Or if it's meant for sex, it's serving a very specialized kink. And look at this."

She parted the bot's hair. Under the blonde filaments was a glassy visual array that extended from the bot's temple, all the way around the head to the other side.

"Whatever this is for, it needs to be able to see in all directions." Agnes draped the bot's garment over her shoulder. "I'd guess Skinless has maxed out the sex bot market and is exploring the market for a generic, multiuse model. Now we know, okay? Not a sex bot, no issues. Show and tell is over. I love you all."

Humans can have sex with anything

Monday morning, far too early. Agnes usually had the mornings to herself, but both Cat and Susanne were shiny and awake, and far too interested in the bot.

"Are you going to mulch this, or trade it on GiftCycle?" Susanne asked.

The Skinless bot stood in the middle of the studio, beside its box. Agnes swiveled her bar stool away from the kitchen counter. Susanne and Cat circled the bot. They looked like a nature vid, mongooses checking out a cobra.

"Neither," said Agnes. "I have to give it back."

"When?" Cat rubbed a lock of the bot's hair between her fingers. "Soon?"

"A week or so."

Susanne placed her palms on the bot's hipbones and pushed. The bot stepped back. Susanne shifted her grip and pulled. The bot stepped forward. She pulled it close to her, so close their noses touched. Susanne tilted her head and sniffed the bot's jawline.

"Smells weird. Not bad. Just weird."

Agnes turned back to the counter. She propped her head on her hand and reviewed the responses to her performance call as she finished her coffee. She was about to check her Tower dashboard, make sure her bots were prepped and ready for the morning rush, when she heard a giggle behind her.

Cat stood behind it with her hand on its forehead, tilting its head back against her shoulder. Susanne knelt on the floor in front of it, gripping its knees. As Cat backed up, the bot's grippy feet shuffled along the floor in an attempt to stay upright.

"What the heck?" Agnes lunged across the room and pulled the bot from their clutches. "You know you can't have sex with this thing, right?"

Susanne looked thoughtful. "It would be a bit restrictive."

"It's got fingers," said Cat. "So no problem there."

"Three days ago, you were accusing me of procuring a sex bot." Agnes threw her hands in the air. "Now you want to molest this poor thing?"

"Everybody likes a challenge," said Cat.

Agnes grabbed the bot's hand and dragged it to her room. She found it a pair of vintage track pants, a fluffy sweater, and a rainbow mask, then dragged it along with her as she walked to work. Makeup a bit slapdash, hair less perfect than usual, but half the car daddies would be taking a long weekend. She counted on Tower to be slow most Mondays, but today she was wrong.

"Vintage car fair on the weekend," said her manager. "Fifties convertibles, sixties sedans, seventies muscle cars. We booked a bunch of new clients and they all want to strut, so let's make the cars look extra pretty today."

Onboarding new cars meant scanning them with the laser mapper—the most ponderous bot in the garage—confirming the data in several bot management systems, creating unique IDs for each car, and installing the RFID tags under the edges of each bumper. The tags didn't like sticking to chrome. Agnes had a workaround but it took time to etch each tag location with a diamond-tipped pen and seat the tag with a pinpoint of archival resin.

She didn't have time to deal with the Skinless bot. It followed her around the garage and watched as she wrangled bots, and slid under cars on her mechanic's creeper, and manually transferred data from the mapper into the garage's governance system. Naturally, she began talking to it.

"I've got to get the tags in exactly the right locations. If the cars were all the same, it wouldn't be a problem. But they're all different."

The spool of tags spilled from Agnes' breast pocket and rolled across the floor. Agnes sighed and slid from under the shark-like prow of a 1960 Lincoln Continental. But before she could get up, the bot chased the spool down and brought it to her.

"Thanks," Agnes said under her breath.

She got the bot on the floor with her. Seating tags was a simple three-step process. The bot learned it in a half an hour, which left Agnes free to manage data, assign maintenance and hygiene protocols, and fix her hair and makeup before checking in with the new car daddies about their schedules and preferences. In the afternoon, she took a few minutes to ping Pilip.

He scrubbed his hands over his face and blinked into the camera. Clearly she'd woken him up.

"Don't forget to rejig the schedule," she said, cheerily. "My performers can't do mornings."

"Right. Why is that, again?" He lunged to his feet and staggered off camera.

"Burlesque isn't for the mornings. I mean, it could be. There's no reason it couldn't. But in general, our audiences don't attend morning performances. It's just not in the culture. You get that, right?"

"I guess I don't really know what burlesque is. Some kind of theater, I think? Italian. With masks and clowns?"

Agnes frowned. She'd spent hours talking with Pilip. She knew more details than she cared about his juggling repertoire, but he didn't even know what kind of art she practiced.

"No," she said coolly. "That's commedia dell'arte."

"Right, so it's like a variety show?" His voice was distant under the sound of running water.

"Now you're thinking vaudeville."

"So what's burlesque, again?" Now he sounded garbled, as if talking through a mouth of toothpaste.

"Striptease."

No reply. Agnes could picture his balls hitting the ground.

"You still there?" she asked.

"Yeah. Uh. You know this is a street performer festival, right? Like, outside. On the sidewalks. In the parks." Pilip sounded strained. And he was still off-camera.

"Yes, I know."

"And you don't see any problem with that?"

"Burlesque dancers are artists. We make art. We perform and entertain. There's nothing objectionable about it, unless you're some kind of prude."

He didn't reply.

"Are you a prude, Pilip?"

"No, but you've got me in a corner. How can I put strippers on the street?"

Agnes hated that term, but she didn't have the time to educate him about the politics of striptease. She gave the camera a crisp, professional smile.

"I don't think you have much choice. Let's go over logistics."

She went through the venues with him. Checked on the locations of green rooms and change rooms, the status of security contractors and support volunteers. She offered to tap her contacts for extra bodies, but he remained cold throughout the rest of the conversation and refused to take her up on any more offers of help.

Agnes told herself she'd have to be okay with that. All she had to do was make sure her performers were safe and supported. Pilip's prejudices weren't her concern.

Everyone needs a second self

"So did Pilip burst a blood vessel in his eye?" Susanna asked that night, at supper.

"Just about," said Agnes. "But I don't care what he thinks. His threat reaction to femme sexuality is none of my business."

"That's weird," said Cat. "You usually care what everybody thinks."

Agnes bent over her plate and twirled noodles around her fork. It felt odd to sit at the kitchen bar with the bot on the other side of the plexiglass wall, perched on the edge of Agnes' frilly bed. After working with the bot all day, she'd become attached to it. Not as a person, but certainly as a useful tool. She wouldn't have gotten through the day without it.

After supper, she'd have to go looking for maintenance info, find a way to access the bot's self-cleaning algorithms. Tower of Cars was tidy, but it was still a garage. The cars might be retrofitted with electric engines, but they still dripped oil. The bot had pancaked its fluffy sweater with dirt, torn holes in the knees of its track pants.

Maybe she should tell it to strip and take a shower? No, the bot needed to stay out of sight. Agnes didn't want Cat and Susanne to get any more horny ideas about it.

With Cat and Susanne's help, Agnes reviewed the long queue of audition vids. They began drinking herbal tea, then coffee, then gin, then finally at at two in the morning, she sent out the festival acceptance letters, with contracts and payment forms. When she woke on Tuesday morning, the festival was forty-eight hours away, and she had a stable of performers to onboard.

"This is doable, right?" she asked the bot.

It was still sitting on the corner of her bed. Tiny cilia on either side of its secondary visual array parted its hair, and a sliver of shiny lens glinted in the sun. She hadn't cleaned it, hadn't changed its clothes, hadn't even paid it more than a moment of attention since getting home from work. It looked like a Victorian street urchin, grimy and neglected.

"Let's wash up," she said.

Not one bit of sexual frisson while showering with the bot. How could there be? It was a thing. Sure, she wanted it clean and operational, but that's not all. She loved it the way a car daddy loved his vintage ride. Did that mean he wanted to stick his dick in an exhaust pipe? No. And same with Agnes. After only one day with the bot, she wasn't sure she wanted to live without it. Ever.

By mid-morning, the bot was doing all of Agnes's grunt work—vacuuming the cobwebs from the garage's beams and corners, moving consumables from storage to the refilling stations, and making the Corvette shine.

The bot was good at buffing, polishing, waxing. Methodical, untiring, and able to apply consistent pressure both hands. All Agnes had to do was teach it to keep wax and polish off the glass, and touch up the wipers and weather stripping.

This left Agnes time to worry about the performer contracts. Most of the dancers had signed and returned them, but Pilip hadn't countersigned them yet, not even one. Was it too early to nag him? He was a late sleeper, but what festival producer slept late two days before their big weekend—or slept at all for that matter? She was just about to ping him when Mason and Avery contacted her.

"It's your grandparents," she said to the bot, and took their call.

"Have you named her yet?" Avery asked.

"No," Agnes said, startled. "Am I supposed to?"

"It's the first thing most people do."

"Okay. Sally. No—Daisy. No—Petunia."

"Cute," said Mason. "How do you like her?"

I love her forever, Agnes thought. "I'd be happier if it came with an owner's manual."

"Seems like you've figured her out pretty well on your own."

"You're monitoring it?" Silly question. Of course they were. She'd probably defaulted away her privacy the moment she took delivery.

"The usage data we collect from these trials is extremely valuable. Does that bother you?"

"I don't mind people watching me, as long as I know who they are so I can look back."

Both salespeople laughed as if she'd made a joke.

She made an excuse and dropped the call. She watched as Petunia corralled a pair of malfunctioning hygiene bots. The bot flipped one of them on its back and held down the reset button. Its crablike legs waved frantically, then went still.

So useful. Even if all Petunia ever did was reboot bots and polish cars, it would save Agnes six hours a week. She had to admit, Skinless had a brilliant product on their hands. Everyone needed a second self to deal with brainless, annoying tasks. But then, anyone who could afford a second-self bot was already paying humans to do that stuff for them.

And there were some annoyances no bot could deal with.

Hi Pilip, just checking on the contracts for my performers. Can you sign and return as soon as you get a chance? I'm starting onboarding tonight.

Agnes ran straight from work to St. James Park, under the shadow of the old cathedral, its neo-Gothic facade now the pedestal for a half-built multi-use tower, its vertical farm already green and growing. Ten dancers clustered around her as she pointed out locations and tagged them on a shared map. After a few minutes, she realized the dancers weren't listening to her. They were all staring at the bot.

Agnes had dressed it in the clothes she wore when constructing scenery and props—paint-stained jeans and a pink hoodie crusted with glitter. The bot returned the dancers' gazes with a pleasant, open expression, just the barest hint of a dimple on each cheek.

"This is Petunia, my second self," she told the dancers. "I'm having her grafted to my hip so Skinless can't take her back."

The dancers laughed. She let them poke at the bot for a few minutes, and then reeled them all in again.

"Bathrooms and change room in the coffee shop." She pointed across the street. "The owner is on board, I just checked. Volunteers will drum up audiences on all four sides of the park. You'll bring your own music and stream to the venue manager's amp."

As they walked toward the next venue, the sun came out. The dancers flashed with color, sequins sparkling, feathers waving. Agnes ran ahead, then turned to trap a few photos of them all walking across the grass.

"You look amazing," she shouted. "Pray for a sunny weekend."

"I'm praying for rain," said a voice from behind her.

Pilip. He looked strained, eyes puffy, shoulders slumped.

"That's natural," she said. "The days before a show, it always feels like everything's falling apart. But it's going to be great, don't worry."

"No, I'm pulling the plug."

Agnes flashed her performers a shaky smile as they gathered around.

"You can't do that," she said.

"It's what I should have done when the feds closed the border."

The dancers murmured and exchanged worried looks.

"But what about your street performers? The local ones?"

"They know it's pointless. You can't revive an art form when conditions don't support it. Nobody performs on the street anymore. The audiences aren't there. People just don't go outside that much. And half the time the weather tries to kill you."

Pilip's eyes were on Agnes's toes, his hands in his pockets. He couldn't even look at her. She should say something conciliatory, mollifying, make him feel better. But she didn't have it in her.

"Are you giving up because you're scared to work with us?"

He gazed toward the far horizon, unwilling to meet her eye.

"You know, I've heard things about you. Not good things."

"That's no reason to kill your festival," said Agnes.

Something nudged Agnes' arm. Petunia stood at her side, hands on hips, head thrown back to look at Pilip from under lowered lids. A belligerent pose, assertive, even aggressive. But the bot hadn't come up with it on its own. It was mirroring her.

"Do you know what I think?" Agnes asked. "You want to give up the fight, but you can't admit it so you're looking for a scapegoat. Blame the audiences, the weather. Blame me. Anything to keep from admitting you're ready to quit."

Petunia squared her shoulders and nodded briskly, as if Agnes had just made a very good point.

"Go ahead and quit," Agnes continued. "But don't take us with you. Transfer your license to me. I'll take over the festival."

"I can't," he said. "The grants aren't—"

"Just the festival license," she interrupted. "I don't care about your stupid grants. Do you think we do this for money? Money's nice, but we do it for art. We always have."

"You can't—"

"Who says I can't? I can do anything I want. Everything I want. Right?"

She turned to her dancers, expecting them to back away from this new version of her, this bossy, bristly Agnes, but they were on her side, grinning and streaming the scene to their friends with hand-helds and shouldercams.

When Agnes jabbed a finger at Pilip, Petunia did too.

"I'll program the whole festival with dancers. You'll see people you never knew existed coming out of their homes. And they're all going to love it."

He opened his mouth and closed it. Then he nodded.

"Three days of street burlesque will change this city," she told him.

She gathered her dancers, linked arms with Petunia, and led them all into the sunlight.

NOTES ABOUT "ALIAS SPACE"

I wrote "Alias Space" in the middle of the COVID-19 lockdown. Figuring out how to fit my Science Fictional ideas around the new reality was a heck of a brain twist. Adjusting to a new creative routine was hard, too. Previously, I'd benefited from a clear border between day job and writing. Day job happened in the office, a fifteen-minute walk from home. Writing happened at my tiny living room desk. Now nearly everything is happening in the same hundred square feet. My spot at the dining table is next to my desk, which is next to my spot on the couch. This was hard at first.

"Are you getting lots of writing done?" asked my newly-retired CEO, via email. "Or is the environment not stimulating enough?"

Stimulating. Hah. Finding stimulation isn't a problem. Ideas are everywhere. I can get character from a dust bunny, plot from laundry. Even after weeks trapped in a small condo, the lockdown wasn't boring. In fact, I'd never been less at risk of boredom in my life. But I thrive on stability, routine—a lot of writers do. When the schedule gets blasted to pieces, it takes a while to readjust.

As I write this, it's the last day of the Nebula Conference, brought brilliantly online by SFWA's dedicated staff and board, with the help of many talented volunteers. Last night I chatted on Zoom with Neil Clarke, editor of Clarkesworld and all-around terrific guy. He said that since the lockdown, the magazine has been getting more than the usual number of submissions, and a great deal of them from people who had never submitted to the magazine before.

This is fantastic news. Though many of those new writers will give up fairly quickly, some will keep trying and will eventually learn to write good stories. When good stories get written—when art gets made where there was no art before—we all win.

I wish all new writers great success. New blood keeps the art alive, and I'm always searching for new favorite reads.

SKIN CITY

FOR KASS, THE WORST THING ABOUT BEING in jail wasn't the food. Sure, lunch was batch-processed and slopped onto partitioned trays, but edible. It wasn't the small shared cell, or the stiff disposable coverall that scraped over her pasties. The worst part was the aesthetics.

The jail took its interior design cues from the late twentieth century. Monochrome. gray walls, gray floors, gray furniture. Kass would have skinned the jail in late nineteenth century Arts and Crafts—soothing and restful to the eye—but as a prisoner, she was totally cut off from the open data stream. When she pinged for data, all she got was a menu of old movies, a selection of single-player games, and a whirring bar showing progress on her indictment. Twelve percent complete. When it got to a hundred, the charges against her would be filed and she'd find out just what kind of trouble she was in.

Kass's elderly cell mate, Janet, snorted while waking up from her nap. She creaked out of bed and hitched herself over to the padded recliner. Kass wheeled the table over and adjusted it so the lunch tray was positioned over the old woman's lap.

"So what're you in for?" Janet reached for her spoon with unsteady fingers.

Kass sighed. "Unrequited love."

The old woman coughed hard, like she was dislodging something from the back of her throat. She snatched a napkin from the side of her tray and raked it over her tongue.

"Just my luck to get stuck with an incurable romantic," she spat.

Kass had first seen her one true love on the slideway ramp at Osgoode Station, coming up as Kass was coming down. Though all Kass could see was a vaguely human-shaped form in a full privacy drape, matte black microfiber from fingertips to eyelashes, she was instantly transfixed. The woman moved through the station as though she owned it, like it was a stage she was in complete control of, and Kass her anonymous, devoted audience. The next day, Kass watched her striding through Queen's Park at twilight, and then later, selecting oranges in the grocery on Dundas. A few long days went by without a glimpse, then she almost ran into the woman walking up Simcoe. Kass had to dodge out of the way to avoid a collision.

"I can't stop thinking about her," Kass told her friends crowded around the cafe tables in the middle of University Avenue.

"You know there's no chance, right?" Trinh said, not unkindly. "She's a privacy nut. She's not going to wink at an open-source mutt who shakes her tits in the street."

"I know," Kass banged her forehead gently on flimsy table. "But I love her."

"Them. You think you're in love, but you're not," said Rafe. "You don't even know their pronouns."

"She's femme for sure. Something about the sashay," said Kass.

"You're adorable, Kass," said Marie-Claude. "But what if she prefers her lovers well-hung and hairy?"

Kass wrapped both hands around her cooling coffee. Marie-Claude had cut right to the heart of her problem. Seen with a logical, dispassionate eye, she knew nothing about the woman and had no way of finding out. But Kass was passionate in everything she did. Over the past few days this stranger had set her world aflame.

"What if she's monogamous and married?" Janie added. "She might like the way you spin your tassels, but won't ruin her life for you."

"What if she just has better things to do?" Trinh added.

"They could be femme to the eyebrows and a cis man." Rafe remained adamant about pronouns. "Sashay or no sashay."

"I know," Kass said with a gentle sigh. "It doesn't make sense, but I can't live without her."

"Whatever you do, be careful. She lives in Fearsville." Angel pointed at the battery of black-windowed towers on the east side of the street, behind the train of bikes streaming up the glideway. "Keep your distance or she'll fire a neuromuscular blocker up your nose."

"There's no such thing as love at first sight," said Janie. Everyone nodded. "Real relationships are built over time. You're projecting a fantasy onto a blank slate."

"You think I'm silly." Kass looked deep into her coffee cup.

"No, honey, just young," said Rafe.

"You don't know how it feels. When she walks by, it's like there's a spotlight shining on her." Kass cupped her palms over her heart. "I may not know her, but I feel it here. She's the most important person in the world."

"That's magical thinking," said Janie.

"No, it's true love," Kass replied.

Marie Claude took Kass's hands and squeezed. "Forget her, or we'll be picking pieces of your broken heart off the sidewalk."

"I know you're trying to protect me, but you're wrong," said Kass with a grin. "I'm going to show you exactly how wrong you are."

Janet was a centenarian—a hundred and twelve years old. Kass did the math. Janet had been born in the twentieth century, just like the jail decor.

"What's it like having a lifetime that spans three different centuries?" Kass asked. "I mean, you lived through so many changes. The last gasp of industrialization. Climate change remediation. The doming of the cities. Rewilding on every continent. The death of scarcity. The privacy wars. What's it like?"

"I got to tell you, I miss doing that." Janet pointed a gnarled finger at Kass.

"Doing what?"

"Sitting cross-legged like your hips won't snap like a well-dried wishbone."

Clearly, Janet wasn't comfortable answering her question.

"I'm a dancer," Kass said. "Flexible."

"A dancer, huh?" Janet's eyes twinkled. "I know what kind of dancers shake it around the city these days. See them on every other corner. Perverts."

Kass stiffened. "People come from all over the world to see Toronto's street burlesque shows. We're a city treasure. If you don't want to see it, you can skin us out."

Janet slapped the tray. Her cutlery clattered. The fork fell to the floor and bounced under Janet's chair.

"An incurable romantic and a pervert. What's the world come to? No privacy, cameras everywhere, and little sluts running around naked."

Kass slipped off her bed and crawled to retrieve the fork. Were all privacy nuts like Janet—imposing their values on everyone? She hadn't considered that the woman she loved might have a problem with Kass being a street burly.

But no. Janet was old, very old, and like many centenarians, she clung to an outdated value system. The woman wasn't old. Couldn't be, not with all that energy and bounce in her walk.

Kass set the fork gently on the side of Janet's the tray. She'd wanted to find out what it was like to be old, and she had her answer. Janet had seen a lot of change, and it scared her.

In Toronto, as in most city-states, the population skinned the city to accommodate their aesthetic preferences, adding banks of greenery, inserting views and vistas, changing the city's shapes, textures, and colors to suit themselves. No city was perfectly designed for all its people, but skinning provided personal customization options. It was an effective solution to the problems created by providing utilities and services at the maximum economy of scale.

People from Fearsville skinned the city too, but their skins deleted people from the cityscape, eliminating the visible population—or at least reducing them to wireframes to avoid collisions. They'd lost the privacy wars, and retreated to their towers to their private, anonymous towers. Many never left Fearsville, and the rest only emerged fully veiled, their IDs masked by a bonded security firm and available only on a need-to-know basis.

"All I have to do is get her to notice me," Kass said. "Then nature can take its course."

Angel laughed. "How? Privacy nuts skin us out of the landscape. Even if you got in her face, all she'd see is wireframe."

"Yeah, but I have a plan."

They were was sharing a bottle of Tecumseth Tower pinot noir under a leafy golden locust tree on Queen Street. A train of cars hummed past, protected by a shimmering bounce field. Mid-day rush over, the street was comparatively quiet. Just enough free space outside Osgood Station for a rec group to kick a soccer ball around. They were loud—five kids, an oldster with a toddler in a chest sling, and two heavily pregnant people supported by mobility aids—all screeching and laughing over imaginary fouls.

"Be careful," said Angel. "My neighbor's cousin was carrying groceries past Fearsville once. She dropped a bag of apples and one of them rolled into their sidewalk setback. Not even into the building, just a piece of land they think is theirs. And when she tried to retrieve it, boom. Right up the nose. She was unconscious for three hours."

"That's an urban legend."

"Maybe," Angel replied. "But the point is, their world view is completely different from ours. When they look around, they see the enemy. What do you see, Kass?"

"Friends I haven't met yet."

"Right. How you going to reconcile that?"

"There are legitimate reasons for people to protect their privacy. They can't all be paranoid."

Angel looked skeptical.

Kass leaned back in her chair and scanned the leaves overhead for inspiration. Then she let her gaze drift to the

Fearsville towers. From the roofs, spindles stretched high to stabilize Toronto's weather dome, their surfaces covered in vertical farms that helped feed their inhabitants.

"Just because someone doesn't like you, doesn't mean they're bad," said Kass.

"Maybe. I guess I just want them to prove it," said Angel.

Kass tipped the last of the wine into their glasses. Then a flash of black caught her eye.

"Shit, there she is," she whispered.

The woman sauntered through Osgoode Station's wide archway, gloved thumbs hooked in the pockets of her billowing privacy wrap. Maybe she didn't want to be noticed, but the posture stretched the loose fabric over her shoulders and chest, emphasizing her breasts. Kass followed her with hungry eyes until she disappeared into one of Fearsville's narrow entryways.

"She's never going to talk to me," she moaned.

"I thought you had a plan?"

Kass lurched to her feet, banging the table with her knees and spilling the last of the wine.

"I do, and I'm starting right now."

Janet grumbled under her breath as she thumbed through the menu of games. Kass wasn't intimidated. In her teens, she'd volunteered at a care home for elderly lesbians that occupied a historic building so old it was actually made of brick, wood, and glass. The building had barely made it through the violent storms of the early twenty-first century, and if Toronto hadn't erected its dome in time, the building and thousands of others would have been flattened by the ten-month superstorm of 2057.

Janet might be narrow-minded and hostile, but Kass knew how to handle her. To make a centenarian happy, all you had to do was ask them to dip into their store of accumulated wisdom. Older people loved to give advice.

"Have you ever loved someone who didn't know you existed?" she asked.

"None of that lovey-dovey shit when I was your age. We swiped right, hooked up, got off, and moved on."

Janet chose an old-fashioned first-person shooter, non-immersive, and set the credits rolling.

"So, you're aromantic?" Kass asked gently.

"I'm not a-anything. I've been married three times."

"You don't believe in love at first sight?"

"That's not love, kid. That's a delusion."

"Not for me." Kass perched on the edge of her bed. "I saw someone and now I know my life will be worthless without them. Anybody you know ever felt that way?"

Janet screwed up her mouth like she tasted something sour. She spat into her wadded napkin.

"Yeah, a few."

"How did it work out?"

"Same as all relationships. One person six feet under, and the other crying."

"I just want her to notice me."

Janet grunted and engaged the game controller. Kass scooped up Janet's discarded lunch tray, passed it through the under-door access slot, and whistled for the hygiene bot. A trio of sweepers slid into the cell and began polishing the floor.

"So you got in her face and got thrown into jail."

"Something like that."

"You're doomed." The old woman cackled.

"What do you think would attract the biggest crowd," Kass asked her roommate Brio. "Prince/ess Pie from Sooper Bloopers or Ksai and Trombo from Team Mucho Bad Manners?"

Brio rolled his chair back from the packed and stacked communal sewing table. He rolled the pointy tip of his beard between his thumb and forefinger.

"Those are both difficult designs to pull off."

It was what he always said when Kass started dreaming up a new costume. Entertainment franchises ruthlessly enforced intellectual property rights on their characters, raking through data for unlicensed skins and squashing pirates under every available legal steamroller. But franchises couldn't do much about analog costumes. They could monitor data streams from city cameras, but search bots were easily dazzled by slight differences in color, photo-iridescent fabrics, and silhouette-disrupting props.

Kass had a Milady Captain Sterling costume with peekaboo cutouts and dissolving panels that put a super-saucy twist on the buttoned-up classic hero. To fool the bots, she performed a hula-hoop routine using a prop painted ultra-matte black. The hoop disrupted the silhouette and also provided a cheap gesture at Milady's ouroboros-like alien familiar.

"Prince/ess Pie, I think." Kass climbed on her stool to reach a bolt of purple fabric from the overhead rack. "I love Ksai and Trombo but my shoulders aren't broad enough for a second head."

"Yeah, but Team Mucho is better for you," Brio said, still fingering his beard. "Prince/ess Pie is for little kids."

"Kiddy stuff is what I want." Kass jumped down. "No skin. Just cute and popular."

"Are you feeling okay?" Brio looked confused.

"Prince/ess Pie will draw a general-interest crowd. Big enough that even someone from Fearsville will wonder what's going on and drop the wireframes to look. The point is to get noticed."

Kass spent two days perfecting her costume, then lugged her portable stage to a plum spot just outside Osgoode Station. She targeted the mid-morning and late-afternoon time windows she'd previously seen the woman in the area, and also captured the younger crowd on their way to and from Queen Street's most popular kittengarden.

In eight performances over four days, she lost herself in the joy of her tiny fans. They screeched louder than any burlesque audience ever could. Each performance, she spun faster, jumped higher, swirling her floating, iridescent purple trouser skirt. Her vest pockets sprouted with flower-like mini-bots, and projectors behind her ears approximated Pie's shimmering whiskers. It was so much fun, she almost forgot why she was there. She began to think maybe kiddy shows were her true calling after all.

And then she saw the woman coming up the slideway ramp. Kass stumbled off the stage and fell to one knee. Her pint-sized audience moaned in sympathy.

The woman's gaze swept across Kass like a searchlight. But she didn't stop. Didn't even pause. When she rounded the corner and disappeared, Kass went hollow with disappointment. But she jumped up and gave the kids a huge smile.

"That's okay, kids. Even a prince/ess falls down sometimes!"

Ten minutes later, a conflict resolution contractor showed up. He waited patiently until Kass pulled off her big finish and the children dispersed.

"Is there a problem?" she asked. "Did I take someone's usual performance spot? I can move, it's no trouble."

"No, you're being indicted. Probably nothing serious, but the city wants you locked up while the charges are pending." He gave her an apologetic half-grin. "It was a great show."

Kass tried to ignore Janet's wholesale murder of fang-faced aliens as the centenarian progressed from one shooter level to the next. She watched her indictment progress bar slowly creep on. When it got stuck at seventy percent, she dismissed it and pulled up an old movie. The Big Sleep was an ancient crime romance, zero immersion, monochrome, and heteronormative as heck, but stylish, and with an undercurrent of daddy-play.

"So, if you've been married three times," Kass said when Janet paused her game to use the toilet, "why are you so negative about love?"

"Your aimbot's stuck, kid. Find another topic."

"There is no other topic. If we don't have people we care about, what's the point of life?"

"Too-too twenty-second century," Janet grumbled. "Too-too happy. Too-too crowded. Too-too cozy. You gotta toughen up. Grow up, too."

When the indictment bot finally slid through the access slot, Janet slapped down the game, abandoning her progress in a tricky level.

"This bot's for you, too-too," she said with a wicked grin. "I want to watch it blow that chirpy smile off your face."

"I'm sure I'll be fine," Kass replied.

The bot whirred over to the bed.

Please confirm that your personal accessibility requirements have been met.

Kass poked the green smiley-face icon.

This indictment bot provides the legal interface for criminal charges. Volunteer justice tribunal members Willnet Lo, Yvonne MacKenzie, and Minnie Mininnewah have agreed to supervise your indictment.

Three faces hove into view. Kass recognized them all. Yvonne and Minnie were established members of Toronto's street art community, and Willnet was with the Bank of Toronto board of trade, responsible for orchestrating IP treaties with sister cities. Kass smiled wide. Minnie nodded, and the other two looked stern. None of them smiled back.

Kassander Gillian Chewinsky, the bot said, *after examining evidence from the City of Toronto surveillance archives, the World Court charges you with fifty-two counts of intellectual property theft. The evidence has been entered into your case file. Please examine it at your leisure. You may now ask questions of the tribunal.*

Kass reached out with a shaking hand and flipped through the stack of bookmarks. Each one showed her performing in her usual spots around the city, with her best, most up-to-date costumes. Working the crowd, charming people, thrilling the tourists.

"But I use bot-dazzling," she said. "I'm careful."

"That only works on bots, honey," Minnie said. "When live investigators get interested in you, it's all over—except the crying."

"But why me? Why now?"

Minnie flipped to the final bookmark. "It must have been Prince/ess Pie. If you ask me, it's pretty sad for a street burly to get hammered for a routine that prissy."

Kass sat on the edge of her bed, hard.

"Someone reported me. Do you…" Kass swallowed, trying to clear the lump that had formed in the depths of her throat. "Do you know their name?"

Minnie shook her head. Yvonne spoke up. "They chose to remain anonymous."

"Privacy freaks," Minnie said under her breath.

Something deep inside Kass crumpled. The woman she loved had turned her in, just like that. But no, she wouldn't believe it. Couldn't believe it. She sat up straight, breathed deep, and relaxed her shoulders with a dancer's practiced grace. She'd get through this.

"What's going to happen to me?" she asked.

Willnet cleared his throat. He wore a red noose-like tie around his neck, standard banker costume.

"The Bank of Toronto is highly supportive of the city's street performance community. No other city-state can claim such an abundant, vivacious home-grown tourist draw, but our treaties are important too. Our trading partners demand we respect their intellectual property rights."

Kass blinked. "What does that mean?"

"It means the city wants to make an example of you," said Yvonne. "I'm really sorry."

Kass should have asked more questions, but she was stunned. She dismissed the bot.

"You got slammed hard," said Janet.

"They won't keep me in jail for wearing a few costumes." Kass tried to sound brave and confident. "When the arraignment bot comes, I'll plead guilty and go home. They'll sentence me to some extra volunteer work, big deal."

"Lemme see your file."

Janet put out her hand like she expected Kass to give her a handful of paper, old-style. Kass shot her the case file, then lay back on her bed and checked the arraignment progress bar. Twelve percent already. It would all be over soon.

"Fifty-two counts." Janet cackled. "If they make them consecutive, you'll never get out."

"They won't do that." Fifteen percent. Kass stretched out on the bed to wait.

"Take it from me. Never plead guilty. Never do what they want. Be sand in the gears of the world. That's the only true freedom."

"I don't believe that." Kass tried changing the subject. "When are you getting out? When do you go back home?"

"This is my home." Janet's grin was ghastly.

"Nice place you got here," Kass joked. "No, really though."

"Remember I said all relationships end with someone six feet under? Not being that person is the only way to survive love." Janet grinned wider, her lips stretched to threads. She drew a gnarled finger across her throat.

"Nobody believes that anymore." Kass lifted herself on her elbows. She'd been making an effort to be kind, but twentieth-century eye-for-an-eye, kill-or-be-killed wasn't just old fashioned, it was plain stupid. "You're a dinosaur, Janet."

"Maybe, but dinosaurs are survivors." Janet's rheumy eye gleamed, and a thrill of fear coursed down Kass's spine.

"You didn't—"

"Kill someone?" Janet hissed. "No. I don't plead guilty, remember?"

Janet went back to her first person shooter. Kass sat with her back against the wall, grimly watching Janet murder her way through level after endless level. What justification could the city possibly have for shutting her up with someone so horrible? Maybe this was her life now. Maybe she would never get out.

When the cell door opened, Kass was curled on the bed, knees to her chest. The doorway framed a figure draped in black, head to toe, emerging from the dim hallway. To Kass, that dark form shone sun-bright, haloed in light. Her love. She'd know her anywhere.

One of the woman's graceful hands rested on an arraignment bot, the other reached out with an open, upturned palm.

"I'm your defense council." Her voice was musical and sweet. She lifted her fingers to the brim of her hood, and when she pushed it back, Kass finally saw the face she'd been yearning for.

"Don't worry," said the love of her life. "I'm getting you out of here."

NOTES ABOUT "SKIN CITY"

Do you believe in love at first sight? I do. I've experienced it. But gosh, it's a difficult concept to sell in fiction. People are more willing to believe in demons or ghosts than they are in love at first sight. They're more attracted to serial killers than loving, trusting souls.

"Skin City" posits a post-Privacy Wars future that is only hinted at in the "Alias Space." This is a subject I'll have to return to in a future story, because the opportunities for drama are endless.

Have you ever noticed that only the people with an unquestioned right to privacy are generally the ones who get so upset about having it threatened? The rest of us have never had any privacy. I grew up the lesbian daughter of a small town lawyer, where every person who saw me on the street or passed me in the grocery store knew my name, my family's history, and a good deal of gossip about us. As an adult, I've come out to everyone with whom I've ever had reason to exchange chit chat about what I'm doing on the weekend. Privacy? I don't even know what it is.

Which isn't to say privacy isn't a real issue. It is. But it's the people who don't have it who need it most. And the people who benefit from unquestioned privacy? They're the ones the world could use a closer look at.

WATERS OF VERSAILLES

-1-

SYLVAIN HAD JUST PULLED UP ANNETTE'S SKIRTS when the drips started. The first one landed on her wig, displacing a puff of rose-pink powder. Sylvain ignored it and leaned Annette back on the sofa. Her breath sharpened to gasps that blew more powder from her wig. Her thighs were cool and slightly damp—perhaps her arousal wasn't feigned after all, Sylvain thought, and reapplied himself to nuzzling her throat.

After two winters at Versailles, Sylvain was well acquainted with the general passion for powder. Every courtier had bowls and bins of the stuff in every color and scent. In addition to the pink hair powder, Annette had golden powder on her face and lavender at her throat and cleavage. There would be more varieties lower down. He would investigate that in time.

The second drip landed on the tip of her nose. Sylvain flicked it away with his tongue.

Annette giggled. "Your pipes are weeping, monsieur."

"It's nothing," he said, nipping at her throat. The drips were just condensation. An annoyance, but unavoidable when cold pipes hung above overheated rooms.

The sofa squeaked as he leaned in with his full weight. It was a delicate fantasy of gilt and satin, hardly large enough for the two of them, and he was prepared to give it a beating.

Annette moaned as he bore down on her. She was far more entertaining than he had expected, supple and slick. Her gasps were genuine now, there was no doubt, and she yanked at his shirt with surprising strength.

A drip splashed on the back of his neck, and another a few moments later. He had Annette abandoned now, making little animal noises in the back of her throat as he drove into her. Another drip rolled off his wig, down his cheek, over his nose. He glanced overhead and a battery of drips hit his cheek, each bigger than the last.

This was a problem. The pipes above were part of the new run supporting connections to the suites of two influential men and at least a dozen rich ones. His workmen had installed the pipes just after Christmas. Even if they had done a poor job, leaks weren't possible. He had made sure of it.

He gathered Annette in his arms and shoved her farther down the sofa, leaving the drips to land on the upholstery instead of his head. He craned his neck, trying to get a view of the ceiling. Annette groaned in protest and clutched his hips.

The drips fell from a join, quick as tears. Something was wrong in the cisterns. He would have to speak with Leblanc immediately.

"Sylvain?" Annette's voice was strained.

It could wait. He had a reputation to maintain, and performing well here was as critical to his fortunes as all the water flowing through Versailles.

He dove back into her, moving up to a galloping pace as drips pattered on his neck. He had been waiting months for this. He ought to have been losing himself in Annette's flounced and beribboned flesh, the rouged nipples peeking from her bodice, her flushed pout and helplessly bucking hips, but instead his mind wandered the palace. Were there floods under every join?

Instead of dampening his performance, the growing distraction lengthened it. When he was finally done with her, Annette was completely disheveled, powder blotched, rouge smeared, wig askew, face flushed as a dairy maid's.

Annette squeezed a lock of his wig and caressed his cheek with a water-slick palm.

"You are undone, I think, monsieur."

He stood and quickly ordered his clothes. The wig was wet, yes, even soaked. So was his collar and back of his coat. A quick glance in a gilded mirror confirmed he looked greasy as a peasant, as if he'd been toiling at harvest instead of concluding a long-planned and skillful seduction—a seduction that required a graceful exit, not a mad dash out the door to search the palace for floods.

Annette was pleased—more than pleased despite the mess he'd made of her. She looked like a cat cleaning cream off its whiskers as she dabbed her neck with a powder puff, ignoring the drips pattering beside her. The soaked sofa leached dye onto the cream carpet. Annette dragged the toe of her silk slipper through the stained puddle.

"If this is not the only drip, monsieur, you may have a problem or two."

"It is possible," Sylvain agreed, dredging up a smile. He leaned in and kissed the tips of her fingers one at a time until she waved him away.

He would have to clean up before searching for Leblanc, and he would look like a fool all the way up to his apartment.

At least the gossips listening at the door would have an enduring tale to tell.

-2-

Sylvain ducked out of the marble halls into the maze of service corridors and stairs. Pipes branched overhead like a leaden forest. Drips targeted him as he passed but there were no standing puddles—not yet.

The little fish could turn the palace into a fishbowl if she wanted, Sylvain thought, and a shudder ran through his gut. The rooftop reservoirs held thousands of gallons, and Bull and Bear added new reservoirs just as fast as the village blacksmiths could make them. All through the royal wing, anyone with a drop of blood in common with the king was claiming priority over his neighbor, and the hundred or so courtiers in the north wing—less noble, but no less rich and proud—were grinding their teeth with jealousy.

Sylvain whipped off his soaked wig and let the drips rain down on his head one by one, steady as a ticking clock as he strode down the narrow corridor. He ducked into a stairwell—no pipes above there—and scrubbed his fingers through his wet hair as he peeked around the corner. The drips had stopped. Only a few spatters marked the walls and floorboards.

The little fish was playing with him. It must be her idea of a joke. Well, Leblanc could take care of it. The old soldier loved playing nursemaid to the creature. Age and wine had leached all the man out of him and left a sad husk of a wet nurse, good for nothing but nursery games.

A maid squeezed past him on the stairs and squealed as her apron came away wet. She was closely followed by a tall valet. Sylvain moved aside for him.

"You're delivering water personally now, Monsieur de Guilherand?"

Sylvain gave the valet a black glare and ran up the stairs two at a time.

The servants of Versailles were used to seeing him lurking in the service corridors, making chalk marks on walls and ceilings. He was usually too engrossed in his plans to notice their comments but now he'd have to put an end to it. Annette d'Arlain was in the entourage of Comtesse de Mailly, King Louis's *maîtresse en titre*, and Madame had more than a fair share of the king's time and attention—far more than his poor ignored Polish queen.

The next servant to take liberty with him would get a stiff rebuke and remember he was an officer and a soldier who spent half the year prosecuting the king's claims on the battlefield.

By the time Sylvain had swabbed himself dry and changed clothes, Bull and Bear were waiting for him. Their huge bulks strained his tiny parlor at the seams.

"What is the little creature playing at?" Sylvain demanded.

Bull twisted his cap in his huge hands, confused. Bear raised his finger to his nose and reached in with an exploratory wiggle.

"Down in the cisterns," Sylvain spoke precisely. "The creature. The little fish. What is she doing?"

"We was on the roof when you called, monsieur," said Bull, murdering the French with his raspy country vowels.

"We been bending lead all day," said Bear. "Long lead."

"The little fish was singing at dawn. I heard her through the pipes," Bull added, eager to please.

It was no use demanding analysis from two men who were barely more human than the animals they were named for. Bull and Bear were good soldiers, steady, strong, and vicious, but cannonfire had blasted their wits out.

"Where is Leblanc?"

Bull shrugged his massive shoulders. "We don't see him, monsieur. Not for days."

"Go down to the cellars. Find Leblanc and bring him to me."

The old soldier was probably curled around a cask in a carelessly unlocked cellar, celebrating his good luck by drinking himself into dust. But even dead drunk, Leblanc knew how to talk to the creature. Whatever the problem was, Leblanc would jolly the silly fish out of her mood.

-3-

"Our well-beloved king is an extraordinary man," said Sylvain. "But even a man of his parts can only use one throne at a time."

The Grand Chamberlain fluffed his stole like a bantam cock and lowered his hairy eyebrows. "The issue is not how the second throne will be used but how quickly you will comply with the request. We require it today. Disappoint us at your peril."

Sylvain suppressed a smile. If royalty could be measured by number of thrones, he was king of Europe. He had at least two dozen in a village warehouse, their finely painted porcelain and precious mahogany fittings wrapped in batting and hidden in unmarked crates. Their existence was a secret even Bull and Bear kept close. To everyone else, they were precious, rare treasures that just might be found for the right person at the right price.

The Grand Chamberlain paced the silk carpet. He was young, and though highborn, titled, and raised to the highest office, responsibility didn't sit well with him. He'd seen a battlefield or two at a distance but had never known real danger. Those hairy brows were actually trembling. Sylvain could easily draw this out just for the pleasure of making a duke sweat, but the memory of Annette's soft flesh made him generous.

"My warehouse agent just reported receiving a new throne. It is extremely fine. Berlin has been waiting months for it." Sylvain examined his fingernails. "Perhaps it can be diverted. I will write a note to my agent."

The Grand Chamberlain folded his hands and nodded, an officious gesture better suited to a gray-haired oldster. "Such a throne might be acceptable."

"You will recall that installing plumbing is a lengthy and troublesome process. Even with the pipes now in place servicing the original throne, his majesty will find the work disruptive."

Installing the first throne had been a mess. Bear and Bull had ripped into walls and ceilings, filling the royal dressing room with the barnyard stench of their sweat. But King Louis had exercised his royal prerogative from the first moment the throne was unpacked, even before it was connected to the pipes. So, it was an even trade—the king had to breathe workmen's stench, and Bull and Bear had been regularly treated to the sight and scent of healthy royal bowel movements.

The Grand Chamberlain steepled his fingers. "Plumbing is not required. Just the throne."

"I cannot imagine the royal household wants a second throne just for show."

The Grand Chamberlain sighed. "See for yourself."

He led Sylvain into the cedar-scented garderobe. A rainbow of velvet and satin cushions covered the floor. The toilet gleamed in a place of honor, bracketed by marble columns.

Something was growing in the toilet bowl. It looked like peach moss.

The moss turned its head. Two emerald eyes glared up at him.

"Minou has been offered a number of other seats, but she prefers the throne." The Grand Chamberlain looked embarrassed. "Our well-beloved king will not allow her to be disturbed. In fact, he banished the courtier who first attempted to move her."

The cat hissed, its tiny ivory fangs yellow against the glistening white porcelain. Sylvain stepped back. The cat's eyes narrowed with lazy menace.

A wide water drop formed in the bend of the golden pipes above the toilet. The drop slid across the painted porcelain reservoir and dangled for a few heartbeats. Then it plopped onto the cat's head. Minou's eyes popped wide as saucers.

Sylvain spun and fled the room, heart hammering.

The Grand Chamberlain followed. "Send the second throne immediately. This afternoon at the latest." The request was punctuated by the weight of gold as he discreetly passed Sylvain a pouch of coins.

"Certainly," Sylvain said, trying to keep his voice steady. "The cat may prefer the original throne, however."

"That will have to do."

When he was out of the Grand Chamberlain's sight, Sylvain rushed through the royal apartments and into the crowded Grand Gallery. There, in Versailles' crowded social fishbowl, he had no choice but to slow to a dignified saunter. He kept his gaze level and remote, hoping to make it through the long gallery uninterrupted.

"Sylvain, my dear brother, why rush away?" Gérard clamped his upper arm and muscled him to the side of the hall. "Stay and take a turn with me."

"Damn you," Sylvain hissed. "You know I haven't time for idling. Let me go."

Gérard snickered. "Don't deprive me of your company so soon."

Sylvain had seen his friend the Marquis de la Châsse in every imaginable situation—beardless and scared white by battle-scarred commanders, on drunken furlough in peat-stinking country taverns, wounded bloody and clawing battlefield turf. They had pulled each other out of danger a hundred times—nearly as often as they'd goaded each other into it.

Gérard's black wig was covered in coal-dark powder that broadcast a subtle musky scent. The deep plum of his coat accentuated the dark circles under his eyes and the haze of stubble on his jaw.

Sylvain pried his arm from Gérard's fist and fell into step beside him. At least there were no pipes overhead, no chance of a splattering. The gallery was probably one of the safest places in the palace. He steered his friend toward the doors and prepared to make his escape.

Gérard leaned close. "Tell me good news. Can it be done?"

"My answer hasn't changed."

Gérard growled, a menacing rumble deep in his broad chest.

"I've heard that noise on the battlefield, Gérard." Sylvain said. "It won't do you any good here."

"On a battlefield, you and I are on the same side. But here you insist on opposing me."

Sylvain nodded at the Comte de Tessé. The old man was promenading with his mistress, a woman young enough to be his granddaughter, and the two of them were wearing so much powder that an aura of tiny particles surrounded them with a faint pink glow. The comte raised his glove.

"I wonder," said the comte loudly, as if he were addressing the entire hall, "can Sylvain de Guilherand only make plain water dance, or does he also have power over the finest substances? Champagne, perhaps."

"Ingenuity has its limits, but I haven't found them yet." Sylvain let a faint smile play at the corners of his mouth.

"Surely our beloved king's birthday would be an appropriate day to test those limits. Right here, in fact, in the center of the Grand Gallery. What could be more exalted?"

Sylvain had no time for this. He nodded assent and the comte strolled on with an extra bounce in his step, dragging his mistress along by the elbow.

The doors of the Grand Gallery were barricaded by a gang of nuns who gaped up at the gilded and frescoed ceiling like baby sparrows in a nest. Sylvain and Gérard paced past.

"You don't seem to understand," Gérard said. "Pauline is desperate. It's vulgar to talk about money, but you know I'll make it worth your effort. Ready cash must be a problem. Courtiers rarely discharge their obligations."

"It's not a question of money or friendship. The north wing roof won't hold a reservoir. If the king himself wanted water in the north wing, I would have to refuse him."

"Then you must reinforce the roof."

Sylvain sighed. Gérard had never met a problem that couldn't be solved by gold or force. He couldn't appreciate the layers of influence and responsibility that would have to be peeled back to accomplish a major construction project like putting reservoirs on the north wing.

"Pauline complains every time she pisses," said Gérard. "Do you know how often a pregnant woman sits on her pot? And how often she gets up in the night? The smell bothers her, no matter how much perfume and rose water she applies, no matter how quickly her maid whisks away the filth. Pauline won't stop asking. I will have no peace until she gets one of your toilets."

"Sleep in a different room."

"Cold, lonely beds are for summer. In winter, you want a warm woman beside you."

"Isn't your wife intimate with the Marquise de Coupigny? I hear she keeps a rose bower around her toilet. Go stay with her."

"The marquise told my wife that she does not cater to the general relief of the public, and their intimacy has now ended in mutual loathing. This is what happens when friends refuse each other the essential comforts of life."

"I'll provide all the relief you need if you move to an apartment the pipes can reach."

"Your ingenuity has found its limits, then, despite your boasts. But your pipes reached a good long way yesterday. I hear it was a long siege. How high were the d'Arlain battlements?"

"You heard wrong. Annette d'Arlain is a virtuous woman."

"Did she tell you the king's mistress named her toilet after the queen? Madame pisses on Polish Mary. Pauline is disgusted. She asked me to find out what Annette d'Arlain says."

Two splashes pocked Sylvain's cheek. He looked around wildly for the source.

"Tears, my friend?" Gérard dangled his handkerchief in front of Sylvain's nose. "Annette is pretty enough but her cunt must be gorgeous."

Sylvain ignored his friend and scanned the ornate ceiling. The gilding and paint disguised stains and discolorations, but the flaws overhead came to light if you knew where to look.

There. A fresh water stain spread on the ceiling above the statue of Hermes. A huge drop formed in its gleaming centre. It grew, dangled like a jewel, and broke free with a snap. It bounced off the edge of a mirror, shot past him, then ricocheted off a window and smacked him on the side of his neck, soaking his collar.

Sylvain fled the Grand Gallery like a rabbit panicking for its burrow. He ran with no attention to dignity, stepping on the lace train of one woman, raking through the headdress feathers of another, shoving past a priest, setting a china vase rocking on its pedestal. The drone of empty conversation gave way to shocked exclamations as he dodged out of the room into one of the old wing's service corridors.

He skidded around a banister into a stairwell. Water rained down, slickening the stairs as he leapt two and three steps at a time. It spurted from joins, gushed from welded seams, and sprayed from faucets as he passed.

The narrow corridors leading to Sylvain's apartment were clogged with every species of servant native to the palace. The ceiling above held a battery of pipes—the main limb of the system Bull and Bear had installed two years before. Every joint and weld targeted Sylvain as he ran. Everyone was caught in the crossfire—servants, porters, tradesmen. Sylvain fled a chorus of curses and howls. It couldn't be helped.

Sylvain crashed through the door of his apartment. His breath rasped as he leaned on the door with all his weight, as if he could hold the line against disaster.

Bull and Bear knelt over a pile of dirty rags on the bare plank floor. Sylvain's servant stood over them, red-eyed and sniffling.

"What is this mess?" Sylvain demanded.

His servant slowly pulled aside one of the rags to reveal Leblanc's staring face, mottled green and white like an old cheese. Sylvain dropped to his knees and fished for the dead man's hand.

It was cold and slack. Death had come and gone, leaving only raw meat. All life had drained away from that familiar face, memories locked forever behind dead eyes, tongue choked down in a throat that would never speak again.

The first time they met, Sylvain had been startled speechless. The old soldier had talked familiarly to him in the clipped rough patois of home and expected him to understand. They were on the banks of the Moselle, just about as far from the southern Alps as a man could be and still find himself in France.

Sylvain should have cuffed the old man for being familiar with an officer, but he had been young and homesick, and words from home rang sweet. He kept Leblanc in his service just for the pleasure of hearing him talk. He made a poor figure of a servant but he could keep a tent dry in a swamp and make a pot of hot curds over two sticks and a wafer of peat. He'd kept the old man close all through the Polish wars, through two winters in Quebec, and then took him home on a long furlough. Sylvain hadn't been home for five years, and Leblanc hadn't seen the Alps in more than thirty, but he remembered every track of home, knew the name of every cliff, pond, and rill. Leblanc had even remembered Château de Guilherand, its high stone walls and vast glacier-fed waterworks.

Close as they'd been, Sylvain had never told the old man he was planning to catch a nixie and bring her to Versailles. Under the Sun King, the palace's fountains had been a wonder of the world. Their state of disrepair under Louis XV was a scandal bandied about and snickered over in parlors from Berlin to Naples. Sylvain knew he could bring honor back to the palace and enrich himself in the bargain. The fountains were just the beginning of his plan. There was no end to the conveniences and luxuries he could bring to the royal blood and courtiers of Versailles with a reliable, steady flow of clean, pure water.

She'd been just a tadpole. Sylvain had lured her into a leather canteen and kept her under his shirt, close to his heart, during the two weeks of steady hard travel it took to get from home to Versailles. The canteen had thrummed against his chest, drumming in time with hooves or footsteps or even the beating of his heart—turning any steady noise into a skeleton of a song. It echoed the old rhythms, the tunes he heard shepherds sing beside the high mountain rills as he passed by, rifle on his shoulder, tracking wild goats and breathing the sweet, cold, pure alpine air.

Sylvain had kept her a secret, or so he'd thought. The day after they arrived at Versailles, he'd snuck down to the cisterns, canteen still tucked under his shirt. A few hours later, Leblanc had found him down there, frustrated and sweating, shouting commands at the canteen, trying to get her to come out and swim in the cisterns.

"What you got there ain't animal nor people," Leblanc had told him. "Kick a dog and he'll crawl back to you and do better next time. A soldier obeys to avoid the whip and the noose. But that little fish has her own kind of mind."

Sylvain had thrown the canteen to the old man and stepped back. Leblanc cradled it in his arms like a baby.

"She don't owe you obedience like a good child knows it might. She's a wild creature. If you don't know that, you know nothing."

Leblanc crooned a lullaby to the canteen, tender as a new mother. The little fish had popped out into the cistern pool before he started the second verse, and he had her doing tricks within a day. Over the past two years, they'd been nearly inseparable.

"Ah, old Leblanc. What a shame." Gérard stood in the doorway, blocking the view of the gawkers in the corridor behind him. "A good soldier. He will be much missed."

Sylvain carefully folded Leblanc's hands over his bony cold breast. Bull and Bear crossed themselves as Sylvain drew his thumb and finger over the corpse's papery eyelids.

Gérard shut the door, closing out the gathered crowd. Sylvain tried to ignore the prickling ache between his eyes, the hollow thud of his gut.

"Sylvain, my dear friend. Do you know you're sitting in a puddle?"

Sylvain looked down. The floor under him was soaked. Bull dabbled at the edge of the puddle with the toe of his boot, sloshing a thin stream through the floorboards while Bear added to the puddle with a steady rain of tears off the tip of his ratted beard.

"I don't pretend to understand your business," said Gérard, "But I think there might be a problem with your water pipes."

Sylvain barked a laugh. He couldn't help himself. A problem with the pipes. Yes, and it would only get worse.

-4-

Sylvain had rarely visited the cisterns over the past two winters. There had been no need. The little fish was Leblanc's creature. The two of them had been alone for months while

Sylvain fought the summer campaigns, and through the winter, Sylvain had more than enough responsibilities above ground—renovating and repairing the palace's fountains, planning and executing the water systems, and most importantly, doing it all while maintaining the illusion of a courtly gentleman of leisure, attending levées and soirées, dinners and operas.

Versailles was the wonder of the world. The richest palace filled with the most cultivated courtiers, each room containing a ransom of art and statuary, the gardens rivaling heaven with endless fountains and statuary. The reputation it had gained at the height of the Sun King's reign persisted, but close examination showed a palace falling apart at the seams.

Sylvain had swept into Versailles and taken the waterworks for his own. He had brought the fountains back to their glory, making them play all day and all night for the pleasure of Louis the Well-Beloved—something even the Sun King couldn't have claimed.

The tunnel to the cisterns branched off the cellars of the palace's old wing, part of the original foundations. It had been unbearably dank when Sylvain had first seen it years before. Now it was fresh and floral. A wet breeze blew in his face, as though he were standing by a waterfall, the air pushed into motion by the sheer unyielding weight of falling water.

The nixie's mossy nest crouched in the centre of a wide stone pool. The rusted old pumps sprayed a fine mist overhead. The water in the pool pulsed, rising and falling with the cadence of breath.

She was draped over the edge of her nest, thin legs half submerged in the pool, long webbed feet gently stirring the water. The little fool didn't even know enough to keep still when pretending to sleep.

He skirted the edge of the pool, climbing to the highest and driest of the granite blocks. Dripping moss and ferns crusted the grotto's ceiling and walls. A million water droplets reflected the greenish glow of her skin.

"You there," he shouted, loud enough to carry over the symphony of gushes and drips. "What are you playing at?"

The nixie writhed in the moss. The wet glow of her skin grew stronger and the mist around her nest thickened until she seemed surrounded by tiny lights. She propped herself on one scrawny elbow and dangled a hand in the pool.

With her glistening skin and sleek form, she seemed as much salamander as child, but she didn't have a talent for stillness. Like a pool of water, she vibrated with every impulse.

A sigh rose over the noise. It was more a burbling gush than language. The sound repeated—it was no French word but something like the mountain patois of home. He caught the meaning after a few more repetitions.

"Bored," she said. Her lips trembled. Drips rained from the ferns. "So bored!"

"You are a spoiled child," he said in court French.

She broke into a grin and her big milky eyes glowed at him from across the pool. He shivered. They were human eyes, almost, and in that smooth amphibian face, they seemed uncanny. Dark salamander orbs would have been less disturbing.

"Sing," she said. "Sing a song?"

"I will not."

She draped herself backward over a pump, webbed hand to her forehead with all the panache of an opera singer. "So bored."

As least she wasn't asking for Leblanc. "Good girls who work hard are never bored."

A slim jet of water shot from the pump. It hit him square in the chest.

She laughed, a giddy burble. “I got you!”

Don’t react, Sylvain thought as the water dripped down his legs.

“Yes, you got me. But what will that get you in the end? Some good girls get presents, if they try hard enough. Would you like a present?”

Her brow creased as she thought it over. “Maybe,” she said.

Hardly the reaction he was hoping for, but good enough.

“Behave yourself. No water outside of the pipes and reservoirs. Keep it flowing and I’ll bring you a present just like a good girl.”

“Good girl,” she said in French. “But what will that get you in the end?”

She was a decent mimic—her accent was good. But she was like a parrot, repeating everything she heard.

“A nice present. Be a good girl.”

“Good girl,” she repeated in French. Then she reverted back to mountain tongue. “Sing a song?”

“No. I’ll see you in a few days.” Sylvain turned away, relief blossoming in his breast.

“Leblanc sing a song?” she called after him.

There it was. Stay calm, he thought. Animals can sense distress. Keep walking.

“Leblanc is busy,” he said over his shoulder. “He wants you to be a good girl.”

“Behave yourself,” she called as he disappeared around the corner.

-5-

Sylvain paced the Grand Gallery, eyeing the cracked ceiling above the statue of Hermes. There had been no further accidents with the pipes. He had spent the entire night checking every joint and join accompanied by a yawning Bull. At dawn, he'd taken Bear up to the rooftops to check the reservoirs.

Checking the Grand Gallery was his last task. He was shaved and primped, even though at this early hour, it would be abandoned by anyone who mattered, just a few rustics and gawkers.

He didn't expect to see Annette d'Arlain walking among them.

Annette was dressed in a confection of gold and scarlet chiffon. Golden powder accentuated the pale shadows of her collarbones and defined the delicate ivory curls of her wig. A troop of admiring rustics trailed behind her as she paced the gallery. She ignored them.

"The Comte de Tessé says you promised him a champagne fountain," she said, drawing the feathers of her fan between her fingers.

Sylvain bent deeply, pausing at the bottom of the bow to gather his wits. He barely recalled the exchange with the comte. What had he agreed to?

"I promised nothing," he said as he straightened. Annette hadn't offered her hand. She was cool and remote as any of the marble statues lining the gallery.

"The idea reached Madame's ear. She sent me to drop you a hint for the King's birthday. But—" She dropped her voice and paused with dramatic effect, snapping her fan.

Sylvain expected her to share a quiet confidence but she continued in the same impersonal tone. “But I must warn you. Everyone finds a champagne fountain disappointing. Flat champagne is a chore to drink. Like so many pleasures, anticipation cannot be matched by pallid reality.”

Was Annette truly offended or did she want to bring him to heel? Whatever the case, he owed her attention. He had seduced her, left her gasping on her sofa, and ignored her for two days. No gifts, no notes, no acknowledgement. This was no way to keep a woman’s favor.

Annette snapped her fan again as she waited for his reply.

It was time to play the courtier. He stepped closely so she would have to look up to meet his eyes. It would provide a nice tableau for the watching rustics. He dropped his voice low, pitching it for her ears alone.

“I would hate to disappoint you, madame.”

“A lover is always a disappointment. The frisson of expectation is the best part of any affair.”

“I disagree. I have never known disappointment in your company, only the fulfillment of my sweet and honeyed dreams.”

She was not impressed. “You saw heaven in my arms, I suppose.”

“I hope we both did.”

A hint of a dimple appeared on her cheek. “Man is mortal.”

“Alas,” he agreed.

She offered him her hand but withdrew it after a bare moment, just long enough for the lightest brush of his lips. She glided over to the statue of Hermes and drew her finger up the curve of the statue’s leg.

“You are lucky I don’t care for gifts and fripperies, monsieur. I detest cut flowers and I haven’t seen a jewel I care for in months.”

Sylvain glanced at the ceiling. A network of cracks formed around a disk of damp plaster. Annette was directly beneath it.

He grabbed her around the waist and yanked her aside. She squealed and rammed her fists against his chest. Passion was the only excuse for his behavior, so he grabbed at it like a drowning man and kissed her, crushing her against his chest. She struggled for a moment and finally yielded, lips parting for him reluctantly.

No use in putting in a pallid performance, he thought, and bent her backward in his arms to drive the kiss to a forceful conclusion. The rustics gasped in appreciation. He released her, just cupping the small of her back.

He tried for a seductive growl. “How can a man retain a lady’s favor if gifts are forbidden?”

“Not by acting like a beast!” she cried, and smacked her fan across his cheek.

Annette ran for the nearest door, draperies trailing behind her. The ceiling peeled away with a ripping crack. A huge chunk of plaster crashed over the statue’s head, throwing hunks of wet plaster across the room. The rustics scattered, shocked and thrilled.

He crushed a piece of wet plaster under his heel, grinding it into mush with a vicious twist, and stalked out of the gallery.

The main corridor was crowded. Servants rushed with buckets of coals, trays of pastries, baskets of fruit—all the comforts required by late sleeping and lazy courtiers. He pushed through them and climbed to a vestibule on the third floor where five water pipes met overhead.

“What have you got for me, you little demon?” he seethed under his breath.

A maid clattered down the stairs, her arms stacked with clean laundry. One look at Sylvain and she retreated back upstairs.

Sylvain had spent nights on bare high rock trapped by spring snowstorms. He had tracked wild goats up the massif cliff to line up careful rifle shots balanced between a boulder and a thousand-foot drop. He had once snatched a bleating lamb from the jaws of the valley's most notorious wolf. He had met the king's enemies on the battlefield and led men to their deaths. He could master a simple creature, however powerful she was.

"Go ahead, drip on me. If you are going to keep playing your games, show me now."

He waited. The pipes looked dry as bone. The seal welds were dull and gray and the tops of the pipes were furred with a fine layer of dust.

He gave the pipes one last searing glare. "All right. We have an understanding."

-6-

Leblanc's coffin glowed in the cold winter sun. Bull and Bear watched the gravediggers and snuffled loudly.

Gérard had taken all the arrangements in hand. Before Sylvain had a moment to think about dealing with the old soldier's corpse, it had been washed, dressed, and laid out in a village chapel. Gérard had even arranged for a nun to sit beside the coffin, clacking her rosary and gumming toothless prayers.

The nun was scandalized when Bull and Bear hauled the coffin out from under her nose, but Sylvain wanted Leblanc's body away from the palace, hidden away in deep, dry dirt where the little fish could never find it. Gérard and Sylvain led the way on horseback, setting a fast pace as Bull and Bear followed with the casket jouncing in the bed of their cart. They trotted toward the city until they found a likely boneyard, high on dry ground, far from any streams or canals.

"This is probably the finest bed your man Leblanc ever slept in." Gérard nudged the coffin with the toe of his boot.

"Very generous of you, Gérard. Thank you."

Gérard shrugged. "What price eternal comfort? And he was dear to you, I know."

Sylvain scanned the sky as the priest muttered over the grave. A battery of rainclouds was gathering on the horizon, bearing down on Versailles. It was a coincidence. The little fish couldn't control the weather. It wasn't possible.

The gravediggers began slowly filling in the grave. Gérard walked off to speak with a tradesman in a dusty leather apron. Sylvain watched the distant clouds darken and turn the horizon silver with rain.

Gérard returned. "Here is the stonemason. What will you have on your man's gravestone?"

"Nothing," said Sylvain, and then wondered. Was he being ridiculous, rushing the corpse out of the palace and hauling it miles away? She couldn't understand. She was an animal. Any understanding of death was just simple instinct—the hand of fate to be avoided in the moment of crisis. She couldn't read. The stone could say anything. She would never know.

Without Leblanc's help, Sylvain's funds wouldn't have lasted a month at Versailles. He would have wrung out his purse and slunk home a failure. But with Leblanc down in the cisterns coddling the little fish, the whole palace waited eagerly in bed for him. And what had he done for the old soldier in return? Leblanc deserved a memorial.

The stone mason flapped his cap against his leg. The priest clacked his tongue in disapproval.

"He must have a stone, Sylvain," said Gérard. "He was a soldier his whole life. He deserves no less."

There was no point in being careless. "You can list the year of his death, nothing more. No name, no regiment."

Sylvain gave the priest and the stonemason each a coin, stifling any further objections.

The gravediggers were so slow, they might as well have been filling in the grave with spoons instead of spades. Sylvain ordered Bull and Bear to take over. The gravediggers stood openmouthed, fascinated by the sight of someone else digging while they rested. One of them yawned.

"Idle hands are the Devil's tools," the priest snapped, and sent both men back to their work in the adjoining farmyard.

An idea bloomed in Sylvain's mind. The little fish claimed she was bored. Perhaps he had made her work too easy. The lead pipes and huge reservoirs were doing half the job. He could change that. He would keep her busy—too busy for boredom and certainly far too busy for games and tricks.

"Tell your wife she won't wait much longer for a toilet of her own," said Sylvain as they mounted their horses. "In a few days she can have the pleasure of granting or denying her friends its use as she pleases."

Gérard grinned. "Wonderful news! But just a few days? How long will it take to reinforce the roof?"

"I believe I have discovered a quick solution."

-7-

The new water conduits were far too flimsy to be called pipes. They were sleeves, really, which was how had he explained them to the village seamstresses.

"Sing a song?" The little fish dangled one long toe in the water. Her smooth skin bubbled with wide water droplets that glistened and gleamed like jewels.

"Not today. It's time for you to work," Sylvain said as he unrolled the cotton sleeve. He dropped one end in the pool, looped a short piece of rope around it, and weighted the ends with a rock.

"Be a good girl and show me what you can do with this."

She blinked at him, water dripping from her hair. No shade of comprehension marred the perfect ignorance of those uncanny eyes. She slid into the water and disappeared.

He waited. She surfaced in the middle of the pool, lips spouting a stream of water high into the air.

"Very good, but look over here now," he said, admiring his own restraint. "Do you see this length of cotton? It's hollow like a pipe. Show me how well you can push water through it."

She rolled and dove. The water shimmered, then turned still. He searched the glassy surface, looking for her sleek form. She leapt, shattering the water under his nose, throwing a great wave that splashed him from head to toe.

How had Leblanc put up with this? Sylvain turned away, hiding his frustration.

As he pried himself out of his soaked velvet jacket, Sylvain realized he was speaking to her in court French. A nixie couldn't be expected to understand.

The next time she surfaced he said, "I bet you can't force water through this tube." The rough patois of home felt strange after years wrapping his tongue around court French.

That got her attention. "Bet you!" She leapt out of the water. "Bet you what?"

"Well, I don't know. Let's see what I have." He made a show of reluctantly reaching into his breast pocket and withdrawing a coin. It was small change—no palace servant would stoop to pick it up—but it had been polished to gleaming.

He rolled the coin between his thumb and forefinger, letting it wink and sparkle in the glow of her skin. The drops raining from her hair quickened, spattering the toes of his boots.

"Pretty," she said, and brushed the tip of one long finger along the cotton tube.

The pool shimmered. The tube swelled and kicked. It writhed like a snake, spraying water high into the ferns, but the other end remained anchored in the water. The tube leaked, not just from the seams but along its whole length.

"Good work," he said, and tossed her the coin. She let it sail over her head and splash into the pool. She laughed, a bubbling giggle, flexed her sleek legs, and flipped backward, following the coin's trajectory under the surface.

He repeated the experiment with all of the different cloth pipes—linen, silk, satin—every material available. The first cotton tube kept much of its rigidity though it remained terribly leaky, as did the wide brown tube of rough holland. The linen tube lay flat as a dead snake, and across the pond, a battery of satin and silk tubes warred, clashing like swords as they flipped and danced.

The velvet pipes worked best. The thick nap held a layer of water within its fibers, and after a few tries, the little fish learned to manipulate the wet surface, strengthening the tube and keeping it watertight.

By evening, her lair was festooned with a parti-colored bouquet of leaping, spouting tubes. The little fish laughed like a mad child, clapping her hands and jumping through the spray. But he didn't have to remind her to keep the spray away from him—not once.

When he was down to his last shiny coin, her skin was glowing so brightly, it illuminated the far corners of the grotto. He placed the last coin squarely in her slender palm, as if paying a tradesman. The webs between her fingers were as translucent as soap bubbles.

"You won a lot of bets today," he said.

"Good girls win." She dropped the coin into the pond and peered up at him, eyes wide and imploring.

He cut her off before she could speak. "No singing, only work."

"You sang once."

He had, that was true. How could she remember? He'd nearly forgotten himself. He had crouched at the edge of a high mountain cataract with icy mist spraying his face and beading on his hair, singing a shepherd's tune to lure her into his canteen. She'd been no bigger than a tadpole, but she could flip and jump through the massive rapids as if it took no effort at all.

She had grown so much in the past two years. From smaller than his thumb to the size of a half-grown child. Full growth from egg in just two years.

But two years was a lifetime ago, and those mountains now seemed unreachable and remote. He wouldn't think about it. He had an evening of entertainments to attend, and after that, much work to do.

-8-

Sylvain had almost drifted off when Annette dug her toes into the muscle of his calf. He rolled over and pretended to sleep.

He had given her an afternoon of ardent attention and finished up splayed across her bed, fully naked, spent, and sweating. Though he was bone tired from long nights planning the palace's new array of velvet tubes, he had given Annette a very good facsimile of devotion and several hours of his time. Surely she couldn't want more from him.

She raked her toenails down his calf again. Sylvain cracked an eyelid, trying for the lazy gaze of the Versailles sybarite. Annette reclined in the middle of the bed draped in a scrap of pink chiffon. The short locks of her own dark hair curled over her ears like a boy's. She had ripped the wig from his head earlier, and he had responded by pulling hers off as well, more gently but with equal enthusiasm.

"No sleeping, Sylvain. Not here. You must be prepared to leap from the window if my husband arrives."

"You want me to dash naked through the gardens in full view of half the court? My dear woman, it would mean my death and your disappointment." He couldn't suppress a yawn. "The ladies would hound after me day and night."

"I forgot that about you," she said under her breath.

Sylvain rolled to his feet and lifted a silken shawl off the floor. He wrapped it around his hips and returned to bed. He lifted an eyebrow, inviting her to continue, but she had begun playing with a pot of cosmetic.

"What did you forget about me?" If she meant to insult him, he intended to know.

She put her foot in his lap. "I forgot that you are a singular man."

That didn't sound like an insult. Sylvain let a smile touch his lips. "Is that your own assessment, or do others speak of me as a singular man?"

"My judgment alone. How many people in the palace ever take a moment to think of anyone other than themselves? Even I, as extraordinary as I am, rarely find a moment to notice the existence of others. Life is so full." She nudged him with her toe.

"In this moment, then, before it passes, tell me what you mean by *singular*." To encourage her, he took her foot in both hands and squeezed.

A dimple appeared on her cheek. "It is a contradiction and a conundrum. By *singular*, I mean the exact opposite. You are at least three or four men where many others have trouble achieving more than a half manhood."

"Flattery. Isn't that my role?"

"I mean no flattery. Quite the opposite, in fact." She dipped her finger into the cosmetic pot and daubed her pout with glossy pigment. Then she stretched herself back on the velvet pillows, arching as he kneaded her toes.

"Sylvain the wit may be a good guest to have at a dinner party but no better than any other man with some quickness about him. Sylvain the courtier contributes to the might of the crown and the luxury of the palace as he ought. Sylvain the lover conducts himself well in bed as he must or sleep alone. I can't speak to Sylvain the soldier or hunter but will grant the appropriate virtues on faith."

"I thank you," he said, kneading her heel.

She fanned her fingers in a dismissive gesture. "All these are expected and nothing spectacular to comment upon. But the true Sylvain is the singular one—the only one—and yet he's the man few others notice."

"And that man is?"

"I don't know if I should tell you. You might stop massaging my foot."

"You enjoy being mysterious."

"The only mystery is how you've gotten away with it for so long. If anyone else knew, you'd be run out of the palace."

"I will stop if you don't tell me."

"Very well. Sylvain, you are a striver."

A lead weight dropped into his stomach. "Ridiculous. I thought you were going to say something interesting, but it is all blather."

She nudged his crotch with her foot. "Don't be insulted. Striving must be in your nature. Or perhaps you were taught it as a child and took it into the blood with your host and catechism. But it will all end in disaster. Striving always does."

He kept his expression remote and resumed stroking her foot.

"You seek to raise yourself above your station," she continued. "Those who do have no true home. They leave behind their rightful and God-given place and yet never reach their goal. It is a kind of Limbo, a choice to begin eternity in purgatory even before death."

"And you have chosen to become a lay preacher. Do you have a wooden crate to stand on? Shall I carry it to a crossroads for you?"

"Oh, very well, we can change the topic to Annette d'Arlain if you are uncomfortable. I find myself a most engaging subject."

"Yes, keep to your area of expertise because you know little of me. I don't seek to raise myself. I am where I belong. The palace would be poorer without me."

"If you remained satisfied with being a lover, a courtier, and a good dinner guest, I might agree with you. Your uncle is a minor noble but I suppose his lineage is solid, should anyone care to trace it, and you're not the first heir to a barren wilderness to manage a creditable reputation at court. But you want to be the first man of Versailles, even at the destruction of your own self and soul. You are striving to be better than every other man."

"That is the first thing you've said that makes any sense."

Sylvain eased her into his lap. He slid his fingers under the chiffon wrap and began teasing her into an eagerly agreeable frame of mind. She would declare him the best man in France before he was done with her, even if it took all evening.

-9-

The monkey clung to Sylvain's neck and hid its face under his coat collar. Sylvain hummed under his breath, a low cooing sound shepherds used to calm lambs.

The dealer had doused the monkey in cheap cologne to mask its animal scent. The stink must be a constant irritation to the creature's acute sense of smell. But it would wear off soon enough in the mist of the cisterns.

Sylvain rounded the corner into the little fish's cavern and tripped. He slammed to his knees and twisted to take the weight of the fall on his shoulder. The monkey squealed with fright. He hushed it gently.

"Work carefully, be a good girl!" The little fish's voice echoed off the grotto walls.

He had tripped over the painted wooden cradle. The little fish had stuffed it with all of the dolls Sylvain had given her over the past week. The family of straw-and-cloth dolls were soaked and squashed down to form a nest for the large porcelain doll Sylvain had brought her the day before. It had arrived as a gift from the porcelain manufacturer, along with the toilets Bull and Bear were installing in the north wing.

The doll's platinum curls had been partly ripped away. Its painted eyes stared up at him as he struggled to his feet.

The little fish perched on the roof of her dollhouse, which floated half submerged in the pool. The toy furniture bobbed and drifted in the current.

“Come here, little miss,” he said. She slipped off the roof and glided across to him. She showed no interest in the monkey, but she probably hadn’t realized it was anything other than just another doll.

“Do you remember what we are going to do today?” he asked. “I told you yesterday; think back and remember.” She blinked up at him in ignorance. “What do you do every day?”

“Work hard.”

“Very good. Work hard at what?”

“Good girls work hard and keep the water flowing.” She yawned, treating him to a full view of her tongue and tiny teeth as she stretched.

The monkey yawned in sympathy. Her gaze snapped to the creature with sudden interest.

“Sharp teeth!” She jumped out of the pool and thrust one long finger in the monkey’s face. It recoiled, clinging to Sylvain with all four limbs.

“Hush,” he said, stroking the monkey’s back. “You frightened her. Good girls don’t frighten their friends, do they?”

“Do they?” she repeated automatically. She was fascinated by the monkey, which was certainly a more engaged reaction than she had given any of the toys Sylvain had brought her.

He fished in his pocket for the leash and clipped it to the monkey’s collar.

“Today, we are adding the new cloth pipes to the system, and you will keep the water flowing like you always do, smooth and orderly. If you do your work properly, you can play with your new friend.”

He handed her the leash and gently extracted himself from the monkey’s grip. He placed the creature on the ground and stroked its head with exaggerated kindness. If she could copy his words, she could copy his actions.

She touched the monkey's furry flank, eyes wide with delight. Then she brought her hand to her face and whiffed it.

"Stinky," she said.

She dove backward off the rock, yanking the monkey behind her by its neck.

Sylvain dove to grab it but just missed his grip. The monkey's sharp squeal cut short as it was dragged under water.

Sylvain ran along the edge of the pool, trying to follow the glow of her form as she circled and dove. When she broke surface he called to her, but she ignored him and climbed to the roof of her dollhouse. She hauled the monkey up by its collar and laid its limp, sodden form on the spine of the roof.

Dead, Sylvain thought. She had drowned it.

It stirred. She scooped the monkey under its arms and dandled it on her lap like a doll. It coughed and squirmed.

"Sing a song," she demanded. She shoved her face nose to nose with the monkey's and yelled, "Sing a song!"

The monkey twisted and strained, desperate to claw away. She released her grip and the monkey splashed into the water. She yanked the leash and hauled it up. It dangled like a fish. She let her hand drop and the monkey sank again, thrashing.

"Sing a song!" she screamed. "Sing!"

Sylvain pried off his boots and dove into the pool. He struggled to the surface and kicked off a rock, propelling himself though the water.

"Stop it," he blurted as he struggled toward her. "Stop it this instant!"

She crouched on the edge of the dollhouse roof, dangling the monkey over the water by its collar. It raked at her with all four feet, but the animal dealer had blunted its claws, leaving the poor creature with no way to defend itself. She dunked it again. Its paws pinwheeled, slapping the surface.

Sylvain ripped his watch from his pocket and lobbed it at her. It smacked her square in the temple. She dropped the monkey and turned on him, enormous eyes veined with red, lids swollen.

He hooked his arm over the peak of the dollhouse roof and hoisted himself halfway out of the water. He fished the monkey out and gathered the quivering creature to his chest.

"Bad girl," he sputtered, so angry he could barely find breath. "Very bad girl!"

She retreated to the edge of the roof and curled her thin arms around her knees. Her nose was puffy and red just like a human's.

"Leblanc," she sobbed. "Leblanc gone."

She hadn't mentioned Leblanc in days. Sylvain had assumed she'd forgotten the old man, but some hounds missed their masters for years. Why had he assumed the little fish would have coarser feelings than an animal?

She was an animal, though. She would have drowned the monkey and toyed with its corpse. There was no point in coddling her—he would be stern and unyielding.

"Yes, Leblanc has gone away." He gave her his chilliest stare.

Her chin quivered. She whispered, "Because I am a bad girl."

Had she been blaming herself all this time? Beneath the mindless laughter and games she had been missing Leblanc—lonely, regretful, brokenhearted. Wondering if she'd done wrong, if she'd driven him away. Waiting to see him again, expecting him every moment.

Sylvain clambered onto the dollhouse roof and perched between the two chimneys. The monkey climbed onto his shoulder and snaked its fingers into his hair.

"No, little one. Leblanc didn't want to go but he had to."

"Leblanc come back?"

She looked so trusting. He could lie to her, tell her Leblanc would come back if she was a good girl, worked hard, and never caused any problems. She would believe him. He could make her do anything he wanted.

"No, little one. Leblanc is gone and he can never come back."

She folded in on herself, hiding her face in her hands.

"He would have said goodbye to you if he could. I'm sorry he didn't."

Sylvain pulled her close, squeezing her bony, quaking shoulders, tucking her wet head under his chin.

There was an old song he had often heard in the mountains. On one of his very first hunting trips as a boy, he'd heard an ancient shepherd sing it while climbing up a long scree slope searching for a lost lamb. He had heard a crying girl sing it as she flayed the pelt from the half-eaten, wolf-ravaged corpse of an ewe. He'd heard a boy sing it to his flock during a sudden spring snowstorm, heard a mother sing it to her children on a freezing winter night as he passed by her hut on horseback. The words were rustic, the melody simple.

Sylvain sang the song now to the little fish, gently at first, just breathing the tune, and then stronger, letting the sound swell between them. He sang of care, and comfort, and loss, and a longing to make everything better. And if tears seemed to rain down his cheeks as he sang, it was nothing but an illusion—just water dribbling from his hair.

-10-

Sylvain stood on the roof of the north wing, the gardens spread out before him. The fountains jetted high and strong, fifteen hundred nozzles ticking over reliably as clockwork, the water spouts throwing flickering shadows in the low evening light.

The gardens were deserted as any wilderness. Inside, everyone was preparing for the evening's long menu of events. Outside, the statues posed and the fountains played for the moon and stars alone.

Sylvain was taking advantage of this quiet and solitary hour to do one final check of the velvet pipes. He had already felt every inch of the new connection, examined the seams all the way to the point where the fabric sleeve dove off the roof to disappear through a gap above a garret window.

Bull and Bear waited by the main reservoir, watching for his signal. There was no point in delaying any further. He waved his hat in the air. The sleeve at his feet jumped and swelled.

Sylvain ran from the north wing attics down several flights of stairs to Gérard's apartments. Pauline greeted him at the door herself. She was hugely pregnant and cradled her belly in both hands to support its weight. Breathless, he swept off his hat and bowed.

"Go ahead, monsieur," Pauline said as she herded him toward her dressing room. "Please don't pause to be polite. I've waited as long as I can."

Not only were the velvet pipes lighter and easier to install, but they could be pinched off at any point simply by drawing a cord around the sleeve. Sylvain waited for Pauline to follow him, then pulled the red ribbon's tail and let it drift to the floor. Water gushed into the toilet, gurgling and tinkling against the porcelain.

Pauline seized him by the ears, kissed him hard on both cheeks, and shooed him away. She hiked her skirts up to her hips even before her servant shut the door behind him.

Sylvain arrived fashionably late at the suite of the Mahmud emissary, a Frenchman turned Turk after years at the Sultan's court. Sylvain saluted le Turque, lifted a glass of wine, and assumed an air of languid nonchalance. Madame and her ladies swept in. Their jewels and silks glowed in the candlelight.

Annette carried Madame's train—a sure sign she was in favor at that moment. Sylvain saluted her with a respectful nod. She dimpled at him and made her way over as soon as the host claimed Madame's attention.

"Is that for me, monsieur?" she asked.

Sylvain glanced at the monkey on his shoulder. "Perhaps, if there is a woman in the room who isn't tired of gifts."

"Jewels and flowers are all the same. This is something different." She caressed the monkey under her chin. It reached for Annette like a child for its mother. "What is her name?"

"Whatever you want, of course."

"I will ask Madame to choose her name. She will love that." Annette cradled the monkey against her breast and nuzzled its neck. "Oh, she smells lovely—vanilla and cinnamon oil."

It was the only combination of scents Sylvain had found to kill the stench of cheap cologne. He allowed himself a satisfied smirk.

Across the room a subtle commotion was building. Le Turque had lifted a curtain to reveal a pair of acrobats, but

Madame was watching Annette and Sylvain. The acrobats were frozen in a high lift, waiting for permission to begin their performance as the musicians repeated the same few bars of music.

"You had better go back. Madame has noticed the monkey and is jealous for your return."

Annette awarded him a melting smile and drifted back to Madame's circle. The ladies greeted the monkey as if it were a firstborn son. Madame let the effusions continue for a few moments and then took sole possession of the creature, holding it close as she turned her attention to the performance.

Sylvain struggled to stay alert, despite the near-naked spectacle on stage. He had barely seen his bed since Leblanc's death, and the warm wine and rich food were turning his courtier's air of languid boredom into the prelude to a toddler's nap. The spinning and leaping acrobats were mesmerizing—especially when viewed in candlelight through a screen of nodding wigs and feathers. The bright silk-and satin-clad backs in front of him dipped as they lifted their glasses to their lips, swayed from side to side as they leaned over to gossip with the friend on the left about the friend on the right, then turned the other way to repeat the performance in reverse. Men and women they might be, but tonight they seemed more like the flamingoes that flocked on the Camargue, all alike in their brainless and feathered idiocy.

At least a flamingo made a good roast.

Sylvain spotted Gérard sneaking into the room, stealthy as a scout. He took his place by Sylvain's side as if he'd been there all evening.

"Thank God, Gérard," Sylvain whispered. "Stick your sword into my foot if you see me nodding off."

Gérard grinned. "It's the least I could do for the man who has brought such happiness to my wife."

The acrobats were succeeded by a troupe of burly Turkish dancers bearing magnums of champagne entombed in blocks of ice. Children dressed as cherubs passed crystal saucers to the guests.

"This will keep you awake, my friend. Champagne cold as a cuckold's bed."

"I've been in such a bed recently. It was quite warm."

Le Turque himself filled Sylvain and Gérard's saucers. "Tonight, you are in favor with the ladies, monsieur."

"Am I?" Sylvain sipped his champagne. The cold, sweet fizz drilled into his sinuses. His eyes watered as he forced back the urge to sneeze.

"So true!" said Gérard. "My own wife is ready to call Sylvain a saint. She has set up an altar to him in her dressing room."

"But I refused the honor," said Sylvain. "I would prefer not to have those offerings dedicated to me."

They laughed. Le Turque gave them a chill grimace.

"My apologies, monsieur," said Gérard. "It is not a private joke, just too coarse for general consumption. We are soldiers, you know, and are welcomed into civilized homes on charity."

Le Turque demonstrated his kind forbearance by topping up both their saucers before moving on to the other guests.

Sylvain studied the champagne and their enclosing blocks of ice as the Turkish dancers circled the room, trailing meltwater on the carpet. The bottles couldn't have been frozen into the ice or the wine would be frozen through. They must be made from dual pieces carved to enclose a bottle like a book. He stopped a dancer and examined the ice. Yes, the two pieces were joined by a seam.

A simple solution, too practical to be called ingenious, but effective. The guests were impressed, even though many of them were fingering their jaws and wincing from cold-induced toothache. Not one guest refused a second glass, or a third, or a fourth. Bottles were being drained at impressive rate.

Annette drew her fan up to her ear and flicked Sylvain a telling glance from across the room. He took Gérard's arm. "Come along; we are being summoned to an audience with Madame."

The royal mistress was dressed in white and silver. Her snowy wig was fine as lamb's wool, her skin frosted with platinum powder. A bouquet of brightly clad ladies surrounded her like flowers around a statue. The monkey slept in her lap. She had tied a silver ribbon around its neck.

The standard palace practice was to praise Madame's face and figure in public and criticize it in private. Sylvain had seen her often, but always at a distance. Now after months of maneuvering, he was finally close enough to judge for himself.

"A triumph worthy of our Turkish friends, is it not?" Madame offered Sylvain her hand. "I shall never be able to enjoy champagne at cellar temperature again. It is so refreshing. One feels renewed."

"Our host has distinguished himself," said Sylvain, brushing her knuckles with his lips. Madame let her fingers linger in his palm for a moment before presenting her hand to Gérard.

"Le Turque is an old man and has resources appropriate to his age and rank," said Madame. "I wonder how young men can become distinguished in the king's gaze."

"Perhaps by murdering the king's enemies on the battlefield every summer?" said Gérard.

The ladies tittered. Madame slowly drew back her hand and blinked. Pretty, thought Sylvain, at least when surprised.

"Excuse my friend, Madame. Cold champagne has frozen his brain."

Madame eyed Gérard up and down. "Everyone respects our valiant soldiers, and your devotion to manly duty is admirable." She turned back to Sylvain. "If your brawny friend the Marquis de la Châsse is content with his achievements, who are we to criticize? But you, monsieur, I know you care about the honor of France both on and off the field of war."

"Every Frenchman does, madame, but especially when he has been drinking champagne," said Sylvain. Gérard lifted his glass in salute.

Madame flicked her fan at Annette. "You may have heard an idea of mine. At first, it was just an idle thought, but now le Turque has thrown down the gauntlet. Is there a man who will accept the challenge?"

"No man could refuse you anything, madame. The rulers of the world fall at your feet."

"I would rush to serve you," said Gérard, "if I had any idea what you meant. Madame is so mysterious."

Madame dismissed Gérard with flick of her fan. "Be so good as to fetch me one of those dancers, monsieur."

"A Turk with a full magnum, Madame?" Gérard saluted her and set off with a jaunty military stride.

Madame shifted on the sofa. She seemed to be considering whether or not to invite Sylvain to sit. Then she lifted the monkey from her lap and set it beside her.

Not nearly so lovely as Annette, Sylvain decided.

"You may not know, monsieur, how highly you are praised. I am told that even when the Bassin d'Apollon was new, fountain-play was a parsimonious affair, the water doled out like pennies from a Polish matron's purse."

She paused to collect dutiful titters from her ladies for this jab at the queen. Perhaps not pretty at all, thought Sylvain. Hardly passable.

"You have found a way to keep all of the fountains constantly alive without pause. Some members of the royal household call you a magician, but the word from the highest level is less fanciful and more valuable. There, you are simply called inspiring."

Sylvain puffed up at the praise. Gérard returned with a beefy Turk. The dancer's fingers were blue from the cold, and he struggled to fill Madame's saucer without dribbling.

"Just like a commander on the battlefield, a woman judges a man by his actions." She lifted the monkey and planted a kiss between its ears. "Any other man would have collared this monkey's neck with a diamond bracelet before presenting it to a lady of the court. We would call that vulgar."

Her ladies nodded.

"You have taste and discernment. So give me champagne, free-flowing and cold. That is a triumph worthy of Versailles." She presented her hand to Sylvain again, then waved him away. The ladies closed around her like a curtain.

"Vulgar, indeed," said Gérard as they retreated. "I've never seen a woman greet a diamond with anything other than screeches of delight. Have you?"

"My experience with diamonds is limited."

"Madame knows it. She was spreading you with icing."

"She wants to secure a valuable ally. Compliments are the currency of court."

Gérard drained his champagne and rubbed his knuckles over his jaw as if it ached. "She just wants to drink champagne at another man's expense. As with most pleasures, it comes with a little pain. She wants the pain to be yours, not hers."

"The champagne fountain is a whim. She will ask me for something else next time."

"Very well. Madame will ask you to do something expensive and original with only a few pretty words as payment. Will you do it?"

Two full glasses of red wine had been abandoned at the foot of a statue. Sylvain fetched them and passed one to his friend. After the sweet champagne, the warm wine tasted flat and murky as swamp water.

"Only a fool would pass up the opportunity."

-11-

"Papa, come play!"

The nixie swam backward against a vortex of current, dodging spinning hunks of ice that floated like miniature icebergs, splintering and splitting as they smashed together. Overhead, the red-and-blue parrot climbed among the fern fronds, screeching and flapping its wings.

As he had suspected, the little fish loved ice. He had once seen a nixie swimming at the foot of a glacier, playing with ice boulders as they calved from the ice field's flank. The nixie had pushed them around like kindling, building a dam that spread a wide lake of turquoise meltwater over the moraine.

"Papa, come play!"

"Papa!" The parrot screeched its name.

Sylvain had purchased the bird from an elderly lady who was moldering in a north-wing garret, wearing threadbare finery from the Sun King's reign and living off charity and crumbs of her neighbors' leftover meals. The parrot was a good companion for the little fish. It was old and wily, and with its sharp beak and talons, it was well equipped to protect itself if she got too rough. It could fly out of reach and was fast enough to dodge sprays and splashes.

"Papa?" The nixie levered herself up the lip of her nest and stared at Sylvain expectantly. "Papa come play?"

Sylvain felt in his pockets for the last of the walnuts. "Here, little one. See if you can lure Papa down with this."

"Bird! Food!" she yelled, waving the walnut aloft. The parrot kited down to the nest and plucked the nut from her fist.

"Come play, Papa?" she asked. She wasn't looking at the bird. Her uncanny gaze was for him alone.

"That's quite enough of that," he said. "The bird's name is Papa, and you'll do well to remember it, young lady."

She leaned close and spoke slowly, explaining. "Bird is Bird, Papa is Papa."

"Papa," agreed the parrot, its beady gaze fixed on Sylvain.

"You are impossible." Sylvain waved at the surface of the pond, which was now carpeted with icy slurry circulating in the slowing current. "Clear away your toys or I'll freeze swimming across."

"Papa go away?"

"The bird is staying here with you. I am going to see about my important business. When I come back, I'll bring more walnuts for Papa and nothing for you. Now clean up the ice."

She laughed and dove. The water bubbled like a soup pot, forcing the slush to congeal into wads the size of lily pads. As the turbulence increased the leaves tilted and stacked, climbing into columns of gleaming ice that stretched and branched overhead.

The parrot flew to the top of a column and nibbled at the ice. It was solid and hard as rock.

"Very impressive," breathed Sylvain.

He had spent the past few days running up debts with the village icemongers and pushing cartloads of straw-wrapped ice blocks down the tunnels. Though she had never seen ice, she had taken to it instinctively, tossing it around the grotto, building walls and dams, smashing and splitting the blocks into shard and slag, and playing in the slush like a pig in mud. But now she was creating ice. This was extraordinary.

"Come here, little one," he said.

Obedient for the moment, she slipped over the surface to tread water at the edge of the nest. Above the water, her pale green skin was furred with frost. Steam snaked from her nostrils and gill slits.

"Show me how you did that," he said.

She blinked. "Show me how, Papa?"

He spoke slowly. "The ice was melted into slush, but you froze it again, building this." He pointed to an ice branch. The parrot sidestepped along the branch, bobbing its head and gobbling to itself. "Can you do it again?"

She shrugged. "You are impossible."

He scooped up a fistful of water and held it out in his cupped hand. "Give it a try. Can you freeze this?"

The little fish peered up at him with that familiar imploring, pleading expression. He could hear her request even before she opened her mouth.

"Sing a song?"

Gifts were one thing but blatant bribery was another. If he began exchanging favor for favor, it would be a constant battle. But he had no time for arguments. He could risk a small bribe.

"I will sing you one song—a very short song—and only because you have been such a good girl today. But first freeze this water."

"One song," she agreed.

Heat radiated up his arm. The water in his fist crackled and jumped, forming quills of ice that spread from his palm like a chestnut conker. He was so astonished that he forgot to breathe for a few moments. Then he drew in a great breath and let himself sing.

The foresters of home played great lilting reels on pipes and fiddles. Their lives were as poor and starved as the shepherds in the meadows above or the farmers in the valley below, but they were proud and honed the sense of their own superiority as sharp as the edges on their axes. Their songs bragged of prowess at dancing, singing, making love, and of course at the daredevil feats required by their trade. The song that came to his lips told of a young man proving his worth by riding a raft of logs down a grassy mountainside in full view of the lowly villagers in the valley below.

He only meant to give her the first verse, but the little fish danced and leaped with such joy that he simply gave himself over to the song—abandoned himself so completely that halfway through the second verse, he found himself punctuating the rhythm with sharp staccato hand claps just as proudly as any forester. He sang all six verses, and when he was done, she leapt into his arms and hugged her thin arms around his neck.

"Papa sing good," she whispered, her breath chill in his ear.

He patted her between the shoulder blades. Her skin was cold and clammy under a skiff of frost. Sylvain leaned back and loosened her arms a bit so he could examine her closely.

Her eyes were keen, her skin bright. She was strong and healthy, and if she was a bit troublesome and a little demanding, it was no more than any child.

-12-

"Annette tells me you had your men run water to the north wing."

Madame reclined on a golden sofa, encased and seemingly immobilized by the jagged folds of her silver robe. Her cleavage, shoulders, and neck protruded—a stem to support her rosebud-pale face. Her ladies gathered around her, gaudy in their bright, billowing silks.

Annette avoided his eye. Sylvain brushed imaginary lint from his sleeve, feigning unconcern. "I believe my foreman mentioned that they had finally gotten so far. I gave the orders months ago."

"Everyone has a throne now. Madame de Beauvilliers claims to possess one exactly like mine. She shows it to her neighbors and even lets her maid sit on it."

"Your throne was one of the first in the palace, Madame, and remains the finest."

"Being first is no distinction when a crowd of nobodies have the newest. No doubt our village merchants will be bragging about their own thrones in a day or two."

Sylvain twitched. He had just been considering running pipes through the village and renting toilets there. Merchants had the cash flow to sustain monthly payments, and unlike courtiers, they were used to paying their debts promptly.

"No indeed, Madame. I assure you I am extremely careful to preserve the privileges of rank. I am no populist."

"And how will you preserve my distinction? Will you give me a second throne to sit in my dressing room? A pedestal for a pampered pet? If a cat has a throne, surely you can give me one for each of my ladies. We shall put them in a circle here in my salon and sit clucking at each other like laying hens."

Her ladies giggled obediently. Annette stared at the floor and wrung the feathers of her fan like the neck of a Christmas goose. Just a few more twists and she would break the quills.

Madame glared at him. Angry color stained her cheeks, visible even through her heavy powder. "If every north-wing matron can brag about her throne, you may remove mine. I am bored of it. Take the vulgar thing away and throw it in the rubbish."

If Sylvain took just two steps closer, he could loom over her and glare down from his superior height. But intimidation wasn't possible. She held the whip and knew her power. If she abandoned her toilet, the whole palace would follow fashion. He would be ruined.

He strolled to the window and examined a vase of forced flowers, careful to keep his shoulders loose, his step light. "My dear madame, the thrones don't matter. You might as well keep yours."

Madame's eyebrows climbed to the edge of her wig. Annette dropped her fan. The ivory handle clattered on the marble with a skeletal rattle. Sylvain sniffed one of the blossoms, a monstrous pale thing with pistils like spikes.

"Is that so," said Madame, iron in her voice. "Enlighten me."

"We need not speak of them further. If possessing a throne conveyed distinction, it was accidental. They are a convenience for bodily necessity, nothing more. Having a throne was once a privilege, but it has been superseded."

"By what?" Madame twisted on her divan to watch him, unsettling her artfully composed tableau. He had her now.

"By the thing your heart most desires, flowing freely like a tap from a spring. So cold it chills the tongue. So fresh, the bubbles spark on the palate. Sweet as the rain in heaven and pure as a virgin's child. I believe you hold a day in February close to your heart? A particularly auspicious day?"

"I do, and it is coming soon."

"You will find your wishes fulfilled. Count on my support."

A slow grin crept over Madame's face. "It's possible you are a man of worth after all, Sylvain de Guilherand, and I need not counsel my ladies against you."

She dismissed him. Sylvain was careful not to betray the tremor in his limbs as he strolled through her apartment. The rooms were lined with mirrors, each one throwing his groomed and powdered satin-clad reflection back at him. He could put his fist through any one of those mirrors. It would feel good for a moment—the glass would shatter around his glove and splinter this overheated, foul, wasteful place into a thousand shards.

But if he showed his anger, he would betray himself. Any outburst would reveal a childish lack of self-control and provide gossip that would be told and retold long after he had been forgotten.

Sylvain found the nearest service corridor and descended to the cellars. He got a bottle of champagne from one of the king's stewards—a man who knew him well enough to extend the mercy of credit. He bought a bag of walnuts and half a cheese from a provisioner's boy who was wise enough to demand coin. The Duc d'Orléans' baker gave him a loaf of dark bread and made a favor of it. Then he slipped out of the palace and made his way to the cisterns.

The little fish dozed on a branch of her ice tree, thin limbs dangling. The bird was rearranging the nest, plucking at fern fronds and clucking to itself.

"You're fancy," the little fish said, her voice sleepy.

Sylvain looked down. He was in full court garb, a manikin in satin, wrapped in polished leather and studded with silver buttons.

He pulled off his wig and settled himself on a boulder. "Do I look like a man of worth to you, little one?"

"Worth what, Papa?"

He grimaced. "My dear, that is exactly the question."

He spread a handkerchief at his feet and made a feast for himself. Good cheese and fresh bread made a better meal than many he'd choked back on campaign, better even than most palace feasts with dishes hauled in from the village or up from the cellar kitchens, cold, salty, and studded with congealed fat. A man could live on bread and cheese. Many did worse. And many went gouty and festered on meat drowning in sauce.

The parrot winged over to investigate. Sylvain offered it a piece of cheese. It nuzzled the bread and plucked at the bag of walnuts. Sylvain untied the knot and the bird flapped away with a nut clenched in each taloned foot.

The little fish stretched and yawned. She slipped from the branch, surfaced at the edge of the pool, and padded over to him.

"Stinky," she said, nose wrinkling.

"The cheese? You're no French girl." He pared a sliver for her. She refused it. "Some bread?"

She shook her head.

"What do you eat, my little fish?" She had teeth, human teeth. Had he been starving her?

"Mud," she said, patting her belly.

There was certainly enough mud to choose from. "Would you eat a fish?" She stuck out her tongue in disgust. "The parrot eats nuts. Have you tried one?"

"Yucky. What's this, Papa?" She lifted the champagne bottle.

"Don't shake it. Here, I'll show you."

He scraped off the wax seal and unshipped the plug. He held it out. She sniffed at the neck of the bottle and shrugged, then took the bottle and dribbled a little on the floor. It foamed over her bare toes.

"Ooh, funny!" she said, delighted.

"It's like water, but a bit different."

She raised the bottle overhead and giggled as the champagne foamed over her ears. It dribbled down her cheeks and dripped from her chin. She licked her lips and grinned.

"Don't drink it. It might make you sick."

She rolled her eyes. "Just water, Papa. Fuzzy water."

"All right, give it a try."

She took a gulp and then offered the bottle to him, companionable as a sentry sharing a canteen with a friend.

He shook his head. "No, thank you, I don't prefer it."

He watched attentively as she played. She drank half the bottle but it had no apparent effect. She remained nimble and precise, and if her laughter was raucous and uncontrolled, it was no more than normal. The rest of the bottle she poured on or around herself, reveling in the bubbles and foam. Sylvain wondered if the ladies of the palace had tried bathing in champagne. If they hadn't, he wasn't going to suggest the fashion. The foamy sweet stuff was already a waste of good grapes.

When she lost interest, she dropped the bottle and arced back into the pool, diving clean and surfacing with a playful spout and splash. A finger or two was left, and when he poured it out, it foamed on the rocks fresh as if the bottle had just been cracked.

He nodded to himself. If the little fish could force water through pipes and sleeves, could make ice and keep it from melting, could chase him around the palace and make him look a fool while never leaving the cisterns, what were a few bubbles?

Sylvain knelt and pushed the empty bottle under the surface of the pool. He had done this a thousand times—filled his canteen at village wells, at farmyard troughs, at battlefield sloughs tinged pink with men's blood—and each time, his lungs ached as he watched the bubbles rise. He ached for one sip of mountain air, a lick of snowmelt, just a snatch of a shepherd's song heard across the valley, or a fading echo of a wolf's cry under a blanket of moonlight. Ached to crouch by a rushing rocky stream and sip water pristine and pure.

"Thirsty, Papa?"

The little fish stood at his side. In her hand was a cup made of ice, its walls porcelain-thin and sharp as crystal. He raised it to his lips. The cold water sparkled with fine bubbles that burst on his tongue like a thousand tiny pinpricks and foamed at the back of his throat. He drank it down and smiled.

-13-

The Grand Gallery streamed with all the nobles and luminaries of Europe, men Sylvain had glimpsed across the battlefield and longed to cross swords with, highborn women whose worth was more passionately negotiated than frontier borders, famous courtesans whose talents were broadcast in military camps and gilded parlors from Moscow to Dublin, princes of the church whose thirst for bloody punishment was unquenched and universal. This pure stream was clotted with a vast number of rich and titled bores with little to do and nothing to say. The whole world was in attendance for the king's birthday, but Sylvain had only glimpsed it. He hadn't left the champagne fountain all evening.

"If you don't come, I'll brain you with my sword hilt. Mademoiselle de Nesle is Madame's sister. If you snub one, you insult both," Gérard said, then added in an undertone, "Plus, she has the finest tits in the room and is barely clothed."

"In a moment."

The fountain branched overhead. Crystal limbs reached for the gilded ceiling and dropped like a weeping willow. Each limb was capped with ice blossoms, and each blossom streamed with champagne.

Madame had offered the first taste to the king, plucking a delicate cup of ice that sprouted from the green ice basin like a mushroom from the forest floor and filling it from a gushing spout. The king had toasted Sylvain and led the gallery in a round of applause. Then the guests flocked eagerly for their turn. They drank gallons of champagne, complained about toothache, and then drank more.

Sylvain had planned for this. He knew the noble appetite, knew the number of expected guests and how much they could be expected to drink. The fountain's basin was tall and wide, and the reservoir beneath held the contents of a thousand magnums. The reservoir was tinted dark green with baker's dye. It was too dark to see through but Sylvain calculated it to be about half full. More than enough champagne was left to keep the fountain flowing until the last courtier had been dragged to bed.

But the guests were now more interested in the king's other gifts—an African cat panting in a jeweled harness, a Greek statue newly cleaned of its dirt and ancient paint, a tapestry stitched by a hundred nuns over ten years, a seven-foot-tall solar clock. The guests were still drinking champagne at an admirable rate but sent attendants to fill their cups. The novelty had worn off.

Sylvain slipped off his glove and laid his hand on the edge of the basin, letting the cold leach into his bare palm. The little fish had been eager to play in the fountain's reservoir, but she'd been inside for hours now and must be getting bored. Still, she had played no tricks. She kept the champagne flowing fresh, kept the ice from melting just as she had agreed. All because he had promised her a song.

"The fountain is fine," Gérard insisted. "We've all admired it. Now come see Madame and her sister."

Sylvain replaced his glove and followed Gérard. Guests toasted him as he passed.

"I need a fountain in my hat," said Mademoiselle de Nesle.

The two sisters were holding court outside the Salon of War, presenting a portrait of tender affection and well-powdered beauty. But their twin stars did not orbit peacefully. Madame held the obvious advantage—official status, a liberal allowance from the royal purse, a large entourage, and innumerable privileges and rights along with her jewels and silks—but her sister had novelty on her side and emphasized her ingénue status with a simple gauze robe. Goodwill bloomed between them, or a decent counterfeit of it, but their attending ladies stood like two armies across an invisible border.

Annette stood apart from the scene, dimples worn shallow. A line of worry wrinkled her brow. Her fan drooped from her elbow. No coy signals tonight, just a bare nod and a slight tilt of her eyebrows. Sylvain followed her gaze to the ermine-draped figure of the King of France.

The two sisters had captured the king's attention. He was ignoring Cardinal de Fleury and two Marshals of the Empire, gazing down from the royal dais to watch his mistress and her sister with obvious interest, plumed hat in his hand, gloved fist on his hip, alert as a stallion scenting a pair of mares.

Sylvain moved out of the king's view. The ladies were on display for one audience member alone, and Sylvain was not about to get between them.

"A fountain in my hat," Mademoiselle de Nesle repeated. "My dear sister says you are a magician."

Sylvain bowed deeply, hiding his expression for a few moments. A ridiculous request. The woman must be simple. Did she think he could pull such a frippery out of his boot?

"The fountain will have its naissance at the peak of my chapeau, providing a misty veil before my eyes."

"But mademoiselle would get wet," Sylvain ventured finally.

"Yes! You have grasped my point. My dress is gauze, as you can see. It's very thin and becomes transparent when wet." She smoothed her hands over her breasts and leaned toward her sister. "Do you not think it will prove alluring, Louise?"

Madame caressed her sister's hands. "No man would be able to resist you, my dear sister."

Mademoiselle laughed. Her voice was loud enough for the opera house. "I care for no man. Only a god can have me."

The king took a few steps closer to the edge of the dais, the very plumes on his hat magnetized by the scene.

Across the room, the Comte de Tessé approached the fountain with the careful, considered step of a man trying to hide his advanced state of drunkenness. The comte waved his crystal cup under the blossom spouts, letting the champagne overflow the glass and foam over his hand. The cup slipped from his hand and shattered on the fountain's base. The comte sputtered with laughter.

"Do you not think it would be the finest of chapeaux, monsieur? A feat worthy of a magician, would it not be?"

The comte was joined at the fountain by a pair of young officers, polished, pressed, and gleaming in their uniforms, and just as drunk as the comte but far less willing to hide it. One leaned over the fountain and tried to sip directly from a blossom spout.

"I think it would be a very worthy feat," Madame said. "Monsieur, my sister posed you a question."

The officers were now trying to clamber onto the fountain's slippery base. The comte laughed helplessly.

"No," said Sylvain.

Madame blinked. Her ladies gasped.

The officer grasped a blossom spout. It snapped off in his hand. His friend slipped on the fountain's edge and fell into the basin. His gold scabbard clanged on the ice. Two women—their wives, perhaps—joined the comte to laugh at the young heroes.

"Excuse me, mesdames."

Sylvain rushed back to the fountain. One snarl brought the two young officers to attention. They scrambled off the fountain, claimed their wives from the comte, and disappeared into the crowd.

The comte's gaze was bleary. "Well done indeed, Monsieur de Guilherand. The palace is ablaze with compliments. But remember it is I who gave you this kingly idea in the first place. As a gentleman, you will ensure I receive due credit."

"You can take half the credit when you bear half the expense," Sylvain hissed. "I'll send you the vintner's bill. You'll find the total appropriately kingly."

The comte turned back to the fountain and refilled his cup, pretending to not hear. Sylvain plucked the cup from the comte's hand and poured the contents into the basin.

"You've embarrassed yourself. Go and sober up."

The comte pretended to spot a friend across the room and tottered away.

Sylvain examined the broken blossom. Its finely carved petals dripped in the overheated air. The broken branch gushed champagne like a wound. Had the little fish felt the assault on the fountain? Had it frightened her? He tried to see through the dark green ice, watching for movement within the reservoir.

"Perhaps we ask too much," said Annette, "expecting soldiers to transform themselves into gentlemen and courtiers for the winter. Many men seem to manage it for more than a few hours at a time. One wonders why you can't, Sylvain de Guilherand."

She posed at the edge of the fountain, fan fluttering in annoyance.

"Perhaps because I am a beast?"

The reservoir ice was thick and dark. In bright sunlight, he might be able to see through it, but even with thousands of candles overhead and the hundreds of mirrors lining the gallery, the light was too dim. He should have left a peephole at the back of the fountain.

"I speak as a friend," said Annette. "Madame is insulted. You have taken a serious misstep."

"Madame has made her own misstep this evening and will forget about mine before morning."

Annette's fan drooped. "True. She has made a play to keep the king's interest, but I fear she'll lose his favor. *Maîtresse en titre* is an empty honor if your lover prefers another woman's bed."

"She'll be naming something vile after her sister next," said Sylvain.

Annette coughed. "You heard about Polish Mary, then?" Sylvain nodded. "It's her way of insulting those she despises. It makes the king laugh."

A shadow moved in the fountain's base, a flicker of a limb against the green ice just for a moment. He should have given the little fish a way to signal him if she was in distress.

"I begin to perceive that my conversation is not engaging enough for you, monsieur."

"I beg your pardon, madame." Sylvain turned his back on the fountain. The little fish was fine. Nixies spent entire seasons under the ice of glacier lakes. It was her element. The fact that the champagne continued to flow was perfect evidence that she was not in distress. He was worrying for nothing. Offending Annette further would be a mistake.

He swept a deep bow. "More than your pardon, my dear madame. I beg your indulgence."

"Indulgence, yes." She looked over her shoulder at Madame and her sister. "We have all indulged ourselves too much this evening and will pay for it."

He forced a knowing smile. "Perhaps the best practice is to let others indulge us. Although a wise and lovely woman once mentioned that most ladies prefer a long period of suspense first. It whets the appetite."

The empty banter seemed to cheer her. Her dimples surfaced and she snapped her fan with renewed purpose.

"Would you join me in taking a survey of the room?" He offered his arm. "I don't beg your company for myself alone but in a spirit of general charity. If all this indulgence will lead to a morning filled with regrets, at least we can offer the king's guests a memory of true beauty. With you on the arm of a beast such as myself, the contrast will be striking."

She glanced at Madame. "I was sent to scold you, not favor you with my company."

"You can always say I forced you."

She laughed and took his arm. He led her through a clot of courtiers toward the royal dais. The king had returned his attention to his most favored guests but displayed a shapely length of royal leg for the two sisters to admire.

"Much better, my dear Sylvain," said Gérard as they approached. "I hate to see you brooding over that fountain. My wife strokes her great belly with the same anxious anticipation. You looked like a hen on an egg."

Sylvain dropped his hand onto the pommel of his sword and glared. Gérard barked with laughter.

"Your friend the Marquis de la Châsse can't manage civil conversation, either," said Annette as they moved on.

"Gérard doesn't need to make the effort. He was born into enough distinction that every trespass is forgiven."

"You sound jealous, but it's not quite accurate. His wealth and title do help, but he is accepted because everyone can see he is true to his nature."

"And I am not?"

"A bald question. I will answer it two ways. First, observe that at this moment, you and I are walking arm in arm among every person in the world who matters. If that is not acceptance, I wonder how you define the word."

"I am honored, madame."

"Yes, you most certainly are, monsieur."

"And your second answer?"

"You are not true to your nature, and it makes people uncomfortable. Everyone knows what to expect from a man like the Marquis de la Châsse, but one suspects that Sylvain de Guilherand would rather be somewhere else, doing something else. Heaven knows what."

Sylvain closed his glove over hers. "Not at all. I am exactly where I want to be."

"So you say, but I do not believe it. Our well-beloved king toasted you this evening. Many men would consider that enough achievement for a lifetime, but still you are dissatisfied."

"We discussed my character before. Remember how that ended?"

A delicate blush flushed through her powder. "I am answering your question as honestly as I can."

"Honesty is not a vice much indulged at Versailles."

She laughed. "I know the next line. Let me supply it: 'It's the only vice that isn't.' Oh, Sylvain. I can have that kind of conversation with any man. I'd rather go home to my husband and talk about hot gruel and poultices. Don't make me desperate."

Sylvain stroked her hand. "Very well. You enjoy my company despite my faults?"

She nibbled her bottom lip as she considered the question. "Because of your faults, I think," she said. "The fountain is successful, the king is impressed with you, and you have my favor. Take my advice and be satisfied."

Sylvain raised her palm to his lips. "I will."

They walked on, silent but in perfect concord. As they circled the gallery, the atmosphere seemed less stifling, the crowd less insipid, the king's air of rut less ridiculous. Even

Madame's poses seemed less futile and her sister's pouts less desperate. Sylvain was in charity with the world, willing to forgive its many flaws.

The guests parted, opening a view of the fountain. A girl in petal-yellow silk reached her cup to one of the blossoms. The curve of her bare arm echoed the graceful arc of the fountain's limbs. She raised the cup to her lips and the crowd closed off his view of the scene just as she took her first sip.

"Nature perfected, monsieur," said a portly Prussian. "You must be congratulated."

Sylvain bowed and drew Annette away just as the Prussian's gaze settled on her cleavage. The king rose to dismount the dais and the whole crowd watched. Sylvain took advantage of the distraction to claim a kiss from Annette, just a brief caress of her ripe lower lip before they joined the guests in a ripple of deep curtseys and bows. The king progressed down the gallery toward Madame and her sister, his pace forceful and intent as a stalking hunter.

Annette slid her hand up Sylvain's arm and rested her palm on his shoulder. A pulse fluttered on her throat. He resisted the urge to explore it with his lips.

"I suppose it is too early to leave," he whispered, drinking in the honeyed scent of her powder.

"Your departure would be noticed," she breathed. "It is the price of fame, monsieur."

"Another turn of the room, then?"

She nodded. They moved down the gallery in the king's wake. The African cat gnawed on its harness, blunted ivory fangs rasping over the jewels. Its attendant yanked ineffectually on the leash.

"Poor thing," said Annette. "They should take it outside. This is no place for a wild animal."

Sylvain nodded. “I have not thought to ask before now, but how is the monkey? Happier, I hope, than that cat?”

“Very well and happy indeed. My maid Marie coddles her like a new mother. They are madonna and child, the two of them a world unto themselves.” She glanced up at him, a wicked slant to her gaze, daring him to laugh. He grinned.

“And what name did Madame give the creature?”

The color drained from her cheeks. “Is that the viceroy of Parma? I would not have thought to see him here.”

“I couldn’t say. He looks like every other man in a wig and silk. Are you avoiding my question?”

“Show me your fountain. I haven’t had the chance to admire it up close.”

The crowd parted to reveal three young men in peacock silks filling their cups at the fountain. One still kept his long baby curls, probably in deference to a sentimental mother.

“There!” Annette said. “Not quite as delicate a tableau as the girl in yellow, but I think I like it better. You must make allowances for differences in taste, and I have always preferred male beauty.”

“I am sure you do. What did Madame name the monkey, Annette?”

“She is called Jesusa. It is a terrible sacrilege and my accent makes it bad Spanish too, but what can I do when I am presented with madonna and child morning, noon, and night? God will forgive me.”

“Madame didn’t name the monkey Jesusa.”

“Don’t be so sure. Madame is even worse a Christian than I am.”

“Very well. I’ll ask her myself.”

Sylvain strode toward the Salon of War. The crowd was thick. The king was with Madame now. The tall feathers of the royal hat bobbed over the heads of the guests.

Annette pulled his arm. "Stop. Not in front of the king. Don't be stubborn."

He turned on her. "Answer my question."

The jostling crowd pressed them together. She gripped his arms, breath shallow.

"Promise you won't take offence."

"Just answer the question, Annette."

She bit her lip hard enough to draw blood. "She named the monkey Sylvain."

He wrenched himself out of her grip and lurched back, nearly bowling over an elderly guest.

"It is a joke," said Annette, pursuing him.

"Does it seem funny to you?"

"Take it in the spirit it was intended, just a silly attempt at fun. It isn't meant as an attack on your pride."

"Madame thinks I am a prize target. Did you laugh, Annette?" His voice rose. Heads turned. Guests jostled their neighbors, alerting them to the scene. "Who else would like to take a shot at me?"

"Sylvain, no, please." Annette spoke softly and reached out to him. He stepped aside.

Sylvain paced in a circle, glaring at the guests, daring each one of them to make a remark.

"I have done more than any other man to make a place for myself at court. I've attended levees, and flattered, and fucked. But worse—I've worked hard. As hard as I can. You find that disgusting, don't you?"

"No. I don't." She watched him pace.

"I've worked miracles. Everyone says so. The magician of the fountains, the man who puts thrones throughout the palace. Everyone wants one. Or so it seems, until everyone has one. Then it's nothing special. Not good enough anymore.

Take it away. Come up with something else while we insult you behind your back."

"Madame is difficult to please." Annette's voice was soft and sad.

"Nothing I do will ever be good enough, will it? Even for you, Annette. You tell me I try too hard, I'm a striver, and I'm not true to my nature." He spread his arms wide. "Well, this is my nature. How do you like me now?"

She opened her mouth and then closed it without speaking. He stepped close and spoke in her ear.

"Not well, I think," he said, and walked away.

The crowd parted to let him pass, opening a view to the fountain. Two of the young men were leaning over the basin. The boy with the curls crouched at the side of the reservoir. Sylvain broke into a run.

The boy was banging on the ice with his diamond ring. The reservoir rang like a drum with each impact.

Sylvain grabbed the boy by the scruff of his neck.

"There's something in there, monsieur," he squealed. "A creature, a monster. I saw it."

Sylvain threw the boy to the floor and drew his sword. The boy scrabbled backward, sliding across the marble. The two friends rushed to the boy's side and yanked him to his feet. They backed away, all three clinging to each other. Behind them a crowd gathered—some shocked, some confused, most highly entertained. They pointed at him as if he were a beast in a menagerie.

Several men made a show of dropping their hands to the hilts of their dress swords, but not one of them drew.

The fountain sputtered. A blossom crashed into the basin, splashing gouts of champagne.

Gérard shoved through the crowd, wig askew, slipping on the wet floor. He skidded into place at Sylvain's side.

The fountain sprayed champagne across their backs and high to the ceiling, snuffing out a hundred candles overhead.

"Go to your wife. Get her out of the palace," said Sylvain.

Gérard ran full-speed for the door.

Sylvain raised his sword and brought it crashing down on the fountain. Ice limbs shattered. Champagne and ice vaulted overhead and fell, spraying debris across the marble floor. He shifted his grip and smashed the pommel of his sword on the side of the reservoir. It cracked and split. He hit it again and again until the floor flooded with golden liquid. Sylvain threw down his sword and shouldered the ice aside.

"Papa?"

The little fish was curled into a quivering ball. Sylvain slipped and fell to his hands and knees. He crawled toward her, reached out.

"It's all right, my little one. Come here, my darling."

She lifted her arms. He gathered her to his chest. She burrowed her face into his neck, quaking.

"Noisy," she sobbed. "Too loud. Hurts. Papa."

Sylvain held her on his lap, champagne seeping through his clothes. He cupped his palms over her ears and squeezed her to his heart, rocking back and forth until her shivering began to subside. Then he pulled himself to his feet, awkward and unbalanced with the child in his arms.

He stepped out of the shattered ice into a line of drawn swords. Polished steel glinted, throwing points of light across the faces of the household guard. Sylvain shielded the child with his body as he scanned the crowd.

The jostling guests were forced against the walls by the line of guards. The plumes of the king's hat disappeared into the Salon of Peace, followed by the broad backs of his bodyguards. Madame, her sister, and their ladies clustered on the royal dais, guarded by the Marshal de Noailles.

De Noailles had personally executed turncoat soldiers with the very same sword that now shone in his hand.

"Let the water go, my little one," Sylvain whispered.

She blinked up at him. "Be a bad girl, Papa?" Her brow furrowed in confusion.

"The water pipes, the reservoirs. Let it all go."

"Papa?"

"Go ahead, little fish."

She relaxed in his arms, as if she had been holding her breath a long time and could finally breathe.

A faint rumble sounded overhead, distant. It grew louder. The walls trembled. Sylvain spread his palm over the nixie's wet scalp as if he could armor her fragile skull. A mirror slipped to the floor and shattered. The guards looked around, trying to pinpoint the threat. Their swords wavered and dipped.

The ceiling over the statue of Hermes bowed and cracked. Plaster rained down on the guests. The statue teetered and toppled. The guests pushed through the guards, scattering their line.

The ceiling sprang a thousand leaks. The huge chandeliers swung back and forth. Water streamed down the garden windows, turning the glass silver and gold, and then dark as the candles sputtered and smoked.

The guests broke through the wide garden doors and stormed through the water streaming off the roof and out onto the wide terraces. Sylvain retrieved his sword and followed, ducking low and holding the little fish tight as he fled into the fresh February night.

He ran across the gardens, past the pools and reservoirs, though the orangery and yew grove. He climbed the Bois des Gonards and turned back to the palace, breathless, scanning the paths for pursuing guards.

Aside from the crowd milling on the terraces, there was no movement in the gardens. The fountains jetted high, fifteen hundred spouts across the vast expanse of lawns and paths, flower beds and hedges, each spout playing, every jet dancing for its own amusement.

"You can turn the fountains off now, little one."

"Papa?" The little fish was growing heavy. He shifted her weight onto his hip, well balanced for a long walk.

"Don't worry, my little girl. No more fountains. We're going home."

One by one the fountains flailed and drooped. The little fish leaned her head on his shoulder and yawned.

The palace was dark except for an array of glowing windows in the north wing and along the row of attic garrets. At this distance, it looked dry and calm.

And indeed, he thought, nothing was damaged that couldn't be repaired. The servants would spend a few busy weeks mopping, the carpenters and plasterers, gilders and painters would have a few seasons of work. Eventually, someone would find a way to repair a fountain or two. The toilets and pipes would stand dry, but the nobles and courtiers would notice little difference. What was broken there could never be fixed.

Dawn found them on a canal. Sylvain sat on the prow of a narrow boat, eating bread and cheese and watching his little fish jump and splash in the gentle bow wave as they drifted upstream on the long journey home.

NOTES ABOUT "WATERS OF VERSAILLES"

Ah. "Waters of Versailles." What a miracle it is. This is the story where, after years of trying, I finally learned to write.

In 2005, I realized that if I didn't give writing a good fair try, it'd be the worst regret of my life. But I had some mountains to climb along the way. First, I had to find a way to shut up my internal editor, which wouldn't let me write a sentence without changing it. Second, I had to learn to ignore the voice in the back of my head telling me I couldn't ever accomplish anything, because I was too [insert any of a hundred insults here].

Throw a rock and you'll hit a writer who had to overcome those same barriers. Few people are self-confident enough to just pick up a pen and write. Most of us struggle. And all I can say to new and aspiring writers is this: The victory is worth it.

I spent years writing trunk novels and trying to wrap my head around writing stories. Then in 2013, I was laid off from my job. It was a huge ego blow, completely unexpected. I was devastated. And if anyone had told me at the time that it was the best thing that could happen to me, I would have been furious. But…it was. The next day, I started rewriting from scratch a story that hadn't worked. "Waters of Versailles" is that story. Everything else in this book came after it.

WHAT GENTLE WOMEN DARE

Liverpool, Midsummer, 1763

WHEN SATAN HIMSELF CAME TO LOLLY, SHE didn't recognize him. She wasn't on her guard—hadn't been for years. Why should she be? Her immortal soul had long since drowned in rum and rotted under gobs of treacle toffee. If any scrap was left, it was too dry and leathery to tempt evil. But even the most pious of parsons wouldn't have recognized the Devil in the guise of a dead woman floating face-down in the Mersey.

Lolly matched her steps with each clang reverberating from St. Nicholas's bell tower. The morning sky was dim and lightless except for a yellow haze to the east, silhouetted by Liverpool's cold chimneys. Over her right shoulder, the glowing lamp of the Woodside ferry skittered across the inky river. A pale streak drifted along the edge of the timber wharf.

Could've been a log or a scrap of sail cloth, but no, Lolly knew death when she saw it. She'd seen plenty and it always made her shiver. An icicle shoved through the living lights of her eyes couldn't chill her more than the sight of a corpse.

Wasn't long before the Wharfinger's men spotted it.

"Hey ho, a floater." George pointed with his pipe stem.

"If we're in luck, the current will carry it out to Bootle," said Robbie. "Then it'll sink into the marsh and be nobody's problem."

They turned back to their dice game. If George and Robbie didn't care about the corpse, Lolly shouldn't either. Still, she stared at it until a sailor appeared at the edge of the timber wharf, stooped and weaving from a long night in a tavern. The sight of him lifted her spirits.

"Mouth tricks here," she called out. "Soft as a tit, wet as a twat, twice as tight, and good for sucking." She licked her gums.

The sailor grinned. He had no more teeth than she did, and the long plait hanging over his shoulder was iron gray all the way to its curly, pig-tail end. The sight of him made her glad. Sailors who lived to get old were often kindly.

"Thart thirsty, old girl?" he asked.

"Not old." She gave him a saucy wink. "Tha might be me da, maybe. Did tha never plug a Welsh ewe?"

He laughed and hitched down his trousers. While she was working, he clutched her head hard, mashing her hat with his grimy fingers. But after, he gave her four pence and a kiss on the cheek. Generous. Lolly always thought she could be rich if only she could line men up in a row, but men, like fish, were shy and catching them took more time than eating.

When she looked for the corpse, it had beached on the mud bar at the corner of the timber wharf. Head, arms, legs, maybe eyes and a mouth under her hair. A woman, for certain. The men had finally put down their dice. George hung off the side of the wharf like a monkey, reaching for the corpse with a boat hook. He snagged it, passed the hook up to his friend, and together they hauled the sodden, streaming form on to the wharf.

George groped the corpse's neck. He pulled off his cap and held it to his chest.

"Cold and fresh," he said.

"Suicide." Robbie swiped off his own cap. "Me missus won't want it. Will yourn?"

George shook his head. "She'd bar the door. That's nobody's honest wife or daughter."

Lolly crept closer. The corpse was naked but for a smock, so flimsy her mottled flesh showed through. When Lolly reached out to touch the wet cloth, George swung a fist at her.

"Get off, tha ol meff."

"Gentle, now. Tarts take care of their own," Robbie whispered to his friend. He swiped a calloused hand over his hair and turned to Lolly. "This here's one of yourn. I'll bring the parson's man by and by, but if tha hant thruppence to pay for burial, just weigh her down and tip her into the river. I'll turn my back if you do."

Lolly shook her head, pretending not to understand.

"A sinking stone solves many a problem," Robbie explained.

He pointed at the nearest pile of ballast gravel and mimed tying a knot in the girl's shift. Lolly stalled until he slipped her a penny, then nodded agreement. Robbie scooped up his dice, and both men retreated to the far end of the timber wharf.

Lolly had a sharp eye for a chance. She wanted the smock. Once she had it in hand, she could just roll the naked corpse back in the river. If the men pulled it out again, she could say the rocks had ripped through the fabric.

Lolly was neither god-fearing nor churchgoing, but stealing from a corpse didn't sit easy in her mind. It seemed to flaunt a rule more basic and ancient than any in the Bible. She looked the corpse over, trying to find a reason to justify taking the one thing it still possessed.

"What's that, mammy?"

Little Meg tottered out of the timber yard, knuckling her eyes and dragging her old red blanket behind her. The wool barely had enough nap left to pick up sawdust.

Lolly knelt and pulled her daughter close.

"Good morning, my Meggie. Did tha dream all night long?"

Meg was warm and damp with sleep. Her eyes were puffy, and she still had that yeast-bread smell of a sleeping child.

Meg yawned. "What's the lady doing?"

"Sleeping, love, just like you." Lolly kissed Meg's ear, and then turned her attention back to the corpse.

The woman was tall, with a breadth of shoulder a young man might be proud of. Her thighs were wide and strong. Her hair stuck to her temples in little half-crescent locks. Her teeth were so even Lolly thought they must be ivory, but no, they were set into her bloodless gums tight as fence posts. Despite the good teeth, when alive she'd been homely, with small eyes, a bulbous forehead, and flat cheeks marred by constellations of pockmarks.

Lolly turned the corpse's hands over and squinted at her fingers and palms. Soft skin, no warts or scars, but before she could think much about what that might signify, the skin on her palms flushed pink. Lolly's gaze darted to the woman's face. Though deathly gray a moment before, now it was flushed. The new skin in each smallpox scar glowed red as a tart's lips.

She was alive, and that meant Lolly had no time to spare. She hiked the smock up the woman's torso, exposing her rapidly pinkening flesh to the rising sun. The wet cloth clung to her skin and rucked under her armpits. The woman's arms flopped as Lolly yanked the smock over her head. She stuffed it under her arm, grabbed Meg's hand, and ran behind the rope shed.

As Lolly peeked around the corner with one eye, the drowned woman propped herself on one elbow. She convulsed twice, retching fluid onto the warped boardwalk. She lay still for a moment, then looked both ways, sharp and quick, slithered to the edge of the wharf, and slipped back into the water.

Lolly had a habit of telling boastful stories about herself. Not lies. Lies could be found out. Stories were different—nobody could prove them untrue. She told a few on her way home that morning, clutching the wadded-up smock under her arm.

First, she told a ship's cook she wouldn't buy his slush because she wasn't hungry. Truth was, both she and Meg were hollow, but those greasy leavings from the salt pork barrel turned Meg's stomach and left her trotting for days. Slush was cheap, but her dear girl couldn't abide it.

On Castle Street, she told a baker she would never take nothing from his basket without paying, even if nobody was watching. Just to prove it, she bought two cream buns for Meg instead of one.

Behind the Punch Bowl Tavern, she told the sleepy girl minding the dregs keg that she didn't mind filling her flask with the drainage from last night's tankards. Salt from a sailor's tongue just made the liquor more tasty. When the girl caught her sipping from the spout, Lolly claimed she was just smelling the dregs and if the girl wanted an extra farthing for a whiff, she'd be happy to pay because she liked that just as well as a gulp.

Walking up the Dale Street hill, Lolly told her daughter she wasn't tired nor limping. She could walk a lot faster if she wanted, but she liked a slow stroll of a morning.

When a pack of rough boys surrounded her in the forecourt of Cable Yard, Lolly told them she had a knife. Fact was, she'd lost it months back. A press gang crimp had heard Lolly knew mouth tricks that would turn a man cross-eyed, and when his curiosity was satisfied, he'd walked away without paying. When she'd tried to cut him, he'd knocked her down, kicked in her ribs, and left her cringing in the sawdust. If a broken rib wasn't enough payment for trying to make a man do what he ought, the Wharfinger punished her too. So angry, he'd actually taken the time to climb down from the pilots' office and cross the dockyards. He tracked her down, and bent back her thumb until it snapped. Took her knife away, too.

The rough boys had all the vim of youth and a good night's sleep, while Lolly was tired and defenseless. A whore without a knife is like a cat without claws—she could hiss or she could run. But Lolly couldn't run. At the first sign of trouble, Meg ducked under her mother's skirt and clamped fast to her leg, gripping her knee like a foremast jack in a hurricane.

Lolly held the smock tight and swatted the boys with her other hand, taking care to protect the flask in her pocket.

"Keep dogging me and I'll cut y'open and give your heartstrings to your mammies," she shouted.

Lolly swung her fist at the tallest boy. He dodged easily. When he began snatching at her hat, Lolly knew it was either that or the flask. She let the hat go. The boys chased it like dogs after a rat.

When Lolly got home, her landlady was up to her elbows in suds in the narrow back yard, with three children crawling four-legged around her, and a herd of two-legged ones scurrying about. Snot ran over their lips like water through a sluicegate.

"Where's tha hat?" asked the landlady as Lolly latched the gate.

"Blew into the river," Lolly answered. Usually she'd tell a better story, but the brawl had left her shaking.

"Doest tha have another?"

"Seems a shame to cover my tresses." Lolly dredged up a saucy smile. Dockside charm never worked with her landlady, but habits are hard to break. "I might go bare-headed."

The landlady pushed her sweat-darkened hair off her brow with a wet forearm and scowled.

"If it's a choice between a new hat and making me happy on rent day, tha knowst which to choose. If we come to blows, it won't be me worst off."

Lolly nodded and trudged up to her room. She knew better than to cross her landlady. She could be vicious. Anyone who expects women to live together happy as Eden before the fall has a poor understanding of human nature. A woman with ten children and a husband sailing the African trade has little enough kindness to spare for her own kin, and certainly none for her tenants.

Meg ate her buns and dandled her straw doll while Lolly spread the smock over her lap for examination. The silk was so fine she couldn't see strands in the weave. No wrinkles, no pulled threads, no seams. Soft as new skin under a blister. It didn't seem fabric at all, more like something grown as one piece. Also, it was perfectly clean, not a scuff or stain. In fact, it didn't seem to hold dirt. Her hands were none too clean, but the grime from her fingers dried and flaked away, leaving no mark behind on the pure white cloth.

She dragged the smock over her face. Off came all the dirt that had built up since she'd last got caught in a rainstorm: salt grime, coal dust, and the crusty flakes of sailors' leavings all embedded in her greasy mutton-fat rouge. She pulled the fabric away and held it out with both hands like a curtain. A ghost of her own self stared back, with rosy cheeks, a red smear for a mouth, and two blank spaces for eyes.

Then the dirt flaked off, and the cloth shone white again.

Lolly slept with the smock wadded under her head like a pillow. It warmed her hands and cooled her brow, cradling her in a cloud of comfort. When she woke, she stripped and pulled it over her head.

Meg ran in from the yard. The child yanked at the smock's edge.

"It's too fine to keep, mammy."

"I'll sell it tomorrow," Lolly said as she pulled on her skirt and belted her bodice over the smock. "When I do, I'll buy thee a cake with sugared plums in all the colors of a rainbow."

On her way back to the wharf, Lolly seemed to float. The fabric glissaded over her thighs. It cupped her shoulders in a cool embrace, and soothed the itch and burn of her flea bites, nicks, blisters, and scabs. From the soles of her feet all the way up to her scalp, Lolly felt fine. When she scratched herself, it was only from habit.

Lolly stopped at the Nag's Head. She asked the landlady for a bun and a bit of bacon rind for Meg, and had her flask filled with the cheapest rum.

"Tha ent dressed for jobbing, little puss." The old man in the chair beside the door blew smoke in her face and leered. He poked his spit-coated pipe stem into the white fabric on her chest. "How doest tha catch fish with nowt jiggling on tha hook?

She batted the pipe away.

"Don't need it. I'm a legendary suckstress. They talk about me in foreign ports."

He kept hounding her, but she hardly noticed. She sauced him back, automatically—*men queue up to give me gravy—nobody gets more mucky than me—even backskuttle jacks shoot milt my way.*

When the landlady brought her flask back, Lolly gave it a shake to make sure she hadn't dropped in pebbles to cheat her. Then she tasted it and grimaced. The rum was so badly still-burnt it could put a wrinkle in her tongue, but it would do.

On the way down Dale Street, Lolly held tight to Meg's hand, careful to protect the child from the carts and wagons.

"That white cloth does look strange," Meg mumbled, her mouth full of bread.

True, the smock was too modest. Sailors liked a high pair of swollen teats. It reminded them of their long-lost mammies.

With one hand, Lolly adjusted her clothing as she dawdled along. If she pulled the cloth slowly, it stretched and stayed that way. By the time she entered narrow, dark Water Street, Lolly looked much as she always did, but stood a little taller. She had a secret next to her skin, and a good one. The smock made her feel clean. Stainless. Prideful. Not the boastful, fake pride she claimed every day, but something truer. Like a pip of gold at the core of a soft brown apple. A secret something that proved she was more than bruises and bluster.

But it also made her scared. What if, at the stroke of midnight, the corpse came back? What if it called her a thief and dragged her to the bottom of the river? Meg would be left frightened and alone with nobody to care for her. The thought was nearly enough to make her run for home.

Soft and quiet, old girl, she thought as she led her daughter through the narrow warehouse alleys crowded with pack mules and porters. Most likely the corpse had never slunk back to the water in the first place. She'd probably imagined it.

Lolly had seen impossible things before. Once, when she'd drunk dregs from a nutmeg barrel, the river had caught fire, kicking up sparks that wove patterns in the sky and set ships aflame. She ran though the dockyards and wharves, terrified, not stopping until she'd tumbled down the saltworks steps. Working mouth tricks had been a torment until her ribs healed.

If she'd imagined the corpse rolling itself back into the water, then it might have lain naked on the wharf all morning. George and Robbie would finger Lolly and call her a thief. The Wharfinger would strip her raw, take the smock, and have her hanged. What would happen to little Meg, then?

If the Wharfinger knew his duty, he'd protect Lolly. She paid him a shilling sixpence every Sunday, which bought her the right to walk back and forth along the timber wharf through wind, rain, and snow. She put coins in his pocket, but he never lifted a finger to aid her or any of the girls. If he did, people would call him a whoremaster.

Best sell the smock, and fast. Put on an innocent face and do her night's work. But no, the smock was her own comfort and joy. She wasn't taking it off. Not now. Maybe not ever.

"All my treasures are here with me." Lolly hoisted her sleepy daughter in her arms and kissed the delicate curl of her ear.

She leaned against the grimy weatherboards of the coal shack at the corner of Brunswick Street, watching the traffic grind along the busy dockside parade. She sipped from her flask and gathered her thoughts.

Where to go, if not homeward? The taverns on the quay and the alleys all around were defended territory. Navy crews landed there, starved for soft company and ready to spend their pay. If Lolly walked those streets looking hopeful, she'd have a knife in her guts before midnight.

"Take me to the churchyard, mammy," Meg said.

Lolly took a deep gulp of acrid rum. St. Nicholas's churchyard was as good a place as any. Nobody's stroll—or everybody's. Not much custom, but if she stood high up on the hill she might catch the eyes of men coming up from the bridewell. She could give herself 'til midnight, then if chances looked bad, she'd settle Meg down to sleep against the church wall and skip up Bath Street all the way to the Fort. Try her luck with the soldiers. She might even creep down Lancellot's Hey in the deep of night and take a squat on the Wharfinger's steps—see how he liked that sauce.

Belligerent thoughts gave her the energy to get moving. When she passed into St. Nicholas's churchyard, Meg squealed and struggled out of her arms. It was her favorite place to play—grass and flowers, bugs and worms. Meg might trip on someone's shinbone sticking up from the turf and if she fell wrong, she could smash her brains out on a gravestone. But a mother can't keep her child in an apron pocket, no matter how much she might want to.

Lolly strolled uphill, weaving through the higgledy-piggledy canted gravestones until she found her favorite seat. Meg scampered about, chasing moths and pulling up harebells by the roots.

When the bells tolled midnight, Lolly was still sitting in the churchyard, and that's where the Devil found her.

The first thing Lolly noticed were the insects. Large ones, the size of her thumb, pitching through the air on glittering, thumbnail-sized wings. At first she thought they were bats—she saw plenty of bats skittering over the river in late summer, when the tide was out and flies swarmed over the mud. These weren't bats. Not cleggs, either—too big—and cockchafers didn't fly in summer. Eight or more of the insects hovered overhead, just past arm's reach. Watching her. They ignored little Meg, though, so that was all right.

Then a stranger entered the churchyard—a woman in dark clothes and a hooded cloak. The insects extended their tiny wings and flew to meet her.

"*Ssssst sssst*," Lolly hissed.

Meg dove under her mother's skirt and wrapped both her arms around her mother's thigh, little fingers digging in deep. Lolly patted her head through the fabric.

The child whispered, *What is it, mammy?*

"Looks like a chapel-hen," Lolly told her daughter. "This one's out all by herself. That's rare. Usually they walk in twos and threes."

She'd seen them before, good women from Liverpool's dissenting congregations. Every so often they'd try to talk Lolly into saving her soul. Sometimes, if Lolly played along, a chapel-hen could be talked out of a few coins.

Lolly knew a prayer. She shuffled toward a gravestone and bent her head in an exaggerated pantomime of piety. When the chapel-hen was close enough to hear, Lolly began praying aloud.

"All fathers dwell in heaven, where a hollow be in tha name."

The woman flipped down her hood, exposing a face white as a skull, with a round forehead and flat cheeks scarred as the moon.

"You took something from us," the woman croaked. Her voice sounded more like a cart wheel on gravel than any human sound.

Get off, Meg. Run, Lolly whispered.

Meg squeezed her mother's leg. *Nay, I'm scared.*

Lolly tried to flee, hobbling along with little Meg under her skirt, perching on her foot. The woman leapt over a row of close-set stones and cut Lolly off.

Nothing to do but brazen it out.

"Who said I took anything?" Lolly shook her fist while backing up slowly. "Nobody, that's who. Don't you tell a lie."

"An argument is unnecessary," the woman squawked. "The garment must be recovered. However, you may continue wearing it for the moment. No doubt it gives you comfort."

Lolly gulped at her flask. For certain, the stranger was the very same drowned woman who had crawled naked into the river. Her voice was otherworldly—inhuman—devilish. A chill shivered over Lolly's flesh, raising goosebumps from her scalp to her toes.

"If I have something of yourn, it's because tha were dead when I found it," Lolly said. "That's salvage, not theft. Like with a shipwreck."

"A compelling argument, well worth taking into consideration." The woman smiled, exposing the straight teeth Lolly had plucked at that morning. "We agree. By the local custom of salvage, you may keep the garment."

"Thart kindly." Lolly grinned. "I get many gifts, but this is my favorite."

"It is not a gift. Neither is it bribery, nor a commercial transaction," the stranger croaked. "The garment was lost. You found it and claim ownership by the customs of your community. Please acknowledge those facts."

Lolly nodded. "It were salvage, like I say."

"Very good. You may address us as Mary Overholt." The woman dipped her head, like one lady might to another. "We welcome your company."

"Goodnight, miss." Lolly shuffled away, taking care to keep Meg concealed under her skirt.

"Wait a moment," Mary squawked. "Would you stay and talk with me, of your own free will?"

Make her pay for it, mammy.

Lolly heard some men wanted to pay for chat, though she'd never met one. If a man could do it, so could a woman.

"I might stay for a good thick coin."

"Bribery would invalidate the results of our conversation." The woman spread her hands. Men used that same gesture men to show they had no money, which was almost always a lie. "Intoxication might invalidate it as well. I'm awaiting the determination."

The stranger's gaze rose to a point above Lolly's head, where the insects circulated. She pursed her lips, then seemed to reach a decision.

"We've determined intoxication is not a barrier to any agreements reached or decisions made. Nearly everyone on this planet carries a disease or condition that impairs their perceptions, and your habits have made you somewhat inured to the effects of intoxicants."

The words might have been in a foreign language, for all Lolly could understand. But she wasn't about to admit ignorance.

"That's right, I'm immured. The Lord Mayor himself gave me a medal for it."

"Excuse me. I will attempt to limit my vocabulary to terms you understand."

"I understand plenty." Lolly bristled. "Like I know tha has a voice like a Bootle organ and a smile to match."

The stranger's pockmarked face contorted in confusion. Lolly's courage soared.

"A Bootle organ is a frog and that were an insult. Will tha take offence now, and leave me in peace?"

"Our invitation was sincere. We would like to talk with you."

"I don't work my mouth for free. Give me a coin or something to eat or I'll be gone."

The woman looked thoughtful again. "Commensality is an important human value and doesn't constitute a bribe. Very well."

Mary pulled a paper bundle from her cloak pocket and placed it in Lolly's outstretched hand.

"That's nice." She raised the packet to her nose and inhaled the heady aroma of treacle toffee. "My one sweet tooth likes a bit of toffee."

Lolly shuffled backward and couched her haunches on a canted gravestone. She stuffed the greasy packet into her pocket, and took a deep swig from her flask.

Ask her who she is and what she wants. And why she speaks so strange, mammy.

"Did tha get a smack in the throat, miss? A woman doesn't croak like that from nothing."

"This voice is an indication of our dual nature." The woman placed her hand on her chest. "This individual is my host. Making my own voice seem human would be deceptive. Our intent is to communicate clearly and truthfully."

Lolly snorted. "Tha best stop talking nonsense, then."

"I will ask my host to help us communicate."

Lolly eyed the silky sheen of the woman's cloak, and the slash pockets along the front seams. If she could get her hands on the cloak and move stealthy, she might find out what else the woman carried, aside from toffee. Lolly scuffed her palms up and down her arms.

"Can I borrow that cloak? It's a bit chill."

With no hesitation, Mary shrugged off the cloak and held it out. The silk lining glowed in the moonlight. Lolly half expected to see claws on the ends of Mary's pale fingers, or webs between the knuckles, but her hands were human, with pearly, neat-cut fingernails showing no hint of grime, as if she'd just come soaped and scrubbed from the bath.

But she had taken a bath, just that morning. And in a very large bathtub indeed.

"How'd tha end in the river?" Lolly asked as she settled the cloak around her shoulders. "Some man object to hearing your nonsense?"

Don't anger her, Mammy. Not while you're getting away with something.

"Don't mean to be uncivil," Lolly added quickly. "If tha has a tale to tell, I'll listen. Won't surprise nor shock me, neither. I heard it all. When women sit together, sad stories start spilling out our holes."

The woman winced and pressed her lips together into a thin line. When she spoke, her voice had changed.

"You make an apt observation," she said. Her voice had turned soft and musical, like a lady who put sugar on her words to tempt others to listen.

"There now," said Lolly. "Did tha cough the frog out?"

"No," croaked the Bootle organ. "As I tried to explain, we are two separate individuals, autonomous but working in cooperation."

"I am an Englishwoman," the lady interjected. "The daughter of a Manchester gentleman. The voice you find unpleasant is not of this world."

"That's true enough," said Lolly.

"To answer your other question," the ladylike voice continued, "Early yesterday morning we attempted conversation with another of your profession. We ran afoul of her procurator. A... A... What do you call a man like that?"

"A pimp?"

"Yes, her pimp. He was in drink, and violent. Murderous." Mary's homely face crumpled like furled sail. "He thought I was attempting to lure the young woman off the streets."

"Was tha?"

Mary raised her hands to cover her eyes for a moment. Lolly took the opportunity to snake her fingers into the cloak's pockets and scoop out the contents. When Mary looked up, Lolly had her hands spread on her thighs, innocent as anything.

"No, we only wanted to talk to her, as I'm talking to you now." Her voice was thick with grief. "I misjudged, and it nearly cost me my life."

"That'll happen if tha crosses the wrong pimp."

No time to finger the treasure, but there was a handkerchief for certain. Probably silk and if so would fetch half a crown. A few other pieces—likely a penknife and a pouch of matches, maybe a little packet of needles and thread. No coins, more's the pity. What else a lady like Mary might carry in her cloak pockets at night, Lolly couldn't imagine. But if Lolly could get away with it, her landlady would be happy about the rent, and little Meg would have a cake.

Lolly swigged from her flask, and then offered it to Mary. She didn't accept—Lolly would have been surprised and regretful if she had—but it was only polite to offer a drink to a mark.

Mary wiped her nose on her sleeve, cleared her throat, and squawked, "This planet—"

"—this world," the lady's sweet voice interrupted.

"This world," the Bootle organ continued, "Has a long history of violent intraspecies competition and colonization. Entire populations are conquered and their lands and resources stolen. We observe this pattern in approximately five-point-five-eight percent of sentient species surveyed. Other species—the vast majority—are parasitic, like my own. Among species like yours, most individuals consider violent conflict as an inevitable mode for intra- and inter-community interaction. Would you agree?"

"Wha?" Lolly hadn't understood one word.

"Do you believe," Mary's sweet voice asked, "That it's natural for people to take the property of others with violence? To steal their homes, land, forests, farms, mines, villages, and towns?"

"Sure," Lolly answered. "If I knew nothing else, I know that. Seen it enough."

"So you agree," the Bootle organ said. "Colonization backed by violence is the norm?"

"If thart asking if those stronger and meaner take what they want from the weaker and meeker, that's a simple-minded question. They do. Here, there, and everywhere."

Under Lolly's skirt, Meg yawned. Her warm breath puffed across her mother's knee.

"If we suggested that the breeding population is also considered a rightful spoil of colonialism, would you agree?"

More nonsense. Lolly gulped at her flask, ignoring the question.

"We are attempting to establish whether you agree that colonialism traditionally includes co-opting the females of the colonized population for propagation."

The lady interjected again. "If you don't keep it simple, she'll never understand." Mary sat beside Lolly on the wide gravestone. "You've heard of the Sabine women, have you not?"

Lolly hadn't, but she nodded anyway.

"In old Rome," Mary continued, "When the men didn't have women, they stole them from their neighbors. What my friend wants to know is whether or not you think that's natural."

"Sure is," Lolly said without hesitation. "Where would they put their pricks otherwise? A man sees something he likes, he's going to skewer it. Otherwise another man will skewer them. That's men, whether babe or bishop. Women are a little different."

"How are women different?" asked the Bootle organ.

"Let me think." Lolly drew the toffee packet out of her pocket and unfolded it. "A woman will kill for a loaf of bread if her children are starving. Some might kill to keep her man. A tart might kill the man who cheats her, or the woman who poaches her stroll. But women don't kill for sport. They don't roam in gangs looking for women to fuck dead. No woman ever set upon a neighbor's young husband and left him bleeding in the woodpile."

Lolly picked off a shard of toffee and slipped it between her gums. The sugar made her head spin. Its flavor was strong as the darkest rum, and just as heady. She tongued it into the pouch of her cheek.

"No woman ever chased a boy around the house, half-strangled him to death, then sent him home to the farm with a necklace of bruises and belly full of bastard. A woman will look the other way if her man does it, though, and that's contusion."

"Collusion." Mary nodded.

"Some say that's the same as if she did the deed herself," Lolly continued. "A woman can be mean and nasty. Some have heavier hands than others, and sharper tongues. But we ent like men."

"Why the inequity?" asked the Bootle organ.

Lolly frowned.

"Why do you think men are more violent than women?" the sweet voice explained.

The toffee dissolved, coating Lolly's mouth in sweet syrup. She savored the flavor for a moment before answering.

"Why we chewing this over, that's what I want to know? Spoils my appetite. If tha wants an opinion, Miss Mary, talk back and forth with tha own self."

"Your opinion is the one we are interested in."

"I don't care why. Nobody does. It's the way of the world."

"What if it weren't the way of the world?" The Bootle organ's voice harshened with urgency. "What if it didn't have to be?"

Take me home, mammy. I'm tired.

The child ought to be wrapped tight in her blanket and snugged into a timber yard alcove, not cowering under her mother's skirt listening to a stranger talk nonsense. No sense in drawing this out. Lolly wouldn't get anything more out of Mary.

"Good night, miss." Lolly shrugged off the cloak.

"You may keep the garment," croaked the Bootle organ. "It's a local product, worthless, and doesn't constitute a bribe. We understand it may be exchanged for currency, but your economic transactions are meaningless."

I don't like her.

Lolly didn't either. Aside from the voice tricks, anyone who gave gifts easily might have a changeable mind. But perhaps Mary hadn't been squeezed dry, not quite yet.

"Why would a fine wool cloak be worth nothing, when tha came chasing after me to find some plain white smock?" Lolly asked.

"It is not a garment, but a piece of technology."

"Does tha have more worthless things to give?"

"Perhaps."

Mary pulled two items from her skirt pockets—a large muslin handkerchief and a little velvet purse. Lolly eyed the purse greedily. Mary tipped the coins into her hand and pocketed them before handing over the empty purse.

Get her shoes.

Lolly laughed. "Maybe you think your boots are worthless too, miss?"

"Yes," Mary said, "But I don't fancy walking on stocking feet."

"True, but does tha need stockings, though?"

Mary touched Lolly lightly on the back of her hand, just the tips of her fingers, light as a moth.

"I would strip to my skin to get you to keep you talking, Lolly. Would you require that of a lady?"

"It's midsummer. Tha wouldn't catch a death." Lolly laughed again, then coughed. When she spat, she took care to aim behind the gravestones, away from Mary.

I don't want to listen to her no more. Meg pinched the skin of her mother's thigh between two little fingers, hard enough to make Lolly's eyes water.

"You stated violence is the way of the world," said the Bootle organ. "I suggest that other options exist."

"If so, I haven't heard them."

Lolly shook the gritty dregs of her flask onto her palm and licked up the last of the liquor. She wiped the grains on her skirt and stood. Meg placed her feet on top of her mother's foot and wrapped her arms around Lolly's thigh. Lolly stumped away, but only got a few steps before Mary blocked her path.

"Just a few more questions. If violence were not the way of the world, would that be better?"

"Sure. Better for lots of people."

"Like whom?"

Like me, mammy.

Lolly coughed again, and wiped the spittle from her lips with the back of her hand.

"Though you insist it's not possible, having admitted it would be desirable, can you say how it might be accomplished?" Mary squawked.

"I can say a lot of things."

"Turn your mind to this specific problem. How could your world be rid of violence?"

Kill the men.

"What's that?" Lolly blurted.

Kill the men, mammy. Like the one who tore into you the day after your own mammy died. Like the pimp who knocked your teeth out. Like the ones who pay you with a smack and a knee to the nose. Like the Wharfinger, even, who makes you walk the soles off your shoes and doesn't keep you safe even though you're his girl and he's your pimp same as any.

Lolly's eyes began to sting.

Like the man who tossed me under that wagon.

"No, little Meggy," she mumbled. "Don't think about the wagon. Don't remember it."

I don't, mammy. But you do. You always think about it.

Lolly nodded. Her little girl in a pool of blood, squashed so flat she could be folded in two. A tall man laughing, specks of blood in his red beard, and everyone on the street pointing at Lolly, saying a mother should keep her child safe.

Kill the men. All of them. They deserve it.

"Kill the men," said Lolly. "All of them."

Mary's shoulders relaxed and she let out a long sigh.

"There," she breathed. "That's nine hundred women, just under the deadline."

Mary placed her hand on Lolly's shoulder.

"Having agreed that violence is a primary mode of social behavior on this planet, and having admitted the results are undesirable, you suggest that this situation could be ameliorated if all men on this planet were killed. Is that true?"

Yes. Tell her, mammy.

"Yes," Lolly said. "I do. That's exactly what I think."

In that moment, Lolly realized who she was talking to. Mary was Satan, the Devil himself in disguise. What other creature could talk so easily about the destruction of man?

"If you knew this project were possible, that the male half of the human population would be exterminated, would you change your opinion?"

Lolly reached down to pat her daughter's head, but Meg was gone. She'd be back, though. Meg always came back.

"No, I won't change my mind."

Mary grinned up at the watching insects.

"Victory," she said in her sweet voice. And when she turned back to Lolly, her smile was so warm, so kind, so glowing with approval that Lolly barely recognized the expression.

"What kind of world will it make?" Lolly asked.

"Nobody knows." Mary took Lolly's hand and squeezed. "But we'll soon find out."

"Can't be worse than this one. If tha wants to kill them all, best get to work. Just one thing." Lolly leaned close and touched Mary's shoulder with her own. "Start with the Wharfinger."

NOTES ABOUT "WHAT GENTLE WOMEN DARE"

Oof. "What Gentle Women Dare" was a struggle. It went through nine versions over three years, all starkly different, though all dealing with Liverpool sex workers in the 1700s. Why the struggle? All I was doing was trying to encompass the entire history of violence against women over the past hundred thousand years of human history, and its links to colonialism and slavery.

Violence against women is an issue that obsesses me. How has humanity survived when women have been raped, murdered, abused, kidnapped, and forced to bear children for the entirety of our history? I think the best way to begin to understand fundamental unanswerable questions is to write fiction about it. We ask *why*, and *why*, and *why*, until something finally gives. The story becomes a framework to hang the question on. We get a tiny bit closer to the answer.

Bouquets to poet, writer, and editor Dominik Parisien for helping dig this story out of a hole. He said, "Why don't you think about 'The Screwfly Solution'?" James Tiptree, Jr. is a huge influence on my work, and turns out that suggestion was exactly what I needed.

THE THREE RESURRECTIONS OF JESSICA CHURCHILL

Content warning: rape, murder, suicide

"I rise today on this September 11, the one-year anniversary of the greatest tragedy on American soil in our history, with a heavy heart…" (Hon. Jim Turner)

September 9, 2001

JESSICA SLUMPED AGAINST THE INSIDE OF THE truck door. The girl behind the wheel and the other one squished between them on the bench seat kept stealing glances at her. Jessica ignored them, just like she tried to ignore the itchy pull and tug deep inside her, under her belly button, where the aliens were trying to knit her guts back together.

"You party pretty hard last night?" the driver asked.

Jessica rested her burning forehead on the window. The hum of the highway under the wheels buzzed through her skull. The truck cab stank of incense.

"You shouldn't hitchhike, it's not safe," the other girl said. "I sound like my mom saying it and I hate that but it's really true. So many dead girls. They haven't even found all the bodies."

"Highway of Tears," the driver said.

"Yeah, Highway of Tears," the other one repeated. "Bloody Sixteen."

"Nobody calls it that," the driver snapped.

Jessica pulled her hair up off her neck, trying to cool the sticky heat pulsing through her. The two girls looked like tree planters. She'd spent the summer working full time at the gas station and now she could smell a tree planter a mile away. They'd come in for smokes and mix; dirty, hairy, dressed in fleece and hemp just like these two. The driver had blond dreadlocks and the other had tattoos circling her wrists. Not that much older than her, lecturing her about staying safe just like somebody's mom.

Well, she's right, Jessica thought. A gush of blood flooded the crotch of her jeans.

Water. Jessica, we can do this but you've got to get some water. We need to replenish your fluids.

"You got any water?" Jessica asked. Her voice rasped, throat stripped raw from all the screaming.

The tattooed girl dug through the backpack at Jessica's feet and came up with a two-liter mason jar half-full of water. Hippies, Jessica thought as she fumbled with the lid. Like one stupid jar will save the world.

"Let me help." The tattooed girl unscrewed the lid and steadied the heavy jar as Jessica lifted it to her lips.

She gagged. Her throat was tight as a fist but she forced herself to swallow, wash down the dirt and puke coating her mouth.

Good. Drink more.

"I can't," Jessica said. The tattooed girl stared at her.

You need to. We can't do this alone. You have to help us.

"Are you okay?" the driver asked. "You look wrecked."

Jessica wiped her mouth with the back of her hand. "I'm fine. Just hot."

"Yeah, you're really flushed," said the tattooed girl. "You should take off your coat."

Jessica ignored her and gulped at the jar until it was empty.

Not so fast. Careful!

"Do you want to swing past the hospital when we get into town?" the driver asked.

A bolt of pain knifed through Jessica's guts. The empty jar slipped from her grip and rolled across the floor of the truck. The pain faded.

"I'm fine," she repeated. "I just got a bad period."

That did it. The lines of worry eased off both girls' faces.

"Do you have a pad? I'm gonna bleed all over your seat." Jessica's vision dimmed, like someone had put a shade over the morning sun.

"No problem." The tattooed girl fished through the backpack. "I bleed heavy too. It depletes my iron."

"That's just an excuse for you to eat meat," said the driver.

Jessica leaned her forehead on the window and waited for the light to come back into the world. The two girls were bickering now, caught up in their own private drama.

Another flood of blood. More this time. She curled her fists into her lap. Her insides twisted and jumped like a fish on a line.

Your lungs are fine. Breathe deeply, in and out, that's it. We need all the oxygen you can get.

The tattooed girl pulled a pink wrapped maxi pad out of her backpack and offered it to Jessica. The driver slowed down and turned the truck into a roadside campground.

"Hot," Jessica said. The girls didn't hear. Now they were bitching at each other about disposable pads and something called a keeper cup.

We know. You'll be okay. We can heal you.

"Don't wait for me," Jessica said as they pulled up to the campground outhouse. She flipped the door handle and nearly fell out of the truck. "I can catch another ride."

Cold air washed over her as she stumbled toward the outhouse. She unzipped her long coat and let the breeze play though—chill air on boiling skin. Still early September but they always got a cold snap at the start of fall. First snow only a few days ago. Didn't last. Never did.

The outhouse stench hit her like a slap. Jessica fumbled with the lock. Her fingers felt stiff and clumsy.

"Why am I so hot?" she said, leaning on the cold plywood wall. Her voice sounded strange, ripped apart and multiplied into echoes.

Your immune system is trying to fight us but we've got it under control. The fever isn't dangerous, just uncomfortable.

She shed her coat and let it fall to the floor. Unzipped her jeans, slipped them down her hips. No panties. She hadn't been able to find them.

No, Jessica. Don't look.

Pubic hair hacked away along with most of her skin. Two deep slices puckered angry down the inside of her right thigh. And blood. On her legs, on her jeans, inside her coat. Blood everywhere, dark and sticky.

Keep breathing!

An iron tang filled the outhouse as a gout of blood dribbled down her legs. Jessica fell back on the toilet seat. Deep within her chest something fluttered, like a bird beating its wings on her ribs, trying to get out. The light drained from the air.

If you die, we die too. Please give us a chance.

The flutters turned into fists pounding on her breastbone. She struggled to inhale, tried to drag the outhouse stink deep into her lungs but the air felt thick. Solid. Like a wall against her face.

Don't go. Please.

Breath escaped her like smoke from a fire burned down to coal and ash. She collapsed against the wall of the outhouse. Vision turned to pinpricks; she crumpled like paper and died.

"Everything okay in there?"

The thumping on the door made the whole outhouse shake. Jessica lurched to her feet. Her chest burned like she'd been breathing acid.

You're okay.

"I'm fine. Gimme a second."

Jessica plucked the pad off the outhouse floor, ripped it open and stuck it on the crotch of her bloody jeans, zipped them up. She zipped her coat to her chin. She felt strong. Invincible. She unlocked the door.

The two girls were right there, eyes big and concerned and in her business.

"You didn't have to wait," Jessica said.

"How old are you, fifteen? We waited," the driver said as they climbed back into the truck.

"We're not going to let you hitchhike," said the tattooed girl. "Especially not you."

"Why not me?" Jessica slammed the truck door behind her.

"Most of the dead and missing girls are First Nations."

"You think I'm an Indian? Fuck you. Am I on a reserve?"

The driver glared at her friend as she turned the truck back onto the highway.

"Sorry," the tattooed girl said.

"Do I look like an Indian?"

"Well, kinda."

"Fuck you." Jessica leaned on the window, watching the highway signs peel by as they rolled toward Prince George. When they got to the city the invincible feeling was long gone. The driver insisted on taking her right to Gran's.

"Thanks," Jessica said as she slid out of the truck.

The driver waved. "Remember, no hitchhiking."

September 8, 2001

Jessica never hitchhiked.

She wasn't stupid. But Prince George was spread out. The bus ran maybe once an hour weekdays and barely at all on weekends, and when the weather turned cold you could freeze to death trying to walk everywhere. So yeah, she took rides when she could, if she knew the driver.

After her Saturday shift she'd started walking down the highway. Mom didn't know she was coming. Jessica had tried to get through three times from the gas station phone, left voice mails. Mom didn't always pick up—usually didn't—and when she did it was some excuse about her phone battery or connection.

Mom was working as a cook at a retreat center out by Tabor Lake. A two-hour walk, but Mom would get someone to drive her back to Gran's.

Only seven o'clock but getting cold and the wind had come up. Semis bombed down the highway, stirring up the trash and making it dance at her feet and fly in her face as she walked along the ditch.

It wasn't even dark when the car pulled over to the side of the highway.

"Are you Jessica?"

The man looked ordinary. Baseball cap, hoodie. Somebody's dad trying to look young.

"Yeah," Jessica said.

"Your mom sent me to pick you up."

A semi honked as it blasted past his car. A McDonald's wrapper flipped through the air and smacked her in the back of the head. She got in.

The car was skunky with pot smoke. She almost didn't notice when he passed the Tabor Lake turnoff.

"That was the turn," she said.

"Yeah, she's not there. She's out at the ski hill."

"At this time of year?"

"Some kind of event." He took a drag on his smoke and smiled.

Jessica hadn't even twigged. Mom had always wanted to work at the ski hill, where she could party all night and ski all day.

It was twenty minutes before Jessica started to clue in.

When he slowed to take a turn onto a gravel road she braced herself to roll out of the car. The door handle was broken. She went at him with her fingernails but he had the jump on her, hit her in the throat with his elbow. She gulped air and tried to roll down the window.

It was broken too. She battered the glass with her fists, then spun and lunged for the wheel. He hit her again, slammed her head against the dashboard three times. The world stuttered and swam.

Pain brought everything back into focus. Face down, her arms flailed, fingers clawed at the dirt. Spruce needles flew up her nose and coated her tongue. Her butt was jacked up over a log and every thrust pounded her face into the dirt. One part of her was screaming, screaming. The other part watched the pile of deer shit inches from her nose. It looked like a heap of candy. Chocolate-covered almonds.

She didn't listen to what he was telling her. She'd heard worse from boys at school. He couldn't make her listen. He didn't exist except as a medium for pain.

When he got off, Jessica felt ripped in half, split like firewood. She tried to roll off the log. She'd crawl into the bush, he'd drive away, and it would be over.

Then he showed her the knife.

When he rammed the knife up her she found a new kind of pain. It drove the breath from her lungs and sliced the struggle from her limbs. She listened to herself whimper, thinking it sounded like a newborn kitten, crying for its mother.

The pain didn't stop until the world had retreated to little flecks of light deep in her skull. The ground spun around her as he dragged her through the bush and rolled her into a ravine. She landed face down in a stream. Her head flopped, neck canted at a weird angle.

Jessica curled her fingers around something cold and round. A rock. It fit in her hand perfectly and if he came back she'd let him have it right in the teeth. And then her breath bubbled away and she died.

When she came back to life a bear corpse was lying beside her, furry and rank. She dug her fingers into its pelt and pulled herself up. It was still warm. And skinny—nothing but sinew and bone under the skin.

She stumbled through the stream, toes in wet socks stubbing against the rocks but it didn't hurt. Nothing hurt. She was good. She could do anything.

She found her coat in the mud, her jeans too. One sneaker by the bear and then she looked and looked for the other one.

It's up the bank.

She climbed up. The shoe was by the log where it had happened. The toe was coated in blood. She wiped it in the dirt.

You need to drink some water.

A short dirt track led down to the road. The gravel glowed white in the dim light of early morning. No idea which way led to the highway. She picked a direction.

"How do you know what I need?"

We know. We're trying to heal you. The damage is extensive. You've lost a lot of blood and the internal injuries are catastrophic.

"No shit."

We can fix you. We just need time.

Her guts writhed. Snakes fought in her belly, biting and coiling.

Feel that? That's us working. Inside you.

"Why doesn't it hurt?"

We've established a colony in your thalamus. That's where we're blocking the pain. If we didn't, you'd die of shock.

"Again."

Yes, again.

"A colony. What the fuck are you? Aliens?"

Yes. We're also distributing a hormonal cocktail of adrenaline and testosterone to keep you moving, but we'll have to taper it off soon because it puts too much stress on your heart. Right now it's very important for you to drink some water.

"Shut up about the water." She wasn't thirsty. She felt great.

A few minutes later the fight drained out of her. Thirsty, exhausted, she ached as though the hinge of every moving part was crusted in rust, from her jaw to her toes. Her eyelids rasped like sandpaper. Her breath sucked and blew without reaching her lungs. Every rock in the road was a mountain and every pothole a canyon.

But she walked. Dragged her sneakers through the gravel, taking smaller and smaller steps until she just couldn't lift her feet anymore. She stood in the middle of the road and waited. Waited to fall over. Waited for the world to slip from her grasp and darkness to drown her in cold nothing.

When she heard the truck speeding toward her she didn't even look up. Didn't matter who it was, what it was. She stuck out her thumb.

September 10, 2001

Jessica woke soaked. Covered in blood, she thought, struggling with the blankets. But it wasn't blood.

"What—"

Your urethra was damaged so we eliminated excess fluid through your pores. It's repaired now. You'll be able to urinate.

She pried herself out of the wet blankets.

No solid food, though. Your colon is shredded and your small intestine has multiple ruptures.

When the tree planters dropped her off, Gran had been sacked out on the couch. Jessica had stayed in the shower for a good half hour, watching the blood swirl down the drain with the spruce needles and the dirt, the blood clots and shreds of raw flesh.

And all the while she drank. Opened her mouth and let the cool spray fill her. Then she had stuffed her bloody clothes in a garbage bag and slept.

Jessica ran her fingertips over the gashes inside her thigh. The wounds puckered like wide toothless mouths, sliced edges pasted together and sunk deep within her flesh. The rest of the damage was hardened over with amber-colored scabs. She'd have to use a mirror to see it all. She didn't want to look.

"I should go to the hospital," she whispered.

That's not a good idea. It would take multiple interventions to repair the damage to your digestive tract. They'd never be able to save your uterus or reconstruct your vulva and clitoris. The damage to your cervix alone—

"My what?"

Do you want to have children someday?

"I don't know."

Trust us. We can fix this.

She hated the hospital anyway. Went to Emergency after she'd twisted her knee but the nurse had turned her away, said she wouldn't bother the on-call for something minor. Told her to go home and put a bag of peas on it.

And the cops were even worse than anyone at the hospital. Didn't give a shit. Not one of them.

Gran was on the couch, snoring. A deck of cards was scattered across the coffee table in between the empties—looked like she'd been playing solitaire all weekend.

Gran hadn't fed the cats, either. They had to be starving but they wouldn't come to her, not even when she was filling their dishes. Not even Gringo, who had hogged her bed every night since she was ten. He just hissed and ran.

Usually Jessica would wake up Gran before leaving for school, try to get her on her feet so she didn't sleep all day.

Today she didn't have the strength. She shook Gran's shoulder.

"Night night, baby," Gran said, and turned over.

Jessica waited for the school bus. She felt cloudy, dispersed, her thoughts blowing away with the wind. And cold now, without her coat. The fever was gone.

"Could you fix Gran?"

Perhaps. What's wrong with her?

Jessica shrugged. "I don't know. Everything."

We can try. Eventually.

She sleepwalked through her classes. It wasn't a problem. The teachers were more bothered when she did well than when she slacked off. She stayed in the shadows, off everyone's radar.

After school she walked to the gas station. Usually when she got to work she'd buy some chips or a chocolate bar, get whoever was going off shift to ring it up so nobody could say she hadn't paid for it.

"How come I'm not hungry?" she asked when she had the place to herself.

You are; you just can't perceive it.

It was a quiet night. The gas station across the highway had posted a half cent lower so everyone was going there. Usually she'd go stir crazy from boredom but today she just zoned out. Badly photocopied faces stared at her from the posters taped to the cigarette cabinet overhead.

An SUV pulled up to pump number three. A bull elk was strapped to the hood, tongue lolling.

"What was the deal with the bear?" she said.

The bear's den was adjacent to our crash site. It was killed by the concussive wave.

"Crash site. A spaceship?"

Yes. Unfortunate for the bear, but very fortunate for us.

"You brought the bear back to life. Healed it."

Yes.

"And before finding me you were just riding around in the bear."

Yes. It was attracted by the scent of your blood.

"So you saw what happened to me. You watched." She should be upset, shouldn't she? But her mind felt dull, thoughts thudding inside an empty skull.

We have no access to the visual cortex.

"You're blind?"

Yes.

"What are you?"

A form of bacteria.

"Like an infection."

Yes.

The door chimed and the hunter handed over his credit card. She rang it through. When he was gone she opened her mouth to ask another question, but then her gut convulsed like she'd been hit. She doubled over the counter. Bile stung her throat.

He'd been here on Saturday.

Jessica had been on the phone, telling mom's voice mail that she'd walk out to Talbot Lake after work. While she was talking she'd rung up a purchase, $32.25 in gas and a pack of smokes. She'd punched it through automatically, cradling the phone on her shoulder. She'd given him change from fifty.

An ordinary man. Hoodie. Cap.

Jessica, breathe.

Her head whipped around, eyes wild, hands scrambling reflexively for a weapon. Nobody was at the pumps, nobody parked at the air pump. He could come back any moment. Bring his knife and finish the job.

Please breathe. There's no apparent danger.

She fell to her knees and crawled out from behind the counter. Nobody would stop him, nobody would save her. Just like they hadn't saved all those dead and missing girls whose posters had been staring at her all summer from up on the cigarette cabinet.

When she'd started the job they'd creeped her out, those posters. For a few weeks she'd thought twice about walking after dark. But then those dead and missing girls disappeared into the landscape. Forgotten.

You must calm down.

Now she was one of them.

We may not be able to bring you back again.

She scrambled to the bathroom on all fours, threw herself against the door, twisted the lock. Her hands were shuddering, teeth chattering like it was forty below. Her chest squeezed and bucked, throwing acid behind her teeth.

There was a frosted window high on the wall. He could get in, if he wanted. She could almost see the knife tick-tick-ticking on the glass.

No escape. Jessica plowed herself into the narrow gap between the wall and toilet, wedging herself there, fists clutching at her burning chest as she retched bile onto the floor. The light winked and flickered. A scream flushed out of her and she died.

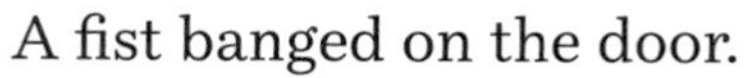

A fist banged on the door.

"Jessica, what the hell!" Her boss's voice.

A key scraped in the lock. Jessica gripped the toilet and wrenched herself off the floor to face him. His face was flushed with anger and though he was a big guy, he couldn't scare her now. She felt bigger, taller, stronger, too. And she'd always been smarter than him.

"Jesus, what's wrong with you?"

"Nothing, I'm fine." Better than fine. She was butterfly-light, like if she opened her wings she could fly away.

"The station's wide open. Anybody could have waltzed in here and walked off with the till."

"Did they?"

His mouth hung open for a second. "Did they what?"

"Walk off with the fucking till?"

"Are you on drugs?"

She smiled. She didn't need him. She could do anything.

"That's it," he said. "You're gone. Don't come back."

A taxi was gassing up at pump number one. She got in the back and waited, watching her boss pace and yell into his phone. The invincible feeling faded before the tank was full. By the time she got home Jessica's joints had locked stiff and her thoughts had turned fuzzy.

All the lights were on. Gran was halfway into her second bottle of u-brew red so she was pretty out of it, too. Jessica sat with her at the kitchen table for a few minutes and was just thinking about crawling to bed when the phone rang.

It was Mom.

"Did you send someone to pick me up on the highway?" Jessica stole a glance at Gran. She was staring at her reflection in the kitchen window, maybe listening, maybe not.

"No, why would I do that?"

"I left you messages. On Saturday."

"I'm sorry, baby. This phone is so bad, you know that."

"Listen, I need to talk to you." Jessica kept her voice low.

"Is it your grandma?" Mom asked.

"Yeah. It's bad. She's not talking."

"She does this every time the residential school thing hits the news. Gets super excited, wants to go up north and see if any of her family are still alive. But she gives up after a couple of days. Shuts down. It's too much for her. She was only six when they took her away, you know."

"Yeah. When are you coming home?"

"I got a line on a great job, cooking for an oil rig crew. One month on, one month off."

Jessica didn't have the strength to argue. All she wanted to do was sleep.

"Don't worry about your Gran," Mom said. "She'll be okay in a week or two. Listen, I got to go."

"I know."

"Night night, baby," Mom said, and hung up.

September 11, 2001

Jessica waited alone for the school bus. The street was deserted. When the bus pulled up the driver was chattering before she'd even climbed in.

"Can you believe it? Isn't it horrible?" The driver's eyes were puffy, mascara swiped to a gray stain under her eyes.

"Yeah," Jessica agreed automatically.

"When I saw the news I thought it was so early, nobody would be at work. But it was nine in the morning in New York. Those towers were full of people." The driver wiped her nose.

The bus was nearly empty. Two little kids sat behind the driver, hugging their backpacks. The radio blared. Horror in

New York. Attack on Washington. Jessica dropped into the shotgun seat and let the noise wash over her for a few minutes as they twisted slowly through the empty streets. Then she moved to the back of the bus.

When she'd gotten dressed that morning her jeans had nearly slipped off her hips. Something about that was important. She tried to concentrate, but the thoughts flitted from her grasp, darting away before she could pin them down.

She focused on the sensation within her, the buck and heave under her ribs and in front of her spine.

"What are you fixing right now?" she asked.

An ongoing challenge is the sequestration of the fecal and digestive matter that leaked into your abdominal cavity.

"What about the stuff you mentioned yesterday? The intestine and the...whatever it was."

Once we have repaired your digestive tract and restored gut motility we will begin reconstructive efforts on your reproductive organs.

"You like big words, don't you?"

We assure you the terminology is accurate.

There it was. That was the thing that had been bothering her, niggling at the back of her mind, trying to break through the fog.

"How do you know those words? How can you even speak English?"

We aren't communicating in language. The meaning is conveyed by socio-linguistic impulses interpreted by the brain's speech processing loci. Because of the specifics of our biology, verbal communication is an irrelevant medium.

"You're not talking, you're just making me hallucinate," Jessica said.

That is essentially correct.

How could the terminology be accurate, then? She didn't know those words—cervix and whatever—so how could she hallucinate them?

"Were you watching the news when the towers collapsed?" the driver asked as she pulled into the high school parking lot. Jessica ignored her and slowly stepped off the bus.

The aliens were trying to baffle her with big words and science talk. For three days she'd had them inside her, their voice behind her eyes, their fingers deep in her guts, and she'd trusted them. Hadn't even thought twice. She had no choice.

If they could make her hallucinate, what else were they doing to her?

The hallways were quiet, the classrooms deserted except for one room at the end of the hall with 40 kids packed in. The teacher had wheeled in an AV cart. Some of the kids hadn't even taken off their coats.

Jessica stood in the doorway. The news flashed clips of smoking towers collapsing into ash clouds. The bottom third of the screen was overlaid with scrolling, flashing text, the sound layered with frantic voiceovers. People were jumping from the towers, hanging in the air like dancers. The clips replayed over and over again. The teacher passed around a box of Kleenex.

Jessica turned her back on the class and climbed upstairs, joints creaking, jeans threatening to slide off with every step. She hitched them up. The biology lab was empty. She leaned on the cork board and scanned the parasite diagrams. Ring worm. Tape worm. Liver fluke. Black wasp.

Some parasites can change their host's biology, the poster said, or even change their host's behavior.

Jessica took a push pin from the board and shoved it into her thumb. It didn't hurt. When she ripped it out a thin stream of blood trickled from the skin, followed by an ooze of clear amber from deep within the gash.

What are you doing?

None of your business, she thought.

Everything is going to be okay.

No it won't, she thought. She squeezed the amber ooze from her thumb, let it drip on the floor. The aliens were wrenching her around like a puppet, but without them she would be dead. Three times dead. Maybe she should feel grateful, but she didn't.

"Why didn't you want me to go to the hospital?" she asked as she slowly hinged down the stairs.

They couldn't have helped you, Jessica. You would have died.

Again, Jessica thought. Died again. And again.

"You said that if I die, you die too."

When your respiration stops, we can only survive for a limited time.

The mirror in the girls' bathroom wasn't real glass, just a sheet of polished aluminum, its shine pitted and worn. She leaned on the counter, rested her forehead on the cool metal. Her reflection warped and stretched.

"If I'd gone to the hospital, it would have been bad for you. Wouldn't it?"

That is likely.

"So you kept me from going. You kept me from doing a lot of things."

We assure you that is untrue. You may exercise your choices as you see fit. We will not interfere.

"You haven't left me any choices."

Jessica left the bathroom and walked down the hall. The news blared from the teacher's lounge. She looked in. At least a dozen teachers crowded in front of an AV cart, backs turned. Jessica slipped behind them and ducked into the teachers' washroom. She locked the door.

It was like a real bathroom. Air freshener, moisturizing lotion, floral soap. Real mirror on the wall and a makeup mirror propped on the toilet tank. Jessica put it on the floor.

"Since when do bacteria have spaceships?" She pulled her sweater over her head and dropped it over the mirror.

Jessica, you're not making sense. You're confused.

She put her heel on the sweater and stepped down hard. The mirror cracked.

Go to the hospital now, if you want.

"If I take you to the hospital, what will you do? Infect other people? How many?"

Jessica, please. Haven't we helped you?

"You've helped yourself."

The room pitched and flipped. Jessica fell to her knees. She reached for the broken mirror but it swam out of reach. Her vision telescoped and she batted at the glass with clumsy hands. A scream built behind her teeth, swelled and choked her. She swallowed it whole, gulped it, forced it down her throat like she was starving.

You don't have to do this. We aren't a threat.

She caught a mirror shard in one fist and swam along the floor as the room tilted and whirled. With one hand she pinned it to the yawning floor like a spike, windmilled her free arm and slammed her wrist down. The walls folded in, collapsing on her like the whole weight of the world, crushing in.

She felt another scream building. She forced her tongue between clenched teeth and bit down. Amber fluid oozed down her chin and pooled on the floor.

Please. We only want to help.

"Night night, baby," she said, and raked the mirror up her arm.

The fluorescent light flashed overhead. The room plunged into darkness as a world of pain dove into her for one hanging moment. Then it lifted. Jessica convulsed on the floor, watching the bars of light overhead stutter and compress to two tiny glimmers inside the thin parched shell of her skull. And she died, finally, at last.

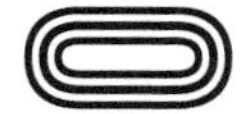

NOTES ABOUT "THE THREE RESURRECTIONS OF JESSICA CHURCHILL"

When I was sixteen, my classmate Shelly Ann Bacsu disappeared. She was certainly murdered; the RCMP found her clothes but not her body. We imagine she was abducted from alongside the highway while walking home in the evening, targeted by an unknown man. Maybe he was known to her, maybe not. What she went through in the hours before she died is unimaginable. I'm pretty sure none of my female classmates have ever gotten over it. I know I haven't. Her murder has never been solved.

Over the years, I've tried to encompass this horror in various ways. In "The Three Resurrections of Jessica Churchill," I've applied September 11 as a framework, drawing an equivalent between those acts of terrorism and the long-term, still ongoing, and barely investigated epidemic of murdered and missing Indigenous women.

This was my first published story. I took some flack for portraying a rape (though nobody ever complained about the murder). Rape is not here for prurience or effect. Horrible violence appears in this story because it happens all the time. Sexual violence is the air women breathe. It haunts me.

If we can't tell stories about the things that haunt us, then we can't tell stories at all.

WE WHO LIVE IN THE HEART

RICCI SLIPPED IN AND OUT OF CONSCIOUSNESS as we carried her to the anterior sinus and strapped her into her hammock. Her eyelids drooped but she kept forcing them wide. After we finished tucking her in, she pulled a handheld media appliance out of her pocket and called her friend Jane.

"You're late," Jane said. The speakers flattened her voice slightly. "Are you okay?"

Ricci was too groggy to speak. She poked her hand through the hammock's electrostatic membrane and panned the appliance around the sinus. Eddy and Chara both waved as the lens passed over them, but Jane was only interested in one thing.

"Show me your face, Ricci. Talk to me. What's it like in there?"

Ricci coughed, clearing her throat. "I dunno. It's weird. I can't really think." Her voice slurred from the anesthetic.

I could have answered Jane, if she'd asked me. The first thing newbies notice is how strange it smells. Human olfaction is primal; scents color our perceptions even when they're too faint to describe. Down belowground, the population crush makes it impossible to get away from human funk. Out here, it's the opposite, with no scents our brains recognize. That's why most of us fill our habs with stinky things—pheromone misters, scented fabrics, ablative aromatic gels.

Eventually, Ricci would get around to customizing the scentscape in her big new hab, but right then she was too busy trying to stay awake. Apparently she'd promised Jane she'd check in as soon as she arrived, and not just a quick ping. She was definitely hurting but the call was duty.

"There's people. They're taking care of me." Ricci gazed blearily at our orang. "I was carried in by a porter bot. It's orange and furry. Long arms."

"I don't care about the bot. Tell me about you."

"I'm fine, but my ears aren't working right. It's too noisy."

We live with a constant circulatory thrum, gassy gurgles and fizzes, whumps, snaps, pops, and booms. Sound waves pulse through every surface, a deep hum you feel in your bones.

Jane took a deep breath, let it out with a whoosh. "Okay. Go to sleep. Call me when you wake up, okay?"

Ricci's head lolled back, then she jerked herself awake.

"You should have come with me."

Jane laughed. "I can't leave my clients. And anyway, I'd be bored."

Ricci squeezed her eyes shut, blinked a few times, then forced them wide.

"No you wouldn't. There's seven other people here, and they're all nuts. You'd already be trying to fix them."

Vula snorted and stalked out of the sinus, her long black braids slapping her back. The rest of us just smiled and shook our heads. You can't hold people responsible for what they say when they're half-unconscious. And anyway, it's true—we're not your standard moles. We don't want to be.

Only a mole would think we'd be bored out here. We have to take care of every necessity of life personally—nobody's going to do it for us. Tapping water is one example. Equipment testing and maintenance is another. Someone has to manage the hygiene and maintenance bots. And we all share responsibility for health and safety. Making sure we can breathe is high on everyone's our priority list, so we don't leave it up to chance. Finally, there's atmospheric and geographical data gathering. Mama's got to pay the bills. We're a sovereign sociopolitical entity, population: eight, and we negotiate our own service contracts for everything.

But other than that, sure, we have all the free time in the world. Otherwise what's the point? We came out here to get some breathing room—mental and physical. Unlike the moles, we've got plenty of both.

Have you ever seen a tulip? It's a flowering plant. No nutritional value, short bloom. Down below ground, they're grown in decorative troughs for special occasions—ambassadorial visits, arts festivals, sporting events, that sort of thing.

Anyway. Take a tulip flower and stick an ovoid bladder where the stem was and you've got the idea. Except big. Really big. And the petals move. Some of us call it Mama. I just call it home.

The outer skin is a transparent, flexible organic membrane. You can see right through to the central organ systems. The surrounding bladders and sinuses provide structure and protection. Balloons inside a bigger balloon, filled with helium and hydrogen. The whole organism ripples with iridescence.

We live in the helium-filled sinuses. If you get close enough, you can see us moving around inside. We're the dark spots.

While Ricci slept, I called everyone to the rumpus room for a quick status check. All seven of us lounged in the netting, enjoying the free flowing oxygen/hydrogen mix, goggles and breathers dangling around our necks.

I led the discussion, as usual. Nobody else can ever be bothered.

"Thoughts?" I asked.

"Ricci seems okay," said Eddy. "And I like what's-her-name. The mole on the comm."

"Jane. Yeah, pretty smile," said Bouche. "Ricci's fine. Right Vula?"

Vula frowned and crossed her arms. She'd hooked into the netting right next to the hatch and looked about ready to stomp out.

"I guess," she said. "Rude, though."

"She was just trying to be funny," said Treasure. "I can never predict who'll stick and who'll bounce. I thought Chara would claw her way back down belowground. Right through the skin and nosedive home."

Chara grinned. "I still might."

We laughed, but the camaraderie felt forced. Vula had everyone on edge.

"We'll all keep an eye on Ricci until she settles in," Eleanora said. "Are we good here? I need to get back to training. I got a chess tournament, you know."

"You always have a tournament." I surveyed the faces around me, but it didn't look like anyone wanted to chat.

"As long as nobody hogs the uplink, I never have any problems," said Bouche. "Who's training Ricci?"

"Who do you think?" I said. We have a rule. Whoever scared off the last one has to train the replacement.

We all looked at Vula.

"Shit," she said. "I hate training newbies."

"Stop running them off then," said Chara. "Be nice."

Vula scowled, fierce frown lines scoring her forehead. "I've got important work to do."

No use arguing with Vula. She was deep in a creative tangle, and had been for a while..

"I'll do it," I said. "We better train Ricci right if we want her to stick."

When Ricci woke up, I helped her out of the hammock and showed her how to operate the hygiene station. As soon as she'd hosed off the funk, she called Jane on her appliance.

"Take off your breather for a moment," Jane said. "Goggles too. I need to see your face."

Ricci wedged her fingernails under the seal and pried the off her breather. She lifted her goggles. When she grinned, deep dimples appeared on each cheek.

Jane squinted at her through the screen. She nodded, and Ricci replaced the breather. It attached to her skin with a slurp.

"How do I look?" Ricci asked. "Normal enough for you?"

"What's the failure rate on that thing?"

"Low," Ricci said.

Point two three percent. Which *is* low unless you're talking about death. Then it's high. But we have spares galore. Safety nests here, there, and everywhere. I could have chimed in with the info but Jane didn't want to hear from me. I stayed well back and let Ricci handle her friend.

"Has anyone ever studied the long-term effects of living in a helium atmosphere?" Jane asked. "It can't be healthy."

"Eyes are a problem." Ricci tapped a finger on a goggle lens. "Corneas need oxygen so that's why we wear these. The hammocks are filled with air, so we basically bathe in oxygen while we're sleeping. But you're right. Without that the skin begins to slough."

Jane made a face. "Ugh."

"There's air in the common area, too—they call it the rumpus room. That's where they keep the fab and extruder. I'm supposed to be there now. I have to eat and then do an orientation session. Health, safety, all that good stuff."

"Don't forget to take some time to get to know your hab-mates, okay?"

"I met them when I got here."

"One of them is Vula, the artist, right? The sculptor. She's got to be interesting."

Ricci shrugged. "She looked grumpy."

I was impressed. Pretty perceptive for someone who'd been half-drowned in anesthetic.

"What's scheduled after training?"

"Nothing. That's the whole point of coming here, right?"

"I wondered if you remembered." A smile broke over Jane's face, star-bright even when glimpsed on a small screen at a distance. "You need rest and recreation."

"Relaxation and reading," Ricci added.

"Maybe you'll take up a hobby."

"Oh, I will," said Ricci. "Count on it."

Yes, I was spying on Ricci. We all were. She seemed like a good egg, but with no recourse to on-the-spot conflict intervention, we play it safe with newbies until they settle in. Anyone who doesn't like it can pull down a temporary privacy veil to shield themselves from the bugs, but most don't bother. Ricci didn't.

Plus we needed a distraction.

Whether it's half a million moles in a hole down below-ground or eight of us floating around in the atmosphere, every hab goes through ups and downs. We'd been down for a while. Some of it was due to Vula's growly mood, the worst one we'd seen for a while, but really, we just needed a shake-up. Whether we realized it or not, we were all looking to Ricci to deliver us from ourselves.

During orientation, Ricci and I had company. Bouche and Eddy claimed they needed a refresher and tagged along for the whole thing. Chara, Treasure, and Eleanora joined us halfway through. Even Vula popped out of her hab for a few moments, and actually made an effort to look friendly.

With all the chatter and distraction, I wasn't confident Ricci's orientation had stuck, so I shadowed her on her first maintenance rotation. The workflow is fully documented, every detail supported by nested step-by-steps and supervised by dedicated project management bugs that help take human error out of the equation. But I figured she deserved a little extra attention.

Life support is our first priority, always. We clear the air printers, run live tests on the carbon dioxide digesters, and ground-truth the readings on every single sensor. It's a tedious process, but not even Vula complains. She likes to breathe as much as any of us.

Ricci was sharp. Interested. Not just in the systems that keep us alive, but in the whole organism, its biology, behavior, and habitat. She was even interested in clouds around and the icy, slushy landscape below. She wanted to know about the weather patterns, wind, atmospheric layers—everything. I answered as best I could, but I was out of the conversational habit.

That, and something about the line of her jaw had me tongue-tied.

"Am I asking too many questions, Doc?" she asked as we stumped back to the rumpus room after checking the last hammock.

"Let's keep to the life-and-death stuff for now," I said.

Water harvesting is the next priority. To get it, we have to rise to the aquapause. There, bright sunlight condenses moisture on the skin and collects in the dorsal runnels, where we tap it for storage.

Access to the main inflation gland is just under the rumpus room. Ricci squeezed through the elasticized access valve. The electrostatic membrane pulled her hair into spikes that waved at the PM bots circling her head. I stayed outside and watched her smear hormone ointment on the marbled surface of the gland. Sinuses creaked as bladders began to expand. As we walked through the maze of branching sinuses, I showed her how to brace against the roll and use the momentum to pull herself through the narrow access slots. Once we got to the ring-shaped fore cavity, we hooked our limbs into the netting and waited.

Rainbows rippled across the expanded bladder surfaces. We were nearly spherical, petals furled, and the wind rolled us like an untethered balloon. The motion makes some newbies sick, and they have to dial up anti-nauseant. Not

Ricci. She looked around with anticipation, as if she were expecting to see something amazing rise over the vast horizon.

"Do you ever run into other whales?" she asked.

"I don't much care for that term," I said. It came out gruffer than I intended.

A dimple appeared at the edge of her breather. "Have you been out here long, Doc?"

"Yes. Ask me an important question."

"Okay." She waved her hand at the water kegs nested at the bottom of the netting, collapsed into a pile of honeycomb folds. "Why don't you carry more water?"

"That's a good question. You don't need me to tell you though. You can figure it out. Flip through your dash."

The dimple got deeper. Behind her darkened goggles, her eyelids flickered as she reviewed her dashboards. Naturally it took a little while; our setup was new to her. I rested my chin on my forearms and waited.

She surfaced quicker than I expected.

"Mass budget, right? Water is heavy."

"Yes. The mass dashboard also tracks our inertia. If we get too heavy, we can't maneuver. And heavy things are dangerous. Everything's tethered and braced, and we have safety nets. But if something got loose, it could punch through a bladder wall. Even through the skin, easy."

Ricci looked impressed. "I won't tell Jane about that."

We popped into the aquapause. The sun was about twenty degrees above the horizon. Its clear orange light glanced across the thick violet carpet of helium clouds below. Overhead, the indigo sky rippled with stars.

Bit of a shock for a mole. I let Ricci ogle the stars for a while. Water ran off the skin, a rushing, cascading sound like one of the big fountains down belowground. I cleared my throat. Ricci startled, eyes wide behind her goggles, then she climbed out of the netting and flipped the valve on the overhead tap. Silver water dribbled through the hose and into the battery of kegs, slowly expanding the pleated walls.

Ricci didn't always fill the quiet spaces with needless chatter. I liked that. We worked in silence until the kegs were nearly full, and when she began to question me again, I welcomed it.

"Eddy said you were one of the first out here," Ricci said. "You figured out how to make this all work."

I answered with a grunt, and then cursed myself. If I scared her away, Vula would never let me forget it.

"That's right. Me and a few others."

"You took a big risk."

"Moving into the atmosphere was inevitable," I said. "Humans are opportunistic organisms. If there's a viable habitat, we'll colonize it."

"Takes a lot of imagination to see this as viable."

"Maybe. Or maybe desperation. It's not perfect but it's better than down belowground. Down there, you can't move without stepping on someone. Every breath is measured and every minute is optimized for resource resilience. That might be viable, but it's not human."

"I'm not arguing." Ricci's voice pitched low, thick with emotion as she gazed at the stars in that deep sky. "I love it here."

Yeah, she wasn't a mole anymore. She was one of us already.

One by one, the kegs filled and began flexing through their purification routine. We called in the crablike water bots and ran them through a sterilization cycle.

Water work done, the next task was spot-checking the equipment nests. I let Ricci take the lead, stayed well back as she jounced through the cavities and sinuses. She was enthusiastic, confident. Motivated, even. Most newbies stay hunkered in their hammocks for a lot longer than her.

We circled back to the rumpus room, inventoried the nutritional feedstock, and began running tests on the hygiene bots. I settled into the netting and watched Ricci pull a crispy snack out of the extruder.

"You must know all the other crews. The ones who live in the..." Ricky struggled to frame the concept without offending me.

"You can call them whales if you want. I don't like it, but I've never managed to find a better word."

She passed me a bulb of cold caffeine.

"How often do you talk to the people who live in the other whales, Doc?"

"We don't have anything to do with them. Not anymore."

"How come?"

"The whole reason we came out here is so we don't have to put up with anyone else's crap."

"You never see the other whales at all? Not even at a distance?"

I drained the bulb. "These organisms don't have any social behavior."

"But you must have to talk to them sometimes, don't you? Share info or troubleshoot?"

I collapsed the bulb in my fist and threw it to a hygiene bot.

"You lonely already?"

Ricci tossed her head back and laughed, a full belly guffaw. "Come on, Doc. You have to admit that's weird."

She was relentless. "Go ahead and make friends with the others if you want," I growled. "Just don't believe everything they say. They've got their own ways of doing things, and so do we."

We checked the internal data repeaters and then spent the rest of the shift calibrating and testing the sensor array—all the infrastructure that traps the data we sell to the atmospheric monitoring firms. I kept my mouth shut. Ricci maintained an aggressive cheerfulness even though I was about as responsive as a bot. But my glacier-like chilliness—more than ten years in the making—couldn't resist her. My hermit heart was already starting to thaw.

If I'd been the one calling Jane every day, I would have told her the light is weird out here. We stay within the optimal thermal range, near the equator where the winds are comparatively warm and the solar radiation helps keep the temperature in our habitat relatively viable. That means we're always in daylight, running a race against nightfall, which is good for Mama but not so good for us. Humans evolved to exist in a day-night cycle and something goes haywire in our brains when we mess with that. So our goggles simulate our chosen ratio of light and dark.

Me, I like to alternate fifty-fifty but I'll fool with the mix every so often just to shake things up. Vula likes the night so she keeps things dimmer than most. Everyone's different. That's what the moles don't realize, how different some of us are.

"I did a little digging, and what I found out scared me," Jane said the next time Ricci checked in. "Turns out there's huge gaps in atmospheric research. The only area that's really well monitored is the equator, and only around the beanstalk. Everywhere else, analysis is done by hobbyists who donate a few billable hours here and there."

Ricci nodded. "That's what Doc said."

Hearing my name perked me right up. I slapped down two of my open streams and gave their feed my whole attention.

"Nobody really knows that much about the organism you're living inside. Even less about the climate out there, and nearly nothing about the geography, not in detail. I never would have supported this decision if I'd realized how..." Jane's pretty face contorted as she searched for the word. "How *willy-nilly* the whole situation is. It's not safe. I can't believe it's even allowed."

"Allowed? Who can stop us? People go where they want."

"Not if it's dangerous. You can't just walk into a sewage treatment facility or air purification plant. It's unethical to allow people to endanger themselves."

Ricci snorted, fouling the valves on her breather and forcing her to take a big gulp of helium through her mouth.

"Not all of us want to be safe, Jane." The helium made her voice squeaky.

Jane's expression darkened. "Don't mock me. I'm worried about you."

"I know. I'm sorry," Ricci squeaked. She exhaled to clear her lungs and took a deep slow breath through her nose. Her voice dropped to its normal register. "Listen, I've only been here a few days"

"Six," Jane said.

"If I see anything dangerous, you'll be the first to know. Until then, don't worry. I'm fine. Better than fine. I'm even sleeping. A lot."

That was a lie. The air budget showed Ricci hadn't seen much of the inside of her hammock. But I wasn't worried. Exhaustion would catch up with her eventually.

"There's something else," Jane said. "I've been asking around about your hab-mates."

"Vula's okay. It's just that lately none of her work has turned out the way she wants. You know artists. Their professional standards are always unreachable. Set themselves up to fail."

"It's not about Vula, it's Doc."

Ricci bounced in her netting. "Oh yeah? Tell me. Because I can't get a wink out of that one. Totally impervious."

I maximized the feed to fill my entire visual field. In the tiny screen in Ricci's hand, Jane's dark hair trailed strands across her face and into her mouth. She pushed them back with an impatient flick of her fingers. She was in an atrium, somewhere with stiff air circulation. I could just make out seven decks of catwalk arching behind her, swarming with pedestrians.

"Pull down a veil," Jane said. "You might have lurkers."

"I do," Ricci answered. "Four at least. I'm the most entertaining thing inside Mama for quite a while. It doesn't bother me. Let them lurk."

But Jane insisted, so Ricci pulled down a privacy veil and the bug feed winked out.

I told myself whatever Jane had found out didn't matter. It would bear no relation to reality. That's how gossip works—especially gossip about ancient history. But even so, a little hole opened up under my breastbone, and it ached.

Only six days and I already cared what Ricci thought. I wanted her to like me. So I set about trying to give her a reason.

A few days later, we drifted into a massive storm system. Ricci's first big one. I didn't want her to miss it, so I bounced aft and hallooed to her at a polite distance from her hab. She was lounging in her netting, deep in multiple streams, twisting a lock of her short brown hair around her finger.

She looked happy enough to see me. No wariness behind her gaze, no chill.

We settled in to watch the light show. It was an eye-catcher. Bolts zagged to the peaks of the ice towers below, setting the fog alight with expanding patches of emerald green and acid magenta.

Two big bolts forked overhead with a mighty *whump*. Ricci didn't even jump.

"What was that?" she asked.

I was going to stay silently mysterious, but then remembered I was trying to be friendly.

"That," I said, "was lunch."

A dark splotch began to coalesce at the spot where the two bolts had caressed each other, a green and violet pastel haze in the thin milky fog. We banked slowly, bladders groaning, massive sinus walls clicking as we changed shape to ride the wind currents up, up, and then the massive body flexed just enough to reveal two petals reaching into the coalescing bacteria bloom.

Ricci launched herself out of the netting and clung to the side of her hab, trying to get a better view of the feeding behavior. When the bloom dissipated, she turned to me.

"That's all it does, this whale? Just search for food?"

"Eat, drink, and see the sights," I said. "What else does anyone need from life?"

Good company, I thought, but I didn't say it.

The lightshow went on for hours. Ricci was fascinated from start to finish. Me, I didn't see it. I spent the whole storm watching the light illuminate her face.

What else does anyone need from life? That was me trying to be romantic. Clumsy. Also inaccurate.

When we first moved out here, my old friends and I thought our habs would eventually become self-contained. Experience killed that illusion pretty quick. We're almost as dependent on the planetary civil apparatus as anyone.

Without feedstock, for example, we'd either starve or suffocate—not sure which would happen first. It has a lot of mass, so we can't stockpile much.

Then there's power. Funding it is a challenge when you're supplying eight people as opposed to eight million. No economy of scale in a hab this size. It's not the power feed itself that's the problem, but the infrastructure. We're always on the move, so the feed has to follow us around and provide multiple points of redundancy. Our ambient power supply costs base market value plus a massive buy-back on the research and development.

Data has to follow us around too, but we don't bother with redundancy. It's not critical. You'd think it was more important than air, though, if you saw us when the data goes down. Shrieking. Curses. Bouche just about catatonic (she's a total media junkie). Eleanora wall-eyed with panic especially if she's in the middle of a tournament (chess is her drug of choice). Vula, Eddy, and me in any state from suave to suicidal depending on what we're doing when the metaphorical umbilical gets yanked out of our guts.

Treasure and Chara are the only ones who don't freak out. Usually they're too busy boning each other.

Without data, we couldn't stay here, either. If we only had each other to talk to, it'd be a constant drama cycle, but we're all plugged into the hab cultures down belowground. We've got hobbies to groom, projects to tend, performances to cheer, games to play, friends to visit.

Finally, as an independent political entity, we need brokers and bankers to handle our economic transactions and lawyers to vet our contracts. We all need the occasional look-in from medtechs and physical therapists. And when we need a new crew member, we contract a recruiter.

"You look tired," Jane said the next time Ricci called. "I thought you said you were sleeping."

Ricci hung upside down in her netting. She'd made friends with the orang. It squatted in front of her, holding the appliance while she chatted with Jane.

"I've been digging through some old work." She dangled her arms, hooked her fingers in the floor grid, and stretched. "I came up with a new approach to my first dissertation."

Jane gaped. Her mouth worked like she was blowing bubbles.

"I know," Ricci added. "I'll never change, right?"

"Don't you try that with me." Jane's eyes narrowed. "You have a choice—"

Ricci raised her hands in mock surrender. "Okay. Take it easy."

"—you can keep working on getting better, or you can go back to your old habits."

"It's not your fault, Jane. You're a great therapist."

"This isn't about me, you idiot," Jane yelled. "It's about you."

"I tried, Jane." Ricci's voice was soft, ardent. "I really tried. So hard."

"I know you did." Jane sucked in a deep breath. "Don't throw away all your progress."

They went on and on like that. I didn't listen, just checked in now and then to see if they were still at it. I knew Ricci's story. I'd read the report from the recruiter. The privacy seal had timed out but I remembered the details.

Right out of the crèche she'd dived into an elite chemical engineering program, the kind every over-fond crèche manager wants for their favorite little geniuses. Sound good, doesn't it? Isn't that where you'd want to put your little Omi or Occam, little Carey or Karim? But what crèche managers don't realize—because their world is full of guided discovery opportunities and subconscious learning stimuli—is that high-prestige programs are grinders. Go ahead, dump a crèche-full of young brilliants inside. Some of them won't come out whole.

I know; I went through one myself.

When Ricci crashed out of the chem program within spitting distance of an advanced degree, she bounced to protein engineering. She did a lot of good work there before she cracked. Then she moved into pharmaceutical modeling. A few more years of impressive productivity before it all went up in smoke. By that time she wasn't young anymore. The damage had accumulated. Her endocrinologist suggested intensive peer counselling might stop the carnage, so in stepped Jane, who applied her pretty smile, her patience, and all her active listening skills to try to gently guide Ricci along a course of life that didn't include cooking her brain until it scrambled.

At the end of that long conversation through the appliance, Ricci agreed to put her old work under lockdown so she could concentrate on the here-and-now. Which meant all her attention was focused on us.

Ricci got into my notes. I don't keep them locked down; anyone can access them. Free and open distribution of data is a primary force behind the success of the human species, after all. Don't we all learn that in the crèche?

Making data available doesn't guarantee anyone will look at it, and if they do, chances are they won't understand it. Ricci tried. She didn't just skim through, she really studied. Shift after shift, she played with the numbers and gamed my simulation models. Maybe she slept. Maybe not.

I figured Ricci would come looking for me if she got stumped, so I de-hermited, banged around in the rumpus room, put myself to work on random little maintenance tasks.

When Ricci found me, I was in the caudal stump dealing with the accumulated waste pellets. Yes, that's exactly what it sounds like: half-kilogram plugs of dry solid waste covered in wax and transferred from the lavs by the hygiene bots. Liquid waste is easy. We vaporize it, shunt it into the gas exchange bladder, and flush it through gill-like permeable membranes. Solid waste, well, just like anyone we'd rather forget about it as long as possible. We rack the pellets until there's about two hundred, then we jettison them.

Ricci pushed up her goggles and scrubbed knuckles over her red-rimmed eyes.

"Why don't you automate this process like you do for liquids?" Ricci asked as she helped me position the rack over the valve.

"No room for non-essential equipment in the mass budget," I said.

I dilated the interior shutter and the first pellet clicked through. A faint pink blush formed around the valve's perimeter, only visible because I'd dialed up the contrast on my goggles to watch for signs of stress. A little hormone ointment took care of it—not too much or we'd get a band of inflexible scar tissue, and then I'd have to cut out the valve and move it to another location. That's a long, tricky process and it's not fun.

"There are only two bands of tissue strong enough to support a valve." I bent down and stroked the creamy striated tissue at my feet. "This is number two, and really, it barely holds. We have to treat it gently."

"Why risk it, then? Take it out and just use the main valve."

A sarcastic comment bubbled up—*have you never heard of a safety exit?*—but I gazed into her big brown eyes and it faded into the clouds.

"We need two valves in case of emergencies," I mumbled.

Ricci and I watched the pellets plunge through the sky. When they hit the ice slush, the concussive wave kicked up a trail of vapor blooms, concentric rings lit with pinpoints of electricity, so far below each flash just a spark in a violet sea.

A flock of jellies fled from the concussion, flat shells strobing with reflected light, trains of ribbon-like tentacles flapping behind.

Ricci looked worried. "Did we hit any of them?"

I shook my head. "No, they can move fast."

After we'd finished dumping waste, Ricci said, "Say, Doc, why don't you show me the main valve again?"

I puffed up a little at that. I'm proud of the valves. Always tinkering, always innovating, always making them a little better. Without the valves, we wouldn't be here.

Far forward, just before the peduncle isthmus, a wide band of filaments connects the petals to the bladder superstructure. The isthmus skin is thick with connective tissue, and provides enough structural integrity to support a valve big enough to accommodate a cargo pod.

"We pulled you in here." I patted the collar of the shutter housing. "Whoever prepared the pod had put you in a pink bodybag. Don't know why it was such a ridiculous color. When Vula saw it, she said, 'It's a girl!'"

I laughed. Ricci winced.

"That joke makes sense, old style," I explained.

"No, I get it. Birth metaphor. I'm not a crechie, Doc."

"I know. We wouldn't have picked you if you were."

"Why did you pick me?"

I grumbled something. Truth is, when I ask our recruiter to find us a new hab-mate, the percentage of viable applications approaches zero. We look for a specific psychological profile. The two most important success factors are low self-censoring and high focus. People who say what they think are never going to ambush you with long-fermented resentments, and obsessive people don't get bored. They know how to make their own fun.

Ricci tapped her fingernail on a shutter blade.

"Your notes aren't complete, Doc." She stared up at me, unblinking. No hint of a dimple. "Why are you hoarding information?"

"I'm not."

"Yes, you are. There's nothing about reproduction."

"That's because I don't know very much about it."

"The other whale crews do. And they're worried about it. You must know something, but you're not sharing. Why?"

I glared at her. "I'm an amateur independent researcher. My methods aren't rigorous. It would be wrong to share shaky theories."

"The whale crews had a collective research agreement once. You wrote it."

She fired the document at me with a flick of her finger. I slapped it down and flushed it from my buffer.

"That agreement expired. We didn't renew."

"That's a lie. You dissolved it and left to find your own whale."

I aimed my finger at the bridge of her goggles and jabbed the air. "Yes, I ran away. So did you."

She smiled. "I left a network of habs with a quarter billion people who can all do just fine without me. You ran from a few hundred who need you."

Running away is something I'm good at. I bounced out of there double-time. Ricci didn't call after me. I wouldn't have answered if she had.

⬭

The next time she talked to Jane, Ricci didn't mention me. I guess I didn't rate high enough on her list of problems. I didn't really listen to the details as they chatted. I just liked having their voices in my head while I tinkered with my biosynthesis simulations.

Halfway through their session, Vula pinged me.

You can quit spying, she said. *None of us are worried about Ricci anymore.*

I agreed, and shut down the feed.

Ricci's been asking about you, by the way, Vula added. *Your history with the other whales.*

Tell her everything.

You sure?

I've been spying on her for days. It's only fair.

Better she heard the story from Vula than me. I still can't talk about it without overheating, and they tell me I'm scary when I'm angry.

Down belowground the air is thick with rules written and unwritten, the slowly decaying husks of thirty thousand years of human history dragged behind us from Earth, and the most important of these is cooperation for mutual benefit. Humans being human, that's only possible in conditions of resource abundance—not just actual numerical abundance, but more importantly, the *perception* of abundance. When humans are confident there's enough to go around, life is easy and we all get along, right?

Ha.

Cooperation makes life possible, but never easy. Humans are hard to wrangle. Tell them to do one thing and they'll do the opposite more often than not. One thing we all agree on is that everyone wants a better life. Only problem is, nobody can agree what that means.

So we have an array of habs offering a wide variety of socio-cultural options. If you don't like what your hab offers, you can leave and find one that does. If there isn't one, you can try to find others who want the same things as you and start your own. Often, just knowing options are available keeps people happy.

Not everyone, though.

Down belowground, I simply hated knowing my every breath was counted, every kilojoule measured, every moment of service consumption or contribution accounted for in the transparent economy, every move modeled by human capital managers and adjusted by resource optimization analysts. I got obsessed with the numbers in my debt dashboard; even though it was well into the black all I wanted to do was drive it up as high and as fast as I could, so nobody would ever be able to say I hadn't done my part.

Most people never think about their debt. They drop a veil over the dash and live long, happy, ignorant lives, never caring about their billable rate and never knowing whether or not they syphoned off the efforts of others. But for some of us, that debt counter becomes an obsession.

An obsession and ultimately an albatross, chained around our necks.

I dreamed about an independent habitat with abundant space and unlimited horizons. And I wasn't the only one. When we looked, there it was, floating around the atmosphere.

Was it dangerous? Sure. But a few firms provide services to risk takers and they're always eager for new clients. The crews that shuttle ice climbers to the poles delivered us to the skin of a very large whale. I made the first cut myself.

Solving the problems of life was exhilarating—air, food, water, warmth. We were explorers, just like the mountain climbers of old, ascending the highest peaks wearing nothing but animal hides. Like the first humans. Revolutionary.

Our success attracted others, and our population grew. We colonized new whales and once we got settled, our problems became more mundane. I have a little patience for administrative details, but the burden soon became agonizing. Unending meetings to chew over our collective agreements, measuring and accounting and debits and credits and assigning value to everyone's time. This was exactly what we'd escaped. Little more than one year in the clouds, and we were reinventing all the old problems from scratch.

Nobody needs that.

I stood right in the middle of the rumpus room inside the creature I'd cut into with my own hands and gave an impassioned speech about the nature of freedom and independence, and reminded them all of the reasons we'd left. If they wanted their value micro-accounted, they could go right back down belowground.

I thought it was a good speech, but apparently not. When it came to a vote, I was the only one blocking consensus.

I believe—hand-to-heart—if they'd only listened to me and did what I said everything would have been fine and everyone would have been happy. But some people can never really be happy unless they're making other people miserable. They claimed I was trying to use my seniority, skills, and experience as a lever to exert political force. I'd become a menace. And when they told me I had to submit to psychological management, I left.

Turned out we'd brought the albatross along with us, after all.

When Jane pinged me a few days later, I was doing the same thing as millions down belowground—watching a newly-arrived arts delegation process down the beanstalk and marveling at their dramatic clothing and prosthetics.

I pinged her back right away. Even though I knew she would probably needle me about my past, I didn't hesitate. I missed having Ricci and Jane in my head, and life was a bit lonely without them. Also, I was eager to meet her. I wasn't the only one; the whole crew was burning with curiosity about Ricci's pretty friend.

When Jane's fake melted into reality, she was dressed in a shiny black party gown. Long dark hair pouffed over her shoulders, held off her face with little spider clips that gathered the locks into tufts. Her chair was a spider model too, with eight delicate ruby and onyx legs that cradled her torso.

"Hi, Doc," she said. "It's nice to meet you, finally. I'm a friend of Ricci's. I think you know that, though."

A friend. Not a therapist, peer counselor, or emotional health consultant. That was odd. And then it dawned on me: Jane had been donating her time ever since Ricci joined us. She probably wanted to formalize her contract, start racking up the billable hours.

When I glanced through her metadata, my heart began to hammer. Jane's rate was sky high.

"We can't float your rate," I blurted. "Not now. Maybe eventually. But we'd have to find another revenue stream."

Jane's head jerked back and her gaze narrowed.

"That's not why I pinged you," she said. "I don't care about staying billable—I never did. All I want to do is help people."

I released a silent sigh of relief. "What can I do for you?"

"Nothing. I just wanted to say hi and ask how Ricci's getting along."

"Ricci's fine. Nothing to worry about." I always get gruff around beautiful women.

She brightened. "She's fitting in with you all?"

"Yeah. One of the crew. She's great. I love her." I bit my lip and quickly added, "I mean we all like her. Even Vula, and she's picky."

I blushed. Badly. Jane noticed, and a gentle smile touched the corners of her mouth. But she was a kind soul and changed the subject.

"I've been wondering something, Doc. Do you mind if I ask a personal question?"

I scrubbed my hands over my face in embarrassment and nodded.

She wheeled her chair a bit closer and tilted toward me. "Do you know what gave you the idea to move to the surface?

I mean originally, before you'd ever started looking into the possibility."

"Have you read Zane gray's *Riders of the Purple Sage?*" I asked. "You must have."

"No." She looked confused, like I was changing the subject.

"You should. Here."

I tossed her a multi-bookmark compilation. Back down belowground, I'd given them out like candy at a crèche party. She could puzzle through the diction of the ancient original or read it in any number of translations, listen to a variety of audio versions and dramatic readings, or watch any of the hundreds of entertainment docs it had inspired. I'd seen them all.

"This is really old. Why did you think I'd know it?" She flipped to the summary. "Oh, I see. One of the characters is named is Jane."

"Read it. It explains everything."

"I will. But maybe you could tell me what to look for?" Her smile made me forget all about my embarrassment.

"It's about what humans need to be happy. Sure, we evolved to live in complex interdependent social groups, but before that, we were nomads, pursuing resource opportunities in an open, sparsely populated landscape. That means for some people, solitude and independence are primary values."

She nodded, and I could see she was trying hard to understand.

"Down belowground, when I was figuring all this out, I tried working with a therapist. When I told him this, he said, 'We also evolved to suffer and die from violence, disease, and famine. Do you miss that, too?'"

Jane laughed. "I hope you fired him. So one book inspired all this?"

"It's not just a book. It's a way of life. The freedom to explore wide open spaces, to come together with like-minded others and form loose knit communities based on mutual aid, and to know that every morning you'll wake up looking at an endless horizon."

"These horizons aren't big enough?" She waved at the surrounding virtual space, a default grid with dappled patterns, as if a directional light source were shining through gently fluttering leaves.

"For some, maybe. For me, pretending isn't enough."

"I'll read it. It sounds very..." She pursed her lips, looking for the right word. "Romantic."

I started to blush again, so I made an excuse and dropped the connection before I made a fool of myself. Then I drifted down to the rumpus room and stripped off my goggles and breather.

"Whoa," Bouche said. "Doc, what's wrong?"

Eleanora turned from the extruder to look at me, then fumbled her caffeine bulb and squirted liquid across her cheek.

"Wow." She wiped the liquid up with her sleeve. "I've never seen you look dreamy before. What happened?"

I'm in love, I thought.

"Jane pinged me," I said instead.

Bouche called the whole crew. They came at a run. Even Vula.

In a small hab, any crumb of gossip can become legendary. I made them beg for the story, then drew it out as long as I could.

"Can you ask her to ping me?" Eddy asked Ricci when I was done.

"I would chat with her for more than a couple minutes, unlike Doc," said Treasure.

Chara grinned lasciviously. "Can I lurk?"

The whole crew in one room, awake and actually talking to each other was something Ricci hadn't seen before, much less all of us howling with laughter and gossiping about her friend. She looked profoundly unsettled. Vula bounced over to the extruder, filled a bulb with her favorite social lubricant, and tossed it to Ricci.

"Tell us everything about Jane," Chara said. Treasure waggled her tongue.

"It's not like that." Ricci frowned. "She's a friend."

"Good," they chorused, and collapsed back onto the netting, giggling.

"I've been meaning to ask—why do you use that hand-held thing to talk to her, anyway?" Chara said. "I've never even seen one of those before."

Ricci shook her head.

"Come on, Ricci. There's no privacy here," Vula said. "You know that. Don't go stiff on us."

Ricci joined us in the netting before answering. When she picked a spot beside me, my pulse fluttered in my throat.

"Jane's a peer counselor." She squeezed a sip from the bulb and grimaced at the taste. "The hand-held screen is one of her strategies. Having it around reminds me to keep working on my goals."

"Why do you need peer counseling?" asked Chara.

"Because I…" Ricci looked from face to face, big brown eyes serious. Everyone quieted down. "I was unhappy. Listen, I've been talking with some people from the other whale crews. They've been having problems for a while now, and it's getting worse."

She fired a stack of bookmarks into the middle of the room. Everyone began riffling through them, except me.

"That's too bad," I said.

"Don't you want to know what's going on, Doc?" asked Chara.

I folded my arms and scowled in the general direction of the extruder.

"No," I said flatly. "I don't give a shit about them."

"Well, you better," Vula said. "Because if it's happening to them, it could happen to us. Look."

She fired a feed from a remote sensing drone into the middle of the room. A group of whales had gathered a hundred meters above a slushy depression between a pair of high ridges. They weren't feeding, just drifting around aimlessly, dangerously close to each other. When they got close to each other, they unfurled their petals and brushed them along each other's skin.

As we watched, two whales collided. Their bladders bubbled out like a crechie's squeeze toy until it looked like they would burst. Seeing the two massive creatures collide like that was so upsetting, I actually reached into the feed and tried to push them apart. Embarrassing.

"Come on Doc, tell us what's happening," said Vula.

"I don't know." I tucked my hands into my armpits as if I was cold.

"We should go help," said Eddy. "At least we could assist with the evac if they need to bail."

I shook my head. "It could be dangerous."

Everyone laughed at that. People who aren't comfortable with risk don't roam the atmosphere.

"It might be a disease," I added, "We should stay as far away as we can. We don't want to catch it."

Treasure pulled a face at me. "You're getting old."

I grabbed my breather and goggles and bounded toward the hatch.

"Come on Doc, take a guess," Ricci said.

"More observation would be required before I'd be comfortable advancing a theory," I said stiffly. "I can only offer conjecture."

"Go ahead, conjecture away," said Vula.

I took a moment to collect myself, and then turned and addressed the crew with professorial gravity.

"It's possible the other crews haven't been maintaining the interventions that ensure their whales don't move into reproductive maturity."

"You're saying the whales are horny?" said Bouche.

"They look horny," said Treasure.

"They're fascinated with each other," said Vula.

Vula had put her finger on exactly the thing that was bothering me. Whales don't congregate. They don't interact socially. They certainly don't mate.

"I'd guess the applicable pseudoneural tissue has regenerated, perhaps incompletely, and their behavior is confused."

Ricci gestured at the feed, where three whales collided, dragging their petals across each other's bulging skin. "This isn't going to happen to us?"

"No, I said. "Definitely not. Don't worry. Unlike the others, I've been keeping on top of the situation."

"But how can you be sure?" And then realization dawned over Ricci's face. "You knew this was going to happen, didn't you?"

"Not exactly."

She launched herself from the netting and bounced toward me. “Why didn’t you share the information? Keeping it secret is just cruel.”

I backed toward the hatch. “It’s not my responsibility to save the others from their stupid mistakes.”

“We need to tell them how to fix it. Maybe they can save themselves.”

“Tell them whatever you want.” I excavated my private notes from lockdown, and fired them into the middle of the room. “I think their best option would be to abandon their whales and find new ones.”

“That would take months,” Vula said. “Nineteen whales. More than two hundred people.”

“Then they should start now.” I turned to leave.

“Wait.” Ricci looked around at the crew. “We have to go help. Right?”

I gripped the edge of the hatch. The electrostatic membrane licked at my fingertips.

“Yeah, I want to go,” Bouche said. “I’d be surprised if you didn’t, Doc.”

“I want to go,” said Treasure.

“Me too,” Chara chimed in. Eddy and Eleanora both nodded.

Vula pulled down her goggles and launched herself out of the netting. “Whales fucking? What are we waiting for? I’ll start fabbing some media drones.”

With all seven of them eager for adventure, our quiet, comfortable little world didn’t stand a chance.

We're not the only humans on the surface. Not quite. Near the south pole a gang of religious hermits live in a deep ice cave, making alcohol the old way using yeast-based fermentation. It's no better than the extruded version, but some of the habs take pity on them so the hermits can fund their power and feedstock.

Every so often one of the hermits gives up and calls for evac. When that happens, the bored crew of a cargo ship zips down to rescue them. Those same ships bring us supplies and new crew. They also shuttle adventurers and researchers around the planet, but mostly they sit idle, tethered halfway up the beanstalk.

The ships are beautiful—sleek, fast, and elegant. As for us, when we need to change our position, it's not quite so efficient. Or fast.

When Ricci found me in the rumpus room, I'd already fabbed my gloves and face mask, and I was watching the last few centimetres of a thick pair of protective coveralls chug through the output.

"I told the other crews you'd be happy to take a look at the regenerated tissue and recommend a solution, but they refused," she said. "They don't like you, do they?"

I yanked the coveralls out of the extruder.

"No, and I don't like them either." I stalked to the hatch.

"Can I tag along, Doc?" she asked.

"You're lucky I don't pack you into a bodybag and tag you for evac."

"I'm really sorry, Doc. I should have asked you before offering your help. When I get an idea in my head, I tend to just run with it."

She was all smiles and dimples, with her goggles on her forehead pushing her hair up in spikes and her breather swinging around her neck. A person who looks like that can get away with anything.

"This is your idea," I said. "Only fair you get your hands dirty."

I fabbed her a set of protective clothing and we helped each other suit up. We took a quick detour to slather appetite suppressant gel on the appropriate hormonal bundle, and then waddled up the long dorsal sinus, arms out for balance. The sinus walls clicked and the long cavity bent around us, but soon the appetite suppressant took hold and we were nearly stationary, dozing gently in the clouds.

On either side towered the main float bladders—clear multi-chambered organs rippling with rainbows across their honeycomb-patterned surfaces. Feeder organs pulsed between the bladder walls. The feeders are dark pink at the base, but the color fades as they branch into sprawling networks of tubules reaching through the skin, grasping hydrogen and channeling it into the bladders.

At the head of the dorsal sinus, a tall, slot-shaped orifice provides access to the neuronal cavity. I shrugged my equipment bag off my shoulder, showed Ricci how to secure her face mask over her breather, and climbed in.

With the masks on, to talk we had to ping each other. I was still a bit angry so no chit-chat, business only. I handed her the laser scalpel.

Cut right here. I sliced the blade of my gloved hand vertically down the milky surface of the protective tissue. *See these scars?* I pointed at the gray metallic stripes on either side of the imaginary line I'd drawn. *Stay away from them. Just cut straight in between.*

Ricci backed away a few steps. *I don't think I'm qualified to do this.*

You've been qualified to draw a line since you were a crechie. When she began to protest again, I cut her off. *This was your idea, remember?*

Her hands shook, but the line was straight enough. The pouch deflated, draping over the skeleton of the carbon fiber struts I'd installed way back in the beginning. I pulled Ricci inside and closed the incision behind us with squirts of temporary adhesive. The wound wept drops of fluid that rapidly boiled off, leaving a sticky pink sap-like crust across the iridescent interior surface.

Is this the whale's brain? Ricci asked.

I ignored the question. Ricci knew it was the brain—she'd been studying my notes, after all. She was just trying to smooth my feathers by giving me a chance to show my expertise.

Not every brain looks like a brain. Yours and mine look like they should be floating in the primordial ocean depths—that's where we came from, after all. The organ in front of us came from the clouds—a tower of spun glass floss threaded through and through with wispy, feather-like strands that branched and re-branched into iridescent fractals. My mobility control leads were made of copper nanofiber embedded in color-coded silicon filaments: red, green, blue, yellow, purple, orange, and black—a ragged, dull rainbow piercing the delicate depths of an alien brain.

Ricci repeated her question.

Don't ask dumb questions, Ricci.

She put her hands up in a gesture of surrender and backed away. Not far—no room inside the pouch to shuffle back more than one step.

The best I can say is it's brain-like. I snapped the leads into my fist-sized control interface. *The neurons are neuron-like. Is it the whole brain? Is the entire seat of cognition here? I can't tell because there's not much cognition to measure. Maybe more than a bacterium, but far less than an insect.*

How do you measure cognition? Ricci asked.

Controlled experiments, but how do you run experiments on animals this large? All I can tell you is that most people who study these creatures lose interest fast. But here's a better measure: After more than ten years, a whale has never surprised me.

Before today, you mean.

Maneuvering takes a little practice. We use a thumb-operated clicker to fire tiny electrical impulses through the leads and achieve a vague form of directional control. Yes, it's a basic system. We could replace it with something more elegant but it operates even if we lose power. The control it provides isn't exactly roll, pitch, and yaw, but it's effective enough. The margin for error is large. There's not much to hit.

Navigation is easy, too. Satellites ping our position a thousand times a second and the data can be accessed in several different navigational aids, all available in our dashboards.

But though it's all fairly easy, it's not quick. My anger didn't last long. Not in such close quarters, especially just a few hours after realizing I was in love with her. It was hardly a romantic scene, both of us swathed head-to-toe in protective clothing, passing a navigation controller back and forth as we waggled slowly toward our destination.

In between bouts of navigation, I began telling Ricci everything I knew about the organ in front of us: A brain dump about brains, inside a brain. Ha.

She was interested; I was flattered by her interest. Age-old story. I treated her to all my theories, prejudices, and opinions, not just about regenerating pseudoneuronal tissue and my methods for culling it, but the entire scientific research apparatus down belowground, the social dynamics of hab I grew up in, and the philosophical underpinnings of the research exploration proposal we used to float our first forays out here.

Thank goodness Ricci was wearing a mask. She was probably yawning so wide I could have checked her tonsils.

Here. I handed her the control box. *You drive the rest of the way.*

We were aiming for the equator, where the strong, steady winds have carved a smooth canyon bisecting the ice right down to the planet's iron core. When we need to travel a long distance, riding that wind is the fastest route.

Ricci clicked a directional adjustment, and our heading swung a few degrees back toward the equator.

What does the whale perceive when we do this? Ricci waggled the thumb of her glove above the joystick. *When it changes direction, are we luring it or scaring it away?*

Served me right for telling her not to ask simple questions.

I don't really know, I admitted.

Maybe it makes them think other whales are around. What if they want to be together, just like people, but before now they didn't know how. Maybe you've been teaching them.

My eyebrows climbed. I'd never considered how we might be influencing whale behavior, aside from the changes we make for our own benefit.

That's an interesting theory, Ricci. Definitely worth looking into.

Wouldn't it be terrible to be always alone?

I'd always considered myself a loner. But in that moment, I honestly couldn't remember why.

⬭

Once we're in the equatorial stream, we ride the wind until we get into the right general area. Then we wipe off the appetite suppressant, and hunger sends us straight into the arms of the nearest electrical storm.

The urge to feed is a powerful motivator for most organisms. Mama chases all the algae she can find, and gobbles it double-time. For us on the inside, it's like an oldstyle history doc. Everyone stays strapped in their hammocks and rides out the weather as we pitch around on the high seas.

I always enjoy the feeding frenzy; it gets the blood flowing.

I'd just settled to enjoy the wild ride when Ricci pinged me.

Two crews tried surgical interventions on the regenerated tissue. Let me know what you think, okay? Maybe now we can convince them to let you help.

The message was accompanied by bookmarks to live feeds from the supply ships. The first feed showed a whale wedging itself backward into a crevasse, its petals waving back and forth as it wiggled deeper into the canyon-like crack in the ice.

The other feed showed a whale scraping its main valve along a serrated ridge of ice. Its oval body stretched and flexed, its bladders bulged. Its petals curled inward then snapped into rigid extension as the force of its body crashed down on the ice's knife edge.

Inside both whales, tiny specks bounced through the sinuses. I could only imagine what the crew was doing—what I would do in that situation. If they wanted to live, they had to leave. Fast.

A chill slipped under my skin. My fault. If those whales died, if those crews died, I was to blame. Me alone. Not the two crews. They were obviously desperate enough to try anything. I should have contacted them myself, and offered whatever false apologies would get them to accept my help.

But chances are it wouldn't have changed the outcome, except they would have had me to blame. Another entry in my list of crimes.

Frost spread across my flesh and raised goosebumps. I tugged on my hammock's buckles to make sure they were secure against the constant pitching and heaving, dialed up the temperature, and snuggled deeper into my quilt. I fired up my simulation model and wandered through towering mountains of pseudoneural tissue, pondering the problem, delving deeper and deeper through chains of crystalized tissue until they danced behind my eyelids. Swirling, stacking, combining and recombining…

I was nearly asleep when I heard Ricci's voice.

"Hey, Doc, can we talk?"

I thought I was dreaming. But no, she was right outside my hammock, gripping the tethers and getting knocked off her feet with every jolt and flex. Her goggled and masked face was lit by a mad flurry of light from the bolts coruscating in every direction just beyond the skin.

"Are you nuts?" I yanked open the hammock seal. "Get in here."

She plunged through the electrostatic barrier and rolled to the far side of my bed. When she came up, her hair stood on end with static electricity.

"Whoa." She swiped off her goggles and breather, stuffed them in one of the hammock pouches, then flattened the dark nimbus of her hair with her palms and grinned. "It's wild out there."

I pulled my quilt up to my chin and scowled. "That was stupid."

"Yeah, I know but you didn't ping me back. This is an important situation, right? Life or death."

I sighed. "If you want to rescue people, there are vocations for that."

"Don't we have a duty to help people when we can?"

"Some people don't want to be helped. They just want to be left alone."

"Like you?"

"Nothing you're doing is helping me, Ricci."

"Okay, okay. But if we can figure out a way to help, that's good too. Better than good. Everyone wins."

Lying there in my hammock, facing Ricci sprawled at the opposite end and taking up more than half of the space, I finally figured out what kind of person she was.

"You're a meddler, Ricci. A busybody. You were wasted in the sciences. You should have studied social dynamics and targeted a career in one-on-one social work."

She laughed.

"Listen." I held out my hand, palm up. She took it right away, didn't hesitate. Her hand was warm. Almost feverish. "If you want to stay in the crew, you have to relax. Okay? We can't have emergencies every week. None of us are here for that."

She squeezed my hand and nodded.

"A little excitement is fine, once in a while," I continued. "Obviously this is an extraordinary situation. But if you keep looking for adventure, we'll shunt you back to Jane without a second thought."

She twisted the grip into a handshake and gave me two formal pumps. Then she reached for the hammock seal.

She would have climbed out into the maelstrom if I hadn't stopped her.

"You can't do that," I yelled. "No wandering around when we're in a feeding frenzy. You'll get killed. Kill us too, if you go through the wrong bladder wall."

She smiled then, like she didn't believe me, like it was just some excuse to keep her in my hammock. And when she settled back down, it wasn't at the opposite end. She snuggled in right beside me, companionable as anything, or even more.

"Don't you get lonely, Doc?" she asked.

"Sometimes," I admitted. "Not much."

Our hammocks are roomy, but Ricci didn't give me much space, and though the tethers absorb movement, we were still jostling against each other.

"Because you don't need anybody or anything." Her voice in my ear, soft as a caress.

"Something like that."

"Maybe, eventually, you'll change your mind about that."

What happened next wasn't my idea. I was long out of practice, but Ricci had my full and enthusiastic cooperation.

Down belowground, I was a surgeon, and a good one. My specialty was splicing neurons in the lateral geniculate nucleus. My skills were in high demand. So high, in fact, that I had a massive support team.

I'm not talking about a part-time admin or social facilitator. Anyone can have those. I had an entire cadre of people fully dedicated to making sure that if I spent most of my time working and sleeping, what little time remained would be optimized to support physical, emotional, and intellectual health. All my needs were plotted and graphed. People had meetings to argue, for example, over what type of sex best maintained my healthiest emotional state, and once that was decided, they'd argue over the best way to offer that opportunity to me.

That's just an example. I'm only guessing. They kept the administrative muddle under veil. Day-to-day, I only had contact with a few of my staff, and usually I was too busy with my own work to think about theirs. But for a lot of people, I was a billable-hours bonanza.

But despite all their hard work, despite the hedonics modeling, best-practice scenarios, and time-tested decision trees, I burned out.

It wasn't their fault. It was mine. I was, and remain, only human.

I could have just reduced my surgery time. I could have switched to teaching or coaching other surgeons. But no. Some people approach life like it's an all-or-nothing game. That's me. I couldn't be all, so I decided to become nothing.

Until Ricci came along, that is.

When the storm ended, the two of us had to face a gauntlet of salacious grins and saucy comments. I didn't blush, or at least not much. Ricci had put the spark of life in a part of me that had been dark for far too long. I was proud to have her in my crew, in my hammock, in my life.

The whole hab gave us a hard time. The joke that gave them the biggest fits, and made even Vula cling helplessly to the rumpus room netting as she convulsed with laughter, involved the two of us calling for evac and setting up a crèche in the most socially conservative hab down belowground. Something about imagining us in wrapped in religious habits and swarming with crechies tweaked everyone's funny bones.

Ricci weathered the ridicule better than me. I left to fill the water kegs, and by the time I returned, the hilarity had worn itself out.

The eight of us lounged in the rumpus room, the netting gently swaying to and fro as we drifted in bright directional light of the aquapause. Water spilled off the skin and threw dappled shadows across the room. Vula had launched the media drones and we'd all settled down to watch the feeds.

More than once I caught myself brainlessly staring at Ricci, but I kept my goggles on so nobody noticed. I hope.

Two hundred kilometers to the northwest and far below us, the seventeen remaining whales congregated in the swirling winds above a dome-shaped mesa that calved monstrous sheets of ice down its massive flanks. A dark electrical storm massed on the horizon, with all its promise of rich concentrations of algae, but the whales didn't move toward it, just kept circulating and converging, plucking at each other's skin.

Three hundred kilometers west lay the abandoned corpses of two whales, their deflated bladders draped over warped sinus skeletons half-buried in slush.

Our media drones got there too late to trap the whales' death throes, and I was glad. But Vula and Bouche trapped great visuals of the rescue, showing the valiant supply ship crews swooping in to pluck brightly colored bodybags out of the air. Maybe the crews put a little more of a spin on their maneuvering than they needed too, but who could blame them? They rarely got a job worth bragging about.

One of Bouche's media broker friends put the rescue feeds out to market. They started getting good play right away. Bouche fired the media licensing statement into the middle of the room. The numbers glowed green and flickered as they climbed.

"Look at these fees," she said. "This will underwrite our power consumption for a couple years."

"That's great, Bouchie," I murmured, and flicked the statement out of my visual field.

Night was coming, and it presented a hard deadline. If the whales didn't move before dark, they'd all die.

Ricci moved closer to me in the netting and rested her cheek on my shoulder. I turned my head and touched my lips to her temple, just for a moment. I was deep in my brain simulation, working on the problem. But I kept an eye on the feeds. When the whales collided, I held my breath. As the bladders stretched and bulged, I cringed, certain they'd reach their elastic limit and we would see a whale pop, its massive sinuses rupture, its skin tear away and its body plunge to splatter on the icy surface below. But they didn't. They bounced off each other in slow motion and resumed their aimless circulation.

Hours passed. Eddy got up, extruded a meal, and passed the containers around the netting. Chara and Treasure slipped out of the room. Vula was only half-present—she was working in her studio, sculpting maquettes of popped bladders and painfully twisted corpses.

Eddy yawned. "How long can these whales live without feeding?"

I forced a stream of breath through my lips, fluttering the fringe of my bangs. "I don't know. Indefinitely, maybe, if the crews can figure out a way to provide nutrition internally."

"If they keep their whales fed, maybe they'll just keep stumbling around, crashing into each other." Vula's voice was slurred, her eyes unfocused as she juggled multiple streams.

"I'm more worried about nightfall, actually," I said.

Ever since we'd dragged ourselves out of my hammock, Ricci had been trying to pry information from emergency response up the beanstalk, from the supply ship crews who were circling site, and from the whale crews. They were getting increasingly frantic as time clicked by, and keeping us informed wasn't high on their list of priorities.

I rested my palm on the inside of Ricci's knee. "Are the other crews talking to you yet?"

She sat up straight and gave me a pained smile. "A little. I wasn't getting anywhere, but Jane's been giving me some tips."

That woke everyone up. Even Vula snapped right out of her creative fugue.

"Is Jane helping us?" Chara asked, and when Ricci nodded she demanded, "Why are you keeping her to yourself?"

Ricci shrugged. "Jane doesn't know anything about whales."

"If she's been helping you maybe she can help us too," said Eddy.

"Yeah, come on Ricci, stop hogging Jane." Bouche raked her fingers through her hair, sculpting it into artful tufts. "I want to know what she thinks of all this."

"All right," Ricci said. "I'll ask her."

A few moments later she fired Jane's feed into the room and adjusted the perspective so her friend seemed to be sitting in the middle of the room. She wore a baggy black tunic and trousers, and her hair was gathered into a pony tail that draped over the back of her chair. The pinnas of her ears were perforated in a delicate lace pattern.

Treasure and Chara came barreling down the access sinus and plunged through the hatch. They hopped over to their usual spot in the netting and settled in. Jane waved at them.

"We're making you an honorary crew member," Eddy told Jane. "Ricci has to share you with us. We all get equal Jane time."

"I didn't agree to that," said Ricci.

"Fight over me later, when everyone's safe." Jane said. "I don't understand why the other crews are delaying evacuation. Who would risk dying when they can just leave?"

Everyone laughed.

"This cadre self-selects for extremists." Eddy rotated her finger over her head, encompassing all of us in the gesture. "People like us would rather die than back down."

"I guess you're not alone in that," said Jane. "Every hab has plenty of stubborn people."

"But unlike them, we built everything we have," I said. "That makes it much harder to give up."

"Looks like someone finally made a decision, though." Ricci maximized the main feed. Jane wheeled around to join us at the netting.

Glowing dots tracked tiny specks across the wide mesa, pursued by flashing trails of locational data. Vula's media drones zoomed in, showing a succession of brightly colored, hard-shell bodybags shunting though the main valves. Sleet built up along their edges, quickly hardening to a solid coating of ice.

"Quitters," Treasure murmured under her breath.

Jane looked shocked.

"If you think you know what you'd do in their place, you're wrong," I said. "Nobody knows."

"I'd stay," Treasure said. "I'll never leave Mama."

Chara grinned. "Me too. We'll die together if we had to."

Bouche pointed at the two of them. "If we ever have to evac, you two are going last."

Jane expression of shock widened, then she gathered herself into a detached and professional calm.

Ricci squeezed my hand. "The supply ships want to shuttle some of the evacuees to us instead of taking them all the way to the beanstalk. How many can we carry?"

I checked the mass budget and made a few quick calculations. "About twenty. More if we dump mass." I raised my voice. "Let's pitch and ditch everything we can. If it's not enough we can think about culling a little water and feedstock. Is everyone okay with that?"

To my surprise, nobody argued. I'd rarely seen the crew move so fast, but with Jane around everyone wanted to look like a hero.

⊂⊃

Life has rarely felt as sunny as it did that day.

Watching the others abandon their whales was deeply satisfying. It's not often in life you can count your victories, but each of those candy-colored, human-sized pods was a score for me and a big, glaring zero for my old, unlamented colleagues. I'd outlasted them.

Not only that, but I had a new lover, a mostly-harmonious crew of friends, and the freedom to go anywhere and do anything I liked, as long as it could be done from within the creature I called home.

But mostly, I loved having an important job to do.

I checked our location to make sure we were far enough away that if the other whales began to drift, they wouldn't wander into the debris stream. Then we paired into work teams, pulled redundant equipment, ferried it to the main valve, and jettisoned it.

I kept a tight eye on the mass budget, watched for tissue stress around the valve, and made strict calls on what to chuck and what to keep.

Hygiene and maintenance bots were sacrosanct. Toilets and hygiene stations, too. Safety equipment, netting, hammocks—all essential. But each of us had fifty kilos of personal effects. I ditched mine first. Clothes, jewelry, mementos, a few pieces of art—some of it real artisan work but not worth a human life. Vula tossed a dozen little sculptures, all gifts from friends and admirers. Eddy was glad to have an excuse to throw out the guitar she'd never learned to learn to play. Treasure had a box of ancient hand-painted dinnerware inherited from her crèche; absolutely irreplaceable, but they went too. Chara threw out her devotional shrine. It was gold and took up most of her mass allowance, but we could fab another.

We even tossed the orang bot. We all liked the furry thing, but it was heavy. Bouche stripped out its proprietary motor modules and tossed the shell. We'd fab another, eventually.

If we'd had time for second thoughts, maybe the decisions would have been more difficult. Or maybe not. People were watching, and we knew it. Having an audience helped us cooperate.

It wasn't just Jane we were trying to impress. Bouche's media output was gathering a lot of followers. We weren't just trapping the drama anymore, we were part of the story.

Bouche monitored our followship, both the raw access stats and the digested analysis from the PR firm she'd engaged to boost the feed's profile. When the first supply ship backed up to our valve and we began pulling bodybags inside, Bouche whooped. Our numbers had just gone atmospheric.

We were a clown show, though. Eight of us crowded in the isthmus sinus, shuttling bodybags, everyone bouncing around madly and getting in each other's way. Jane helped sort us out by monitoring the overhead cameras and doing crowd control. Me, I tried not to be an obstruction while making load-balancing decisions. Though we'd never taken on so much weight at once, I didn't anticipate any problems. But I only looked at strict mathematical tolerances. I'm not an engineer; I didn't consider the knock-on effects of the sudden mass shift.

In the end, we took on thirty-eight bodybags. We were still distributing them throughout the sinuses when Ricci reported the rescue was over.

That's it. The cargo ships have forty-five bodybags. They're making the run to the beanstalk now.

Is that all? If the ships are full, we could prune some feedstock.

Everyone else is staying. They're still betting their whales will move.

When the last bodybag was secured so it wouldn't pitch through a bladder, I might have noticed we were drifting toward the mesa. But I was too busy making sure the new cargo was secure and accounted for.

I pinged each unit, loaded their signatures into the maintenance dashboard, mapped their locations, checked the data in the mass budget, created a new dashboard for monitoring the new cargo's power consumption, consumables, and useful life. Finally, I cross-checked our manifest against the records the supply ships had given us.

That was when I realized we were carrying two members of my original crew.

When Ricci found me, I was pacing the dorsal sinus, up and down, arguing with myself. Mostly silently.

"If you're having some kind of emotional crisis, I'm sure Jane would love to help," she said.

I spun on my heel and stomped away, bouncing off the walls.

She yelled after me. "Not me though. I don't actually care about your emotional problems."

I bounced off a wall once more and stopped, both hands gripping its clear ridged surface.

"No?" I asked. "Why don't you care?"

"Because I'm too self-involved."

I laughed. Ricci reached out and ruffled her fingers through the short hair on the back of my neck. Her touch sent an electric jolt through my nerves.

"Maybe that's why we get along so well," she said softly. "We're a lot alike."

Kissing while wearing goggles and a breather is awkward and unsatisfying. I pulled her close and pressed my palms to the soft pad of flesh at the base of her spine. I held her until she got restless, then she took my hand and led me to the rumpus room.

Bouche lounged in the netting, eyes closed.

"Bouchie is giving a media interview," Ricci whispered. "An agent is booking her appearances and negotiating fees. If we get enough, we can upgrade the extruder and subscribe to a new recipe bank."

I pulled a bulb out of the extruder. "She'll be hero of the hab."

"You could wake them up, you know."

"Wake up who?" I asked, and took a deep swig of sweet caffeine.

"Your old buddies. In the bodybags. Wake them up. Have it out."

I managed to swallow without choking. "No, I don't think so."

"Maybe they'll apologize."

I laughed, a little too hard, a little too long, and only stopped when Ricci began to looked offended.

"We can't wake them," I said. "Where would they sleep until we got to the beanstalk?"

"They can have my hammock." She sidled close. "I'll bunk with you."

We kissed then, and properly. Thoroughly. Until I met Ricci, I'd been a shrunken bladder; nobody knew my possible dimensions. Ricci filled me up. I expanded, large enough to contain whole universes.

"No. They're old news." I kissed her again and ran my finger along the edge of her jaw. "It was another life. They don't matter anymore."

Strange thing was, saying those words made it true. All I cared about was Ricci, and all I could see was the glowing possibility of a future together, rising over a broad horizon.

Twilight began to move over us. We only had a little time to spare before we recalled the media drones, wiped off the appetite suppressant, and left the other crews to freeze in the dark.

We gathered in the rumpus room, all watching the same feed. Whales circulated above the mesa. Slanting sunlight cast deep orange reflections across their skins, their windward surfaces creamy with blowing snow. Inside, dark spots bounced around the sinuses. If I held my breath, I could almost hear their words, follow their arguments. When I bit my lip, I tasted their tears.

"More than a hundred people," Jane said. "I still don't understand why they'd decide to commit suicide. A few maybe, but not so many."

"Some will evac before it's too late." Vula shrugged. "And as for the rest, it's their own decision. I can't say I would do anything different. And I hope I never find out."

I shivered. "Agreed."

"It doesn't make sense," Jane said. "Someone must be exercising duress."

"Nobody forces anyone to do anything out here, any more than they do down belowground," said Treasure.

"Yeah," said Chara. "We're not crechies, Jane. We do what we want."

Jane sputtered, trying to apologize.

"It's okay," Eddy told her. "We're all upset. None of us really understand."

"The whales still might move," said Bouche. "They can spend a little time in the dark, right Doc?"

I set a timer with a generous margin for error and fired it into the middle of the room. "Eight minutes, then we have to leave. The other whales will have a little more than thirty minutes before they freeze at full dark. Then their bladders burst."

Chara and Treasure pulled themselves out of the netting.

"We're not watching this," Chara said. "If you want to hang overhead and root for them to evac, go ahead."

We all waved goodnight. The two of them stumped away to their hammock, and silence settled over the rumpus room. Just the whoosh and murmur of the bladders, and the faint skiff of wind over the skin. A few early stars winked through the clouds. They seemed compassionate, somehow. Understanding. Looking at those bright pinpoints, I understood how on ancient Earth, people might use the stars to conjure gods.

I put my arm around Ricci's shoulders and drew her close. She let me hold her for two minutes, no more, and then she pulled away.

"I can't watch this either," she said. "I have to do something."

"I know." I drew her hand back just for a moment and planted a kiss on the palm. "It's hard."

Vula nodded, and Jane, too. Eddy and Bouche both got up and hugged her. Eleanora kept her head down, hiding her tears. The electrostatic membrane crackled as Ricci left.

"Do you know some of the people down there, Doc?" asked Jane.

"Not anymore," I said. "Not for a long time."

We fell quiet again, watching the numbers on the countdown. Ricci had left her shadow beside me. I felt her cold absence; something missing that should be whole. I could have spied on her, see where she'd gone, but no. She deserved her privacy.

The first little quake shuddering through the sinuses told me exactly where she was.

I checked our location, blinked, and then checked it again. We were right over the mesa, above the other whales, all seventeen of them. Wind, bad luck, or instinct had brought us there—but did it matter? Ricci—her location mattered. She was in the caudal stump, with the waste pellets, and the secondary valve.

No. Ricci, no. I slapped my breather on and launched myself out of the rumpus room, running aft as fast as I could. *Don't do that. Stop.*

I lost my footing and bounced hard. *You might hit them. You might...*

Kill them.

When I got to the caudal stump, Ricci was just clicking the last pellet through the valve. If we'd dumped them during the pitch and ditch, none of it would have happened. But dry waste is light. We'd accumulated ten pellets, only five kilograms, so I hadn't bothered with them.

But a half-kilo pellet falling from a height can do a lot of damage.

I fired the feed into the middle of the sinus. One whale was thrashing on the slushy mesa surface, half-obscured by the concussive debris. Two more were falling, twisting in agony, their bladders tattered and flapping. Another three would have escaped damage, but they circulated into the path of the oncoming pellets, Each one burst in turn, as if a giant hand had reached down and squeezed the life out of them.

Ricci was in my arms, then. Both of us quaking, falling to our knees. Holding each other and squeezing hard, as if we could break each other's bones with the force of our own mistakes.

Six whales. Twenty-two people. All dead.

The other eleven whales scattered. One fled east and plunged through the twilight band into night. Its skin and bladders froze and burst, and its sinus skeleton shattered on the jagged ice. Its crew had been one of the most stubborn—none had evacuated. They all died. Ten people.

In total, thirty-two died because Ricci made an unwise decision.

The remaining ten whales re-congregated over a slushy depression near the beanstalk. Ricci had bought the surviving crews a few more hours, so they tried a solution along the lines Ricci had discovered. Ice climbers use drones with controlled explosive capabilities to stabilize their climbing routes. They tried a test; it worked—the whales fled again, but in the wrong direction and re-congregated close to the leading edge of night.

In the end, the others evacuated. All seventy got in their bodybags and called for evac.

By strict accounting, Ricci's actions led to a positive outcome. I remind her of that whenever I can. She says it doesn't matter—we don't play math games with human lives. Dead is dead, and nothing will change that.

And she's right, because the moment she dumped those pellets, Ricci became the most notorious murderer our planet has ever known.

The other habs insist we hand her over to a conflict resolution panel. They've sent negotiators, diplomats—they've even sent Jane—but we won't give her up. To them, that proves we're dangerous. Criminals. Outlaws.

But we live in the heart of the matter, and we see it a little differently.

Ricci did nothing wrong. It was a desperate situation and she made a desperate call. Any one of us might have done the same thing, if we'd been smart enough to think of it.

We're a solid band of outlaws, now. Vula, Treasure, Chara, Eddy, Bouche, Eleanora, Ricci, and me. We refuse to play nice with the other habs. They could cut off our feedstock, power, and data, but we're betting they won't. If they did, our blood would be on their hands.

So none of us are going anywhere. Why would we leave? The whole planet is ours, with unlimited horizons.

NOTES ABOUT "WE WHO LIVE IN THE HEART"

Humans are rapacious colonizers. We will move into any habitat, any niche, even if it's dangerous. Even if it's the sinuses of a space whale, and you can't really control where that whale is going.

This story, and "Intervention," are, so far, my only two forays into first person point of view. In both stories, when I began drafting, I wanted to use the point-of-view characters to tell someone else's story. Then halfway through each first draft, I realized I was breaking my own rule about what makes a story. Or rather, it's Howard Waldrop's advice, which works for me so well that I've made it into a rule: *A short story should be about the most important thing that ever happened to the main character.*

Though both Doc in "We Who Live in the Heart" and Jules in "Intervention" are not gendered, readers tend to assume that Doc is a man and Jules is a woman—just because Doc is a surgeon and Jules raises children. In both stories, I left their gender identities unexplicit. I can't quite articulate the reason. It just feels right.

I reread "We Who Live in the Heart" when I'm feeling unhinged. There's something about Doc that grounds me. I feel more like myself after being in their head.

A HUMAN STAIN

PETER'S LITTLE FRENCH NURSEMAID WAS JUST THE type of rosy young thing Helen liked, but there was something strange about her mouth. She was shy and wouldn't speak, but that was no matter. Helen could keep the conversation going all by herself.

"Our journey was awful. Paris to Strasbourg clattered along fast enough, but the leg to Munich would have been quicker by cart. And Salzburg! The train was outpaced by a donkey."

Helen laughed at her own joke. Mimi tied a knot on a neat patch of darning and began working on another stocking.

Helen had first seen the nursemaid's pretty face that morning, looking down from one of the house's highest windows as she and Bärchen Lambrecht rowed across the lake with their luggage crammed in a tippy little skiff. Even at a distance, Helen could tell she was a beauty.

Bärchen had retreated to the library as soon as they walked through the front door, no doubt to cry in private over his brother's death after holding in his grief through the long trip from Paris. Helen had been left with the choice to sit in the kitchen with two dour servants, lurk alone in the moldering front parlor, or carry her coffee cup up the narrow spiral staircase and see that beauty up close.

The climb was only a little higher than the Parisian garret Helen had lived in the past three months, but the stairs were so steep she had been puffing hard by the time she got to the top. The effort was worthwhile, though. If the best cure for a broken heart was a new young love, Helen suspected hers would be soon mended.

"We had a melancholy journey. Herr Lambrecht was deeply saddened to arrive here at his childhood home without his brother to welcome him. He didn't want to leave Paris." Helen sipped her cooling coffee. "Have you ever been to Paris?"

Mimi kept her head down. So shy. Couldn't even bring herself to answer a simple question.

Peter sat on the rug and stacked the gilded letter blocks Bärchen had brought him. For a newly-orphaned child, he seemed content enough, but he was pale, his bloodless skin nearly translucent against the deep blue velvet of his jacket. He seemed far too big for nursery toys—six or seven years old, she thought. Nearly old enough to be sent away to school, but what did Helen know about children? In any case, he seemed a good-natured, quiet boy. Nimble, graceful, even. He took care to keep the blocks on the rug when he toppled the stack.

She ought to ask him to put the blocks in alphabet order, see how much his mother had taught him before she had passed away. But not today, and probably not tomorrow, either. A motherless, fatherless boy deserved a holiday, and she was tired from travel. The servants here were bound to be old-fashioned, but none of them would judge her for relaxing in a sunny window with a cup of coffee after a long journey.

They *would* judge her, though, if they thought she was Bärchen's mistress. She would be at Meresee all summer, so she needed to be on good terms with them—and especially with Mimi.

"We traveled in separate cars, of course. Herr Lambrecht is a proper, old-fashioned sort of gentleman." Helen stifled a laugh. Bärchen was nothing of the sort, but certainly no danger to any woman. "The ladies' coach was comfortable and elegant, but just as slow as the rest of the train."

Still no reaction. It was a feeble joke, but Helen doubted the nursemaid ever heard better. Perhaps the girl was simple. But so lovely. Roses and snow and dark, dark hair. Eighteen or twenty, no more. What a shame about her mouth. Bad teeth perhaps.

Helen twisted in her seat and looked out the window. The Meresee was a narrow blade of lake hemmed in tight by the Bavarian Alps. Their peaks tore into the summer sky like teeth on a ragged jaw, doubled in the mirror surface of the lake below. It was just the sort of alpine vista that sent English tourists skittering across the Alps with their easels and folding chairs, pencils and watercolors.

The view of the house itself was unmatched. Helen had been expecting something grand, but as they had rowed up the lake, she was surprised she hadn't seen Bärchen's family home reproduced in every print shop from London to Berlin, alongside famous views of Schloss Neuschwanstein and Schloss Hohenschwangau. Schloss Meresee was a miniature version of those grand castles—tall and narrow, as if someone had carved off a piece of Neuschwanstein's oldest wing and set it down on the edge of the lake. Only four stories, but with no other structure for scale it towered above the shore, the rake of its rooflines echoing the peaks above, gray stone walls picked out in relief against the steep, forested mountainside. Not a true castle—no keep or tower. But add a turret or two, and that's what the tourists would call it.

No tourists here to admire it, though. Too remote. No roads, no neighbors, no inns or hotels. From what Helen could see as she sat high in the fourth floor nursery window, the valley was deserted. Not even a hut or cabin on the lakeshore.

She'd never been to a place so isolated. Winter would make it even more lonely, but by then she would be long gone. Back in London, at worst, unless her luck changed.

When she turned from the window, Peter had disappeared. The door swung on its hinges.

"Where did Peter go?" Helen asked.

Mimi didn't answer.

"To fetch a toy, perhaps?"

Mimi bent closer to her needle. Helen carried her coffee cup to the door and called out softly in German. "Peter, come back to the nursery this instant." When there was no answer, she repeated it in French.

"I suppose Peter does this often," Helen said. "He thinks it's fun to hide from you."

Mimi's lips quivered. "Oui," she said.

"Come along then, show me his hiding places."

The nursemaid ignored her. Helen resisted the urge to pluck the darning from Mimi's hands.

"If I were newly orphaned, I might hide too, just to see if anyone cared enough to search for me. Won't you help me look?" Helen smiled, pouring all her charm into the request. A not inconsiderable amount, to judge by the effect she had on Parisian women, but it was no use. Mimi might be made of stone.

"To hell with you," she said in English under her breath, and slammed the nursery door behind her.

It was barely even an oath. She knew much filthier curses in a variety of languages. Her last lover had liked to hear her swear. But no more. That life had cast Helen off. All she had left in Paris were her debts.

The clock chimed noon. When it stopped, the house was silent. Not a squeak or creak. No sign of Bärchen or the servants, no sound from the attics above or the floors below. She padded over to the staircase and gazed down the dizzying stone spiral that formed the house's hollow spine. Steps fanned out from the spiral, each one polished and worn down in the center from centuries of use.

"Peter," she called. "Come back to the nursery, please."

No reply.

"All right," she sang out. "I'm coming to find you."

Who could blame the child for wanting to play a game? Peter had no playmates. She could indulge him, just this once. And it gave her a good excuse to snoop through the house.

By the time Helen had worked her way through the top two floors, it was obvious that the servants were outmatched by the housekeeping. The heavy old furniture was scarred and peeling, the blankets and drapes threadbare and musty, the carpets veiled with a fine layer of cobwebs that separated and curled around her every footstep. The surfaces were furred with a fine white dust that coated the back of her throat and lay salty on her tongue. After a half-hour of wiggling under beds and rifling through closets and wardrobes, she was thirsty as if she'd been wandering the desert.

In old houses, the worst furniture was banished to the highest floors. As Helen descended, she expected the furnishings to become newer, lighter, prettier, if just as dusty. In the main rooms, the ones Peter's mother would have used, the furniture was the same: blackened oak carved into intricate birds, fish, and beasts. The sort of furniture that infested Black Forest hunting lodges, but raw and awkward, as if one of the family's great-uncles had taken up a late-in-life passion for wood carving and filled the house with his amateur efforts.

Still, if she could get the servants to clean it properly, she might adopt the large sitting room as her own. She could teach Peter just as well there as in the nursery. It would save her from climbing up and down stairs all day long. And though the sofa was backed by a winding serpent with a gaping maw, it was still a more likely setting for seducing a nursemaid than a drafty nursery window seat.

Under one of the beds she found a thin rib from a rack of lamb, riddled with tooth marks. Somewhere in the house was a dog. She'd have to take care to make friends with it.

Still no sign of Peter. Perhaps he was a troubled child, despite his placid looks. If so, this summer wouldn't be the holiday Bärchen had promised. She'd found him in a booth at Bistro Bélon Bourriche, drowning himself in cognac. Within five minutes, he'd offered to pay her to join him for the summer at his family home and teach his nephew English. It would be easy, he said. Bärchen knew how badly she needed money. He was always so kind—famous for his generosity among the boys of Montparnasse and Pigalle.

Helen tapped the rib in her palm as she descended to the ground floor. There, the staircase widened and spread into the foyer, forming a wide, grand structure. At the back of the foyer, the stairs continued through a narrow slot in the floor. To the cellars, no doubt. Exploring down there would be an adventure.

Helen's trunk still sat by the front door, waiting for the steward to bring it upstairs. On the near side of the foyer, tobacco smoke leaked from the library. It smelled heavenly.

She hadn't been able to afford cigarettes for months. She'd almost ceased yearning for the taste of tobacco, but her mouth watered for it now. Bärchen would give her a cigarette, if she asked for one. But no. She wouldn't disturb him. He had kept a brave face all through their journey. He deserved some time alone with his grief.

She padded into the murky parlor opposite the library and pulled aside the heavy green drapes, holding her breath against the dust. The sun was high above the mountains. The lake gleamed with light. Dust motes swarmed the air. The sunlight turned the oak furniture chalky, the heavy brocade upholstery nearly pastel. The walls were festooned with hunting trophies—stuffed and mounted heads of deer, wild goats, even two wolves and a bear. Their glass eyes stared down through the cobwebs as if alarmed by the state of the housekeeping.

She skated her finger through the dust on the windowsill. P-E-T-E-R, she wrote in block letters. When she began the boy's lessons there'd be no need for work books and pencils. Any flat surface could be used as a slate. It might embarrass the servants into doing their work.

Stepping back from the window, her foot jittered over a lump on the floor. Two tiny bones nestled under the carpet's green fringe—dry old gnawed leavings from a pair of veal chops. She tucked them in her pocket with the lamb bone. Then in the dining room she found a jawbone under a chair—small, from a roast piglet. She put it in her pocket.

Helen found her way to the kitchen at the back of the ground floor. An old woman chopped carrots at the table, her wrinkled jowls quivering with every blow of the knife. Beside her, the steward crouched over a cup of coffee. He was even older than the cook, his skin liver-spotted with age. They watched as Helen poured herself a glass of water from the stoneware jug.

"Peter likes to play games," she said in German. "I can't find him anywhere."

The cook began fussing with the coffee pot. The steward kept to his seat. "We haven't seen the boy, Fräulein York."

"I hardly expected bad behavior from him on my very first morning at Meresee."

"The boy is with the nursemaid. He is always with the nursemaid." The steward's tone was stern.

"How can you say that? He's certainly not with her now." She brushed cobwebs from her dress. "I've searched the house thoroughly, as you can very well see."

"You must continue to look for him, Fräulein," the steward said.

The cook bit into a carrot. Her jowls wobbled with every crunch.

They were united against her, but it only made sense. They were old country people and she was just an English stranger in a dirty, dusty dress. Raising her voice would win her no friends.

"Could you bring my trunk up to my room?" She smiled brightly. "I'd like to change out of my traveling clothes."

"Yes, Fräulein York," the steward said.

The cook went back to chopping carrots. The steward sipped his coffee. Did they expect her to retreat now?

"There is still the matter of Peter," Helen said.

The cook's knife slipped. Carrots scattered across the floor.

"The French girl takes care of the boy." The cook's words were barely understandable, some kind of antique form of Bavarian. "He's not allowed in the kitchen."

The steward's mouth worked, thin lips stretching over his stained teeth.

"Is that true?" Helen asked the steward. "Why not?"

The steward covered the cook's hand with his own. "The boy's welfare is your business now, Fräulein."

Helen found Peter at the back of the freezing cellar, hunkering in front of a door set deep into rock. The walls were caked with frost. The boy's breath puffed like smoke.

"Aren't you cold?" she asked. "Come back upstairs now."

"*Bitte*, miss," the boy said. He wedged two fingers under the door, then crouched lower, head bobbing as he worked them deeper and deeper. His hair was neatly parted, two blond wings on either side of a streak of skin pale as a grub.

Whatever he was up to, whatever he thought he was going to find on the other side of the door, he was fully engrossed by it. Helen let him have his fun for a few minutes while she poked around the cellar, ducking under the low spines of the vaulted ceiling. On the wall opposite the door, bottles were stacked into head-sized alcoves in pyramids of six. She wiped the dust off a few labels. French, and not that old. Champagne, Bordeaux, Burgundy. More than three hundred bottles. Enough to last the summer.

The cellar smelled salty. It must have been used for aging and preserving meat, in the past. The cold air's salty tang flooded her dry mouth with spit. What she wouldn't give for a piece of pork right now, hot and juicy. Her stomach growled. Perhaps the cook could be persuaded to let her explore the kitchen larder.

Helen wandered back to the boy. "Come along, Peter, that's enough. Mimi is waiting for you."

The light from her candle jittered across the brass plate bolted to the door's face. The tarnished metal was crusted with frost. She stepped closer, lifting her candle. It was a shield—griffins, an eagle, a crown.

She nudged Peter's foot with her toe. "Time to go back upstairs." He was stretched out on his belly now. "Peter, come along this instant." An edge came into her voice. She was tired of being ignored by everyone in the house.

He pulled something from under the door and put it in his mouth.

"Stop that." She grabbed Peter's collar and hauled him across the cellar to the stairs. He pitched forward onto his hands and knees. The object popped out of his mouth and bounced off the bottom step.

Helen picked it up and turned it over in her palm. It was a tiny bone, slender, fragile, and wet with spit.

She stared at Peter. "That's disgusting. What are you thinking?"

"Mama," he sobbed. His thin shoulders quivered under the velvet jacket. "Mama."

Remorse knifed through her. She tossed the bone aside, scooped him into her arms, and hauled him upstairs. "Hush," she said, patting his quaking back as he sobbed.

Tobacco smoke leaking from the library had turned the air in the foyer gray. Her trunk still crouched by the front door.

Helen lowered Peter to his feet. He was heavy. She couldn't possibly carry him up to the nursery. She'd be gasping.

Helen squeezed his bony shoulders. "You're a good boy, aren't you?" He wiped his nose on his sleeve and nodded. "Good, no more crying."

She lugged the trunk upstairs and dropped it in her room. Then she took the boy's hand and called up the spine of the staircase for Mimi.

When her pretty face appeared at the top of the spiral, Helen shooed the boy upstairs.

"Take care of him, won't you?" Helen said. "There'll be no lessons today. Not tomorrow, either. Then we'll see."

"Oui," Mimi said.

When Bärchen came to dinner he was already drunk. The scarlet cheeks above his brown beard were so bright it looked like he'd been slapped.

"So many letters. My brother's desk is stuffed to bursting." Bärchen offered Helen a cigarette. "I can't understand them. I have no head for business, Mausi."

Helen blew smoke at him. "You always say that, but you seem to manage your own affairs well enough."

"I must go to Munich for advice. I'll be back soon, I promise. Two days at most."

"Don't stay away too long. You'll come back to an empty wine cellar and a pregnant nursemaid."

He giggled. "If that happens, it must be God's will."

Helen opened her mouth to make a joke about the furniture, but managed to stop herself in time despite the free flow of wine. The dining room chairs were particularly awful. Each one was topped by a sea serpent, thick and twisting, with staring eyes faced with mother-of-pearl. Under it was a rudely-rendered pair of human forms, male and female. And beneath them were thumb-sized lumps the shape of fat grubs. They dug into the small of Helen's back.

Portraits glared down at the table from the surrounding walls. Wan blond children with innocent, expressionless faces. Handsome, smiling men and women, brown-haired and robust just like Bärchen. And sickly-looking older people, prematurely-aged, with smooth gray skin and straggly black hair framing hollow, staring eyes.

When the clock struck seven, they were halfway into the third bottle of claret. Bärchen was diagonal in his chair.

"Time for me to play *pater familias.*" He called out, "Mimi! *Ici!*"

Mimi appeared at the door, clutching Peter's hand.

"Now, Mimi," Bärchen slurred in French. "Is Peter behaving well? Is he in good health?"

"Oui," said Mimi.

Helen watched close as the girl spoke. Yes, some of her teeth were missing, but how many? Helen pretended to yawn, making a dramatic pantomime of it and sighing ecstatically.

Mimi's eyes watered as she tried not to yawn in response. When her lips curled back Helen caught a quick glimpse into her mouth. Her front teeth were gone, gums worn down to gleaming bone. Candlelight glinted on metal wire twisted through her molars.

Mimi clapped her hand over her mouth. Helen reached for a cigarette and pretended she hadn't noticed. Poor girl. Nothing more sad than young beauty in ruin.

"Peter, come here," Bärchen said.

With rough hands, he examined Peter's fingernails and scalp, looked into his ears, then pried opened his mouth and poked a finger along his gums.

She knew what that felt like. Her father had done the same. His fingers had tasted of ash and ink.

One of Peter's front teeth was loose.

"You're losing your first tooth," he said. "Does it hurt?"

Peter shook his head.

Bärchen wiggled it with the tip of a finger. "Let's pluck it out now, and be done with it."

Peter ran to Mimi and hid his face in her skirts.

"Oh come, Peter." Bärchen laughed. "I'll tie it to the doorknob with a bit of string. It'll be over in a moment."

Peter clutched Mimi's waist.

"No? Then we'll get an apple and you can bite into it like this." He mimed raising an apple to his mouth and chomping down. "You can do that, can't you?"

"No, Uncle." Peter's voice was muffled against Mimi's hip. The girl had backed against the wall and was inching toward the door. Bärchen was taking this too far.

"It's late, Herr Lambrecht," Helen said. "Let the girl take Peter to bed."

"Well then. The tooth with fall out on its own and then this will be yours." Herr Lambrecht put a silver coin on the table. "Miss York will keep it for you."

Mimi and boy slipped out the door.

"How was my performance?" Bärchen asked. "Was I convincing?"

"Very. I can hardly believe you never had children."

"God forbid." Bärchen shuddered and drained his wine glass. "Did I ever tell you about my nursemaid? Bruna was her name. She was devoted to me. You would have liked her. Very pretty. But like Mimi, not much of a talker. Not like you."

"Nothing can keep me from saying what I think." Helen reached into her pocket and set the bones on the stained tablecloth. "For example, your servants are lax," she said.

He shrugged. "What can be done? They're old. Who would choose to live here, if they could be anywhere else?"

After dinner they took their wine out the front door and onto the wide front terrace. Evening stars twinkled above looming mountains and a lakeshore veiled in mist. The three sides of the terrace stepped straight down into the water, like a dock or jetty. The skiff bobbed alongside, tied to an iron ring.

That morning, the water had been an inky sapphire, the color so brilliant it seemed to cling to the oars with Bärchen's every stroke. Under the darkening sky it was tar black and viscous. In the distance, a dark object broke the surface, sending lazy ripples across the water. Helen squinted.

Bärchen followed her gaze. "Just a log, that's all. I have a present for you."

He pressed a silver cigarette case into her hand. It was her own—she'd pawned it for rent money three months ago. And it was full—forty slender cigarettes, lined up with care.

She grinned. "If we were back at the Bélon Bourriche, I could put on a pair of tight trousers and sing you a song, as many a young man has done. But you don't want me sitting in your lap any more than I want to be there. So I'll just say thank you."

"It's nothing. Will you be happy here, Mausi?"

"Of course. It's so beautiful. Though I'm not sure how long I can stand to live in a place where nobody appreciates my jokes."

He laughed. "Meresee is beautiful, but it can be a little confining. I'll show you." He led her to the edge of the terrace to peer around the side of the house. Its walls jutted straight down into the water, raising the house's profile far beyond the shore. Behind, the steep mountainsides advanced on the lake, threatening to topple the house into the water.

"You don't want to fall in. It's deep, and so cold it'll knock the breath right out of you." He braced himself against the wall with an unsteady hand.

"I suppose this was a fortress, once," said Helen. "Holding the border of some medieval Bavarian principality."

Bärchen patted the wall. "A fortress, yes, but it never protected a border. It protected the salt."

"Your family had salt mines?" Helen asked. No wonder Bärchen was wealthy.

"The mines belonged to the Holy Roman Emperor. The crown owed much of its wealth to Meresee. More precious than gold, once, this salt. My family protected it."

Bärchen peered over the edge of the terrace. The water clung to the sides of the house. A shadowed stain crept up the foundation.

"Don't fall in," he repeated. "In winter it's somewhat safer. When the ice forms, you can ski across the lake, or skate, if the snow has blown away. But even then, you must be careful."

She laughed. "You've convinced me. I'll be careful to be far, far from Meresee by winter."

"Of course, Mausi." Bärchen forced a chuckle. "Naples for the winter. Neapolitan widows like tall Englishwomen like you. Or Athens, if you please. The world is open to us. We are rich, happy, and at liberty."

Bärchen was trying too hard to be jolly.

"Your new responsibility is eating at you, isn't it, Bärchen?" She threaded her hand through the crook of his arm and drew him gently away from the water's edge. "Why worry? Send Peter away to school. In England, many boys are sent away at his age."

"Maybe you're right. After the summer, if you think he's ready. I'll take your advice."

"What do I know about children? Next to nothing—I told you so in Paris. You couldn't find a less experienced fraud of a governess."

Bärchen patted her hand. "You're a woman. It will come naturally to you."

"I doubt that very much." Helen pulled her hand away. "But how much damage can I do in one summer? I'll teach him a little English at least."

"That's fine, Mausi. Do your best."

She grinned. "Are you sure you're not his father? Peter favors you."

"A family resemblance." The last trace of dusk drained behind the mountains, and Bärchen's mood darkened with the sky. His gaze fixed on the floating log. "If you think I'll develop a father's feelings, you're wrong." Bärchen's deep voice rose to a whine. "It's not fair to shackle me to a child that's not mine. And it's not fair to the child, either. He should have a mother's love—devoted and selfless."

"What happened to his mother?"

"It was grotesque. She swelled larger than this." Bärchen held his arms out, encircling a huge belly. "How many babies can a woman's body contain? Twins are common, triplets not unheard of. I can't imagine how women survive even one, can you?"

Helen shook her head. Sour wine burned the back of her throat.

"My brother's fault. He should have been more careful than to get so many babies on his wife."

"I don't think it works that way," Helen said.

"It does in our family. One is fine. They should have been content with Peter and stopped there. But no, they had to have more children. And now they've all joined our family in the crypt."

Bärchen stared at the house's foundation stones. Helen followed his gaze.

"Do you mean there are tombs in your cellar? The door in the cellar leads to a crypt?"

He nodded. "I'll go there too, eventually. Not soon—I'm still young." He shrugged his broad shoulders. "I try not to think about such things. Paris makes it easy to forget."

A chill breeze stirred the water. She put her empty wine glass down and chafed her arms. "And your brother?"

"My brother couldn't live without his wife. He had to join her."

"Let's go in, it's getting cold." Bärchen shook his head. "I can't leave you out here alone," she insisted, pulling on his elbow. "You're too melancholy."

"Don't worry about me, Mausi," he laughed. "I have no urge to join my family. I love my life in Paris too much to give it up yet."

At the door she stopped, half in, half out of the house.

"Do you know what happened to Mimi's mouth?" she asked.

"I heard it was an accident," he said, and turned back to the lake.

Bärchen left at the first light of dawn. Helen's pounding headache woke her just in time to spot him from her bedroom window, rowing across the lake in the skiff, pocking the water's surface with each frantic pitch of the oars. She'd never seen him move so quickly, put so much of his bulky muscle to work. It was as though he were escaping something.

Anxiety wormed through her breast. If she called out to him, he'd turn around and row back. But the window latch was stuck, the claw cemented into the catch with years of dust and grit. She struggled with it for a minute, and then gave up. Her head throbbed, her mouth was coated in grit, and her eyes felt as though they'd been filled with sand. She crawled back to bed and shoved her head under her pillow.

When she finally ventured up to the nursery in the afternoon, Mimi was sitting in the window seat, needle and thread idle in her lap. The boy was nowhere to be seen.

Helen joined Mimi in the window seat. "How long have you been caring for Peter, Mimi?"

The girl shrugged.

"I suppose when you first came here, you ransacked the house every time he hid from you."

"Oui," said Mimi.

"But you're tired of it. He's older now. He should know better."

Mimi hung her head. One lone tear streaked over the rose of her cheek and dropped to her collar, staining the cotton dark.

Helen longed to wipe her knuckle along that soft cheek, lift the dregs of the tear to her lips as if it were nectar. But no. That might be fine in a sodden Pigalle bistro, but not here. She'd only frighten the girl.

She rested her palm on Mimi's knee, just the lightest touch. "Stay here, I'll get him."

Helen found Peter sitting on the edge of the terrace, legs extended, trying to reach his toes into the water. He leaned back, balancing on his arms, and squirmed closer to the edge.

Helen's heart hammered. She bit the inside of her cheek to keep herself from calling out—a sudden noise might startle him. She crept closer, poised to run and grab him if he fell. When the boy turned his head toward her, she kept her voice low and calm.

"Come here, Peter."

He ignored her. She slowly edged closer.

"Come away from there, please."

When he was within reach she snatched him up, hauled him to the front of the house and set him down on the doorstep. She gripped his arms firmly and bent to look him in the eye.

"Peter, you can't keep running off, do you understand? It's dangerous. What if you'd fallen into the lake?"

"*Bitte*, miss." The boy scuffed his foot. The light bouncing off the lake seemed to leach the color from his skin.

"*Yes, Miss York*. That's your first English lesson. Repeat after me, *Yes, Miss York*."

"Yes, Miss York," he said.

"Good," she said.

He raised his hand to her cheek. He gave her one brief caress, and then snaked two of his fingers into her mouth.

Helen reeled backward. Her arms pinwheeled. She grabbed for the door handle but missed. When she fell, she raked her shin along the doorstep's edge.

Peter stood over her and watched as she keened in pain, clutching her leg and rocking on the ground like a turtle trapped on its back. She rolled to her side and wadded her skirt around her leg to sop up the blood.

When she could stand, she grabbed his hand and yanked him upstairs, lurching with every step and smearing blood in a trail up the steps. Mimi met her on the upper landing. Helen shoved the boy into her arms, dropped to the floor, and raked up her skirts. Blood poured down her leg and into her shoe. Her shin was skinned back, flesh pursed around gleaming bone. She fell back on one elbow, vision swimming.

Mimi guided her to a chair and lifted her skirts. Helen flinched, but Mimi's touch was soft, her movements quick and gentle. She ran out of the room for a moment, then returned with rags and a jug of water. As Mimi cleaned her wound, Peter cowered in the window seat. Helen kept a close eye on him. He was crying again, silently, his mouth forming one word over and over again. *Mama.*

Mimi put the final tuck into the bandage, then squeezed Helen's knee and looked up, her brown eyes huge.

"Merci," Helen breathed.

Mimi smiled. Lips peeled back over gaping gums. Wire wormed through pinholes in her back teeth. Helen recoiled. She grabbed the edge of the table and hauled herself to her feet. She stumped over to the window seat, grabbed Peter's shoulders and shook him hard.

"That's enough," she yelled. "No more games. No running off on your own. Understand?"

The boy sobbed. She lowered her voice, trying to reach a source of calm, deep within her. "Don't be afraid, Peter. I'm not angry anymore. What do you say?"

"Yes, Miss York."

"Very good. I understand you miss your mother and father. It hasn't been very long since they died, but it will get easier, with time."

"*Bitte*, miss," the boy said. "Mama and Papa died many years ago."

The cook and steward blocked her questions. In between their one-word answers, they commented to each other in an impregnable Bavarian dialect, gossiping about her, no doubt, as if she weren't even there. And why shouldn't they? She was acting like a madwoman, limping around the kitchen, waving her arms and yelling at them in every language she knew.

Helen took two deep breaths, and tried again.

"A few days ago, in Paris, Herr Lambrecht told me his brother had just passed away. He had to travel to Meresee and take responsibility for his nephew, the house and the family finances. Is that true?"

"Yes, Fräulein," said the steward.

There. Everything was fine. The knot in Helen's chest loosened. "But Peter just told me his father and mother have been dead for years."

"Yes, Fräulein," said the steward.

"How can you say that?" Helen longed to grab him by the throat, shake him until he rattled. "How can both those things be true?"

The steward ran his tongue over his stained teeth. "It's not my place to contradict either Herr Lambrecht or his nephew."

It was no use. She stumped up to the nursery. Mimi and Peter stood in the middle of the rug, waiting for her.

"Peter, play with your blocks. I want to see them in alphabet order when I return." She pointed at the blocks. "*Ah—bey—tsay.*"

He knelt on the carpet and began stacking the blocks, obedient for the moment. She didn't trust him, though. She wedged a chair under the handle of the door, trapping them both inside. Then she stumbled downstairs to the library. It was locked, but one stubborn shove and the lock gave way.

The desk was abandoned, cubbyholes dusty, drawers empty except for old pen nibs, bottles of dried ink and a silver letter opener shaped like two entwined sea serpents. *So many letters, I can't make sense of them*, Bärchen had said. Had he taken everything away to Munich?

It made no sense. Why would Bärchen lie to her? He knew how desperate she was. No more friends to borrow from, nothing left to pawn. She would have followed him across the world. She had no other option.

She lit a cigarette and pulled hot smoke deep into her lungs. By the time it had burned down to her knuckle, she was sure the mistake was nobody's but her own. It was typical of her—always too busy searching for the next joke to listen properly. Bärchen had said his brother was dead, but not newly dead. He said Peter's mother had died in the spring, but not this spring. She'd made assumptions. Hadn't she?

There was one way to find out.

"The crypt key." Helen held her hand out to the steward, palm up. "Give it to me, please."

"I don't have it, Fräulein."

"Of course you do. You're the steward. Who else would have it?"

He flipped his jacket open and turned his pockets inside out. "I only have this." A blue and white evil eye medallion spun at the end of his watch fob. "You should have one of these, Fräulein. It keeps you safe."

Helen ransacked the house for keys and limped down the cellar stairs. Her mouth began watering as soon as she smelled the salty air. She lit a cigarette. It dangled from her lips as she tried each key in turn. None fit the crypt's lock. She leaned on the door with all her weight but the heavy iron hinges didn't even shift. She squinted through the keyhole. Only darkness.

She lowered herself to the floor and threaded her fingers under the door. A feathery shift of air drifted from below, ruffling her hair. It smelled delicious, sea-salty and savory, like a good piece of veal charred quickly over white-hot coals and sliced with a sharp knife into bleeding red pieces.

Her fingers brushed against something. Forcing her hands under the door, she caught it with the tips of her fingers, drew it out. It was a tiny vertebra, no bigger than the tip of her finger. Helen held it close to the candle flame, turning it over in her palm. It was brown with dried blood. The canal piercing the bone was packed with white crystals. She picked at them with her fingernail. Salt.

There was something else under the door, too—a tooth coated in a brown blush of blood. A tendril of frozen flesh hung from its root.

Helen limped upstairs. The chair she'd leaned against the nursery door was wedged so tightly the feet scratched two fresh scars into the floor as she dragged it away.

Peter waited in the doorway. Mimi was curled up in the window seat.

"Is this yours?" She showed him the tooth.

"No, miss." He skinned his lips back. His loose tooth hung from his gum by a thread.

"Where did it come from, then?"

He blinked up at her, eyes clear and innocent. "*Bitte*, miss, I don't know."

Tall as he was, in that moment he seemed little more than an infant. His voice was quite lovely. The effect of a slight childish slur on those German vowels was adorable.

"Do you know where the key to the crypt is?"

"No, miss."

"Have you been inside the crypt?"

"No, miss."

He was just a child; children had no sense of time. Did he even know the difference between a month and a year? She'd gotten herself worked up over nothing. The steward and cook had taken a dislike to her, but it was her own fault. She should have taken care to make friends with them. But no matter. Bärchen would be back in a few days, and the summer would continue as planned.

Helen brought Mimi and Peter their dinner, barricaded them in the nursery, then helped herself to a bottle of claret from the steward's pantry. She set it on the dining room table beside her dinner plate. No corkscrew, and she hadn't found one while searching through the house for keys. The steward must have hidden them. She hadn't seen any cigarettes, either. She'd have to ration the ones in her cigarette case until Bärchen came home.

She called for the steward. When he didn't come, she fetched the silver letter opener from the library and used it to pry the cork from the bottle. She lifted the bottle to her mouth like a drunk in a Montparnasse alleyway. The wine burned as it slipped down her parched throat.

Helen put the letter opener in her pocket and took her plate and the wine bottle out to the terrace. The air was fresh with pine. The first evening stars winked overhead between clouds stained with dusk. A hundred feet off the terrace, the floating log bobbed. Slow ripples licked the terrace steps.

She had almost drained the wine bottle when the log was joined by another. The breeze carried a whiff of salt. The two logs seemed to be moving toward her, eel-sinuous. Starlight glistened off their backs as they slipped through the water, dipping under and then breaking the surface in unison like a pair of long porpoises.

The bottle slipped from her hand and smashed on the terrace. Shards of glass flew into the lake.

The logs turned to look at her.

Helen scrambled into the house and slammed the door. She ran to the parlor and began dragging an oak chest across the floor, rucking up the rug and peeling curls of varnish from the floor. She pulled it across the foyer, scraping deep scars across dark wood. By the time she'd barricaded the front door, she was dripping with sweat. Her wounded leg throbbed with every shuddering heartbeat.

She crept to the parlor window and peeked between the drapes. Only one creature was visible, floating just beyond the edge of the terrace. It looked like a log again, but she knew better. She'd seen them. Two long, inky serpents raising their heads from the water, their maggot-pale eyes hollow and staring.

Just a log, that's all.

The log flipped. Water poured across its back. Its mouth split open. Starlight revealed hundreds of teeth, wire-thin and hooked.

Just a log, that's all.

Bärchen was a liar.

The cook and steward sat at the kitchen table, heads down over their dinner, one candle burning between them.

"I suppose you'll tell me there are no serpents in the lake. Herr Lambrecht says they're logs, and it's not your place to contradict him." She threw her arms wide. "If one of those monsters bit off your leg and Herr Lambrecht said it hadn't, you'd agree with him."

"Would you like another bottle of wine, Fräulein?" the steward asked.

"Always." She pounded her fist on the table, rattling their dinner plates. "But I'd rather know how badly Herr Lambrecht lied to me, and why."

The steward shrugged and turned back to his meal.

Helen ransacked the kitchen drawers and piled instruments on the table—knives, forks, even a slender iron spit—everything she could find that was long and slender and strong. She wrapped them in a rag, grabbed the candlestick from the table, and lugged everything downstairs.

Delicious, salty air roiled out from under the door, stronger than before. Helen's stomach growled. She lit a cigarette and rolled up her sleeves.

The white coating on the walls and door wasn't frost; it was salt. She scraped the crust off the eye of one of the griffins. It wadded up under her fingernail, dense and gritty.

Helen licked the salt off her finger and slipped a filleting knife into the keyhole. She could feel the latch inside, and bumps that must be a series of tumblers. They clicked as she guided the knife tip back and forth. The blade sawed at the corners of the keyhole, carving away fine curls of brass. But the knife was too wide, too clumsy.

She tried the iron spit next. It left a patina of sticky grease on her palms. She attacked the lock with each instrument in turn, whining with frustration. She knocked her forehead on the door, gently, once, twice.

A chill played over her bare skin. Gooseflesh prickled her arms. Sour spit flooded her mouth.

Finally, she drew the letter opener out of her pocket and fed its tip through the lock, leaning into the door as if she could embrace its whole width. She peeked into the keyhole, hand by her cheek like an archer with a drawn bow.

She licked salt from her lips. The lock clicked. The door opened an inch, hinges squeaking.

A little wet bone bounced across the floor and hit her foot. She turned.

Peter was right behind her.

Candlelight flickered over his round cheeks and dimpled chin, the neatly combed wings of pale hair framing his face. He was just a child. Orphaned. Friendless. She'd already given him her sympathy. Didn't he deserve her care?

"Hello." She kept her voice gentle. "How did you get out of the nursery?"

"*Bitte*, Miss York. The door opened."

The chair must have fallen. She hadn't wedged it hard enough.

Peter stared at the crypt door. She should take him back upstairs, tell Mimi to put him to bed, but he would just come down here again. And wasn't this his own home?

"Do you know what's behind this door, Peter?"

"Mama," he said.

"Yes, that's what your uncle told me. Not just her, but your whole family—all of your ancestors, in their tombs. Do you know what a tomb is?" He shook his head. "A big box made of stone, usually. Or an alcove in a stone wall, sometimes. Usually family crypts are in cemeteries or churches. But your family—"

She hesitated. *Your family is strange,* she thought. She needed to find out exactly how strange.

"Are you sure you want to see your mother's tomb?"

Peter nodded.

The air that rushed out as she opened the door had a meaty, metallic tang. Her stomach roiled with hunger; her vision swam. She shielded the candle flame with her body. Peter took her hand and led her into the crypt.

Helen had seen crypts before. They didn't frighten her. At age five she'd seen her mother shut away in a Highgate Cemetery tomb. She'd kissed her first girl in the crypt at St. Bride's, after stealing the key from the deacon. And she'd attended parties in the Paris catacombs, drank champagne watched by thousands of gaping skulls.

But this was no crypt.

The passage opened into a wide cavern, its walls caked with salt crystals and honeycombed with human-sized alcoves, rough indentations hacked out of the rock with some primitive tool. Some were deep, as if they might be passages, some gaped shallow and empty, and others were scabbed over with a crusted mess the color of dried blood, leaking filth down the crystalline walls. One of these was just over her left shoulder. Tiny bones were embedded in the bloody grime. It smelled like fresh meat.

A few—just a few here and there—were furred over with cobwebs the same bloodless pale pink as Peter's skin.

At the bottom of the cavern, a wide pool of oily water quivered and sloshed.

"Mama," Peter said. "Papa."

"I don't think they're here, Peter," she whispered, pulling him back toward the door.

His hand slipped from her grasp. He ran to a cobwebbed alcove and plunged his hand deep inside. She grabbed his jacket and pulled him away. The strands clung to his arm, stretched and snapped. When his hand appeared, he held tight to a squirming grub the size of his head. His fingers pierced its flesh; the wounds dripped clear fluid.

Its eyes were dark spots behind a veil of skin. Its tiny, toothless maw opened and closed in agony.

"Brother," Peter said. He raised the grub to his lips and opened his mouth.

Helen swatted it out of his hand. The grub rolled across the floor of the cavern and plopped into the pool.

She ran, dragging Peter behind her by his elbow.

Helen slammed the door and braced it with her shoulder, throwing her weight against it as she jabbed the lock with the letter opener. Getting the door open had been sheer luck. She'd never get it locked again, not if she worried at it for a hundred years.

She couldn't believe her stupidity. Opening doors that should stay shut. Going places she didn't belong. Trusting Bärchen, as if she actually knew him. As if he were human.

"Stupid, stupid, stupid," she said under her breath.

The lock clicked. She fell to her hands and knees, weak with relief. Pain shot up her leg. Her vision darkened.

Peter lifted the candle. "Yes, Miss York?"

She sucked air through her teeth and wrenched herself around to sit with her back against the door. She would get away from Peter, run as fast and as far as possible. Into the mountains, into the forest, anywhere but here. But she didn't think she could stand. Not yet.

"Do you remember your mother? Your father? Do you know what they are?" Monsters, with hollow staring eyes. Her voice rose to a shriek. "Do you know what you are?"

"No, Miss York. I know you."

He sat at her feet and slipped his hand into hers. His fingers were sticky with fluid from the grub. It stank like rot, like old meat turned green and festering with maggots. Her gorge rose once, twice. She took two convulsive gasps for air and then the stench changed. Her stomach growled. She raised Peter's fingers to her mouth and licked them clean, one after another. Then she sucked the last of the juice from his sleeve.

There was more on the other side of the door, puddled on the stone floor. She could open the door again. But Peter looked so tired. His eyelids were puffy and the skin under each eye was stained dark with exhaustion.

"Come here," she said, and the boy climbed right into her open arms.

Helen watched Mimi undress Peter and tuck him into bed. When the nursemaid tried to leave the bedroom, Helen stopped her.

"No. We're staying here. Peter can't be alone. We have to take care of him."

Mimi hung her head.

"Do you understand?"

"Oui."

"I don't think you do. You let Peter go—every time. You don't even try to stop him. Why don't you care for him? He's just a child."

The boy watched them, hands folded between cheek and pillow. Mimi stared at the floor. A tear streaked down her cheek.

"We have to keep Peter safe, you and I, so he can grow up healthy and strong like his uncle. And then like his parents, out in the lake." Helen sighed. "I wish we could talk properly, you and I."

"Oui."

"Wait here," she said.

Helen ran to fetch a pencil and paper. When she returned, Peter was asleep.

"Tell me why you let him go."

Mimi fumbled with the pencil. She couldn't even hold it properly, and the only mark she could make on the paper was a toppling cross inside a crude shape like a gravestone.

Mimi's lower lip quivered. A tear dropped onto the paper. Helen took the pencil from Mimi's shaking fingers. "It doesn't matter," she said.

Mimi climbed onto the bed and lay beside Peter.

Helen pulled a heavy chair in from the hallway and slid it in front of the door. It might not keep him from getting out, but if he tried to drag it away the noise would wake her. Then she kicked off her shoes and climbed onto the bed, reaching around Mimi to rest her palm on Peter's arm.

The girl was crying. Her back quivered against Helen's chest.

"It's all right," Helen whispered, holding her close. "Everything is going to be all right."

Mimi cried harder.

Helen expected to be awake all night, but Peter was safe, the room was warm, the bed cozy, and Mimi's sobs were rhythmic and soothing. Helen slipped into sleep and tumbled through slippery dreams of inky shapes that writhed and grasped and tore at her skin. When she woke, the moon shone through the window, throwing the crossed shadows of the windowpanes over the rug. Her leg throbbed. The clock struck four. And Peter and Mimi were both gone.

On the pillow lay two bright pieces of copper wire, six inches long, worried and kinked, their ends jagged. The pillow was spotted with blood.

Helen ran down to the kitchen and fumbled with a candle, nearly setting her sleeve on fire as she lit it on the oven's banked coals. She plunged downstairs, bare feet on the freezing steps, and when the smell hit her she stumbled. She slipped on a bone and nearly sent herself toppling headfirst.

She panted, leaning on the wall. The smell pierced her. It coiled and drifted and wove through her, conjuring the last drip of whiskey in her father's crystal decanter, the first strawberries of summer, the last scrap of Christmas pudding smeared over gold-chased bone china and licked off with lazy tongue swipes. It smelled like a sticky wetness on her fingers, coaxed out of a pretty girl in the cloak room at a Mayfair ball, slipped into a pair of silk gloves and placed on a young colonel's scarlet shoulder during the waltz.

The smell was so intense, so bright it lit the stairwell. The air brimmed with scents so vast and uncontainable they poured from one sense to the next, banishing every shadow and filling the world with music.

Helen fell from one step to the next, knees weak, each footstep jarring her hips and spine. Her vision spun. The cellar brimmed with haloes and rainbows, a million suns concentrated and focused through a galaxy of lenses, dancing and skipping and brimming with life.

The only point of darkness in the whole cellar was Mimi.

The nursemaid crouched in front of the crypt door. She humped and hunched, ramming her face into the wood as if trying to chew through it. The threshold puddled with blood.

Mimi's jaw hung loose. It swung against her throat with every thrust. Her nose was pulped, upper lip shredded, the skin of her cheeks sloughed away.

The remains of her teeth were scattered at her feet.

Helen grabbed her foot with both hands and heaved, dragging her away. Mimi clawed at the floor, clinging to the edges of the stones with her shredded fingernails.

"Miss York?"

At the sound of Peter's voice, the air cottoned with rainbows.

Peter stood at the head of the stairs, lit by a euphoria of lights. It cast patterns across his face and framed his head in a halo of sparks.

Mimi threw her head back and screamed, her tongue a bleeding live thing trying to escape from a gaping throat, a cavitied maw that was once the face of a girl.

Mimi lunged up the stairwell. Helen chased her.

"Peter, run!" Helen howled.

Mimi threw her arms around the boy. The huff of breath through her open throat spattered the walls with blood. She lunged down the hall, dangling Peter like a rag doll. Helen pitched after her, grabbing at the nursemaid's hair, skirt, sleeves. In the foyer she caught hold of Peter's leg and yanked the boy away.

Mimi dug her fingernails into the heavy chest and pulled. It scraped over the floor, throwing splinters across the foyer.

She yanked the door open and turned. Blood puddled at her feet. Her tongue wagged from deep in her throat. She raised her arms, as if yearning for Peter to enter her embrace.

Helen clutched Peter to her chest. She forced his head against her neck so he couldn't see his nursemaid's pulped face.

Mimi yowled. Then she plunged out the door and clattered across the terrace. At the edge of the water she teetered for a moment, arms wheeling. In the moment before she fell, an inky shape welled up from the water. Its jaws welcomed her with barely a splash.

The boy knelt on the nursery window seat beside Helen, his nose pressed to the window pane. Two sinuous forms floated in the lake, lit by the pale rays of dawn poaching over the mountaintops.

"Come sit over here." Helen patted the stool in front of her.

When the sun broke over the peaks, Peter's mother and father were gone, sleeping the day away at the bottom of the lake, perhaps, or in the crypt pool, keeping watch over their precious, delicious children.

Helen kept Peter by her day and night. She barely took her eyes off him, never left his side. To him she devoted all her care and attention, until her lashes scraped over dry and pitted eyeballs, her tongue swelled with thirst, and her ears pounded with the call from below.

The scent slipped into her like welcome promises. Lights spun at the edge of her vision, calling, guiding her down to the cavern.

At night, the serpents tossed back and forth in the waves, dancing to the rhythm shuddering through the house. She didn't have to look out the window to see them; every time she blinked they were behind her eyelids. Beckoning.

Helen made it three days before she broke. When her pen turned clumsy, when her handwriting dissolved into crude scratches, she was past caring. The crypt was all she could think of. Hunger gushed through her, overflowing and carrying her down each flight of stairs as if floating on a warm river to the source of everything left in the world worth wanting.

Her hands were too clumsy to open the door, but it didn't matter. She could eat her way through it. The scent itself was nourishment enough. Every bite was a blessing. She drowned herself in it. Gave herself over until her mind hung by a thread.

Her world collapsed into pain when Peter pulled her out of the cellar. She resisted, a little, but she couldn't fight him. Not if it might hurt him. When he got the wires through what was left of her teeth and jaw and twisted them tight, the light abandoned her, the call receded, the house darkened.

"Will you be all right now, Miss York?" Peter asked.

"Oui," she said.

NOTES ABOUT "A HUMAN STAIN"

When I started drafting "A Human Stain," I was feeling cocky. I decided to try pushing the envelope, write a bit faster. Though speed works for some writers, it certainly doesn't for me. When I force a draft along, it moves in the wrong direction.

Legendary editor Ellen Datlow put me through five revisions of "A Human Stain" before she bought the story. And they weren't minor revisions, either. They were huge. Each took days.

The story was a vague mess, but Ellen saw something in it and kept after me to revise. She asked questions: "Why is this happening?" "What does this look like?" "What's the story behind this?" Not because she wanted the answers, but because she wanted *me* to have the answers. Each time, I thought I did, but when I got honest with myself, I didn't.

Revising "A Human Stain" taught me not to rush. Any story worth telling will take as long as it takes. For me, rushed writing means rushed thinking, and that leads to mistakes. This story also taught me that being specific is everything. A story doesn't have to be overloaded with detail, but each one should work overtime.

"A Human Stain" won the Nebula Award in 2018, and I have never been so surprised. Gratified, certainly, and so happy, but shocked. The trophy sits on my dresser, and you can bet I give it an incredulous and appreciative look every single morning. It's a good reminder that if we're lucky, persistence pays off.

ACKNOWLEDGEMENTS

I AM DEEPLY INDEBTED TO SO MANY PEOPLE for their kindness, generosity, support, and love. First, all thanks to my wife Alyx Dellamonica, who makes all things possible. Thank you to my agent Hannah Bowman, who always has my back.

Bouquets and much thanks to Yanni Kuznia, Bill Schafer, and everyone at Subterranean Press for making this beautiful book, and to Lauren Saint-Onge for the cover of my dreams.

Thank you to brilliant, dedicated editors Ellen Datlow, Neil Clarke, Sheila Williams, Jonathan Strahan, Irene Gallo, Lee Harris, Vera Sun, Renne Chon, Lynne M. Thomas, Michael Damian Thomas, Eric Desatnik, Ann VanderMeer, Andrew Liptak, Anna Yeatts, and Jen R. Albert.

Thank you, dear friends Linda Carson, Jeffe Kennedy, Peter Watts, Caitlin Sweet, David Nickle, Madeline Ashby, Dominik Parisien, Derek Künsken, Sarah Pinsker, K.M. Szpara, Zandra Renwick, Claude Lalumiere, Margo MacDonald, Titus Androgynous, Delicia Pastiche, Charlie Jane Anders, Annalee Newitz, Ed Campbell, and Gisella Giordano.

Thank you to my family, Sandra Robson, Bill, Rhonda, and Kendal Robson, Sue and Bob Christie, and Sherelyn, David, Beau, and Tate Tocher.

And finally, thank you to my teachers, role models, and inspirations Walter Jon Williams, Michael Bishop, and Connie Willis.

PUBLICATION INFORMATION